HOME IS WHERE THE HEART IS

Going down to the drawing room, Madeleine paused for a moment on the shadowy stairs. She stood with cocked head, absorbing the new feel of the house—the child asleep in her room. Archie and Lisa both here, and Cecil carrying the baby who would be the first grandchild. But more important even than all this was the knowledge that the cloud of disapproval which had hung over her all through her years here had lifted and dispersed. Charles's mother, Charles himself had gone. She took a long breath of a different air.

ONYX

ROMANCE FROM THE
PAST AND PRESENT

☐ **LAMIA by Georgia Taylor.** Lamia, a beautiful and passionate witch, is a shunned and feared outcast in 16th century France. Together with three ardent and powerful patrons, she must brave the perils and persecutions of a pitiless and superstitious world to shield the dazzlingly desirable, wondrously wild Lamia from the vengeance of those who would destroy her—and all her enchanting world. (179714—$4.99)

☐ **DEVOTED by Alice Borchardt.** Elin, a daughter of the Forest People, was mistress of the forbidden powers granted by the old gods. Owen, the warrior-bishop, was his people's last hope against the invading Viking horde, and against the powerful ruler who would betray them. They came together in a love that burned through all barriers in a struggle to save France. "Love and treachery . . . a marvelous, irresistible novel."—Anne Rice

(403967—$6.99)

☐ **LILY A Love Story by Cindy Bonner.** Lily Delony has no reason to doubt the rules of virtue and righteousness she has been brought up with until she meets the man who turns her world—and her small town—upside down. The odds are against her forsaking her family for an unknown future with an outlaw who shoots first and thinks later. (404394—$4.99)

☐ **THE DREAMSTONE by Liane Jones. The Award-Winning National Bestseller.** What was the strange and powerful link between Jane Pridden, a beautiful young 1990s woman from North Dakota and Ceinwin, a young girl from a twelfth-century Welsh village? A dark menace shadowed them both . . . a haunted love that bridged eight centuries and . . . spanned two continents. "Love swept them through the vortex of time—with passion that knew no limits, no law . . . Enthralling, sexy."—*New Woman* (178521—$4.99)

☐ **DUCHESS OF MILAN by Michael Ennis.** Once upon a time, in fifteenth-century Italy, two women faced each other with a ruthlessness and brilliance no man has ever matched. Enter their world of passion and evil in Italy's most dazzling and dangerous age! "Two young women who had the power to change history . . . Be prepared . . . you won't want to put this one down."—Jean M. Auel (404289—$5.99)

*Prices slightly higher in Canada

DRUMVEYN

Alexandra Raife

AN ONYX BOOK

ONYX
Published by the Penguin Group
Penguin Books USA Inc., 375 Hudson Street,
New York, New York 10014, U.S.A.
Penguin Books Ltd, 27 Wrights Lane,
London W8 5TZ, England
Penguin Books Australia Ltd, Ringwood,
Victoria, Australia
Penguin Books Canada Ltd, 10 Alcorn Avenue,
Toronto, Ontario, Canada M4V 3B2
Penguin Books (N.Z.) Ltd, 182–190 Wairau Road,
Auckland 10, New Zealand

Penguin Books Ltd, Registered Offices:
Harmondsworth, Middlesex, England

Published by Onyx, an imprint of Dutton Signet,
a division of Penguin Books USA Inc.
Previously published in Great Britain in a Michael Joseph Ltd. edition.

First Onyx Printing, May, 1997
10 9 8 7 6 5 4 3 2 1

REGISTERED TRADEMARK—MARCA REGISTRADA
Printed in the United States of America

PUBLISHER'S NOTE
This is a work of fiction. Names, characters, places, and incidents
either are the product of the author's imagination or are used
fictitiously, and any resemblance to actual persons, living or dead,
events, or locales is entirely coincidental.

For the "big house."

Chapter One

Madeleine stood on the step, listening to the sound of Archie's car going fast down the drive to the river. She shivered in the dank February air, inescapably reminded of the desolation of the day four months ago when he had been the last to leave after his father's memorial service. Then she had merely had to deal with facing solitude; now she had somehow to come to terms with the news Archie had just brought, and the shock and repugnance she had done her best not to let him see.

As she went in, closing the heavy door behind her, cutting off the sound of the car, she was thankful at least that Charles would never have to know about it. She found she was trembling as she went across the hall with her quick light step, and into the drawing room, the accepted prison of her winter afternoons.

A pair of sofas like drop-sided coffins flanked the white marble and polished steel fireplace. At the end of one, cut off from the heat by its high arm, was an indentation in the faded blue brocade, needlework and reading glasses beside it. One cushion from the row poised on their corners at mathematical intervals was set square, squashed. Her place. She sat down, knees together, fingers laced in her lap, elbows pressed tightly in to her sides.

The room was warmer than it usually was just after lunch, she registered gratefully. The enormous radiators, halfway through their creeping climb from morning chill to bedtime comfort, had been helped out by Archie's attack on the fire. Platt liked to build it up with a black scree of dross before he went off duty for the afternoon, designed to last till he appeared to take away the tea tray. Madeleine never touched it, but Archie had driven the poker into its bowels and with a firm heave had produced leaping flames.

Archie. If only he could have stayed longer today, given her more chance to assimilate what he had driven all this way to tell her. If only he could get up here more often. This was the first time she had seen him since the day of the memorial service. Her mind turned to it again, for Charles had been somewhere behind her thoughts ever since Archie had told her what he had come to say—though thankfully she had managed to catch back the automatic exclamation, "But whatever will your father say?" And though she was not conscious of the evasion, letting her thoughts turn back to Charles allowed her to put off for a little longer examining the implications of this new and appalling development.

The day of Charles's service had been so different from today, mellow golden October sunlight flooding the glen. In fact it felt to her as though they had hardly had a fine day since. How pleased she had been that Archie had chosen so unerringly, so surprisingly, exactly what his father would most have wanted—the short simple service by the loch, with only family and Drumveyn

estate people and a few of his closest lifelong
friends present. His shooting friends. Charles had
had no other interest in recent years. It had felt
so strange, entertaining them in the house after
the service, and it had been difficult to find anything to say to them, so out of touch had she
become with everyone. Once she and Charles had
been part of the friendly dining circle of the big
houses and old families in this and the neighboring glens. How had it all died away? In recent
years they had gone nowhere, seen no one, and
never invited anyone to Drumveyn.

Looking back on the service she saw the scene
objectively, as though she was watching it from
the lawn, standing above the slope where the
shrubs and rhododendrons had been allowed to
get out of hand, looking across the stretch of open
grazing to water which on that day had reflected
a sky of unbroken blue.

She saw the little group of figures, each assuming the stance of respect, punctiliously still and
silent, dark-clad against the yellowing grass at the
water's edge fenced off from stock. She saw herself standing there, in her black cashmere and
black court shoes, heels digging into the grass; no
one could have guessed her strange feeling of
being unable to touch anything or anyone around
her, the extraordinary, unexpected feeling of
lightness, liberation, guilt.

She saw herself standing between Archie and
Lisa. The children. A small smile twisted. Hardly
children; Archie was nearer thirty than twenty,
Lisa was twenty-five. Each was flanked by the
partner who, Madeleine recognized with sad-
ness, had drawn them farther than ever from
Drumveyn.

Lisa, tall and well built, dwarfed her mother. And she stood up straight now, the resentful slouch of her teens gone. She was beautifully dressed, beautifully groomed. The wide-brimmed hat suited her, its angle perfect on her glossy dark-brown hair. What had happened, Madeleine thought with a pang, to the happy boisterous child, and equally to that fat scowling teenager? Hard as Madeleine found it to make any but the most superficial contact with Howard she had to admit that he had been a remarkably beneficial influence on her gauche daughter.

He was there in his appointed place beside Lisa, his well-fed bulk as immaculately dressed as his wife's firm figure, his fair hair still exactly as he had brushed it, his expression saying, "I am prepared to be here," but no more. Madeleine remembered that her thoughts had wandered away from what the minister was saying, wondering with a vague anxiety about this marriage Lisa had made, a marriage so unlike anything her mother would ever have envisioned for her. Materially it seemed excellent—the Surrey house which sounded quite luxurious, the time-share in Antigua, the holidays abroad—but it was still hard to imagine Lisa in that world. She had so loved Drumveyn when she was younger. Was she happy? She seemed utterly wrapped up in Howard, aware of him all the time, and by contrast, her mother had observed with regret, oddly awkward with her friends here on the estate. They would make allowances, of course.

And Howard? He was always so self-contained and certainly in public never displayed any warmth or affection. In fact it seemed to Madeleine that he treated Lisa more as a possession than a partner, speaking to her with an offhand authority which her mother found patronizing. Even today, at this service for her father, there was no sign of tenderness.

And was it he who was refusing the baby Lisa so much wanted?

Madeleine's thoughts checked with a jerk, scrambled, hunted hastily for a different memory. In the silence after the minister's voice, not sonorous enough for this outdoor setting, had died readily away, Archie had walked with his steady tread out onto the frail jetty carrying the urn. Madeleine recalled with a small smile how carefully he had done his homework even though the wind was the merest light breath and the water barely moving. What had his thoughts been? Ashes, flimsiest, lightest of substances. The father he had fought with and then refused to fight with any longer, simply making his home elsewhere. And choosing Cecil for his wife.

Now that Archie had gone out on to the jetty, Cecil was next to Madeleine, but she had made no move to fill the empty space. She, even more than Howard, was so completely alien to Drumveyn, absorbed in her artist's world of color and beauty. Madeleine found her frankly alarming and knew it must be her fault as much as Cecil's that in two years no friendly footing had been established between them. Cecil's expression now was perfectly correct, but untouched by any feeling for Charles whom she had always treated with the most damning courtesy.

Had she and Archie arrived at their decision even then? Madeleine suddenly wondered. Had they perhaps wanted to talk to her about it, but supposed she would be numb and grieving? Certainly Archie had given no hint of it in the talk they had had the next morning before he and Cecil left.

They had walked down to the loch together in the hazy morning light, with the sun just beginning to shred and disperse the silvery trails of mist across the water, neither referring to yesterday's service, but drawn as it were to review it again, each putting it into their own private perspective.

"You'll be all right?" Archie had turned to look into her face, his eyes concerned.

"Of course I shall. Quite all right." In fact she hardly knew how she would be. Her fluttering mind had scarcely absorbed the fact of Charles's death, and all she could really see ahead was a huge but not disagreeable emptiness.

"You know, of course, that the house is your home—always." Drumveyn was now his. She could hear in his voice his dislike of even having to say this to her.

"Darling Archie. But one day you may want to live in it yourself." Unimaginable to think of Cecil there. "But for the time being, I should be grateful . . ."

Her mind reeled from the idea of living anywhere else. Her whole adult life had been spent in this house, with scarcely a night away from it. Yet the thought of being in it alone seemed strange too. It had been Charles's house, not hers.

"You mustn't even think like that. It's your home. I wouldn't dream of your moving out. I mean it." Archie's voice had been urgent, his eyes full of loving concern for her. "I wish I could be here with you for a bit longer but Cecil has a— well, actually, I have to be off again quite soon—

but you mustn't worry about anything, nothing will change."

Nothing will change. The words rang in her head now like a sentence. She looked round the high formal room, conscious of how it dwarfed her, of how rigidly she was sitting, and she tried at last to face squarely the news Archie had brought. She had been careful to make no protests which she would later regret, had assured him, and Cecil via him, of her support.

But gradually she began to see that perhaps she had not done as well as she had thought. Archie had not made the round trip of nine hundred or so miles to have her hide her true feelings and dredge up correct social responses. He had come to try and share with her how he and Cecil felt, to make her understand if he could why they had made this decision. It had been so good of him to come. He was so busy, just back from one job and off again to Spain tomorrow. Generous Archie, he had made the time, which Cecil had not found herself able to do. And he had expected delight and warmth; had the right to expect them.

She had failed him. How much of her reaction had stemmed from the ingrained habit of seeing everything through Charles's eyes? Still, after all these months, her first thought had been that he would have been outraged. How completely subservient to his views she had allowed herself to be, she realized objectively for the first time. But she had been so young when she married him, her thoughts hurried on in instant self-defense, so daunted by this big dark house and its implacable routines. Would she have asserted herself more if there had been only Charles to face up to? He after all had been absorbed in his outdoor life, his shooting and fishing and stalking, and probably would not have concerned himself too much about minor changes. But there had not only been Charles at Drumveyn when she came here twenty-eight years ago; there had been Charles's mother, and the house, irrefutably and without discussion, had been hers.

A dull thumping made Madeleine jump shatteringly. The afternoon silence was always so complete, Platt and Mrs. Platt in their own quarters, peace restored after the morning coming and going of cleaning, bringing in logs, post arriving, tea drinking and the interminable phoning by gamekeeper, grieve and shepherd from the extension in the kitchen passage. Was some job being done on the house that she hadn't been told about? She was by now so unused to anyone arriving uninvited—Charles had seen to that—that it took another series of thumps before she thought of the door. The bell should have been put through to Platt's flat; he must have forgotten. (Platt, teeth out and shoes off, smoking more nicotine stains onto his fingers, enjoyably trawling through catalogues of electrical appliances to see what he could get for his daughter's birthday on the estate account, had not switched the bell through to the flat since last October).

Madeleine almost went to fetch him before it occurred to her that she could open the door herself. An unknown woman was standing half turned away on the wide step, a large woman in trousers, gray hair escaping from an anorak hood which hid her face as she surveyed the dripping trees crowding the gravel sweep. Someone with a collecting tin?

"Good afternoon. Can I help you?" Madeleine asked in her gentle voice.

"Yes, get the bell fixed," said the stranger cheerfully, turning toward her and adding briskly as Madeleine blinked in surprise, "Come on, Mads, get a grip."

Only one person had called her that since she left school. Madeleine stared astounded into the heavy-featured, smiling face under the straggles of hair. "Joss? *Joss!*" It couldn't be, of all the people in the world, it couldn't really be Joss, just when she so desperately needed—

"Maybe in this part of the world you don't call this rain but I'm getting pretty damp out here."

"Joss, oh Joss, come in. I just can't believe it, it's so wonderful." They had never hugged or kissed, and the long habit of constraint was too strong for Madeleine to clutch her and drag her inside bodily as she longed to do.

"I should have phoned, but well, you know . . ." Joss hunched her thick shoulders out of her damp anorak and slung it across the table in the middle of the hall. Even in that moment Madeleine snatched it away from the polished wood and the bronze of Charles's father's wolfhounds.

"Oh, sorry, love, I'm a bit out of touch with all that stuff," said Joss, unrepentant.

"I'll leave it here." Heady defiance, lost on her guest, to lay the jacket over a chair and not hang it at once in the gunroom.

"Not many changes here," Joss commented without enthusiasm, tramping after her into the drawing room and heading for the fire.

"But Joss, why didn't you let me know you were coming? It doesn't matter a bit, of course,

I'm thrilled to see you, but I didn't even know you were in the country."

Joss, her heels on the marble ledge around the hearth, thrust her broad beige needlecord bottom toward the flames. "Thought I was longing for some mist and coolness, but February in the Highlands may turn out to be a bit much."

"You're only just back? You're terribly brown anyway."

"Leather," Joss said resignedly, swiveling around to peer into the mirror above the mantelpiece. "What's the rest meant to be for?" she added, jerking her neck-up reflection at the huge expanse reaching away to the ornate plasterwork of the cornice.

"Getting the view twice over, I think." The top half of Madeleine's head bobbed beside Joss's and together they contemplated the image of the dim room, the mizzle of rain against the long windows, the looming trees. They let out a little simultaneous gust of laughter. It struck Madeleine that she had almost forgotten how that felt.

"That's better," Joss remarked, looking carefully into the small face at her shoulder. Made up with care, this morning by the look of it. Shadows under the eyes too dark to be concealed. Fine lines around eyes and mouth, flesh beginning its downward trend to blur the delicate jawline, gray wings in the ever-tidy hair. Not bad though, Joss decided. She's a year younger than I am, forty-six then. But what was unexpected was the look of distress, of grief still fresh. Had she minded so much about that selfish cold-blooded husband of hers?

"Joss, why did you stop writing? You promised to give me your address when you moved and you never did. Where have you come from now? And, which is much more important, how long can you stay?"

"I heard about Charles," Joss said abruptly. "Jane Burns-Moore works for OW now, in head office. I saw her as I came through London. She still reads her *Times*, evidently. I'm sorry, Mads. And I'm sorry I didn't know at the time so that I could have written."

Jane Burns-Moore. Light glinting on the bumps of tight pale plaits, gym-slip straining over fat haunches. Did the images of the bored eye during prayers never fade? Madeleine's mind dodged, reluctant to turn to Charles.

"Four months ago now." Strange that her mind should have been dwelling on it this very afternoon. She saw again those little dark figures by the bright water, the slow swell of the moor across the loch, the hills beyond the amazing soft blue of autumn.

"I should have kept in touch," Joss was saying. "How are you coping? Are you OK?" The old protectiveness seemed so natural to them both that they were not even aware of it.

"I'm absolutely fine." Too prompt, too cheerful.

"Um. And the family?"

"Oh, Joss, what a shame! Archie was here today, you've only just missed him." Nevertheless her mind floundered to think of Joss arriving a couple of hours earlier, the two shocks coinciding.

"Pity. I'd like to have seen him." Joss had always got on well with the easygoing schoolboy, absorbed in interests that matched her own. "Is he still based in London?"

"He and Cecil. Yes." Move on hurriedly. "Lisa and Howard are in Surrey, Englefield Green.

Howard's away on business a great deal, of course, but otherwise they lead a tremendously busy social life. Lisa seems to love it all. How is your mother, Joss?" It was too soon to risk any questions that might reach to the raw new shock. Of all the people she knew, and she had had ample time in the last few months to realize that that meant almost no one, Madeleine could talk about it to Joss, but after—how long had it been, ten, eleven years?—intimacy must be reestablished at its own pace.

"Mum? She died last year. That's partly why I'm back, house and so on. No, it's all right, you don't have to say all the right things. You know relations were always pretty strained. I'll fill you in presently, but I'll tell you what, right now I could kill for a cup of tea."

"Oh, Joss, of course. I'm sorry. I should have— Platt always leaves a tray." In spite of herself Madeleine glanced at the French mantel clock on its ormolu column. She always made herself wait till four-thirty, the customary time. If she didn't, the gap between tea and dinner was too long.

"Don't tell me that two-faced misery is still on the go?"

"I don't know what I'd do without him," Madeleine protested.

"Huh. Where's this tray then?"

There was no reason to wait today, Madeleine thought, her spirits lifting.

"This kitchen hasn't changed one jot since I first came here," Joss said in disbelief, staring around at its narrow windows and dark wooden cupboards towering to unscalable heights. "The year you were married and I was doing A levels."

So much of their lives in that one sentence. Each

smiled, acknowledging the pleasure of references that needed no spelling out.

"Nonsense, it's been painted at least twice," Madeleine insisted.

"Yes, always the same color though." Joss eyed with disfavor the cream walls beaded with condensation, the worn beige formica of the worktops.

"And there's a food processor and a—" Madeleine gazed around in the hope of spotting something else.

"And a what?" Joss jeered, and they laughed.

On the table lay a tray, elaborately set, beside it an antique enamel tea caddy, cake tin, and prosaic packet of oatcakes. For one person, every day. Familiar rage rose in Joss, followed by the menopausal wave of heat whose discomfort she was only just beginning to learn to accept. She made herself stand still, take a grip on the anger, allow the surging heat to subside. Whatever new life she attempted would be unendurable if she allowed these pointless and furious comparisons.

Madeleine took the fluted Spode teapot and hot-water jug from tray to Aga, poured a little water from the simmering kettle into each, and swilled it around as solemnly as a child who had just been taught the rite. Why didn't that fool Platt leave the pots and the caddy by the kettle in the first place, Joss thought with renewed irritation, watching Madeleine trot to the sink to pour out the water, then back to the table to spoon in the tea. Or why didn't Madeleine think of objecting, come to that.

With caddy spoon poised Madeleine remembered to say, "Oh, Joss, this is Earl Grey. Would you rather have Indian?"

"Is there any?" Joss had not meant to sound so derisive, but Madeleine didn't notice.

"I know there must be because the staff have it," she said, and Joss shook her head again at the spectacle of Lady Napier, oblivious of any irony, questing eagerly along her own kitchen shelves in search of a teabag.

Chapter Two

Joss, discovering the sofas to be more or less rooted where they stood and unable to find a chair she could shift, lugged a footstool to the hearth and added a cushion. While Madeleine poured the tea, she propped another couple of logs on the fire. "Blood's thin," she said, not exactly in apology.

She topped up the teapot with hot water and stood it on the hearth, wrenched the lids off the cake tin and biscuit barrel which she had brought in, ignoring the plates Platt had left beside them, and dropped them on the floor. "Cake for you, Mads?"

"I don't really eat cake."

"Oh? What do you do with it then?" asked Joss, licking lemon buttercream off her broad thumb.

"Platt puts it out."

"Well, who's it made for?"

"Oh, there's always cake," Madeleine said vaguely.

For Platt Inc. No, don't go down that road, Joss warned herself, you're going to meet this at every turn. Silently, she handed up the biscuits to Madeleine, who after a moment's hesitation took a small oatmeal fragment that might have pleased a dog.

Joss took off her distressed trainers and tossed them aside, loosened one khaki loop sock from where it was stuck between her toes and stretched out her feet beside the teapot. The drawing room at Drumveyn was not accustomed to such behavior.

Their friendship had always been improbable. All they had originally had in common was being reluctantly detached from very different backgrounds by ambitious mothers and sent off to a pretentious little boarding school in north Shropshire—and their loneliness there.

For Felicity Holgate, Mortimers was the cheapest form of private education she could find which, while not too far away, kept a teenage daughter conveniently out of sight.

Amy Barnes, Joss's mother, had more positive but no less self-interested motives. Having won a scholarship to grammar school herself, she had been made to leave at sixteen to help in her parents' ironmongery business, and had spent many bitter years despising everything around her before noticing that her chances of changing her situation were dwindling fast. Choice was limited, and marriage to a traveler in carpet sweepers and brushes, who used home as a place for collecting clean clothes, sleeping off Saturday night at the pub and putting away gargantuan Sunday dinners, hardly improved her lot and did nothing for her self-esteem. But it gave her a daughter and to her all hopes could be transferred; for her sake the long hours in the shop could still be endured and every penny saved.

So forth went Joss to repair matters, poor lumpy morose Joss, who wanted only to be left alone to read and go for solitary walks and hoover information about anything and everything into her greedy brain. She found herself instead shut up for weeks at a time with a hundred and fifty twittering females with affected accents and empty heads, expected to sing and dance and play cricket and wear two pairs of knickers and go to church on Sundays, and make do with library and lab facilities a good deal less adequate than she would have found in the local comprehensive.

From the first she had refused to be made miserable over her vowel sounds and her homemade clothes and sarcastic public reminders to use a fork for her pudding, which she didn't call pudding anyway, and she had found malice soon abandoned in the face of her indifference. But nothing had ever softened her contemptuous hatred for the place.

Madeleine remained apart for different reasons. Anxious to do her best, she was forever baffled by the magical way everyone else seemed to know where to go and what to do. On hockey field and cricket pitch, pouring along the polished corridors in quacking groups, screaming guardedly around the record player in the common room over the current pop idol, they all seemed to have some mysterious key to what was going on which she never found.

All she lived for was release to the mellow brick William and Mary ex-farmhouse on the Welsh border, where her mother's social aspirations exceeded her father's income (as an architect in a small local firm) on a regular basis. There, oblivious of tensions and warning signs, Madeleine could be sure of long stretches of time when no one expected anything of her but to be invisible.

Memories were of long quiet hours in various ref-
uges—the walled garden, the warm tomato-
scented greenhouse, her blue-and-white bedroom
where no one ever came, and the tackroom which
was slowly turning into a lumber room now that
her cross Welsh pony had been sold in spite of all
her pleas, where she secretly gobbled up a term's
worth of *Woman's Own* and Mills and Boon filched
from the kitchen.

Misfits as she and Joss both were at Mortimers,
they made no overtures toward each other but
gradually over the years a habit of being together
developed. Escaping to a favorite retreat neither
minded finding the other there, after a while
drawing comfort from the familiar undemanding
presence, and a friendship formed that made
school almost bearable.

It was strong enough to survive after Madeleine
had left Mortimers and Joss had watched appalled
as she was pitched without delay into the marriage market. Felicity Holgate saw a pretty, biddable daughter as her best chance for a future meal
ticket and all the years of clutching at county coat-
tails had to pay off now. She was well aware that
she had no time for finesse; the façade could be
kept in place for a few months more at most.

She could hardly believe her luck in capturing
a Scottish baronet with an estate still bolstered by
sound Edinburgh rents. Never mind that he was
sixteen years older than the childishly immature
Madeleine, or so lazy that he had been thrown
out of Eton, a feat in itself, or that questions might
reasonably be asked as to why he had never married before—he had taken the bait. Dazed by her
achievement, Felicity did not realize that Charles
himself was under orders to find a wife and start

breeding, nor that her complacent plans for moving into Drumveyn would be shattered on her first nightmare visit there once Charles and Madeleine were back from their honeymoon. Her co-mother-in-law, a generation her senior, was in residence and in power. Felicity Holgate was a lightweight beside her, a mere beginner. She fled the field without a thought for her daughter's plight under this régime.

Her own marriage was over, the house sold, Madeleine's father in Chicago with a gravelly-voiced, hard-drinking American widow who had shared a gun in a syndicate he belonged to, and she herself was soon to run out of houses where she could sponge and play cards and get her hands on the gin she had not even realized she needed so badly.

Charles had loathed Joss of course, but her visits to Drumveyn were the one issue on which Madeleine was prepared to be stubborn. And Joss was concerned enough to come, and sensible enough to hold her tongue, more or less, when she got there. For Madeleine, conscientious and compliant as ever, was doing her best to adapt to her formidable new situation.

She had been genuinely attracted to Charles, for not all her mother's unsubtle maneuvering would have made her marry him if she had not thought life with him would be better than any alternative on offer. He had been quite good-looking in those days in a conventional way, fair-haired and fair-skinned, tall, the later flabby heaviness kept at bay by his hours on river and hill. And he had made an effort to be agreeable, relieved to find someone as unalarming as Madeleine thrown in his way, perhaps not precisely meeting his mother's criteria, but certainly acceptable by this stage. His chief concern was to have the whole business settled and get back to his own pursuits without further interruption. As to sex, he had always considered it on the whole a waste of effort, but he thought it might be rather pleasant to have this pretty and good-natured little creature on hand, without the trouble and expense of pursuit.

Madeleine in her own way had felt much the same. She had never felt at ease with her contemporaries, who awed her with their casual assurance. And she had wanted to do as her mother wished, though hopes of pleasing her seemed as vain as the hopes of childhood. Above all, the terrifying question of What To Do when she left school would be safely removed for ever.

She accepted without question Lady Napier's presence at Drumveyn and her continued control of house and staff, garden and estate—even her continued use of the title without modification. It was school all over again, the earnest effort to learn the rules, do the right things—one of which was producing Archie within the first year of her marriage, when she was still eighteen.

Carrying her flight bag upstairs after tea—guest, not hostess, had thought it might be a good idea to get some heating going in her room—Joss was nearly overpowered by the old distaste which came rushing back. The same lifeless smell, the same damp-yellow-sand carpet and the dingy matte-white walls, the dark paintings too depressing to examine, the pointless objects in their unchanging places on the console tables along the corridors, the meager lighting, cold that met you like a steel door—all conjured up too clearly the hostile spirits of the past, their power undiminished, watching, assessing, rejecting as unworthy.

The old lady had moved to Edinburgh years ago, but it had obviously never occurred to Madeleine to change anything. Or perhaps Charles wouldn't allow it. Or perhaps they were hard up by now.

Why did I come back to this bloody awful place? she asked herself, as Madeleine opened the door to one of those characterless Drumveyn bedrooms you could never tell apart. High dark mahogany furniture, colors long ago drained from carpets and curtains, heavy white cotton embroidered bedspread. Counterpane, she heard Lady N. Senior amend tartly.

"It will probably take awhile to come through," Madeleine said, feeling the stone-cold ridges of the huge radiator with a hopeful hand.

"It probably will," Joss assented. "How about a couple of hot water bottles?"

"Platt will put them in as soon as he comes back."

Exactly as of old, conversation was parceled out by the slow-paced routine. Platt came to remove the tray, his martyred butler act a lot less subtle these days, Joss observed. An unannounced visitor, a disreputable van at the door, a bedroom arbitrarily allotted without reference to him, there was only fish for one and Mrs. Platt had already been having her say about that, and someone had been meddling with his fire. It was all in the pursed lips, the not-quite-silent gathering up of cups, the, "Of *course* I remember Miss Barnes."

Then the question of changing for dinner. Did Madeleine really go through that rigmarole, alone, night after night?

"I've nothing to change into, sorry," Joss said
flatly. "So can I be let off the bath till my room's
warmed up a bit?"

"Oh, Joss, I'm sorry. Would you like to use my
bathroom? Or perhaps we could put a heater—"

"Can't I just have a bath when I go to bed?"
When it will do most good, Joss added mentally,
having suffered many chilly nights in this house.

"Would you prefer to do that? Then you won't
mind being left on your own for a while? Would
you like the television on? Or here's the *Times*.
Platt will give you a drink if you'd like one."

No question of Madeleine not having her own
bath, Joss noted with amusement. "Look, just
buzz off," she told her tolerantly. "I'll watch
telly." But within minutes the blank faces of refu-
gees, a close-up of the huge eyes of a starving
baby, brought her angrily to her feet to turn it off.

The dining room was full of uncomfortable associations. The Dowager Lady Napier had done
much of her claw sharpening here. A female biolo-
gist at a red brick university had been an excellent
scratching post. At nineteen, twenty, Joss had not
found it easy to deal with, especially as she knew
Madeleine would suffer if she fought back as she
yearned to do.

Now as then, dinner took forever. How could
Madeleine bear it? Physically, as much as anything else; Platt's brown-stained fingers, the dan-
druff on his collar, his unpressed striped trousers.
Tinned consommé, Melba toast. Sherry offered, refused. A tiny, tiny roll of haddock and a lot of
egg sauce. Steak suspiciously spongy. How had
that been thawed out? Joss wondered. Madeleine
appeared not to notice. Platt had opened wine.
"I'm sorry, your ladyship. I made sure it would

be required." Sorbet which had been in and out of the freezer. A savory offered, Platt daring them to accept. Cheese—cheddar.

Madeleine ate two mouthfuls of this, one mouthful of that, talked brightly, producing acceptable topics from long habit, while in another part of her brain the news Archie had brought clamored for attention. Charles had never wanted to leave Drumveyn, of course, but perhaps later in the year she would go down and see Cecil, stay with Lisa.

Yes, it was surprising, wasn't it, she agreed with Joss, that Lisa had chosen London to live in when she left school, she had always seemed such a country person. . . .

Archie had enjoyed his university work, but his present job, which took him to all kinds of awful places making soil analysis surveys and reports, seemed to suit him even better. . . .

She asked of course about Joss's work. "I don't think I ever heard why you left the Sudan. And didn't you get some kind of promotion?"

"They made me a field coordinator, if you can call that promotion," Joss said brusquely, her face darkening. We left the Sudan because they were shooting relief workers as they got off the plane. How could she begin to make Madeleine understand, any of it? "Look, I'm sorry, I'd like to forget about it for a while if you don't mind," she said frowning, with a dismissive shake of her head more for her own thoughts than for the questions, and Madeleine quickly turned to reminiscences of school.

When we're alone we'll talk, each promised herself, but to their dismay they found that, even when Platt had finally gone and the big house was silent around them, their ease together was only surface deep. Certainly Madeleine knew she was as far as ever from being able to broach the subject that was so tormenting her.

I should have gone straight to the cottage, Joss thought frustratedly, half listening as Madeleine told her about her mother, now divorced for the fourth time and living with a greenkeeper in Vale do Lobo. This place just winds me up tighter and tighter. I must get away tomorrow.

Madeleine looked devastated when she said so, her face sagging in distress. "Surely not so soon, Joss? I need you. Don't leave me alone again."

"I'll be back soon, I promise. It's just that I need time to think, a bit of space."

"You could be alone here. I'd leave you in peace."

"I've just got to be on my own."

She registered with wry admiration Madeleine's swift response, putting Joss's needs before her own. "Of course you must want that. The conditions you work in, the things you see every day, it must be a nightmare. I do understand."

No, you don't understand, you haven't a clue, Joss thought wearily as she hunched her big body in pants and T-shirt around the hot water bottle she had refilled from the tap, and tried not to touch one inch more of the icy linen sheets than she had to. You don't even know what's going on outside your own front door. You have become one of them, a Napier. They did their work well.

And along the corridor Madeleine lay in her hand-stitched Victorian nightdress, hair brushed and face creamed, neat, straight and wakeful on her side of the big bed. The safe cocoon she had lived in had survived Charles's death; it had not survived today's events. She felt adrift, lost, the ground gone from under her feet. Terror at her own inadequacy filled her as thoughts of Archie and Cecil poured anxiously back. Would she ever be able to give them what they expected from her?

Chapter Three

Archie knew he would find Cecil at her studio, the long high light-flooded room overlooking changing dockland where she had lived before they were married and which she too often, in his view, used as a retreat still. "Twenties aesthetic," he called it, not unkindly. Decorated with her cherished Omega Workshops collection of hand-painted screens, candleshades, pottery and fabrics, with the Sonrel "Couronne de Fleurs Blanches" glowing against its dark green wall, he could admire its beauty but couldn't have lived in it.

"Did she understand at all?" Cecil came quickly to meet him.

"It would have helped if you'd come with me."

"She hates it." Cecil's eagerness changed to instant coolness but Archie saw and understood the lift of her chin as she hid disappointment in indifference.

He put his arm around her and drew her gently against him, enjoying as he always did the feel of the slight flexible collection of bones in contrast to his own muscular bulk. "We knew she'd need time to accept it."

"What did she say?"

He sighed, leaning his head against her wet-seal dark hair. "Those things she perceived to be correct. She did her best."

"I want her to love this baby."

"So that it has a grandmother's love, part of the specification?"

Cecil twisted in the circle of his arm, fluid as a cat, and looked searchingly into his eyes, level with her own hazel-green ones dramatically enlarged by professional make-up. "Anyone else would have said that sarcastically. It's part of it, of course."

"I know," he said gently, cupping a hand around her head to draw her cheek against his own. Cecil, the product of a marriage which had split apart when she was very small, had never known the stability of a family, and she wanted it desperately for her own child.

"I want Madeleine to enjoy having a grandchild too." Cecil hoped, but did not say, that it might be a way to bring her closer to his mother, with whom she had so far failed to establish any contact or understanding.

"She's anything but happy about it now, I'm afraid," Archie admitted. "The words, 'But what would your father have said?' were quivering in the air, though to give her her due she managed not to say them out loud. But she does find it impossible to discuss such matters. I couldn't get through to her—partly that wall of convention and so-called civilized behavior she's built around herself which makes her at least a generation out of date, and partly that old fool Platt padding about all the time. It's a pity we're not nearer. It would help if she could feel more involved."

"I know, but we really can't go rushing up and down to Scotland all the time, there's so much on hand just now. I'm absolutely up to my eyes—the Fitzroy Crescent job is going to be colossal—which reminds me, look what's just arrived—''

She was off to her work table, reaching for a portfolio with gloating pleasure, the baby forgotten. Archie walked quietly down the room after her. Had she turned and seen his face she would have been surprised to find an aching longing there.

Joss didn't leave Drumveyn the next morning. Overnight snow had swept the west coast and was now spreading eastward across the Grampians. Platt suppressed this news, knowing that Madeleine never turned on radio or television in the morning, and wanting Joss with her shrewd stare out of the house as soon as possible. Joss, however, had gone out to put her kit in the van, taken one look at the sky and come in to turn on the television.

There was no point in setting off. She was relieved in a way to have the decision made for her, since her conscience had been nagging her. Though God knows what we'll do with ourselves, she thought resignedly, as breakfast wound on its laborious way.

"We mustn't be back late from our walk as it's Mr. Maclaren's Tuesday," Madeleine warned her as they left the frigid dining room.

Did she still walk every morning, not from choice or pleasure or if the weather lured her out, but because that had always been the rule? It sounded like it. "Who's Mr. Maclaren?"

"Don't you remember? The factor? He comes up from the Edinburgh office every other week. I think you must have met him, he's looked after the estate for years."

"Oh God, that anemic-looking old woman. Don't tell me you still put up with him?"

"Well—" It had never occurred to Madeleine that she didn't have to. "He brings the wages, collects invoices and so on, has a look at what needs doing on the estate, sees the grieve and the keeper . . ."

"And what do you talk about at lunch?"

"Well, any work being done. Repairs, plans . . ." And Mr. Maclaren's digestion and Mrs. Maclaren's heart murmur.

"Oh yeah," said Joss, supplying them for herself.

Madeleine laughed. "Let's go and put our boots on."

They walked briskly in the gray and white landscape under a bulging goose-breast sky, Madeleine's face going pink, Joss's going mauve. Drumveyn House stood on a jut of ground between the river and a tumbling burn which fed the loch below the garden. They went up the farm road which climbed behind the house to the steading a quarter of a mile away, past a block of conifers Joss had seen planted, down the path by the burn, around the loch and back up the front drive. The Drumveyn exercise circuit. Joss wondered as she watched Madeleine step out dutifully if she ever looked around her any more.

Platt met them with the news that Mr. Maclaren would not be coming because of the "inclement conditions." Platt, however (if they didn't keep him hanging around too long giving them lunch), had decided to go down to Muirend, their nearest shopping town a few miles down the glen.

"But are you sure that's wise?" Madeleine asked doubtfully but courteously. "If the forecast is so bad?"

"I've the household shopping to think of, my lady." Did Madeleine really not mind that patronizing tone, Joss wondered. "If the weather worsens I may not be able to make my usual run tomorrow." Chez Platt they were out of videos, breaded scampi, oven chips and six-packs.

The snow reached Drumveyn by mid-afternoon. Platt phoned at five to say the glen road was closed. He and Mrs. Platt booked themselves into the Benmore Hotel (three stars), had a five-course dinner and two bottles of Beaujolais which seriously disagreed with them, quarreled all night and kept the bill for Mr. Maclaren.

It was as much their absence as the scream of the wind, the dizzy whirl of flakes against the windows and the early darkness which gave Joss and Madeleine an enjoyable sense of beleaguerment.

"It's fairly chucking it down," Joss reported, taking a last look out before yanking the cord of the heavy curtains with a vigor that rushed them together in a draughty flurry. "We're on our own, Mads."

"It's quite exciting, though I'm glad you're here. I don't think I'd have enjoyed it much on my own."

"It's a nice change to feel thoroughly irresponsible. Though do you suppose the miserable Platt will have left us anything to eat? More likely had to go shopping because he'd run out of everything."

"Oh, there must be something," Madeleine protested, beginning to look faintly worried.

"Have you ever cooked a meal in your own kitchen, just as a matter of interest?"

"Well, not a *meal.*"

"What then?"

"Marmalade. Eggs in aspic."

"Very sustaining."

How nice it was to giggle with no one to disapprove, Madeleine found herself thinking, conscious of knots of tension loosening as they began light-heartedly to hunt for food. She had to be deterred, however, from embarking on a meal along the usual Drumveyn lines.

"Look, forget the soup-fish-meat business," Joss told her, "and forget the dining room. What's wrong with baked beans on toast in front of the fire?"

"Oh, please not baked beans!"

"Well, here's a couple of trout. How about those with brown bread? There's about a kilo of cheddar here and there must be some fruit somewhere."

They built up the fire in the drawing room, pulled a low table in front of it, retrieved Joss's footstool which had been put back in its place by Platt, fetched another from the library, brought in the food and began on the trout with a definite feeling of midnight feasting. They had agreed on wine but couldn't find the cellar key. However, a trawl had revealed plenty of alcohol in one form or another, to Madeleine's surprise, and she settled for white wine from a box found in the little room where inside and outside staff did all their tea-drinking, while Joss chose lager.

And suddenly they were talking, the questions not so different from yesterday's but the answers on a new level.

"You feel guilty, don't you, doing this?" Joss's

jerk of the head took in the plates on the carpet, the half-burned backbone of a trout she had thrown onto the fire, the lager can on the hearth.

Madeleine didn't deny it. "Twenty-eight years," she reminded her.

"What will you do?"

"I haven't begun to think. I mean literally. Since Charles died I've just gone on from day to day, exactly as before. It's quite easy to do; the framework has never altered. And with a place this size there are always day-to-day problems, things breaking down, someone off work, decisions, about this and that which give the illusion of being busy. In the summer there's the garden. But it's all just getting through time. To you it must seem ludicrous, criminal even . . ."

"I hadn't realized Charles had meant so much to you?"

"Charles?"

Your husband. But it was not the moment for teasing. "You looked wretched when I arrived yesterday."

"Not about Charles. To be honest I scarcely think of him, as a person, though I suppose I still mentally refer everything to him. No, yesterday it was something else . . ."

Her voice had changed, as though she was talking to herself. She gazed into the fire, her face looking pinched and tired. Joss gave her time.

"Archie and Cecil are going to have a baby."

Joss frowned at the tone and refrained from leaping in with, "But that's marvelous, isn't it?" She waited quietly.

"They don't seem able to—have one of their own," Madeleine explained, speaking with an effort. "So Cecil is having one—artificially." She jibbed at the complete phrase.

"They've decided that's the best answer for them?" Joss was beginning with business-like interest when Madeleine raised eyes huge with distress and revulsion to hers. "Oh, Mads, poor love, you hate it, don't you?"

"It's disgusting," Madeleine burst out. "Archie's wife—to think of another man's—to be accepted as his child, and not be part of him—" She broke off, her whole body shuddering involuntarily. "Joss, it's obscene to me, the whole idea. A stranger. Who? What do we know about him?"

"Try not to think of it as another man's seed." Madeleine shuddered, closing her eyes.

Joss tried again. "It's just clinical, like—" What will not make her shudder? "—like a routine check-up. Start to think of it as a baby, look ahead to the child that will be."

"But what sort of child? It should be Archie's, with his character, looking like him."

"But they must have discussed all this?"

"Cecil wants the experience of giving birth, of bonding. You know how intense she always is."

Joss knew nothing about Archie's wife except that she was an interior designer already well known in her field, and from the wedding photograph that Madeleine had enclosed in a letter that she was dark and skinny, aloof of expression and exotic of dress.

". . . so ice-cold, everything planned and ordered and always, always successful. Work and marriage quite separate. She still uses her professional name, Cecil Kerevan."

"But that's not unusual."

"She's kept on the studio flat where she used

to live—it's miles from their house in Richmond and when Archie's away she often sleeps there."

"Perhaps if she's deep in some job that's more practical than going back and forth. But does the marriage work? Are they happy?"

"They appear to be. But it all seems so *odd*!" A mother's baffled cry.

"Well, if they're happy . . . But presumably the baby will change their life-style a bit?"

"Archie says Cecil is waiting to see how pregnancy affects her, what the hormonal changes dictate."

"She sound like a pain in the butt to me."

"No, she's not, she's charming. Don't snort, she really is. She just likes to make her own evaluation of everything. I suppose nothing will change much for a while anyway. Archie's in Spain this week and then he goes back to Bahia very soon to do a final report on the effects of some irrigation scheme. That's the part he likes best—what he calls the people side of the job."

"Talk about the baby. Do you mind that one day it might inherit all this, for example?"

Madeleine looked startled. "Goodness, I hadn't got as far as that."

"That it will be your grandchild?"

"But it won't be!"

"Won't Archie want you to see it that way?"

They talked on, while outside the whine of the storm gradually died, and Joss, not without relief, pushed her own problems aside. How many women today, of our generation, she wondered, would have been quite so shattered at this development? Madeleine's life here at Drumveyn was more outlandish than her daughter-in-law's, if only she knew it.

The ticking of the dying radiators, the graying fire, a seeping chill, stirred them in the end.

"Gracious, ought I to lock anything?" Madeleine exclaimed, coming back to reality as they stood up stiffly, realizing they were cold.

"Burglars and rapists out and about on their cross-country skis?" Joss mocked.

Madeleine laughed. "But there must be something we should do. Platt always sees to that sort of thing."

"You should sack Platt, you know."

"Sack him? Whatever for?" Madeleine asked blankly.

"To see how you get on without him."

"No, thank you very much, I've quite enough to worry about just now as it is."

"Lisa's life sounds pretty satisfactory, anyway," Joss offered encouragingly.

"Oh, yes, no problems there," Madeleine agreed. Except that we are strangers, she amended sadly to herself.

When Madeleine heard her door open she thought that the road had been cleared and the Platts were back. But it was Joss with the tray, crashing it down with a casualness that Platt at his most petulant could not have matched.

"God, this room's even colder than mine," Joss complained, going to drag back the curtains. "Not all that much snow, surprisingly enough. It must have stopped when the wind dropped during the evening. Impressive drifts though."

"Joss, you are good," Madeleine exclaimed, hoisting herself up in the bed. "Not just tea, actual breakfast." Which she never ate.

"Bit of a mistake bringing it up here, I'm begin-

ning to think. I hadn't reckoned on the tempera-
ture you put up with. Do you want a sweater
or something?"

"This will do, thanks."

"A bed jacket? For Pete's sake, do they still
make those things?" Joss lifted a cumbersome
electric fire out of the hearth, brought it to the full
extent of its flex toward the bed and switched on
both bars. "Give me the eiderdown." Cross-legged
on the bed with it draped around her shoulders,
she dipped soldiers into her boiled egg and
plunged back without preliminaries into last
night's conversation.

"Why can't Archie and Cecil have a baby of
their own? You didn't say."

"Archie apparently is—has a low sperm count."
Madeleine rushed this out so primly that Joss let
loose a shout of laughter which tipped the tray
and involved a lot of floundering to get the eiderdown back into place.

"You are priceless. You look as though you'd
bitten on something nasty. Poor old Mads, married for nearly thirty years and two kids and you
have to steel yourself to pronounce the word
sperm."

"I don't find it a normal breakfast-time topic,
certainly," Madeleine retorted.

"OK, but I was thinking about the baby while
I waited to get up. So if that was the problem—
and Archie's away three-quarters of the time in
any case—Cecil probably worked out the opti-
mum age for motherhood and decided not to wait
any longer. I've been thinking about you too, and
how much you mind about it."

"If they could just have adopted a child. That's
surely more normal," Madeleine cried.

"You mean so that the baby could be the product of two strangers, instead of one stranger and your son's wife?"

Madeleine stared at her, knife with triangle of butter in one hand, fragment of toast in the other, and began to laugh. "Oh, Joss, thank heavens you turned up to talk sense to me. And to be honest, I do understand something of why Cecil is so determined to have a child of her own. Archie's told me about her own childhood; she never seems to have had any happy family life at all, so I can see that this matters a lot to her."

"You should get her to talk to you about it—what on earth is that?"

Their isolation roared and throbbed to an end as the tractor with blade on arrived from the farm to clear the snow from the courtyard and then go down the drive to the glen road, which had already been swept by the Council plow.

Mr. Maclaren's office phoned to say he would be leaving shortly and Madeleine had just started to panic about lunch when Platt appeared, pallid and red-eyed, urgently needing to find fault with all that had been done or had not been done.

"Poor Platt looks quite exhausted," said Madeleine.

Joss shook her head.

She would have stayed another night but lunch finished her. All the fuss would have been more bearable if the food had been better, she thought angrily, discovering the blackened underside of her chop. And Madeleine didn't seem to notice that at his own level Maclaren treated her with the same patronizing dismissiveness as Platt.

The conversation rambled on as it must have

done on every alternate Tuesday since the beginning of time—the disastrous price of sheep, the crippling exchange rate which was keeping American shooting parties at home, the cost of repairs, wage increases . . . Madeleine showed dutiful concern in it all, but Joss couldn't imagine that she felt any real fear that her sheltered world would ever be under threat.

"Do you really think it's a good idea to set off so late, Joss? Wouldn't it be better to wait till morning? You can't possibly hope to get all the way tonight and even if you managed it, wouldn't it be rather horrid to arrive at an empty cottage in the dark?"

"No, honestly, I'll just push off. I can always b. and b. somewhere if the roads are too bad."

"Drumochter is open, I believe," Platt interposed.

Thank you, Platt.

"But this cottage, isn't it very remote?" Madeleine worried on. "And wasn't there much more snow in the west than we had here?"

"I'll get there. Walk, if necessary."

Going out to the van with her, Madeleine begged, "Come back as soon as you can bear to, Joss. It's going to be hard being alone again, just as I was before."

It was a more explicit plea than she was usually prepared to make and for a moment Joss hesitated. But hadn't she resolved that from now on she was going to consider her own wishes for a change? Hadn't that been part of her decision? And for Madeleine, apart from Archie's bombshell, nothing had fundamentally changed.

"Just a couple of weeks, Mads, then I'll be back, I promise. Anyway, you'll be all right now that the road's open and things are back to normal.''

''Yes, of course I will.'' But they both knew that Madeleine had not been worrying about the storm.

Chapter Four

In the deep seat of the Mercedes the child looked like a doll tucked into the seat belt. Uncomplaining, she had sat silently through the miles, mostly with her head turned away and pressed back against the seat, staring sideways at the drab winter landscape, or more probably from her angle at the drab winter sky.

I mustn't go on thinking of her as "the child," Lisa told herself, but it seemed to preserve anonymity, keep at just bearable distance the shattering events of the last two days. All she must concentrate on now was getting them both safely to Drumveyn, the only possible refuge she could turn to.

It was a long time since she had seen it in that light, the haven longed for through endless school terms. Archie there as the perfect companion, always involved in a new interest when she had just caught up with the last one, but tolerant, accepting her, sharing the long days out of doors with the ponies, the boat, their friends among the estate families.

Somewhere in her teens that had all changed. Archie had made an early transition into an adult world. Cheerful, outwardly casual but in fact quite determined, he had come and gone as he pleased, leaving her behind at last. The father who had petted and spoiled her when she was small had become bored by her. Grannie too had become increasingly caustic with the years, eying the large clumsy teenager with open distaste. "Size seven shoes! The child's a freak." The crisp damning voice echoed down the years.

And hearing it again Lisa knew she had checked at the part that really mattered. Why had her mother not intervened? She had become so— muted—never arguing with Grannie or protecting them from her sharp tongue, deferring to their father in everything. No, it had been more than that. Her mother had found a towering awkward daughter, bursting out of her clothes and banging into the furniture, dismaying and disappointing. Vividly still, Lisa remembered her own hopeless envy for her mother's light step and smooth dark hair, the neat small feet, the well-kept hands.

There had been one brief period of hope. Grannie, saying there were friends with whom she wished to re-establish contact before they died (their views on this were not given), had moved to Edinburgh and settled into a somber flat overlooking Bruntsfield golf course. There she had taken up bridge and central heating and alcohol in an intensive way and had only lasted a couple of years.

The way had seemed clear for a new understanding between Lisa and her mother, but somehow they had achieved only edgy frustration, with Lisa being rude and Madeleine looking hurt. Her mother's chief concern had still been that everything should be done exactly as her father liked it, which meant the way Grannie had done it, and

Drumveyn had become more stifling with each year that passed.

It was Archie who had got her away from it all, pushing her into doing a secretarial course, ordering her to lose weight and keeping a kindly eye on her during his erratic appearances in London. She had dieted frantically, done well on the course. She had made friends, gone out with men. London had been full of size seven shoes. She had landed a job in an employment agency (not that it had called itself that) which placed management high flyers. Howard had been a client.

With an exclamation of helpless frustration as her thoughts came back inevitably to the focus of pain she had been trying to forget, she woke up to where she was, sweeping up the outside lane with the needle on ninety. Shaking, she let the speed drop back, pulled into the center lane and found she had broken into a sweat of fear, remembering how she had driven blindly home from the airport through the torrent of morning traffic two days ago after Howard had . . .

Back swarmed the images, the incredible agonizing facts. Howard's unmoved face as he told her what he had decided, must have been planning for weeks, months; his awful efficiency as rapidly and calmly he detailed the arrangements he had made to end their life together; his absolute lack of emotion, as though in his mind he had already moved on, away from her, and any emotional response from her would be merely irritating.

The house itself, which he said he had given her, had felt subtly changed when she had somehow reached it. The tap of her heels as she crossed the parquet had sounded hollow, no longer a familiar daytime sound, as though familiarity had been stripped with one violent gesture from everything.

For a long time she had sat at the desk where she spent hours a week planning and recording their complex entertaining and keeping the careful household accounts Howard insisted on. She had stared numbly at the scatter of objects, as though hoping to find something there which would fix and steady her reeling thoughts.

The room behind her contained nothing that was hers alone; nothing of her character. Large and light, with the undertone of soft gold that Howard liked, each piece of furniture selected and placed by an expert paid to know what he was doing, with its Chinese rugs, its nineteenth-century seascapes, the formal flower arrangements Howard insisted on all the year round, it was entirely his.

As she had sat hunched there, still in the grip of shock, her mind had focused on one point, as though the rest was too much to take in. He had asked her to drive him to Heathrow, just as usual. He had let her think everything was normal, had accepted as his right that one last convenient service from her.

It had taken so few minutes, sitting in the car outside the terminal, to tell her of the obliteration of their life together. He had planned it so meticulously and she knew he would have closed all doors, left no clues. Appeal to the company, to the other directors, those background powers of her marriage, for information about where he had gone, what he planned, would be useless. Impossible, in fact, for the company no longer existed; he had wiped it out with everything else.

After a while she had moved, going through without conscious purpose to his study. There the computer faced her, her rival for his time and attention. She had smiled wryly at the thought, begun to laugh and instantly been in tears, caught up in terrible racking weeping, clutching his chair, barely able to stand. After a while she had gone up to lie on her bed, their bed. Everything in the room was utterly normal, all the ordinary personal belongings still there, announcing dual possession, the married state.

It had been dusk before she had crawled off the bed, her eyes raw and smarting, and gone downstairs through the warm immaculate house, the hall sweet with the scent of hyacinths. In the kitchen she had begun to make coffee in the Cafetière, then remembered she didn't like the Cafetière, the coffee was never hot. With a careless sweep over the sink she had emptied out water and grounds, dropped the jug in the bin, rebelling in that rough gesture against the extreme order of the house and the years of believing that by achieving perfection she would please.

She had found the Nescafé Mrs. Porter used and paused spoon in hand. Had Howard sacked Mrs. Porter? He hadn't mentioned it, but of course there was the file he had given her, with the registration documents for the car, insurance policies, television license, all the trivia normally dealt with by his office. Perhaps Mrs. Porter would be in it too. But Mrs. Porter might have something to say about that, her tired brain had suggested, struggling for normality.

Sleep had been impossible. She could not escape the insistent questions. Where had she gone wrong? She had tried so hard to be exactly what he wanted her to be. They had been happy, hadn't they, *hadn't* they? And even in her bewilderment and growing anger she had wanted the comfort of his solid body, his arms.

Morning had brought more practical worries. She would have to tell her mother, Archie and Cecil. People. And then what? Her life had been marriage to Howard. Everything she did, said, thought, wore, cooked, and bought had been tied up with him. House, garden, friends, golf, holidays—all had been of his choice, all accepted eagerly by her because she had never had the confidence to create a style of her own.

She had got up and dressed eventually, wandering aimlessly through the silent house but, as though already feeling that it could offer her nothing, ending up again and again staring out of the drawing room window at the beds of rose stumps circled by tarmac, the rock garden cold with gravel and professional planning which sloped down to the road and the village green.

In those awful moments at the airport when she had desperately appealed to him, not so much asking why he was leaving her as urgently needing to understand why if he could do this he had chosen her in the first place, he had been devastatingly explicit.

"You were exactly what I needed at the time—the company still had a long way to climb in those days, if you remember. Baronet's daughter, young, naive, adaptable—you were perfect. And you're a handsome creature, Lisa, don't forget that. You did an excellent job and I'm grateful to you."

"But weren't we happy?" she had cried wildly. "Didn't you love me?"

But that he had refused to answer, handing her

the file he had prepared with a brisk, "You'll need these," snapping shut a new briefcase across his knee.

Need them? MOT certificates? The boiler manual? Why had she not hit him over the head with them, refused to let him go, insisted on—what?

She leaned her forehead on the pane with a groan, shutting her eyes. When they had first met she had been so sure he had wanted her, as she was, for herself. He had said he liked her height and she had walked tall, glowing with new confidence and happiness. She had happily accepted the style he had chosen for her and had felt attractive for the first time in her life.

She had seen it too as a chance to please her mother. No drugs or rebellion or undesirable lovers for her, but a good-looking prosperous husband in his thirties, his career established, Hawks Club, Old Canfordian (Charles said he'd never heard of the place). No one could disapprove now.

She had felt the hopeless tears threaten again and blinked fiercely, staring out across the blanched grass of the green. They played cricket there in the summer. A city cab was prowling slowly along the far side.

Howard had made, as the phrase went, ample provision for her. And she still had her own allowance, now paid by Archie, which she never touched. Had Howard intended her to stay on here, in this house, alone? Doing what? Chasms of purposeless time gaped before her. Without him to look after she had no function.

She had been startled to see the taxi turning into the drive below her. Howard! One second's dizzy, crazy hope. It had all been some cruel joke after all. She had rushed madly through the orderly room, across the hall, tugged open the studded oak door. In the instant of seeing that an unknown child was standing there, a suitcase at her feet, Lisa had realized also that the taxi was heading out of the gate.

"Hey, hang on! There's some mistake. You've come to the wrong address. Stop! Come back!"

The taxi had vanished. From the step the small girl had regarded her silently, eyes huge with apprehension, then with shy politeness had offered the letter she held ready in her hand.

Chapter Five

I should talk to her, Lisa thought with guilty
compunction, glancing worriedly at the still little
figure, but even to have her here beside me hurts.
I don't want to look at her or speak to her. I just
want to get to Drumveyn.

The child had looked arrestingly foreign, standing there on the doorstep, watchful and nervous
in the overcast winter light. Eight, nine? Very
slight and straight, with a long slender neck and
blue-black hair cut stylishly short. Her lemon yellow pleated skirt and cropped jacket, strap shoes
and white knee-length socks, were far too light for
the bitter day.

"I'm sorry, you must have come to the wrong
house. Who brought you here?" Lisa had demanded, infuriated at having to concentrate on
any extraneous problem.

In answer the child had made another little of-
fering movement with the envelope in her hand.

"Oh, well, it may tell me something, I suppose,"
Lisa had muttered crossly, taking it. It said simply
"Lisa" above the address. The writing was Howard's. The worst part had been trying to cope with
what it told her in front of the child, equal victim
of his stupendous egotism and inhumanity, who
had sat obediently where she was told and drawn

on some amazing reserve of stoicism to hold off tears.

"... of us all, you were the one who really longed for a baby. Although I always promised you we'd start a family later I knew I would never want it. A child makes me feel trapped, and I would never willingly let that happen to my life again. Justina didn't intend to have Cristi and to be honest her arrival caused so many problems that she never became reconciled to her. We should have had her adopted straightaway but we didn't foresee all the complications ahead. I know you are a generous and warm person, and I think you will love her as part of me . . ."

Blinding rage had seized Lisa, as with a violent slam of her fist she crushed the letter against her palm, the cold, reasonable, unbelievably arrogant letter. Then she had seen the child flinch and had taken a desperate hold on herself.

"Stay here." She'd heard her own sharp tone and tried again. "Please sit here quietly for a moment, you're quite safe. I'll be back very soon, but I must . . ."

Somehow she had scrambled from the room, got as far as the stairs and collapsed there, drawing deep breaths in an effort to keep calm. After a moment or two, knowing the wound had to be probed, she had made herself smooth out the letter and read on. "You will by now have met Cristi, and will realize that she was born before you and I met, which may make it easier for you to accept her . . ."

What? Lisa had closed her eyes and pressed her forehead against the cold wrought-iron of the banister. Had he been married all along to the mother of this child? Had her own marriage never existed?

A slight sound had roused her. The child had followed her to the drawing room door. She had not touched it, but was looking through the gap of a few inches Lisa had left, as though not wishing to disobey orders but needing to be sure she was not alone. As Lisa looked up she had said nothing, but made a tiny movement, almost imperceptible, which said, "Don't reject me."

Howard's child. I cannot bear to look at her, Lisa had thought. I must get her out of the house. I cannot, *cannot,* believe he thought I would keep her here.

The child had watched her, keeping very still— the only adult presence she could turn to. Lisa wondered what on earth was going through her mind.

"It's Cristi, isn't it?" she had made herself ask with a huge effort.

"Maria-Cristina really. But Daddy always calls me Cristi."

Daddy. Calls me, present tense. Always . . . But she is not to blame, don't pour out your rage on her.

"Well, look, we'll work something out. You're quite all right and you mustn't worry. I'm called Lisa."

"Yes—Lisa, I am to stay with you."

"Well, no, I don't think that will be—"

"In the letter. Daddy said that's what he would arrange. While he and Mummy are away." She spoke natural and effortless English, with a trace of accent.

"I haven't read all the letter yet." But her hands had been shaking too hard to find the place, her mouth suddenly out of control, and as the child watched her gravely Lisa had realized how terrifying it would be for her if she broke down. What can I do with her, where can I send her? she had wondered in panic. I can't bear to question her and uncover more pain. In any case it would be unthinkable to ask her about Howard. But I can't cope with this alone. I can't face those eyes. I must take her home.

Home. Unhappy associations forgotten, that was how Drumveyn had looked to her in that desperate moment. And this morning they had set out, without questions from Cristi or explanations from Lisa.

She had read the whole of Howard's letter now, steadily, right through, more than once. He and Justina (his wife? Or am I still his wife? Or is some other quite different unknown person his wife?) had decided to break all ties and make a completely fresh start. What a bland little cliché that was, Lisa thought, anger boiling up again as she drove. His everyday tone was staggering. He had accomplished what he had set out to do in the UK, he had written; had made a killing in fact (how apt) and had never been much good at sticking to anything once he had made a success of it. Do I come into that category? she wondered with aching bitterness. There was no place for Cristina in his new life and he felt that to send her to Lisa would make some amends for his desertion. He used the word without apology or shame.

In fact he seemed on the whole to think Lisa had done rather well out of their time together. As he saw it, he had turned her into a good-looking, elegant, socially competent woman and had left her very comfortably off. As in widow. When she read this the suspicion had crossed Lisa's mind that he was actually unbalanced. His total self-absorption was surely abnormal and his readiness to give away his own child, which is what he seemed to be attempting, seemed wholly incredible.

Two days ago he had been with her, breezing into the house full of his usual energy and enthusiasm, telling her about an old acquaintance he had run into in the City who had done surprisingly well and might be a valuable contact, tapping away at his computer after dinner, coming yawning to bed saying it sounded as though the weather would be better in the morning and his flight would hopefully be on schedule. Then he had got into bed and drawn her toward him in their own comfortable way of lying, one arm under her neck, his other hand warm on her belly.

Don't, don't . . .

He had said he was flying to New York. Most of his business trips took him there. But did they? Had they? Everything now was open to question. It was always he who had done the phoning when he was away, though he had always left Lisa a contact number. She had prided herself on never using it, pleased when he had said, "Thank God you aren't one of those hounding wives." Would the number have existed if she had tried it, she wondered now.

So humiliation and jealousy matter more than losing him, she mocked herself, in an effort to hold on to some objectivity and fend off threatening hysteria.

The child had flown from Rio the day before yesterday. Her mother had left home two days before. Howard could have gone anywhere, under any name. An unknown lady, it appeared, had escorted Cristi on the flight and had spent the night in London with her, not at a hotel, but in what Cristi called an *apartemento*. Did that belong to Howard? No one else, it seemed, had been there.

No clues, in that, no hint of anyone on whom the child could be off-loaded. The thought of tangling with the Brazilian Embassy was rejected as soon as it came into her head. Archie, the one person who would have been any use, had his answerphone on with the usual airy, "back sometime," message. Cecil's was on too, and though Cecil was quite probably there listening Lisa had found it impossible to formulate any coherent message through her, slamming the receiver down with an angry exclamation.

In her desperation to get away she had barely given a thought to shutting up the house, to what to take or even whether the child was in any state for another journey. She had started to phone Mrs. Porter, realized she couldn't face explanations and instead had scribbled a vague note and left a check. Perhaps Howard had already sent her one. She knew she should warn her mother—one did not arrive at Drumveyn unannounced—but she couldn't face it. She would phone from somewhere on the way.

She was well up the M1 before she remembered that she hadn't set the security alarms, sacred routine. She slowed down, horrified, then accelerated again defiantly. If the house really was hers let it be burgled, burned down or blown up. If she had been alone she would have bored on and on up the motorway, but looking again at the child beside her, not so erect now in the big seat, her conscience woke at last. What was going on in that shapely little head, what terrors and doubts, what longing for her mother, for home and her known world? And in more basic terms, was she hungry, thirsty, needing the loo? I may hate her for being Howard's child, Lisa thought with shame, but surely I can't hate the child herself. And for now I'm all she has.

She turned into the next service area, filled the tank and parked. Then they set off together, heads down against a gritty fume-laden wind which whirled rubbish against them, plucked at their hair, made their eyes water and bent the child's body into a struggling bow. Lisa looked down at the screwed-up wretched face and angry compassion seized her. And I think I'm suffering! She reached out her hand and the child clutched it gratefully.

The unclean, gushing, door-banging loos alarmed Cristi. She looked terrified when Lisa propelled her into a cubicle, peering with wide anxious eyes through the gap as Lisa pulled the door to, but saying nothing. Had she ever been in a public loo before?

"It's all right. I'll be here, just outside." Presumably she's old enough to cope, Lisa thought crossly, unable to face any intimate contact and ashamed of herself.

"Can I really have anything?"

"Anything you like."

"Coca-Cola?" Like a flash.

"If that's what you want."

It was the first time Cristi had smiled. All fears forgotten she gazed rapturously at the motorway cakes and wrapped biscuits and filled rolls, sniffed in the smell of frying and cheap coffee, beamed at having her own tray and helping herself. People waited tolerantly while she made her choice, amused.

Lisa found herself incapable of eating, nauseated by the fuggy food-smelling air. Watching Cristi dealing neatly with beefburger and chips, carefully copying (after a quick look for permission) a small boy at the next table who was lashing on the tomato ketchup, blissfully sucking up her coke through a straw, thick sooty lashes fanning her cheeks, Lisa acknowledged at last that she was beautiful.

She had closed her mind to it, as though ignoring it helped to refute the child's existence. Now she made herself take in the details of the delicate bone structure, the poise of the head, the creamy skin flushed with heat and excitement, the blue sheen of her hair. Where was Howard's fair-to-mouse English coloring in all this? Her mother must be lovely. It was said; she had formed the words in her mind.

And with this new awareness of the child as a person came belated respect. How good she had been; no tears, no arguments, no protests, just doing her best to accept whatever came next in this sequence of outrageous adult manipulation. She had earned some consideration.

"I haven't told you where we're going, have I?"

The dark eyes flicked wide and fixed on her; the happy gobbling in the tilted coke bottle cut off.

"I'm taking you to my home, where I lived when I was a little girl—"

"To leave me?" Sharp enough to turn a couple of heads.

"No, I won't leave you, I promise. I'll be there

with you. It's a long way still, though. It will take all day to get there."

The child watched her.

"My mother is there," Lisa went on, casting about for some reassurance to offer. And what is *she* going to say about all this? Cristi was silent. With an effort Lisa added, "Your father has been there, to stay, several times."

The small face lost its wariness, the eyes lit up with interest.

"Are you called Cristi Armitage?" Lisa asked. She had not realized she needed so urgently to know the answer to that.

The child looked puzzled. "Cristi Thomas. In Portuguese it is *Tomás*," she added, with the helpful courtesy of the well brought up child. Was that her mother's name, or a name Howard used?

"Can you remember your address at home?"

Cristi rattled it off glibly. Yes, she went to school, in the mornings, at the convent of the *Espírito Santo*. No, she had no brothers or sisters. (Well, that's a relief.) Uncles, aunts, cousins? She nodded but looked doubtful. Her grandparents didn't live in Rio but in Campo Novo, a long way away.

"And who lives at home, in your house?" I will not question her about her mother, or about Howard, Lisa swore to herself again, but we shall have to know who we can contact once I get to Drumveyn.

The big eyes stared at her for a moment, then the tears suddenly welled. "Isaura," Cristi wailed, "Isaura is there. I want Isaura."

"Oh, Cristi." With an unexpected lump in her throat Lisa moved hastily around the table to sit beside her and put an arm around the narrow shoulders. Cristi burrowed her head against her without hesitation and sobbed.

"Who is Isaura?" Lisa asked gently after a moment.

"*A criada*," Cristi gasped out.

"Your nanny?"

"The maid. My maid. She is with me always. She cried at the *aeroporto* when I had to go away. I want Isaura."

Holding her quietly, stroking the gleaming hair, Lisa thought grimly, I should be shot. She's worn out, this is no time to start asking questions. And I didn't even think of bringing anything so that she could sleep in the car.

She bought a rug and Cristi perked up at being allowed to choose from a selection of horrid little foam cushions decorated variously with Batman, Mickey Mouse and dinosaurs. Though at first she resisted moving to the back of the car, evidently feeling it was too far from Lisa, she did agree after another halt to lie down across the back seat and she was asleep before the car was back on the road.

Then Lisa forged on without stopping again, her mind moving forward with dread to the next set of problems. She had not telephoned. She had gone to do so, had even dialed the number, then the thought of hearing Platt's voice and having to wait while he put the call through to her mother, picturing Drumveyn as clearly as though its atmosphere was already reaching out to engulf her, had defeated her. How could she possibly explain Cristi's presence without all the emotions she was tamping down erupting? She mustn't think of any of that yet, she must just get there, because there was nowhere else to go.

The lights picked up a ridge of grimy snow along the verge of the A9. It had not occurred to her to check on road conditions—in the south too long. But though the banks of snow were higher as she turned left for Muirend and Glen Ellig the road was clear and the Drumveyn drive when at last she reached it had also been swept.

Then a different apprehension seized her and she felt her stomach clench with an all too familiar nausea which had nothing to do with the events of the last two days. The one-time joy of coming home from school, crossing the river, swinging up through the trees toward the house, had long ago been overlaid by the reluctance of adolescence and adulthood. Drumveyn had come to represent demands to be something she was not, endless personal challenges she could never meet. She had the absurd feeling that she was turning again even now into that ungainly teenager.

I hate this place, what am I doing here? she asked herself in panic. And there's not a light to be seen, they're all in bed, this will cause chaos. But the child, I must get her off my hands, I can't deal with looking after her or the business of sending her back on my own.

Then with a shock she remembered that her father would not be there. She had not been back since his memorial service and was scarcely used yet to the idea of Drumveyn without his repressive presence. She felt a vast unashamed relief that she would not have to face him tonight.

In the dark house ahead there was only her mother, whom she had failed to warn of their arrival and now expected to welcome her son-in-law's cast-off child.

Lisa pulled up at the door and switched off the

engine, putting on the interior light to check on the child. Dead to the world. Setting her mouth firmly, she got out of the car and went to rouse the sleeping house.

Chapter Six

Madeleine had been watching News at Ten. Normally she would have been in bed by this time, but having Joss in the house had broken the pattern. Though they hadn't talked much about Joss's work with her relief organization, One World, it had been enough to jolt Madeleine's conscience and she had promised herself that she would try harder to keep in touch with international affairs. Only her mind had been so preoccupied with Archie and Cecil and the baby that she had begun by missing the nine o'clock news.

Now she was in a state of mesmerized confusion, coming into every crisis in the middle. However, so strong was Joss's influence she had fetched the atlas from the library and looked up what references she could remember, with a growing suspicion that she and the atlas had grown old together.

She didn't hear the car, nor the bell ringing in the kitchen where Platt was fetching the pudding, untouched by Madeleine, which he had forgotten to take through to the flat for a final bed-time treat.

Intending to make his indignation clear as he announced Lisa, he was forestalled as she swept past him saying, ''Mother still up? Yes? All right,

Platt, I'll just go on," all her attention concentrated on the moment of confrontation.

Madeleine lifted her head from the atlas, startled and rather frightened to hear voices in the hall at this time of night, and the next moment Lisa was in the doorway, an open appeal in her face which was quite uncharacteristic of her confident, even dictatorial adult self.

"Darling, what is it? Whatever's happened?" Madeleine sprang up, the atlas crashing to the floor. She felt her heart racing with shock, but was only fleetingly aware of it, all her concern concentrated on Lisa. "What's wrong?"

"I know I should have phoned. I did mean to, well I did try, but then I just couldn't."

"Of course that doesn't matter—"

"Will there be luggage, my lady?" Platt interrupted from the door. "And will a room be needed? Not having had any notice . . ."

Madeleine felt rare anger. "Thank you, Platt, I'll let you know in a moment."

He didn't move. "It is very late, my lady. Perhaps if I could be told of any requirements."

"I'll ring," said Madeleine briefly, and to Lisa, "Come and sit down, darling." She longed to put her arms around her but didn't dare. Whatever could be wrong, to bring her here so unexpectedly at this time of night, so wild-looking and exhausted? The groomed and enameled look she had perfected since her marriage had disintegrated. There could only be one explanation and, distressed as Madeleine was to see her daughter in this state, she felt a flicker of relief. She had never been at ease with Howard and had disliked his attitude to Lisa, who had become more inac-

cessible than ever under the veneer of materialism
he had applied.

"I'm not on my own," Lisa blurted out, the moment the door had shut with a thud behind Platt.

"Howard."

"No, not Howard."

She's found another man, Madeleine thought in
panic. I must say the right thing. Thank heavens
Charles isn't here. I wish Joss was, though.

"Look, I can't—come out to the car," Lisa
begged, unable to find the words to explain Cristi.

"Of course, darling. But I'm sure it will be perfectly all right." That was what one had to say,
whatever it was.

Platt was hovering in the kitchen corridor, making the point that this was all very irregular and
personally inconvenient.

Cristi hardly stirred as Lisa drew her gently
along the seat toward her, and flopped limply forward on to Lisa's shoulder as she was lifted out.
Madeleine, speechless, looked from the child to
Lisa and back again.

"I can't tell you," Lisa said over Cristi's lolling
dark head. "I'm sorry, I just can't tell you yet."

In the light Platt had put on over the door they
stared at each other for one long uncertain moment, oblivious of the freezing air and the cold
striking through their shoes from the snowy
gravel. Then Madeleine remembered how two
days ago she had failed Archie, remembered the
resolutions made after Joss left. All that mattered
now was that Lisa was in need and that that need
had brought her to Drumveyn.

"That's perfectly all right," she said firmly.
"You don't have to tell me a thing. Give her to
me, and let's go inside."

Following her in, Lisa felt aggression and defensiveness deflate in weak relief, Cristi was transferred to other hands, safe hands. And she herself, amazingly, was not required to explain, to utter aloud the words it was going to hurt so much to say . . .

"It will be a little awkward about beds, my lady. Mrs. Platt has gone to bed already. It is nearly eleven after all." Platt, confident that he had grounds for resentment, did nothing to moderate his indignant tone.

"Lisa, this child has hardly stirred. Wouldn't it be best not to wake her? We'll put her on the drawing room sofa while we get something ready. Though I'm not sure the nursery will be—"

"Oh, not the nursery!" Lisa's voice cracked out sharply. "Those rooms are so spooky, we hated them."

Taken aback by this reaction, Madeleine made herself put it aside for later inspection, along with the guilty thought that she had never so much as suspected there was a problem.

"Well, the Gray Room has just been used—"

Platt again interposed. "As Miss Barnes only decided to leave after lunch, there has naturally been no time to—"

"Mother, look, I don't think she should sleep alone. She's only just arrived. Everything's strange to her. She'd be better in with me. How about the Thorburn Room, that's got two beds." But she spoke with the exasperation of someone forced to accept something they don't like, and looked at the child with such reluctance, almost distaste, that Madeleine frowned, aware of undercurrents she didn't at all care for.

"I should like to know what has been decided

as soon as possible, my lady." Platt had followed them.

"Please bring the luggage in from the car, then wait in the kitchen, Platt. I'll let you know what's needed when I am ready."

She had never spoken to him in such a tone in all the years he had been at Drumveyn. She faced him resolutely, and for the first time really took in his unhealthy pouchy skin, his badly cut hair, the unbrushed jacket he had dragged on to answer the door but had not bothered to button. More than that, she looked into his eyes and saw the hostility there.

He decided to outface her, sure of his power. "Well, I should like to get started, if you don't mind, my lady. This is something of an imposition, as I'm sure you'll agree."

Madeleine felt a slow anger begin to burn. "No, Platt, it's no such thing. My daughter has come home. I expect her to be looked after no matter what time of the day or night she arrives. I can't think of the last time anything was expected of you or Mrs. Platt outside your normal working hours. In fact, perhaps it would be a good idea to get Mrs. Platt up while you're waiting, as we shall certainly need food of some kind."

Lisa was as thunderstruck as Platt at this speech, having no way of knowing that Madeleine's determination not to fail one of her children again had driven her to this first fierce grasping at authority.

When Platt had gone, silenced for once, Lisa looked down at Cristi, her mouth tight, then said with an effort, "I'm not sure I can bear to have her with me after all. I know it's awful of me but

I just must be free of her—I can't tell you—" Her voice was wavering, a muscle jumping in her jaw.

"Lisa, you don't have to tell me anything," Madeleine told her swiftly. "She can come in with me, that's the obvious answer. Platt can make up the bed in the Gray Room for you. The bed's aired and the heating has been on for a couple of days. Joss was here, as you'll have gathered."

"Joss." Lisa groped, the name belonging to a long-ago life before the cataclysm of yesterday. Miss Barnes had meant nothing. "Oh, yes, Joss, I remember. But do you mean you'll put Cristi in father's dressing room?" The idea seemed more repugnant even than the dark nurseries with their lurking terrors.

"I really meant have her in my bed. It's absolutely huge. I'd never know she was there."

"In your *bed*?" Lisa was incredulous. As a child her mother's room had been a forbidden area, a door to be knocked on, a hushed place to enter as a treat and to gaze upon in awed fascination. She had hardly ever seen her mother in bed and it would have been unthinkable to get in beside her. No cuddles or romps in the principal bedroom of Drumveyn where the martyred withdrawal of Grandmother was still a living memory and dim Lady Napiers past seemed to hover in ghostly disapproval.

Madeleine flushed, hesitating. Perhaps she had over-reacted and the suggestion was absurd. Then, with perceptions sharpened by the events of the last two days, she realized what lay behind Lisa's scandalized tone. She had denied herself physical contact with her children, acceding to the view that letting them cling would make it harder for them when they had to go away to school. To be demonstrative had been frowned upon.

Now she looked at Cristi, still wrapped in the crude colors of the cheap rug, remembering the light weight she had briefly held in her arms. What possible reason could there be not to take this weary little creature into her bed? What was a bed? A padded shelf, with coverings to keep out the cold, not some citadel or shrine.

"It seems the sensible answer," she said briskly. "Then Platt can take himself off. After he's produced some food, of course."

The little flash of humor amazed Lisa almost more than the unexpectedly practical decision about the bed, and did them both good.

"Do you know, suddenly I'm absolutely ravenous," she declared. "I haven't been able to eat a thing all day."

What on earth has been happening in her life, Madeleine wondered fearfully, then reminded herself quickly that she didn't need to know. Not now, anyway, not tonight. A tentative relief that she seemed to be coping warmed her.

It was Madeleine who carried Cristi upstairs and began carefully to undress her, while Lisa rummaged in Cristi's suitcase and found a ribbed cotton jersey to go over the flimsy nightdress. I should have made her put that on hours ago, she thought guiltily, recalling the freezing wind when they had stopped to eat. She thought seeing Madeleine's pursed lips that she must be thinking the same, but nothing was said.

In spite of Madeleine's gentleness Cristi woke and for the first time was not prepared to be cooperative. In the big bed she looked wispy, pale and scared and she was absolutely determined not

be to left alone. Who could blame her, Lisa
thought, glancing around the somber room with
its towering furniture and its faraway shadowy
turret corners.

"It's not fair to leave her," she said wearily.
"She must be wondering what on earth is going
to happen to her next."

"Then Platt can bring supper up here. I think
I'd like something too." That might induce Lisa to
eat. "And we'll ask him to bring in another fire."

"Good for you," said Lisa vigorously, amused
in a way she would not have believed possible on
this endless and awful day.

Trying to relax her tense muscles at last in the
bed aired by Joss, she reviewed with slightly hysterical disbelief the scene in her mother's room—
she and Madeleine picnicking on omelettes and
coffee, Cristi sufficiently revived to put away two
large slices of cake and some Drumveyn Jersey
milk which she pronounced *maravilhoso*, with two
electric fires humming out the kilowatts and her
mother so astoundingly matter-of-fact about it all.
She must tell Archie—Archie, sending Cristi back
to Brazil—Howard—

Groaning, she twisted and turned.

Chapter Seven

From the hotel in Dingwall Joss phoned the farmer who kept the key to the cottage. Thank God farmers at least got up at a reasonable hour, she thought sourly, prowling the foyer, watching through the glass doors of the dining room a yawning girl with turnip-top hair and a grubby sweatshirt reaching to the hem of her skirt dropping handfuls of wrapped butter portions onto the tables.

"Oh, but we'll surely be able to put you up the track," the slow Highland voice had assured her, with a tinge of reproach that she could have imagined there would be any difficulty. "There is snow to be sure, but nothing out of the way. You just look in at the house . . ."

Today, she told herself, today at long last I shall be alone, beyond the power of that scruffy little waitress who won't give me breakfast till she's ready, or the unctuous Platt, or politicians or bureaucrats or colleagues to make rage surge up. Beyond the need to listen or respond. No pressures; no demands. Just silence and time, thinking my own thoughts.

In the little house in Richmond Cecil leaned against the cool tiles of the bathroom wall, her skin damp and her knees trembling after her first bout of morning sickness. And I chose this, she thought in disbelief, wanted "the whole experience." She managed a weak giggle. Thank goodness Archie wasn't here to see her like this. But at once she said aloud, "No, he should be here. We should be sharing this." About to go to bed last night at the studio in Chandlers Yard she had missed him so much that she had got into her car and come home instead. Assailed as she always was when he was away by the fear that something might happen to him and he would never have known how she truly felt about him, she had felt a compelling need to be as near to him as she could. Coming into the house she had closed her eyes and breathed in the essence of him. "Traveler's terracotta" she had labeled this house when they first met, in answer to his "twenties aesthetic," but the moment of entering it never failed to arouse in her a positive, physical pleasure.

So why when they were together did that nervous incapacity to show her true feelings overtake her? With Archie, direct and honest, steadfastly loving and utterly to be trusted, surely her fear of the evanescence of human feelings could finally be shed? This baby was supposed to reinforce their commitment to each other. Bearing it was meant to ensure bonding. Yet deep in herself she was aware still of reserve, doubt, the inability to give. She had got into their bed with its richly colored Portuguese woven covering, and held Archie's pillow to her face and breathed in the faint good smell of him, but the dread that even having the child would bring no solution was stronger than the comfort this gave her.

* * *

Lisa woke disorientated in the Gray Room at Drumveyn. She had never slept here, even coming home as a married woman. Crash—back came the realization she had held off for one waking moment.

What next? She struggled to think of what must be done. The child must be sent back. For the first time she saw how she had added to the difficulties of this by running for Drumveyn. Archie would have something to say about being dragged all the way up here, since Archie was the one who would have to sort it out.

And then? But for the larger question concerning herself she had no courage yet. She would get up, go out, as she used to do. She pulled out the few clothes she had stuffed hurriedly into her bag. Surrey "country" clothes, useless here. Would everything she had left in her room have been thrown out? But that was not the Drumveyn way. Huddling a too-thin dressing-gown around her she padded rapidly along the freezing corridors.

Drawers sticking with damp, Grannie-ish smell of mothballs. Shirts, sweaters, breeches, all with the depressed look unworn clothes acquire no matter how carefully put away. Dragging out what she needed, leaving the drawers open and spilling over, she hurried back to the relative warmth of the Gray Room.

Madeleine had woken early, conscious at once of the child's body warm against hers, and of her own acceptance of that closeness. How she had wept, poor little Cristi, waking and finding herself in this strange place, wanting someone called "Isaura." Rejecting the slightest touch, beside herself with exhaustion and longing for home, it had taken a long time to comfort her. But gentleness and patience had won, and she had at last accepted Madeleine's arms and hiccoughed and sobbed herself to sleep again.

Madeleine herself had slept fitfully, long unused to sharing her bed, her mind going over and over the implications of Lisa's arrival. Who was this child? Where was Howard? What had so shaken her competent assured daughter? Bossy daughter, she thought, with a little spurt of amused love and honesty.

If only Joss had stayed. If only Archie weren't in Spain. Cecil's baby—did Lisa know about that yet? And what on earth would Charles have said if he had been here when Lisa burst so dramatically into the drawing room last night. How he would have interrogated and hectored her. What an uproar there would have been about the rooms, the time of night, the lack of warning.

How frightful Platt had been though. How dared he complain about being asked to stay up late for once, wretched man. Did he expect her to send Lisa away? At any minute now he would arrive with her tea, open the curtains, go through the ritual morning exchanges.

He comes into my bedroom, she thought with astonishment. That repellent man comes in here, while I'm in bed, every day of my life—and never till this moment have I questioned it. That is the way it's always been. I lie here waiting, often awake for hours before he appears, and after he has gone I wait a little longer, because if I arrive downstairs before nine there is nowhere for me to go. The drawing room is cold and Mrs. Platt doesn't dust it till breakfast has gone in. No other rooms are used. After breakfast I am expected to remove myself from the house. I can't come up here again because by now Mrs. Platt is making the bed and cleaning. By eleven I may resume possession of the drawing room, where the *Times* will be waiting and Platt will bring coffee. No wonder Joss couldn't bear it.

Madeleine slipped carefully out of bed and leaving the door open went to dress in the bathroom, a cozy haven with its enormously thick hot towel rail and pipes. There were things to do and to decide today. She noted detachedly that she felt no trepidation, only a very great determination to evade nothing.

Turning after a final check in the mirror she heard the child stir, saying something in the light burbling voice babies use when they wake alone. Going into the bedroom she saw Cristi sitting up, looking with interest at the sweater she was holding out from her chest in two peaks.

"I've been sleeping in my jersey," she said. This fact seemed to be more arresting than the unknown room or the presence of Madeleine.

"I'm afraid it's rather a cold house," Madeleine said, sitting on the edge of the bed—against all the rules—and smiling at this prosaic opening. "Do you remember where you are? Lisa, Mrs. Armitage, brought you here last night."

"This was her house when she was a little girl?"

"That's right. What do you call her?"

"Daddy said I should call her Lisa because she is young."

From Madeleine had come the principles which had not allowed Lisa to question the child. She in her turn could not do so.

"And I think you should call me Madeleine." Why had she made that choice? She wasn't young.

But Lady Napier seemed a person oddly remote today.

"*Madalena?*" The child looked pleased at the name. Was that Spanish or Italian? That blue-black hair.

"Let's see what sort of day it is." Madeleine went to open the floor-length blue silk curtains, faded down their edges to a horrid gray-beige she hadn't realized was so dingy. There had been a fresh fall of snow—

"*Neve!*" exclaimed an ecstatic voice behind her. "Snow! It is snow, isn't it? Really, really snow?" With a thud of flying feet the child was beside her, nose pressed to the pane. "Daddy told me about it, and sledging and skiing. Oh, it's so beautiful. Look, on the trees. And there are *montanhas*—"

"Goodness, you'll freeze!" Madeleine scooped her up, for half a second wondering if the child would resist. But Cristi scarcely seemed to notice, simply applying her face to the window again, leaning forward out of Madeleine's arms in rapturous excitement.

"Come on, I'll wrap you up in my dressing gown—" Laughing, turning from the window with Cristi in her arms, conscious of all sorts of things simultaneously—that the morning was glorious, that the child's slight body had fitted readily against her own, that the anguish of the night seemed to be forgotten, that it was good to look after someone again—she met the disapproving face of Platt, coming in after his perfunctory tap with a tray whose contents made no concession to the presence of the child.

He was sulking. He slapped down the tray, pointedly straightened the curtains Madeleine had drawn, opened those at the other window, abstained from his customary comment on the weather since she had had the effrontery to look out for herself, ignored Cristi and withdrew with what could only be called a flounce.

Madeleine laughed. "Would you like some milk, Cristi? Do you remember having some last night?"

"I almost remember," Cristi said, struggling to separate dream and half-dream. "And coming in the car. Where is Lisa?"

"Sleeping, I expect. It was late when you got here. Now hop back into bed and keep warm. I'll fetch a tooth-mug and you can have some milk while I have my tea."

"And a biscuit?"

Lisa went fast up the slope toward the steading. The skim of new snow on the drive already showed the tracks of vehicles, and one set of footprints—Jackie Mowat, going down for the school bus which would take her to Muirend. The tractor had also gone down, taking hay to the sheep on the low ground by the loch. And the Land Rover, by the look of it. What day was this? Thursday. Malkie then, collecting rubbish bags from around the estate to be left at the end of the drive for collection. It was a small private pleasure to interpret like this the well-known comings and goings of home.

The sun had been up for an hour or more but its light was still gilt-pale, the long shadows it cast blue across the snow. She felt the air blade-keen on her cheek. In spite of everything exhilaration seized her. To be here, back in this spacious bright landscape, gulping in the heady air, dressed in these clothes (and how gratifying that the breeches had had to be dragged in around her waist), in her own comfortable boots which had been still in their place in the gunroom, made the shocks of the last two days seem unreal and faraway.

Knocking the snow off her boots against the porch of the Galloways' cottage, her nose wrinkled at a nostalgic blend of smells: mud, working clothes, nests of sacking under the seats where the dogs waited for Donnie, whiff of the disinfectant Jean used to sluice the stone flags, acrid tang of wooden walls rotting under years of this treatment.

With her hand on the knob, for she had never knocked on the door at this house, she had a sudden moment of doubt. Since her marriage to Howard she had been so cut off from these friends of her childhood. She remembered the constraint of her father's memorial service, when she had felt so out of keeping with the whole scene, as though Mrs. Armitage had nothing to do any longer with the girl who had grown up here.

Then giving herself a little shake, for after all it was Mrs. Armitage who was the remote unreal figure now, she tapped and went in, calling a greeting as she used to. Jean turning from her blue-enameled Calor gas cooker, the cat vanishing through a slit of window, the children at the table looking up in surprise, Radio One, morning smell of a fire not long lit, bacon frying, clothes drying on the pulley, were all part of life for ever.

And Jean's welcome had not changed. "Lisa! Well, that's the last person I expected to see walking in. We didn't know you were expected. Come away in, it's great to see you."

Shy greetings from Dougal and Jill. Lisa didn't

know them as well as she had their older brother
Donald, now working on a farm near Killin.

Jean scooped school bags off a chair. "Here, sit
in about. It's a wee bit sharp this morning, what
would you say to some porridge? You'll not
bother making it down with you, I'll be bound.
Dougal, don't waste your time cutting out that ad,
I've told you you're not getting . . ."

"I'm starving," Lisa admitted, relaxing gratefully in the unchanged easiness of it all. Explanations, in whatever degree, could come later. For
now there was the big bowl of oatmeal porridge,
the Jersey cream every house on the estate had its
share of, and Jean's strong tea in a thick blue-
banded mug.

"Now you two, for the last time, get yourselves
down that road. One of these days Allie'll no wait
for you and you'll find yourselves walking." Dougal and Jill were still at the glen school, which
Lisa herself had attended for three pre-exile years.

They were bundled off, Dougal's reading book
discovered after they had gone, Jean screeching
after him through the window, clatter of boot-
nails as he came tearing back for it, then he and
Jill going down the brae running and sliding.

"Donnie'll be in any minute," Jean said. "I
swear he waits in back of the steading till
they've gone."

"I'll see him later. I ought to get back."

"For your second breakfast. I see nothing's
changed."

They laughed. These bowls of porridge went
back more than twenty years. But she's fined
down a lot, Jean thought, remembering the fat
schoolgirl whose only solace had been food,
who had many a time sat at this table and

put back meals Donnie himself wouldn't have been ashamed of.

"And are you to be up for a while?" she asked. "Your mother will be glad of the company." Reproof clear in her voice; acceptable and accepted.

"I'm not sure yet," Lisa answered. God, how I want to stay, she realized, startled at the violence of the wish. From here how alien that Surrey house seemed, to live in it again unimaginable. "I won't be off for a day or two anyway. I'll come up soon and catch up properly on all the news, I promise. But for now I'm afraid that I've come begging."

Chapter Eight

"The first thing is to find something for you to wear," Madeleine was saying worriedly, going through Cristi's clothes again. They were all the same; little dresses and suits in pastel colors and light fabrics, beautifully made; delicate hand-made underwear more suitable for a trousseau than an eight-year-old; elegant shoes and sandals and belts.

"Isn't it enough? Isaura thought—"

A tap at the door. "Can I come in?"

Cristi, still in bed, blinked at a new Lisa. In her dark green breeches and sweater, with glowing cheeks and ruffled hair, she looked half the age of the harried grown-up of yesterday.

"Look what I've brought." With a swing of her arm Lisa cast across the bed jeans, woollen tights and polo-neck, socks and slippers, and a soft Shetland sweater in pink and cream knitted by Jean and hardly worn as yet by Jill. "They're all going to be on the big side but they'll do till we can take you shopping."

Cristi gazed at the clothes in silence and for one anxious moment both Lisa and Madeleine thought she was going to reject them out of hand. Then a beaming, incredulous smile spread across her face.

"For me? I am allowed to wear bluejeans?" She made it one word. "I can put them on now?"

They were late for breakfast and Platt made his displeasure clear. Madeleine was hardly aware of it. It was wonderful to have Lisa here, looking in those clothes like the girl marriage to Howard had so radically altered, and after her walk up to the farm seeming less tense and desperate than she had been last night. What had brought her here in that state? Ask nothing, Madeleine reminded herself, recalling only too clearly the exasperation the mildest question could unleash. She found herself wishing that Joss was there for support, then pushed the thought away firmly.

Lisa found, now that she was freed from responsibility for Cristi, that she could accept her presence without the agony of humiliation that had tormented her yesterday. Here at Drumveyn, looking so different from the sophisticated little creature who had turned up on her doorstep, it was possible to see her as a problem quite separate from Howard's departure.

It was a relief to both Lisa and Madeleine to concentrate their attention on Cristi. Every so often she would look down at herself in joyful wonder, oblivious of her rolled-up sleeves, the safety pins in her waistband, the fact that Jill's sweater came nearly to her knees. She was sitting to one side of her chair so that she could casually swing her leg and admire her jeans and the sheepskin slipper dangling from her toe.

It was amazing how her ebullience resurfaced when she felt secure. She was fascinated by everything, from the cumbersome epergne on the sideboard to the quilted lining for the second egg in the base of her egg-cup; from the Lalique grouse to the horn spoon for the heather honey. It was clear she was used to servants, for of Platt she took no notice at all.

Her main concern, however, was for the snow. "Isaura says that sometimes there is snow at my grandfather's *fazenda* where she lived when she was a little girl. But I'm not allowed to go there and I've never seen it. Can we walk in it? Does it hurt your shoes?"

"I've borrowed boots for you," Lisa told her, "though I think you're going to need all of Jill's socks together to keep them on."

"Should we go out now, quickly, before it goes away?"

"It won't vanish, don't worry," Lisa promised her, as they rose from the table and Cristi went straight to the window. "I know we must talk," she added hastily in a low voice to Madeleine. "I should have told you last night what all this is about—"

"You don't have to tell me anything," Madeleine interrupted quickly. "Not a thing that you don't want to. Truly. I'm only thankful that you came."

"You've been marvelous," Lisa said in gratitude but also with a note of surprise which did not escape her mother. "I don't know what I'd have done."

They both glanced at the little hand-me-down figure rapt at the sealed-up French window which no one ever used.

"I must phone Archie," Lisa said. "Could you possibly take—?"

"But darling, he's in Spain, away in some tiny village."

"But I have to talk to him! He must come up."

"Well, Cecil is bound to have a number for him. Is it very urgent? I believe he's due back early next week."

"I *must* talk to him." Inhibited by Cristi's presence, Lisa gazed at her mother in anguish.

"Oh darling." Hating to see that look, not wanting to intrude, dreading a clumsy gesture that would do more harm than good. Madeleine floundered. Unwelcome memories rushed back of the days in Lisa's teens when Grannie had departed for Edinburgh and the way had seemed open for some new rapport. They had never achieved it, and Madeleine could remember all too clearly her own sense of guilty inadequacy.

Then she rallied. Whatever this crisis was, Lisa had turned to her and she would offer any help she was capable of. "You go and talk to Cecil, Lisa. Phone from the drawing room. I'll look after Cristi."

"Mrs. Platt won't have finished the drawing-room yet, my lady," Platt put in, resting the corner of the tray on the table so near Lisa that she was obliged to move. To her admiration her mother ignored him. That must be a first, Lisa thought, entertained momentarily by this new scenario.

Mrs. Platt, secure in her right of tenure, flittering her feather duster along the top of a picture light which she would certainly not have touched in the ordinary way, said complacently, "I shall be ten minutes yet, my lady, at least."

"Then please leave the rest," said Madeleine, going to the fire.

"Well, it won't be very convenient to do it later," Mrs. Platt began huffily. "I shall have my—"

"Leave it altogether, thank you," said Madeleine.

"*And* she's lit the fire," Mrs. Platt reported indignantly in the much disaffected kitchen.

The years rolled back as Madeleine helped Cristi into Jill's gumboots and smiled as she giggled at her suddenly enormous feet. To be here in the gunroom which smelled of a hundred years of damp tweed and leather and gun-oil and boots and ancient game bags, once more wrapping up a child to go out in the snow, seemed to wipe out intervening memories, the beginnings and ends of solitary walks, and the dragging reluctance to go along the corridor and back into the quenching disapproval of the house.

Cristi, puffed as a robin in a gay quilted jacket, spikes of black hair sprouting around her bright face under a red woolly hat, brought back to Madeleine all the winter beauty of Drumveyn, fresh and poignant. To watch her print the first footsteps on the blank sunlit page of the lawn, cautious at first then ecstatically running, taste snow on her tongue, open her eyes wide with astonishment when Madeleine made a snowball and threw it at her, recaptured lost delights. Yet this had been here, all the time.

Madeleine drew a deep breath. Whatever her dismay at Cecil and Archie's decision, whatever trouble Lisa was facing, there had to be answers. The sense of liberation she had felt on the day of Charles's memorial service surged back. Then she had pushed it guiltily away; now she acknowledged it. She would do her best to help the children, but she was answerable to no one but herself for her success or failure.

Lisa came down the steps from the terrace.

"Cecil was at home for once. She says it's hopeless trying to contact Archie during the day but they have an arrangement that she calls in the evening at half past six if she wants to talk to him. She's letting me use her time tonight—though she said it can take ages to get through."

"That's good of her. And does she know when Archie will be back?"

"A bit vague, as usual, he never does say. Mondayish, she thought. So it looks as though you're stuck with us for a few days," she added, suddenly gauche. "Is that all right?"

"You know it is. As long as you like—" A shriek drew their attention to Cristi and they laughed to see her spluttering free of a douche of snow from a released spruce branch.

"She's Howard's," Lisa said abruptly. "He's gone off with her mother. They don't want her."

Cristi came running across the lawn, head back and face screwed up with the snow still on it so that they could see.

Madeleine felt as though her mouth had opened and shut and hoped it hadn't. Huge questions spun in her brain.

"There are little marks in the snow, like drawing," Cristi cried, doing her best to stand still while Lisa brushed the snow off her, beating the woolly hat against her thigh and cramming it back on Cristi's head with firm hands.

"Birds," said Madeleine, pulling herself together, though her voice sounded odd. "We'll come and look."

Cristi darted off.

"Lisa, my poor love—"

"Don't!" Lisa said violently. "I can't bear it."

Madeleine checked, feeling rebuffed for a second, then telling herself fiercely, forget all that, just feel what she feels, understand it for her. You don't matter, Lisa does.

"Why don't we go down to Muirend and buy Cristi a pair of jeans of her own?" she suggested. Saying, be here, safe and quiet and loved, for as long as the need is there, and no one will ask anything.

Lisa stopped and looked at her, her strong-featured face vulnerable with relief and gratitude. "Thanks," she managed awkwardly, but no more.

Madeleine's hand lifted toward her, lost courage. They both moved on quickly to examine the tracks Cristi was excitedly pointing out.

Archie Napier, pushing away the first draft of his report on the impact a small dam would have on this impoverished Spanish village, let his thoughts, as always, turn to Cecil. And, as always, there came at once the little twist of uncertainty. Not doubt of her faithfulness, or of her commitment to him and their marriage, but the much deeper sense of her fundamental elusiveness.

It seemed that he always had to get past this first little stab, and reassure himself once again that he had won her. How soon would he be able to get back? He should have this wrapped up by Saturday if all the various meetings went to plan. He fell into a dream of Cecil waiting for him at home, and remembering the rush of delight he always felt to see her car outside the house, felt instant sharp desire.

With that pang of longing came the memory of her pregnancy. One way of dealing with the problem, he thought ironically, desire fading. They had talked over every aspect of the decision but he knew he had agreed to it in the end because Cecil so desperately wanted it. That desperation had disturbed him. She didn't admit to it but it ran like a thread through all their discussions, and he couldn't understand it. She was five years older than he was, so he could see that she felt more urgency about having a child, and he knew her need to create the family she herself had lacked, but he still felt they could have gone on trying for a little longer. He wanted a child, but he wanted the child she bore to be his.

He moved restlessly. This was all settled; it was bloody ridiculous to go over and over it like this. But there was a little core of dread in him that just as he'd stopped wanting her a moment ago at the thought of that embryo growing inside her, so he would be unable to make love to her when they were together again.

The noise from the primitive and meagerly stocked bar next door was growing. He should go along and have a drink and a chat—always useful. But he sat on, his mind dogged by another thing about having this baby that bothered him. He had found himself repelled by the unemotional way Cecil had planned and organized it all. Clinical technically it had to be, but she also seemed to *feel* clinical about it. He had needed delight from her when the pregnancy was confirmed, to establish for him a mood he knew he could not with the best will in the world create for himself. Cecil had got out her diary and worked out her forward schedule, with great satisfaction it is true, but with none of the euphoria he had expected.

Perhaps if he could persuade her to spend time at Drumveyn she would slow down, begin to transfer her attention from work to the baby, and all those feelings of joy and anticipation would develop and could be shared. And there were other reasons why he wanted her at Drumveyn. Principally he wanted her to let Madeleine get used to the idea of the baby, and accept it if possible without repugnance. Though his own mind had barely accepted the thought, this baby would one day, in the normal course of events, inherit Drumveyn. Would Madeleine have got as far as that yet in her thinking, and if so, how would she feel about it?

Then, whether Cecil liked it or not, he and she now owned the place. Technically it would be the baby's home. Cecil herself was Lady Napier, though she refused to use the title or even the name. He wanted her to share in the plans he had for the estate. His father had run it in the old style, shooting and stalking enjoyed exclusively by family and friends, farming methods scarcely changed since Archie was a boy, timber regarded as sacrosanct. Hardly a penny had been spent on the cottages and farm buildings. There had been no new planting, tracks and bridges were poorly maintained, fences and gates patched with anything that came to hand.

Cecil must not keep herself at a distance from all these concerns. If he could make her feel involved now, because of the baby, perhaps in the end it might be something they could share. Archie himself had no plans to live all the time at Drumveyn. The years of conflict with his father had left their mark. Also the house with its encircling trees and damp-stained harling and dank gloom brought back the morbid feeling of imprisonment he had endured as a boy. In any case, it was his mother's home and he was not going to ask her to move out. But he had a plan for making essential changes and improvements on the estate without being there on a permanent basis himself. He had allowed a tactful interval to pass after his father's death but spring was coming and work should begin. He must talk to his mother and he wanted Cecil with him when he did.

Chapter Nine

It was a long time since Madeleine had bought children's clothes and she had never bought them in Muirend. Ill at ease in the scruffy little shops, she was ready to find everything they offered repellent.

Lisa was no help, in the grip of delayed shock as the fact of Howard's departure sank in at last. She felt as though she was on a madly shunting train, jarred and flung about with nothing to cling on to. She nodded mutely to every suggestion Madeleine made and her face was such an ominous shade of olive green that her mother began to work out where the nearest loo might be.

Cristi saved the situation. She had chattered freely as Lisa drove down the glen, elated by her new surroundings but also quite willing to talk about home, the wild homesick grief of the night forgotten. Apart from the constant background presence of the maid Isaura it seemed that she had led a solitary life and an unnaturally enclosed one, hardly ever out of the house once she came back from school, with no one to play with and rarely seeing her cousins or other members of the family. Her mother slept late, "arranged herself" and went out. When Daddy was there they both went out.

Cristi had been prepared for some time for this "visit" to her father's country—Madeleine saw the wrench of pain on Lisa's face when this became clear. She had been told she was to live in England for a while as she was half English and she had looked forward to it as a lonely child looks forward to boarding school. No one had said anything about Scotland but Cristi thought it was even better. She took it for granted that when her parents came back life would be as before.

Now she was thrilled to be allowed to choose her own version of the borrowed clothes—did she spend her whole life in those elegant little dresses?—but Madeleine was interested to see the distinctive look she achieved, going every time for the most subtle colors available. In "bluejeans" that fitted her and a high-necked amber sweater she surveyed herself in speechless delight. Clutching parcels, beaming with happiness, she left a wake of smiles behind her.

She wanted to look at other children, into shop windows, at the Council roadmen tarring the road, at dogs tied up outside the supermarket and babies in prams. She was wide-eyed at being led through a meal shop with open sacks and high wooden shelves and a table covered with cheeses to a stone-walled restaurant with an open fire.

Madeleine, hoping black coffee might brace Lisa, though not sure she shouldn't have got hold of a large brandy instead, was relieved to find the place still existed.

"Every time I come to Muirend they've flattened something to make a new carpark or run up another supermarket," she remarked. Chatting to cover Lisa's punch-drunk silence also glossed over a matter on her conscience. She had allowed herself to grow afraid of driving. When she had to go to Muirend, or much worse down the terrifying A9 to Perth to have her hair done, Platt took her. Today she had been thankful that Lisa had driven down in the Mercedes as a matter of course. But she knew it was something she was going to have to deal with.

"Now, Cristi, lots of lovely things for you to choose from."

Cristi gave the matter her serious attention. Thank goodness the child was here, Madeleine caught herself thinking, then smiled wryly at the irony of that, since as far as she knew the child herself was the problem.

They were late for lunch. Platt didn't waste time on hints this time. "I would just like to say, my lady, that I hardly think it satisfactory. I was not advised that lunch was to be late so I carried on with my normal routine. Mrs. Platt has had everything ready for more than half an hour."

Even Lisa came out of her stupor to gaze at him in frowning surprise.

Madeleine felt her cheeks grow warm. Her voice shook slightly as she said, "I realize we are later than usual, Platt, but just this once I'm afraid you will have to accept it. We'll come in straight away."

Platt let it hang for one moment, as though expecting more of an apology than this, then backed down, unmollified but not ready for an open fight.

Lunch was tense. Lisa hardly said a word and Madeleine talked quietly to Cristi and left her in peace.

Platt waylaid Madeleine as they left the dining room. "And will nursery tea be required, my lady? It will be extra work of course, and I don't think we can be expected to cover everything, just the two of us."

Hateful little man, Madeleine thought wrathfully. Three of us to look after and Ivy Black, the estate handyman's wife, comes in to clean and iron and mop what were traditionally known as the back passages. But in fact she had not thought about Cristi's supper—or about where she would sleep. But wherever she slept she couldn't be put to bed and left there alone.

"Cristi," she called after the small figure darting off to look at her new belongings. "What time do you go to bed at home?"

"Eleven o'clock," said Cristi swiftly, then with an engaging grin, "or ten o'clock sometimes."

"Cristina will have dinner with us," Madeleine told Platt, and went on into the drawing room leaving him muttering because he had nothing to object to.

Lisa was standing in front of the fire, hands gripping the edge of the mantelpiece, forehead down on her knuckles, eyes shut.

Madeleine went to her quickly. "Darling, you look worn out. Are you sure you're all right?"

Fatal question. Even as she asked it she braced herself for the impatient, "Of course I'm all right, don't fuss."

Lisa didn't raise her head, merely rocked it helplessly on her hands.

"Oh, darling." Madeleine's throat constricted in pity. "Why don't you go and have a sleep? I'll bring up a hot water bottle. Just try to forget everything for a while."

"I shouldn't dump Cristi on you—"

"Don't be silly. I love having her here. We shall

find plenty to do." But how were they to find the opportunity to talk, if Lisa should want to?

"I have to ring Archie."

"I'll wake you in plenty of time. Do go up, you look absolutely at the end of your tether." She wanted to lead her away, tuck her up, lap her with tenderness, but she knew that would never be permitted. Enough that Lisa wearily agreed to go up to her room, saying she didn't need a bottle, and disappeared with a heavy stumping walk that made her mother ache with compassion.

Cristi was contentedly occupied in arranging her new clothes along the sofa in different combinations. How easy she is, Madeleine thought gratefully, and how different this room looks with her in it.

"Do you like books, Cristi?"

"English stories?" Eager pounce.

"The books Lisa had when she was your age."

"Oh!"

"We'll have to wrap up well."

The child thought this very funny as in jackets and scarves they explored the shelves of the old day nursery.

While Cristi pored over the picture of the Lost Boys in bed and Michael in the laundry basket (to be able to give her this for the first time!) Madeleine opened the door to the night nursery.

Spooky. Had there been fears every night, shapes in the shadows, familiar sounds and objects that became threatening in the darkness? Why had they never said? Because at Drumveyn such weaknesses were scorned. She must talk to Joss about it when she came back.

"How would you like to return the clothes we

borrowed and meet Jill?" Madeleine asked Cristi
as they went laden downstairs, with a promise to
put some heating on in the nursery so that another
day Cristi could examine the toys and ride the
rocking horse which had much impressed her
with its friendly eye and dappled flanks and worn
red saddle. ("My cousins ride when they go to
my grandfather's *fazenda* . . .")

"Could we?" Cristi asked eagerly. To meet another little girl!

Unlike Lisa, Madeleine phoned Jean Galloway
first. It was years since she had been inside the
Steading Cottage. She saw Jean occasionally, passing on the drive or in the village. They waved and
greeted each other with a little burst of goodwill,
genuine but leading nowhere.

When Madeleine first came to Drumveyn
Charles's mother was continually in and out of
every house on the estate and had hauled her
along too.

"You must learn all this," she had instructed,
though clearly without much hope of success, and
Madeleine had done her best to tie unpronounce-
able place names to tenants, shepherds, keepers
and strange creatures called orramen, learn huge
families by heart and acquire a vocabulary of hog
and gimmer, gralloch and hummel, garron and
hirsel. After her mother-in-law had moved to Edinburgh she had with shy new eagerness gone to
call on the estate wives alone, but had found it
impossible to believe that she was anything but a
dreadful nuisance to them.

They would stop whatever they were doing, so
that she was always conscious of something off
stage burning, cooling, boiling or spoiling, take off
overalls and push back straggling hair, apologize

for the mess, sweep a few items from one spot to another, eject animals and round on children, make tea and explain why they hadn't baked. Madeleine would ask questions, read how fatuous they were in the politely blank faces, call the latest baby the wrong name and escape with burning cheeks, aware of contempt and relief behind her.

Why should she assume she could turn up unannounced in these women's houses when it would be unthinkable for them to come to hers? She had quietly dropped the whole patronizing business, telling herself that at least Archie and Lisa were welcome everywhere.

Walking up to the farm with Cristi, she realized that all these households were as remote to her now as Muirend had seemed this morning. She had thought Cristi's life restricted, her own was remarkably like it.

This porch is falling to pieces, she observed idly before she remembered that it had something to do with her. How good it was to feel a child's hand in hers again as they waited.

Jean was flustered, the room tidy, the children, just in from school, coming to their feet with subdued, "Good afternoon," but not quite bringing themselves to add, "my lady," and shooting guilty glances at their mother as she pinched her lips at the omission. Their eyes swiveled to Cristi, standing close to Madeleine and still holding her hand, watching them with tense uncertainty.

"We were so grateful for the loan of these—"

"Oh, but you should have kept them, there was no hurry. Jill wasn't needing them, were you, Jill?"

Shake of the head from Jill, too fascinated by

the newcomer to be drawn by this kind of adult prompting.

"We just needed warm things till we could go shopping. We went into Muirend this morning. Cristi had nothing suitable with her—it was very good of you, we did so appreciate—shall I put them down here?"

"Oh, anywhere will do. Here, I'll take them. Jill, put these wellies by the back door. And so this is Cristi?"

What had Lisa told Jean this morning?

Cristi stepped forward to shake Jean's hand, giving a little bob which made Jill open her eyes.

"Jill—and Dougal, isn't it? How are you both getting on at school?" Oh, don't, Madeleine wailed inwardly, listen to yourself. They'll hate being asked, and what can any child ever reply to that anyway?

"Fine," said Dougal.

Jill gazed at Cristi.

"Could they take Cristi out in the snow?" Madeleine asked, and caught Cristi's quick upward eager glance. "It's such a thrill for her, she's never seen it before today. Or have they just come in? Are they about to have tea?"

"Oh, they'll not get their tea till their father comes in. They're generally out till then anyway now that the days are drawing out a bit."

Suddenly animated, the children plunged for jackets. After one fractional moment of alarmed resistance Cristi detached herself from Madeleine's side.

"Nothing rough, mind, Dougal. You see and take care of her."

"I know." Gruff, indignant.

"We've new puppies," said Jill, pausing to look into Cristi's face as though to assess her reaction.

The blaze of excitement could not be mistaken. In that second Cristi was gone, transferred from Madeleine's charge to the children's though she had not yet taken a step.

"Don't be too long now! They'll be all right," Jean added comfortably as the door slammed behind them. "Dougal's got a good head on him."

She had made drop scones. Madeleine wondered how busy she had been when she phoned. While the tea was being made she looked around the kitchen—dark and poky, kitchen and living room in one, old Triplex grate, tiny gas cooker to supplement it, clothes drying on a pulley. Charles had not only refused to spend money modernizing the houses but would never let the occupants do any work on them for themselves.

Cristi hesitated on the concrete path. The others were already off across a stretch of churned and trodden mud which she couldn't believe anyone would be allowed to walk in, boots or no boots. All the years of Isaura's scolding about a creased dress or scuffed shoes, the endless washing, ironing, pressing and sponging; the instilled disgust for the squalor and poverty glimpsed on the drive to school; her mother's aura of dressmaker, hairdresser, manicurist, checked her for one teetering moment.

Dougal turned and saw her hesitating. He had not needed to be told that this foreign-looking wee girl was not of the same robust stuff as his sister Jill.

"Here, gie's your hand," he said, going back to her.

The stubby strong hand stretched out to her, the

unfamiliar resiny air in her nostrils, the edge to
the wind coming off snow, nip of declining winter
day, pungent admix of dung, bruised straw, wet
stone, new-wool smell of her sweater, whipped
up in Cristi a swift exhilaration. Suddenly she felt
brave, reckless, ready for adventure. The component smells and sights of the moment were to stay
with her for the rest of her life, along with the
moment in the draughty byre when Dougal put a
squirming puppy into her hands and she felt the
warm skin of its round stomach on her palm,
stroked the soft fuzz of coat, looked at the tiny
paddling paws and milky eyes and understood its
helplessness.

Chapter Ten

By foregoing the party the entire village seemed to want to throw for him, since they were convinced that by simply digging his inspection pits and producing his report he would magically bring lush crops to their arid fields and ease and prosperity to them all, Archie made it to Madrid for a standby flight on Saturday night.

As he had longed to see it, Cecil's car was parked outside the house. Letting himself in and going straight upstairs, waking her gently, wrapping her in his arms as she took in his presence, he was seized by need for her.

"God, it's wonderful to be back."

"I missed you." She clung to him, burrowing her face into his chest.

"And I missed you. I always miss you," he said fiercely, crushing her to him. She so rarely said it; he felt his heart soar. "Let go a moment, darling. I'll go and have a quick shower—"

"Don't, don't," she implored him, wanting all the male and traveled and real smell of him.

It never lessened, that breath-stopping delight in the moment of gathering her against him, welding the slight silky smooth body to his. Following it always came a need for total possession, a determination that this time . . . He would try to blot

it out of his mind, as though it was an admission
that their lovemaking would be less than perfect.
She was a wonderful partner, exciting and respon-
sive, faking nothing, withholding nothing. It was
afterward that she eluded him, in the moments of
assuaged descent. Even with her body still beneath him, his cock a soft curl inside her, he
would feel her slipping away, the face a moment
ago contracted in the absorption of orgasm cool
again, self-possession regained. He could hold on
to her body, she would make no move, but she
had gone. And sooner or later he would wake to
feel her slipping out of bed. He would whisper in
unashamed anguish, "Don't go, don't leave me,"
and she would answer lightly, as though the passion just shared had never existed. "Can't sleep,
sorry—I'll only disturb you."

He didn't want to think of this as he began the
delicious process of awakening her, but inevitably
he did, and tonight he found himself also remembering, exactly as he had dreaded, the alien life in
her womb.

"Must be tired," he muttered presently. "Sorry,
love." It had never happened before, and sick and
dismayed he buried his face in her neck and
was still.

It's the child, Cecil thought in a flash of terror.
What have I done? She stroked his thick hair,
smoothed her hands down the muscular back, saw
that to say it didn't matter might suggest she
hadn't wanted him, said instead, "Go to sleep,
darling, you must be exhausted, that drive and
then the flight after a day's work. We'll make
lovely lovely love in the morning . . ."

But when morning came she had gone, not to
Chandlers Yard as in fact she sometimes did,

driven by a need she hated and didn't understand to be on her cool own once more, but to the small spare room, where the bed was the only space clear of maps, files, rock specimens, climbing gear, wetsuit and the miscellany of many journeys.

They talked little as Archie drove north, though they rarely had such a stretch of time to themselves. Cecil had not wanted to come.

"I know absolutely nothing about estate things, and you can't imagine how much I have to do here. That spiral staircase is turning into a complete nightmare—"

"I want you to be there."

Perhaps because it was so unusual between them for him to insist on what he wanted; perhaps because of what had happened last night, gnawing at them both this morning when making love had not been on the program, she had agreed.

She hated Drumveyn, but at least Archie's father with his chilly eyes and dominance by divine right would not be there, crushing the life out of any conversation before it began, putting Archie down whenever he opened his mouth, letting Madeleine run around after him like some supernumerary butler.

And this business of Lisa and Howard and the child. Why did they expect Archie to sort out everything for them? Why couldn't they deal with it themselves?

"Will you have to leave for Bahia earlier than you'd planned because of this Howard business?"

"It looks as though I'll have to take the child back. First finding out exactly where I'm taking her."

"What an extraordinary setup."

"Howard always was a bastard."

"I didn't know you thought that."

"Seemed pointless to say so, since he and Lisa appeared to be making a go of it."

How many other things did moderate tolerant Archie suppress?

It was part of the success of their marriage that he believed people should be free to live and behave according to their own principles and needs. Success? Cecil thought again of that moment of disbelief and loss last night when she had realized that her expectant body was not going to receive its sweet satisfaction. What had she done?

Madeleine went to the kitchen to say that Archie and Cecil would arrive in time for dinner.

She had not rung because Platt had his breakfast after dining room breakfast and she had not wanted to disturb him. On the other hand Mrs. Platt, who had put the call from Archie through, would be incensed if she wasn't told about extra mouths to feed at the first possible moment.

And it is my kitchen, Madeleine had reminded herself, pushing back the heavy swing door.

Platt, in his shirt sleeves with tie dangling, was picking bacon out of his teeth with his fingernail, his chair pushed back and a plate of what he hadn't fancied from a heap of sausages, bacon, beans, tinned tomatoes and frizzled eggs shoved away across the table. Crusts of white bread indented with large bites were tossed down beside it. A jar of Silver Shred with a knife in it and a messy carton of Flora with the wrapping of a sliced loaf trailing across it flanked the teapot, against which was propped yesterday's *Sun*.

Platt took his finger out of his mouth and sucked the last pallid shred of bacon free. "I was

having my breakfast, my lady." Definitely not
an apology.

"I'm sorry to disturb you, Platt, but I wanted
to let you know at once that—" Archie and Lisa
were known by their Christian names to everyone
on the estate who had been there since their childhood. But times change. "Sir Archie and Lady Napier are coming to stay for a day or two. They'll
be here for dinner." Lady Napier. Then who am
I? The question brought a feeling not of redundancy but of freedom; she must examine that
when she had time.

Both Platts rushed into bitter complaint. No
warning, which rooms would be needed, how
were they expected, and on a Sunday . . .

By their own choice, since it was liberally reflected in their wages, they followed more or less
the same routine every day, except that at least
once a week they went out and left Ivy to give
Madeleine lunch, and on Sunday evenings put out
for her cold meals of varying gruesomeness.

"It will be quite enough to make up the beds
in the Thorburn Room and put bottles in and the
heating on. You won't need to do any cleaning,
Ivy will be in tomorrow to see to that."

". . . that room's not been used since Sir
Charles's funeral, there's the water to turn on, all
that wing was closed down for the winter, Malkie
will never manage on his own and Sandy Black
won't be best pleased to be called out on a Sunday, the pheasant won't do five . . ."

"I'm sorry it will mean extra work." Madeleine
hadn't expected Cecil to come and had intended
to put Archie in Charles's dressing-room. "Isn't
there time to take out another pheasant? We could

ask Malkie's mother to help with the vegetables and the pots."

"Malkie's mother? I'm not having her in my kitchen."

"Then I think you will just have to manage." Am I really asking very much? The truth was she didn't know.

"Well, I must say, my lady, Mrs. Platt and I both feel we're being extremely put upon," Platt began pompously. "I can't be expected to organize the workload when there's people turning up here, there and everywhere without the slightest warning. You can't produce meals out of thin air, my lady, though you may not realize it," with a horrid joviality, "and then there's the kiddie, all the work with her being here."

Cristi? No more cooperative and civilized child ever existed. There had been the bed brought from the nursery and put up in Madeleine's room, the mattress aired in the boiler room for a day. Lisa had helped Platt with that because of Mrs. Platt's back.

Madeleine held in her anger, made sure her voice was steady. "Well, I think just for today we shall be able to manage, and tomorrow we can make other arrangements if you think it necessary."

"Well, I'm sorry but I don't think that's quite good enough, my lady."

What did he mean? Feeling threatened and vulnerable, her heart beginning to beat uncomfortably, Madeleine met his red-veined calculating eyes.

"We're employed here as butler and cook, if I may say so. But here we are doing the cleaning and shopping and scullery work and all the rest out of the goodness of our hearts, knowing how you're placed. But we do feel we're being taken a loan of, and we're not very happy about it."

"But—" Madeleine found words had deserted her. For years now, since Charles's mother had left and all entertaining at Drumveyn had ceased, things had gone on in this way.

"We feel if we're to be taken advantage of like this we must seriously think of moving on," Platt continued, watching her closely. Frighten her; she couldn't turn this place on her own for five minutes and she knew it. He had his eye on the estate cottage he intended to retire to but it had begun to dawn on him lately that life wasn't going to be quite so cushy without Drumveyn electricity and oil and telephone and petrol and the household accounts to draw on. Some extra cash put away would be very handy.

"Move on?" Madeleine scarcely understood what he meant. Platt was as much a part of Drumveyn as the cold, the smell of birch wood fires, the meager lighting and the musty unchanged air.

He misread the blank note in her voice. She'd be at her wits' end without him. "In fact, my lady, matters are so unsatisfactory that I think it best if Mrs. Platt and I give notice right away." That should be good for a bob or two, he thought with vicious satisfaction. Mrs. Platt nodded righteously at his shoulder, feeling somehow that they had scored.

Madeleine breathed in the smell of dirty fat and cigarettes in her kitchen, looked from Platt's watchful jaundiced face to Mrs. Platt's broad gloating one, and her eye fell on that slimy bread wrapper trailed across the margarine tub. A little bubble of pure uncomplicated rage burst inside her.

"Then I accept your notice. Of course I understand that you will have to find another post or somewhere to live. Shall we say three months?"

Platt was literally winded. For the space of five long seconds he could find neither breath nor words, his brain scudding about trying to pin down how he had been tricked.

"We just think we should get more," Mrs. Platt rushed in. "With all we have to do. And we should be paid triple for Sundays, that's the law. We're owed a lot for that already."

"Shut your face," Platt hissed at her in ugly fury. What else would she come out with from his endless diatribes in the privacy of the flat?

"Well, obviously you're dissatisfied," said Madeleine, not sure how she was managing to keep her voice so calm, but detachedly pleased about it. "You are quite right to give notice and I shall let Mr. Maclaren know in the morning so that he can take the necessary steps."

The sounds of unleashed fury which broke out behind her as she walked down the corridor were rather satisfactory. She thought perhaps Joss might have been proud of her.

Chapter Eleven

"I've done something dreadful."

Lisa, one hand on Cristi's shoulder to steady her, the other twirling a long wool scarf around her neck from above, paused with raised brows.

Cristi, used to being looked after and docile under Lisa's casual treatment, stood still with her chin raised and looked at Madeleine out of the tail of her eye.

"I've sacked Platt."

"What?" Lisa dropped the end of the scarf and Cristi scraped it off her face and looked from one to the other, sensing drama but somehow not disaster.

"Have you honestly?" There was no mistaking the hope in Lisa's voice.

"Well, not sacked exactly. He gave notice and I accepted it. It was a try on, I think, but anyway, I took it."

"But that's marvelous. I never thought you'd do such a thing. That little toad of a man, really going at last?"

I didn't have the least idea she felt like that, one part of Madeleine's brain recorded for later discussion with Joss. "I can't quite believe it myself, but it seems to have happened."

"And you won't change your mind?"

Memory of Platt's hectoring voice, the avarice and triumph in his eyes. "No, I won't change my mind."

"Oh, Mum." Most unexpectedly Lisa stepped forward and gave her a brusque hug, the first contact they had had for a long, long time. And that Mum, too, was impulsive and new. It had always been Mummy, then awkwardly Mother when Howard had scoffed, then really nothing. Grannie had objected forcefully and sarcastically when Archie had taken to Mum, but he hadn't seemed to hear. Lisa had lacked the courage to copy him.

"You don't think I'm quite mad?"

"I think it's the best thing that's ever happened at Drumveyn." Apart from Grannie leaving, that is; and, a small cold voice added, father dying. "But how did all this happen so suddenly?"

"Oh, I haven't even told you—sorry, darling— Archie and Cecil are coming up today. They're on their way now. I went to the kitchen to say they'd be here for dinner and all this blew up like a hurricane. I suppose now there'll be a good deal of unpleasantness to put up with."

She didn't guess how much. She innocently believed that notice would be worked out, that Mr. Maclaren would make the correct arrangements taking into account the years the Platts had been at Drumveyn, and that for the time being everything would go on much as before.

Not so. The Platts rushed headlong into full-scale outrage. Thrown on the scrap-heap, after all they'd done, the best years of their lives, turned out without a roof over their heads . . . They phoned their son, they phoned their daughter, who as it was Sunday at once rushed up from

Cumbernauld and Stirling to fuel the crisis and have their say. They also demanded interviews with Madeleine.

"You don't have to talk to them. It's none of their business," Lisa insisted.

"I'd just like to be sure they know what was actually said and make it clear that we shall look after Platt and Mrs. Platt till they find somewhere else to live. But I won't have them in my drawing room," Madeleine added with a new grim resolution that much impressed Lisa.

An orange van with "Tracy 'n Reg for Fruit 'n Veg" on its side obscured most of the corridor window. The sitting room of the flat was furnace hot and full of cigarette smoke. It was Eddie Platt, full of rancor after the years of having to keep to one small slice of this huge house, envying all Archie and Lisa had and did, who leapt in first. "You can't do this, you know. Dad can get you for unfair dismissal."

One of his many jobs had been with the DSS. He was now more settled, however, his job with a debt collection agency providing him with a satisfaction in dealing with the misfortunes and downfall of others which he found quite addictive.

Madeleine looked at his pale ferret's face under sleeked back yellow-ginger hair and raised her eyebrows at this threat. Eddie, goaded by her silence, launched into a tirade about legitimate grievance, compensation and redundancy payments, to which Madeleine listened quietly. Tracy his sister, always an uncommunicative child, fended off with one arm the demands of her son who had his elbows hooked over the arm of her chair so that his feet were free to kick its side, and stared with dislike at Madeleine over the head of a baby sucking noisily at a huge flaccid breast. Madeleine felt affronted by the sight of it then reminded herself that these were their quarters.

Platt was nodding with satisfaction at every third word of Eddie's while Mrs. Platt added a subnote of gulping sobs. Tracy's husband kept his eyes carefully on *Rawhide* with a "Keep me out of it" expression.

What shook Madeleine was the open hostility in the room, the hatred that had been hidden under Platt's servility, and the resentment of Eddie and Tracy, whose noise, mess and general destructiveness she thought the family had tolerated rather well over the years. She concentrated, speaking quietly, on the one vital fact. Platt had given notice; she had accepted it. She also pointed out that though she believed he was required to give one month's notice she was making the flat available to him for three.

Then she turned and left, hoping they would not see that she was trembling. She drew deep breaths of cool air coming back into the main part of the house and for once was glad of it.

"Gracious, I thought they'd eat you alive." Lisa was full of admiration. "What did you say to them?"

"That it was Platt's decision. It was all very much on the 'take them for every penny you can get' level."

"What a nightmare they are. Honestly, what *do* they think?"

Madeleine caught sight of Cristi's face, almost as tense and anxious as on the evening of her arrival. "Oh, they're just indignant. They'll get over it. Funny thing, though, Platt seems to have forgotten all about coffee."

She was pleased to see Cristi's smile when Lisa laughed and added, "Though actually I see it's nearer lunch time. I suppose there's not much hope of that either. And we may find ourselves making beds for Archie and Cecil yet—"

The drawing room burst open, not with a butler's touch, and Eddie Platt stood there, lager can in hand, his belligerence more defiant in these surroundings in spite of himself. "My dad wants a word with you."

"Eddie, how dare you!" Lisa began wrathfully, but Madeleine checked her.

"Eddie, if your father wants to speak to me he can come and do so."

"You're not going to get away with this, you know."

Madeleine glanced at Cristi, watching open-eyed. "Lisa, I think it might be a good idea to phone Jean. How would you like to have lunch with Jill and Dougal today, Cristi?"

"Are you going away?" Cristi asked instantly.

"We're not going anywhere, I promise you. Lisa will go up to the farm with you. Eddie, tell your father I am here in the drawing room if he has anything to say to me."

Eddie, disconcerted to find that the old familiar order of things still retained its power, retreated swearing and muttering.

Lisa started Cristi on her way to the farm but let her go on alone as she was by this time proud of doing, saw Dougal and Jill emerge from some lair and come racing down to meet her, and turned back to the house full of a lively anticipation. Her mother was a different person now that Father wasn't there to overshadow her. Who ever would have thought she'd take on old Platt like that, and Eddie too? What was more, there seemed every chance she would stick to her decision. Nice surprise for Archie. Lisa didn't realize that she hadn't thought of Howard for hours.

"How about some food to sustain you for the next round?"

How agreeable it was to be teased. "But Lisa, surely you don't think they're going to make things any nastier, do you?"

"I'm sure they'll do their best. Shall we go and see what there is?"

Remarkably little, was the answer to that.

"They really are the limit," Lisa said furiously, slamming the door of the ransacked fridge.

"Heavens, dinner, Archie and Cecil! Do you suppose Mrs. Platt ever got that extra pheasant out?"

"Are you serious?"

"Then whatever are we going to give them?"

"There must be something in the freezer. Let's go and have a look."

The freezers were out in the old game larder, which meant a trek across the courtyard and freezing half to death searching the muddled depths.

"Will a pheasant defrost in time?"

"We'll find something smaller. What's this, do you think? Partridge?"

"Too small surely?"

"Woodcock? If I could find a couple of those. God, nothing labeled, nothing dated. Complete chaos. Bloody man. Look at all the junk kicking around in the bottom. Oh, some wheaten rolls, that makes me feel at home. A sliced loaf, age unguessable. This bag feels like some kind of vegetable. Right, we might as well poison ourselves with this lot as anything else."

They made poached eggs on toast for lunch. "Can't think why they left those," Lisa remarked. "And luckily for us they don't like Stilton or fruit."

Madeleine was struck by how alive and even cheerful she looked, her own problems temporarily pushed aside.

"It's so good to have you here," she said impulsively. "It would have been ghastly dealing with all this without you."

"It wouldn't have happened if I hadn't come," Lisa pointed out, unable to show how pleased she was.

"Then I'm even more glad you did," her mother said, then they became self-conscious and quickly turned to discussing whether they could face the kitchen again to make coffee.

Mingled sounds of revolution and carousal floated from the flat for an hour or two more, then there came much to-ing and fro-ing and calling of raucous voices outside.

"I do believe the cavalry are leaving," Lisa observed.

Banging of car doors, shouts, engines revving. Silence.

"I don't expect we'll see much more of Platt and Mrs. Platt today."

"Shall we get out of the house for a while and forget them? We could go up and see if Cristi and the Galloway children would like to go for a walk."

But as they went out by the gunroom door they saw across the courtyard that the door to the flat was open, and the inner door beyond it. Every light was on but there was an unmistakable air of desertion. The doors of the garage Platt used also gaped wide; his Escort was gone.

"We'd better have a look," said Madeleine, concerned.

The flat looked like the aftermath of a burglary crossed with a three-day party.

"Talk about the sack of somewhere or other," Lisa remarked with awe as they looked into each gutted room, all heaters going full bore, the bare bones of such Drumveyn property as wardrobes and cupboards emerging from a silt of litter.

"They've gone," Madeleine said stupidly.

"Looks like it," Lisa agreed jubilantly, then looked at her mother more doubtfully. For as long as she could remember Platt had been at the core of Drumveyn domestic life and appalling as he had been it would be hard for her mother to imagine the house functioning without him. "Look," she said encouragingly, "we'll cope. There must be plenty of people on the estate who will help out till we can get someone else—"

Madeleine swung around on her, her face alight. "I'm not even thinking about all that yet. He's gone! He has really and truly gone, that odious, odious man. I feel like a balloon that wants to get free and float away, anywhere I like. Let's turn everything off in here and shut the door and forget the horrible place even exists."

"Good idea. And we'd better shut his garage too. It looks like a scrapyard."

Tossed down in the middle of the courtyard they found the household keys.

Chapter Twelve

As dusk gathered in the bare little room Joss sat and listened to the quietness, boring into it with her mind. Beyond the occasional soft settling of the wood fire there was no sound. The wind had died as evening came and the cottage stood too high up the bare slope of field above the loch for her to hear its slow wash on the shell shingle of the beach.

She had achieved what she wanted and she had achieved nothing; had freed herself of all demands but found no peace. She was too intelligent and too honest not to recognize that a few days of solitude would not resolve the turmoil of self-doubt and anger that had been boiling up in her for months. She couldn't go back. The scale of it had defeated her in the end, and restless though her conscience was, she knew that she had had enough. Compassion was exhausted, dried up, expended. She could not revive it.

She looked around the room, at the mock-goatskin hearth-rug, the mock-tapestry sofa and chairs with wooden arms and flimsy legs, the small black and white television she had not had the courage to turn on, the maltreated oak table with the four almost matching chairs tucked around it—luxury for her and for the other OW workers who holidayed thankfully here. I couldn't enjoy real comfort now, she thought. I wouldn't know how to be extravagant, not with any pleasure. Yet I have the money my mother worked so hard for, and my grandparents before her.

She had given a large chunk of it to One World, but even by then her commitment had been less certain. Five years ago she would have handed over the lot without a second thought. Now she had seen too much of the mismanagement, the leaching away of funds, the looting and armed terrorization. She had begun to hate not only those representatives of government who found their way so rarely into the camps, the journalists, the famous who made donations, came for a day, held a baby, made news, vanished, but also the volunteer aid-workers, even her fellow veterans. She knew this swelling pointless rage revealed a deficiency in herself but she was unable to master it.

But to give up, walk away, stop caring. No one did that. Could she live with the guilt? And would she be able to create for herself some "normal" life, re-establish ordinary human relationships? Sitting alone in this silent cottage was not the answer. She must find somewhere to live, and work.

But first she must go back to Drumveyn. All week she had thought of Madeleine alone in that dismal house under the thumb of the ghastly Platt, worrying about failing Archie, worrying about the baby. Poor Mads, she needed a bit of support. Did she ever look ahead at her life and shudder at the prospect, Joss wondered. Would she welcome Joss being somewhere within reach, if that could be achieved, or would she want to cling to her isolation? For Joss, Madeleine was the only focal point of contact and friendship she had in the country, and she needed it badly. First thing in the morning she would pack up and go back.

It was almost dark when Archie pulled up at the door of Drumveyn. The place looked if possible more dead than ever. "Come on," he said to Cecil, "let's see if we can get in without putting up Platt."

No light in the hall, nor, more surprisingly, in the drawing room, whose door stood open. Only the dim light from the corridor that led to the kitchen.

"Mum must be dressing for dinner," he said, dropping their bags at the foot of the stairs. "Have to ask Platt where they're putting us after all."

Cecil wandered after him, looking around her with a shiver of loathing at the Drumveyn beige on beige. Then as Archie pushed open the kitchen door she heard laughter, with the high note of a child above the rest.

Archie stood riveted, staring at a scene he would never have imagined finding in this house, and Cecil came to look over his shoulder.

The kitchen was warm and busy. Madeleine with a tea-towel around her waist was peeling apples; a child in a sweater the color of dying bracken was kneeling on a high stool beside her, patterns of apple peel on the table in front of her, dark head turned to where Lisa was standing with her hand on the door of the old potato-peeling machine. As Archie watched she opened it for a second and a couple of potatoes flew like bullets across the room to thud into a cupboard door. They all laughed, the child's voice rising in an ecstatic squeal.

Archie had never suffered much nostalgia for

Drumveyn but a memory came back vividly of
times when he and Lisa had persuaded a kitch-
enmaid to do just this, and their joy in the forbidden trick.

"Things seem a bit out of control here," he remarked, coming in smiling.

"Archie!"

Madeleine dropped her apple and knife and
came quickly forward to welcome them, and Archie had time to notice as he reached to hug her
that she looked quite different from a week ago,
her face alive, her hair for once bouncing out of
its smooth order, the tea-towel striking a most rak-
ish note for her.

"Darling! And Cecil! Come in. How lovely to
see you. We're rather busy at the moment, as you
can see—making dinner!"

She tried to be casual and sounded as triumphant as a child who can't wait to spring a delicious surprise.

"So I see. What on earth's going on? Where are
Platt and Mrs. P? And this must be Cristi."

Lisa came forward grinning. She hardly looked
the emotionally devastated sister he'd been called
in to succor either. That awful lunch-at-the-Ritz
look she'd affected since her marriage had gone,
and she was back in her old moleskin breeches
and check shirt and gilet and looked about
eighteen.

"Remember the old tattie rumbler?" she said.
"It still works. Hello, Cecil."

Cristi slid down from her stool and came forward to be introduced with shy formality.

What a little stunner, Archie thought, gravely
shaking hands and taking in the striking coloring
and the fine lines which jeans and sweater could

not disguise. It flashed through his mind not only that this was the most improbable offspring for Howard but that she was just such a child as Cecil might have—as he and Cecil might have, he amended carefully.

In the rush of welcome and explanations one thing was clear to him—the atmosphere of the house had radically altered. Never in all his memory had this kitchen felt friendly and human. Opening the door on that laughter had been a tremendous surprise.

"So what's happened to Platt? Is he ill?"

"Even better," said Lisa. "Walked out, gone for good. Can you believe it?"

"Gone? Do you really mean it? What happened?"

As Madeleine and Lisa both plunged into the story and Cristi looked from one to the other, fascinated by their excitement, Archie stopped them. "No, look, hang on. This has to be worth celebrating properly. Why don't I bring up a couple of decent bottles—or would you rather have a G and T, Cecil?" He had asked her once if she thought it was still all right to drink alcohol; he wouldn't ask her again.

"Oh, drinks, that's right, and heavens, the drawing room fire, we've forgotten all about it!" exclaimed programed Madeleine.

"Well, if no Platts are about to appear what's wrong with here? It's the only room in the house that's ever warm anyway—sorry, Mum."

"Here?" Not only redolent still of Platt power, but really rather a mess with dinner half prepared.

Lisa laughed at her. "You're not going to make us eat in the dining room, surely?"

I've walked in on the wrong play, Archie

thought. I've come racing up here because all is tragedy and crisis—what on earth is going on?

"It would suit me never to have to eat a meal in the dining room again," he admitted. "I hate it."

What sort of Frankenstein's castle have I brought them up in, Madeleine wondered.

"Where's the cellar key?" Archie was asking. "Gin for you then, Cecil, yes? Can you round that up, Sleazy, and chuck a few logs on the fire while you're at it so the drawing room's bearable later on. I don't think we're going to persuade Mum to spend the entire evening in the kitchen."

How many years since he had used that much-fought-over nickname? "Archie, come off it," Lisa protested, and Cristi giggled, enjoying adult teasing and sensing released tension in them all.

"Guess where we found the keys," said Madeleine, producing them. "Tossed down in the courtyard by our departing friend."

"Probably meant to go off with them and then thought better of it."

"Or someone made him see sense."

"Wait, wait, hold the story," Archie ordered, hurrying off to the wine cellar.

Cecil draped herself on a kitchen stool, looking tolerant and temporary.

"Oh, Cecil, I'm so sorry. You'll want to go up to your room. I'm afraid it's been rather sketchily cleaned, but the beds are made and it should be warming up a little by now. Shall I take you up?"

"Oh please, don't bother," Cecil said in her cool way. "A drink first would be lovely."

She had never lost that air of the well-conducted guest. She and Archie had been married for two years but she never seemed a member of the family. That has to be my fault, Madeleine thought with her new perception. And in reality this is Cecil's house; an odd thought indeed.

The potatoes which hadn't been fired across the room and the pheasant, less the bacon eaten by the Platts which should have draped its breast, were in the oven, the woodcock (one of which had turned out to be snipe) waiting to join them. Crumble topping made by Mrs. Platt before the simple news of two more for dinner had left her without job or home, was put over the apples. Cream came down from the farm with supplementary supplies of milk.

Cecil slipped away to have a bath, but Madeleine, privately defying she didn't know who, and also too busy to bother, sat with Archie, Lisa and a Cristi very thrilled by these new developments, and they started on one of the bottles of Chablis Archie had brought up.

"No time for red," he said regretfully. "There's some marvelous stuff there. Do you know, I think that's the first time I've ever been down there on my own. No Platt with pursed lips sniffing at my elbow." And no father, he added mentally, in actual pain when he had to take a bottle from the racked dozens he had so much grudged opening.

"Archie! I've just realized something. Oh, how truly awful." His mother was staring at him in consternation.

"What?" She looked really shaken. She couldn't have read his thoughts but he felt guilty just the same.

"Platt. Accepting his notice."

"What about it? Best day's work you ever did, I should have thought. Or are you worried about running the house without him?"

"No, no, it's not that. But Platt, the house, everything—they're yours. Platt wasn't my employee, I had no right—" It was the first time the reality of Archie's ownership had come home to her. He had never referred to it, never hinted at it, since the morning they had walked down to the loch after Charles's service. "Oh, how dreadful of me."

"Mum, are you mad? Don't even think about it." Archie was so concerned that he got up quickly and came around the table to her. He had intended to talk to her about plans, and his cherished idea for the estate which looked as though it might just come off, but he had first meant to make sure she never had a moment of this sort of doubt.

"This house is your home," he said urgently. "Nothing has changed. You know I told you that—I want you to feel totally certain of it. Nothing could have pleased me more than seeing the back of Platt but if you had wanted to keep him on—even if you want him back—shut up, Lisa—that's entirely up to you."

"But the whole place, the estate—" I must have been asleep since Charles died, Madeleine thought despairingly. What have I been doing all these months, shut up in some selfish cocoon, half dead myself?

"Look, I wanted to talk to you about all that," Archie said urgently. "I was planning to come up when I was back from—from the next trip—" (what had they told Cristi?) "—but now that Cecil and I are here perhaps we could go into a few things together. If you're happy with that?"

"I want to," said Madeleine, fiercely for her.

Chapter Thirteen

Talk they did, decamping to the drawing room when dinner was over and the dishwasher loaded.

"But what did they do?" Madeleine asked. "Two of them, evening after evening?"

"Good question," answered Archie, taking with him the gin bottle and what was left of the Chablis while Lisa brought the coffee. "We didn't have starters or a savoury, of course."

"All right, tease if you like, but everything seemed to get done so easily."

Archie and Lisa exchanged a quick grin. Madeleine had done a little light basting of the birds, been so concerned about hot plates that no one could touch them, and admitted she couldn't make gravy, a job Archie had taken over. Lisa had done the rest—though Cecil had murmured, "Cinnamon?" as the topping was about to go on the crumble.

Madeleine went up to put Cristi to bed and give her the bath they'd missed out before dinner. This had become a favorite time—mingled memories and keen immediate pleasure. The warm scented bathroom, comfortable in its cumbersome old-fashioned way, the gaily chattering child with her perfectly made body, small hands delicate as butterflies chasing the Chanel soap, black hair in wet points on her slender neck, added up to an intimacy it was going to be unbearable to lose. Holding the big towel wide and wrapping the laughing wriggling fish of the child in it, Madeleine faced what she had been doing her best to ignore all evening—that Archie's arrival brought very near the prospect of never seeing Cristi again, and that she minded very much indeed.

She stayed till Cristi fell asleep which nowadays, with all the excitements of Drumveyn life, took no time at all. And had Cristi woken she was quite capable by now of finding her way downstairs if necessary. This was one child for whom the house held no terrors.

Going down to the drawing room Madeleine paused for a moment on the shadowy stairs. She stood with cocked head, absorbing the new feel of the house—the child asleep in her room, Archie and Lisa both here, and Cecil, carrying the baby who would be the first grandchild. (There hasn't been a moment yet to tell her I'm pleased, I must make the opportunity to talk to her.) But more important even than all this was the knowledge that the cloud of disapproval which had hung over her all through her years here had lifted and dispersed. Charles's mother, Charles himself, Platt— those eternally disparaging faces—had gone. Platt! She had actually allowed that noxious little man to rule her life, never questioning his strictures or putting a stop to his veiled sneers. She took a long deep breath of a different air. She wished that Joss had stayed to share this but looked forward with a quite new relish to telling her all about it. And with the greater awareness that all the new events and demands of the last few days had brought, she wondered too how Joss was faring and whether when she returned she would be more ready to talk about her own life.

"So what's the story, Lizzie?" Archie asked, after they had heard about his skirmishes with Spanish bureaucracy, swapped a few Platt stories and Cecil had parried well-meaning inquiries from Madeleine about her work.

Cecil had been unable to relax. All the exuberance over Platt's departure seemed merely childish to her, and she was baffled and irritated by the light-hearted mood when they had been dragged up here because Lisa's life was supposedly falling apart. She wanted the baby to be talked about, she wanted to be asked how she was. Morning sickness, which she had got through privately this morning, unable after all to let it be something shared with Archie, made it so real. These changes were actually taking place in her body. Yet on the other hand she felt defensive, ready for her motives to be misunderstood.

Madeleine, rebuffed once, was nevertheless working up courage to open the subject when Archie plunged into Lisa's problems. How different the brother/sister relationship from the parent/child one, she reflected ruefully, amused in spite of herself. No worries for Archie about being rebuffed, or being thought inquisitorial. He was sympathetic, would do everything in his power to help, but he could demand with that cheerful bluntness, "So what's the story?"

Madeleine was horrified to discover just how ruthless Howard had been. She had asked no questions since Lisa arrived, feeling that peace and privacy were the first essentials, glad when Lisa went off revisiting old haunts on the estate, though mostly avoiding people. Surprisingly though, Lisa had spent quite a lot of time with Cristi, digging out the sledge for her, letting her go with her on her shorter walks, taking her up to the nursery to look at its battered treasures and choose books and take wild rides on dappled Kelpie.

But through it all Madeleine had observed with helpless pain Lisa's hurt bewilderment, as though she could not comprehend why such a blow had been dealt her, and she had longed to abandon the passive waiting role and offer sympathy.

Now for the first time Lisa detailed the lengths to which Howard had gone. It seemed that with Archie listening quietly, his good-natured face very grave, she could bring herself to admit the finality of it.

"Poor old Liz," he said gently, when her voice tailed wretchedly away. "You didn't deserve this."

Madeleine was startled to see Lisa raise an arm to her face and roughly wipe away tears with her cuff. She had not cried till now. Yet somehow with Archie there it seemed natural; his large compassion covered everything.

"What we need to know," he said after a pause, "is what you want. Are you going to look for him?"

Lisa stared into the fire, her strong jaw set, her lips compressed. "He's with Cristi's mother," she got out finally. "That's the answer to that, isn't it?"

"Yes, I think it is," Archie said slowly. "And he's left you a good deal, materially, so you don't need to trace him to try to get financial support or anything of that kind. Also, legally, he's free to go."

"But am I married?" Lisa burst out passionately. "Don't I have a right to know that?" Madeleine's heart ached at the pain in that cry.

"I think we ought to try and establish that," Archie agreed. "We'll have to try the Brazilian end, check out a possible existing marriage."

"And Cristi must go back. I can't possibly cope with her. How could Howard have thought I could bear to have her?"

What must it be like, Cecil wondered, to have a child like Cristi suddenly, as it were, given to one? Surely, even apart from the bizarre circumstances, it would be impossible to accept and love her totally? Even adopting a newborn baby would not, could not, be the same as giving birth? She stirred restlessly. That had been her conviction; too late to question it now. Her thoughts roved back over the rootless lonely years and she made no effort to drag them back.

". . . but Cristi must have family in Brazil?" Madeleine was saying.

"By the sound of it they don't have much to do with her," Lisa replied. "It makes me wonder if perhaps Howard isn't married to her mother. Christ, where does that leave me? And who else might there be?" That torturing question.

"Well, tomorrow I'll find out all I can from Cristi and do some phoning," Archie said. "There must be someone I can talk to. But I don't think we should tell her she's going back until something has been decided. She seems so happy here."

"She's got to go back." It was as though the Cristi who was Howard's daughter was quite separate in Lisa's mind from the child who had taken to life at Drumveyn with such zest, who came running down from the farm with pink cheeks and muddy boots, full of news about Jean plucking a chicken and new calves and Dougal's black eye after a fight at school.

"I understand that," Archie said gently. "Don't worry, I'll take care of it."

"And I can't go back to that house," Lisa announced defiantly, almost wildly. "Nothing on earth will make me, whatever happens. You must sell it for me, Archie. Howard gave it to me. There's a whole file with a new lawyer's address, everything. I don't know where I shall go or what I shall do, but I'm never going to set foot in that house again."

"OK, calm down, there's no reason you ever should. That's the simplest thing in the world to deal with."

"You must stay here, darling," said Madeleine, filled with loving pity. "You know that you can, don't you, for as long as you like—if you want to, that is. Just whatever you want."

And as Lisa nodded, unable to speak, but reaching a hand for a moment toward her mother in acknowledgment, Madeleine remembered again that the house was, strictly speaking, no longer hers. "Oh Archie, and Cecil of course, that's all right, isn't it?"

"For God's sake!" Archie sounded most uncharacteristically impatient. "Don't keep saying that, don't even think it. But since we've reached this point—" He glanced at Lisa, leaning back in the corner of the sofa with her hand propping her chin and partly concealing her telltale quivering lips. It might not be a bad idea to give her other things to think about. And Cecil, who had accepted Madeleine's inclusion of her with a polite smile, would she support him, or hold herself separate as she had done all evening, whether deliberately or not he couldn't tell. "You've achieved the one thing I didn't quite know how to tackle," he went on, turning to his mother. "Booting out Platt. Perhaps it's opened the way to the next step—booting out Maclaren."

"Mr. Maclaren?" Madeleine felt quite dizzy. Mr. Maclaren looked after everything, was oracle, arbiter, holder of the purse-strings.

"Look, I didn't want to barge in too soon after father died," Archie said, leaning forward with his elbows on his spread knees, speaking with an urgency that reminded Madeleine of his passionate boyhood enthusiasms. "And I don't want to upset your life in any way, Mum, so just say if you mind."

"Go on, I want to hear," Madeleine said. She found that she did. An exciting wind of change was blowing, and she was eager for it.

"Well, I've been having a look at the estate accounts and the way the place is run," Archie began. (When had he done that? He was flashing about all over the world yet he always found time to fit in things he thought important, like driving up here to tell her about the baby last week—was that only last week?) "I have to say it's pretty alarming. No, I don't mean we're broke or anything drastic like that, but the estate hardly washes its face and it's badly run down. But quite apart from the cash side, I don't like the way it operates. Nothing's changed since grandfather's day. A sporting estate run for the pleasure of the owner, except that no one's even enjoying the shooting and stalking these days. But there are more serious aspects. What's happening to the birds of prey? When did we last plant any trees? Who decides what chemicals we spray, where and how often? Who's interested in preserving wildlife habitats? Who's looking at the changes in the red deer population and adapting our policy to meet them?"

How full of vigor he is, Madeleine thought. How deeply he cares about things. And he's honest and direct. How marvelous it will be to have him running things. And how disgraceful that I cannot answer a single one of his questions and I have "lived" here for twenty-eight years.

"But what will Mr. Maclaren say?" she asked, and realized how banal the question sounded after his eagerness. "I mean, that's all wonderful, darling, really, but—"

Archie laughed, relaxing. "He'll still be employed, Mum, we're not putting him in the dole queue with Platt. The Edinburgh office will still administer the Edinburgh property." He glanced across at Lisa, seeing that she had regained control. "God comes to lunch every other Tuesday," he added reminiscently, drawing her back into the conversation.

"Wasn't it a nightmare?" she rushed in gratefully. "I really thought for years that Mr. Maclaren owned everything and doled out the pocket money, even to Grannie."

"But how will you—?" Madeleine began, unable to envisage this overthrow of the mighty.

"There's someone I know quite well who I think I might just be able to get hold of, a partner in a firm that handles several farms and estates. He's a member at Rosemount so I sometimes see him

there, and his sons went to Loretto. One of them
was in my house in my last year as a matter of
fact and came out and did a stint on the Camargo
dam—he was pretty useful too. Anyway, I've
heard on the drums that Tom Ferguson might be
considering going freelance. If he does I want him,
if he'd consider such a proposition as Drumveyn
in its present state. He may already have something set up of course, because he's highly experienced and he must know just about everyone in
the county."

"Does he live locally?" Madeleine asked. "Would
we have met him?"

"Probably not. He grew up near Aberfyle where
his father was the local GP and apparently quite
a well-known character. Tom could make an enormous input here plus, and this is what makes me
really keen on him, he's very much into the conservation aspect. If we could get him to take over
I think he could put the place back on its feet in
the way I want."

"Well, that sounds excellent," Madeleine said.
So the same system would go on, she thought
rather flatly, with some other dried-up factor in
the place of Mr. Maclaren. "I do realize there must
be someone. You'll have to go on living in the
south—there's Cecil's work to consider as well as
your own—" She turned smiling to Cecil. I must
say something about the baby; it's awful that she's
been in the house for hours and it's never even
been mentioned. This business with Platt, then
Lisa's affairs.

But Cecil still gave nothing, and it was Archie
who answered. "We do hope to be up a lot more,
though. As time goes on Cecil will have to cut

back on the work, and we were rather planning, if you agree, that later on she could be here."

"Oh, that's a long way ahead," Cecil said lightly, speaking for almost the first time since dinner. "And talking of work, would you mind if I did some quick phoning, Madeleine? I hadn't expected to come up quite so soon and I really ought to—" She glanced at the telephone beside Madeleine's writing table. "But of course I don't want to disturb you. Perhaps—"

"You'll freeze to death in the kitchen corridor," said Archie. It was all the expression he would give to his disappointment.

"It won't take long."

She came back, after nearly an hour, only to make her excuses and vanish toward bed. She detested the Drumveyn bedrooms so much that normally she would wait for Archie. Now she slipped away, leaving him feeling that he had failed, and Madeleine full of guilt.

"Archie, I haven't said one word to Cecil about the baby. Shall I go up now, before she—?"

"Leave it, Mum," he told her wearily. "Time in the morning."

When he went up, not long afterwards, Cecil made no move. He didn't think she was asleep.

Chapter Fourteen

For a groping moment as Madeleine woke the memory that something wonderful had happened fused Charles's death and Platt's departure into one in her mind. Shocked, she rushed past this revelation.

The day stretched ahead, beguilingly empty. Empty? What was she thinking about? The house was full of people—and bare of food. There were rooms to clean, beds to make, all the complicated and mysterious machinery of the day's routine to be set in motion. She beat down a flurry of panic; she might be useless but Archie and Lisa weren't.

She looked across at the small bed and jerked up hastily on one elbow. Empty. Had Cristi gone along to Lisa's room? What time was it? Goodness, after eight—she never slept till now. No yellow fingers slapping down the tray, straightening the cup, turning the handle of the teapot a millimeter nearer to her hand, no padding feet crossing the room to the windows in the inevitable sequence. She threw back the bedclothes with an eagerness she hadn't felt for years.

"She hates what I've done."

"Cecil, no, there were just so many other things to talk about."

"But it's going to be your child, her grand-child . . ."

Cecil looked as white as the bath whose edge they were perched on, a sheen of sweat on her skin, olive circles under her eyes.

Archie, holding her steady with one arm, dabbed gently at her pale face with the corner of a towel. "We were just going to talk about it when you took off."

"I had to phone."

"I thought you'd done all your phoning before we left."

"There's so much to arrange."

He let it go, drawing her close. She had not used the bathroom adjoining their room, clinging instinctively to privacy, but he had heard her go, seen her urgency and had guessed and followed her. Not without a moment's struggle. He hated, and despised himself for hating, these first signs of her condition. He didn't want her beautiful well-cared-for body to lose its sleek perfection. He, who was supposed to care for people, for life. If it were his own child changing her, would that be different? But he knew he must take some positive step, now, to share in it all. If he rejected any part of the process the ground could never be regained. He had gone after her, and seeing her racked and limp and trembling had forgotten his reluctance.

"It was absolutely pointless my coming any-way," Cecil said drearily against his shoulder.

"I'm glad you came. The right moment will come to talk to Mum. She needed a bit of time to get used to the idea. And I want you here when we talk plans. Platt buggering off has created the perfect opportunity. A new estate factor is going to be an important change. We, you and I, must decide how we want to run the place."

"You know it's not my scene."

"I thought you wanted to spend more time here during your pregnancy?"

"Oh, well, I did, but not yet. Later, when I'm earthbound."

Archie didn't persist. He understood very well that in theory Drumveyn was part of the pregnancy plan but that all Cecil's instincts pulled her still to London. She was full of contradictions. If he had made her happy, if he had been able to provide the baby, would all these needs in her have become a coherent whole? She didn't understand that last night the baby had not been talked about not only because of the day's upheavals and Lisa's problems and the question of Cristi, but also because she invited no affection, made no openings. How could he help her?

Lisa woke to a brief sense of peace. Talking to Archie had clarified many things she had not had the courage to face before. Peripheral things like possessions were not important, She had known at the airport when Howard explained to her what he intended to do that she had lost him. He had already gone, then, and somewhere deep in her mind she had known but refused to admit that he had never loved her. She had needed to believe that their life together was perfect.

Numb and floundering, she had found at Drumveyn a comfort she had not hoped for. Her mother's reticence had been balm and Cristi, whose presence should in theory have added to her pain, had with her innocent enthusiasm and goodwill actually helped.

At least the decision had been made to sell the Surrey house. Archie had made it sound so straightforward that she felt it had already gone. And a decision about where to live could wait. The climate of Drumveyn was so different—and without Platt would be more different still—that it would be quite bearable to stay here until she could decide what to do next.

Then over relief crawled a tide of fear—stay here doing what? And for how long? And then? An endless tunnel of time stretched away before her, dark and menacing. Her life had no direction or purpose; she did not even know who she really was. The person known as Mrs. Armitage, evolved by Howard and for Howard, had no existence without him.

Pulling on her waxed jacket and the boots whose muddiness she now prized was still a thrill for Cristi. She had a stiff tussle with the key of the gunroom door which opened to the courtyard, managed to turn it with both hands then found she couldn't shift the bolt at the bottom. What would Dougal do? Looking around her, she spotted the boot-jack. With one lucky swipe she caught the bolt and drove it back.

Exuberant and breathless, she pulled the door. She did not exactly think that what she was doing would be forbidden, but she was savoring a novel impulse to lawlessness. She fled away, past the garages, past the store crammed with dusty heavy old kitchen relics where the sledge lay once more across the beams, past old wash-house, log store, stables, toolhouse, gardener's shed, potting shed and slatted game larder, all by now explored.

Running up the track to the farm she felt wildly

happy, dazzled by adventure. Every day here things happened, new excitements offered, and the small luxurious house in Rio behind its high walls, with its ironwork grilles at the windows, its gleaming marble floors, its small paved garden with camellias and magnolias in tubs, seemed very far away.

Jill and Dougal were coming now, walking separately as though they had been arguing. They forgot whatever the quarrel had been when they saw her.

"Whatever are you doing here?" Dougal demanded, not at all sure she should be out on her own like this.

"Where are you going?" Jill asked curiously.

"I came to meet you."

"But we've to go to school."

"I'll come to the bus with you." No need to say she was pretending she would get on it too and be carried off to school with them, to do whatever they did there.

"Well, I suppose it'll no' matter but mind you go straight back when we've gone," warned Dougal.

"I could carry your schoolbag," Cristi offered Jill.

"Suits me," said Jill, swinging it off.

"Is it true the Platts are away then?" Dougal asked.

This dramatic piece of news occupied them for a while, though Cristi knew little more than they did. When they reached the bridge they stopped to race sticks, a game Dougal and Jill found it hard to believe Cristi didn't know. They told her that the pair of black and white birds who'd flown up from the parapet were oystercatchers, and pointed out for her the curlew with its long curved beak and sweet fluting call.

"That's the first time I've heard him this year," Dougal said. "Everything's back early with the mild winter we've had. There's peesies down on the new plow—there, along the river. Do you ken what plowing is?" He was fascinated by her ignorance of his world, and by what she told them of her own. "See those fat buds, that's elder. And these tiny wee red knobs, do you see them, they'll be wild roses."

"We get frogspawn here," added Jill. "Where this water lies. Do you know frogspawn? Did you never keep tadpoles in a jar? And there'll be lambs soon, do you know lambs?"

"Not for another five weeks," Dougal amended.

"That's soon."

"No, it isna'—"

"Run, run," Jill shouted, "here's the bus."

"Now you go straight home, mind," Dougal instructed Cristi as he helped her out of the straps of Jill's bag. She looked very small as he watched her from the window, waving at the minibus with a longing face. Maybe he should have taken her to the big house on the way down. But she had a fair amount of sense, considering, and she'd not be off Drumveyn ground.

"It really is rather disgusting," Madeleine warned Archie, as they went along the passage to Platt's flat.

"We could get Malkie's mother to come and clean up."

"It hardly seems fair to ask her to do it," Madeleine demurred. "Perhaps we should get some commercial cleaners in."

"I think they're people too," Archie remarked mildly. It was still a fresh pleasure to hear her laugh like that. "Besides, Ailsa might be glad of the money."

He was right, Madeleine knew, and she should have thought of it herself.

"It'll need a lot more than cleaning," Archie said when he had had a look. "Have to be redecorated right through. We can decide about that when we know what we're going to do with it."

Madeleine had taken it for granted that they would look for another cook/butler couple. Why did she find it so hard to shake off set patterns, she asked herself impatiently. All kinds of possibilities were open to them now.

"Look, I think I should go down and see Tom Ferguson today if I can get hold of him," Archie was saying. "I'll have to tackle the Cristi business this afternoon, good Brazilians being in bed at present. You're sure you're happy about dumping Maclaren? I don't want to do anything you're not entirely in agreement with."

"I'm afraid he'll be terribly hurt."

"And he has also been terribly incompetent. But that wasn't what I was asking you."

"Yes, I'm happy. I know I've been complacent and oblivious and scarcely realize yet the state things are in, but I do see that we need to put our house in order, and I'm glad you're going to do it."

"Good," he said, putting an arm around her and giving her a powerful squeeze from which she emerged short of breath but very pleased. "You've made a pretty good start yourself, if I may say so. Though the next thing might be to get in a few supplies," he added as they came into the kitchen and he surveyed the meager breakfast Lisa had cobbled together.

Cristi raced in, cockahoop, spilling all about her escape, hitting the door, wearing a bag, looking for frogs' paws and waving to the bus, and they sat down to breakfast laughing, enjoying her.

"Are we all going down to Perth?" Archie asked, coming back from phoning Tom Ferguson and arranging a meeting for eleven. "Cecil, you'll come and meet Tom, won't you?" It was vital that she was included from the beginning. "What about you, Lizzie?"

"I'd better do some shopping, I suppose."

"Would you mind if I didn't come?" Madeleine asked. "I want to walk about the house."

They knew exactly what she meant.

Only a week since I told her about the baby and she was so shocked and upset and so determined not to let me see how she felt, Archie thought. And now I feel so close to her. Cristi has had a lot to do with it. And Joss, he was sure, when she was here. He had always had a lot of time for Joss who when he was growing up had been the one person in the adult Drumveyn world he could talk to about the interests closest to his heart.

"Then Cristi could stay with you?"

"We'll have a lovely time, won't we, Cristi?"

"Except you'll have no lunch," Lisa reminded her. "Those unbelievable scavengers."

"Then we'll go to the village and get—some sausages."

No one who had not known Madeleine's lifestyle at Drumveyn could have grasped the revolutionary quality of this announcement.

"God, don't go mad, Mum, will you?"

Did we ever laugh like this, Lisa wondered.

When we were very small, perhaps. A long time ago.

Madeleine and Cristi went into every room of the house that morning. To a certain extent normality had reasserted itself; Ivy Black had come in as usual and was cleaning and making beds; Malkie was bringing in logs; vehicles were coming and going in the courtyard; tea was being brewed. But the mood of the house was irrevocably altered. Though technically Archie and Cecil's it was more hers this morning than it had ever been, Madeleine thought, as she wandered on, feeling weightless and relaxed, looking with an objective eye at dispirited fabrics and worn carpets, messy cupboards and chaotic storerooms.

Charles's belongings were untouched in his dressing room; clothes that had belonged to his parents and even his grandparents were still carefully put away in unused rooms. Furs, boots, ball gowns with bodices stiff as birdcages, dress kilts, uniforms, hats in hat-boxes, yellowed kid gloves, boxes of new handkerchiefs and stiff collars, feathers and scarves and pearl-tipped hatpins and bizarre costume jewelry—Cristi was in heaven.

When they were too cold to look at any more they decided to go to the village. Apart from needing food there had been no Platt to make the sacrosanct daily run for his cigarettes and everyone's papers. Ah—driving the Volvo. Madeleine felt a little check of fear, then realized it was more than fear, it was association. Well, she must get over it. But as she went out with the keys, telling herself not to be a fool, she saw Jock Anderson the gamekeeper turning one of the estate pickups in the courtyard.

"Jock, are you very busy?" she called to him.

Charles would have been furious that she should even think of taking one of the men away from his work. Never had she dared do such a thing.

Jock turned off his engine and got out hastily, with the formal manners all the estate people used for her.

"You couldn't run us down to the village?" she asked.

"I could, my lady. In fact, I was just away down for the papers myself, seeing that Mr. Platt is no longer with us." Deadpan, no emphasis in his voice, so how did she know so certainly that he thoroughly approved.

"Good, then we'll come too." She could have asked him to fetch what she wanted; that would have been normal. But this was a different day, different times.

Chapter Fifteen

"In a way I've brought you down here under false pretenses," Tom Ferguson said, pulling forward for Cecil an Edwardian mahogany armchair with a torn seat and fine marquetry detail she longed to examine. Not a country girl, this wife of Archie Napier's, he decided, enjoying the stalking model's walk as she crossed the office and the delectable legs as she sat down, disposing her fine-boned limbs with one assured movement.

"How's that?" Archie asked. Securing Tom's expertise and experience was a crucial part of his plans; but it would not be like Tom to have let them come down for nothing.

Tom looked for a moment out over the crocuses and the greening grass and blossoming trees of the North Inch, then turned to face Archie. "I'm thinking of resigning."

That was why Archie was here. It was the man he wanted, not the firm. He studied Tom thoughtfully. He looked incongruous in this paper-dredged room, a well-built man of medium height with a healthy outdoor look about him. He moved with the energy of the heedlessly fit and there was no gray yet in the dark hair around his bald brown pate. But there was more which appealed to Archie. Tom's brown eyes held kindness and humor, his voice was easy, his whole manner one of relaxed good sense.

"Go on," said Archie.

"Oh, getting more senior and so on. More and more time spent in the office. But the chance to handle Drumveyn might be enough to make me stay on. I've a pretty good idea of what you want to achieve, and I know how you feel about balancing traditional methods and conservation. It would be a fascinating challenge to try and pull the place around, given its present state." He smiled and Archie grinned back with a little rueful chuck of his head. Of course Tom Ferguson would know how Drumveyn had been run down; his minute knowledge of the whole area was a byword.

"I understand you want to shift the estate affairs from Mathieson and Marr," Tom went on, "but I'm not sure how committed you feel to bringing them to us. Or if you'd consider an alternative?"

"Such as?" Archie held down his eagerness and spoke quietly.

Tom took the plunge. "I've been thinking of freelancing."

Archie's grin broadened. "That's why I'm here. Only I wasn't sure how definite that was."

"Trust you to have your ear to the ground."

"But would Drumveyn be enough to keep you going? I don't think it's a full-time job."

"I wasn't looking for one. I was thinking perhaps of a couple of smaller places, being more mobile, getting a bit more fresh air. I don't need a huge salary. I'm on my own now and the boys are more or less independent. I thought I'd like some time to myself."

What had happened to the wife Archie dimly remembered meeting at some long ago dinner party? Dim had been the word, certainly as to looks.

"Then resign," he said. "Take us on."

Tom opened and shut his mouth, then his weathered face creased in a smile of pure pleasure. He held out his hand. Nothing was said. Cecil, her attention wandering, had pulled out her diary and was re-checking the week's schedule. Could she persuade Archie to drive down tonight? She didn't even know a deal had been made.

"Perhaps we'd better do the rest of our talking over lunch," Tom said. Cecil wondered why they laughed.

Archie had mixed success with his calls to Brazil. He and Cecil and Lisa had had lunch in town with Tom Ferguson, and had come home to find Madeleine and Cristi high on enterprise and independence. They had burned their sausages, eaten yogurt out of cartons and failed to get the dishwasher to start because they hadn't shut the door properly. They were sitting side by side at the kitchen table studying the manual with equal noncomprehension when the others staggered in with Lisa's wholesale shopping. Lisa undertook to keep Cristi out of the house while Archie did his telephoning, aware that she wanted to avoid pain for herself as well.

The mother superior of the convent school Cristi had attended had been fighting a bitter battle with the Tomás lawyers over unpaid fees and had no hesitation in telling Archie who they were. She also told him that the house of Señora Tomás was shut up and for sale, and rather unexpectedly was able to provide the name and address of her father.

The lawyers supplied him with the startling information that the papers giving Cristi up for adoption had been finalized in every respect except for Lisa's signature, and had been sent to the address in Englefield Green on the day Howard left England. They were not prepared to put Archie in touch with any member of Señora Tomás's family.

"But surely her grandparents would accept her if you took her to them?" Madeleine protested with concern.

"They can be very ruthless, these aristocrats from the old families. They've always had such power, still have on their own land. I think I'll need to find out from Cristi what her contacts with the family have been so that I can try the best prospects first."

"Could the lawyers perhaps find the maid Isaura?"

"I asked that bossy old nun about her—apparently she's gone back to the ranch at Campo Novo."

"Yes, now I come to think of it, Cristi told me she'd been brought up there."

"I shouldn't think she'd be in any position to help. If she flouts the *patrào* she'll jeopardize the livelihood of her entire family, if I know anything about the system."

"What about the other servants—would they be able to tell us anything?"

"I'd have to go and hunt for them. The house is on the market. Howard and Justina don't intend to come back for Cristi, that much seems clear.

God, how can they abandon her, a child like that? Well, any child, but she really is pretty special."

"I know, it's hard to believe. Unbearable. You couldn't leave it for this evening, though, Archie?" Madeleine begged with sudden urgency. "She'll never sleep if we spring all this on her now. Can it wait till tomorrow?" She knew in her heart that she wanted to delay, however briefly, the moment when Cristi would have to go. That was what Archie had come for, she knew, to take her home, but suddenly it was all happening too quickly.

"I don't see why not, I'll deal with it as soon as Tom has gone."

Madeleine realized that Archie wanted to sort out the management of the estate without delay, but she could have done without the Maclaren lunch routine all over again. It would have to be dining room lunch—what could they give him? Thank goodness Lisa was here to cope.

Joss found she was driving more and more slowly. She had one last windswept walk and looked her fill at the bare and solid shapes of the Torridon hills. Then she had packed up, cleaned and tidied and shut the door on her austere little refuge. There was nothing more to be gained by staying and there was poor old Madeleine needing company and support. But the reluctance to walk once more into that dreary old house had deepened with every mile she'd driven south.

But if she didn't go to Drumveyn, what alternative was there? Some awful hotel. And beyond tonight, some rented room or furnished flat while she looked for a place to live. If only she had some focal point, a landscape that meant something to her, a calf country to return to. A town would be unendurable, that much was certain. But would Madeleine think it a bit much if she looked for something in the glen or around Muirend? It was the only link she had. That was awful, to have reached her age, to have believed she was such a good sort, and to have *one* friend. I've grown so antagonistic, she thought. I didn't even notice it was happening. Angry inner harangues about everything and everyone; how can I stop them, slow myself down?

She felt such antipathy building up as she turned into the Drumveyn drive that she stopped the van on the bridge, got out and leaned for a moment on the cold stone parapet. How the air had changed since she was here a week ago. Even in that short time the evenings had lengthened, and were full of birdsong she was sure she hadn't noticed before. A pair of mallard flew low over the water, rose above the screen of alders along the bank, disappeared calling. Let the moment be enough; surely I've learned that by now.

A small girl opened the door to her. Madeleine's voice, cheerful, almost unrecognizable, called "Did you manage, Cristi—oh, you did, well done."

Lights, music from somewhere, a hand above Cristi's opening the door wider, Madeleine's face appearing around it, looking arrestingly different.

"Joss how perfect! I thought you were staying for two weeks. Come in, I'm so pleased you've come back. This is Cristi. Cristi, Miss Barnes, my great, great friend since I was only a little bit older than you."

That child curtseyed to me, Joss thought blankly, out of the whirl of surprising things.

"Come on, we're in the kitchen."

"Hang on—am I in the wrong house here?"

Madeleine laughed, refusing explanations, trotting ahead briskly.

Joss gazed thunderstruck at the scene in the kitchen, shook her head like someone coming up after a dive, took another look.

"You remember Archie and Lisa?"

Archie neatly dismembering a chicken, Lisa grating cheese.

"Cecil I think you haven't met." A slim dark girl who looked out of place in a jacket of big gray and white squares and brief black skirt raised rubber-gloved hands in greeting and went back to polishing a copper jelly-mold.

"But what's—where's—?" Joss floundered.

"Joss, good to see you," Archie greeted her warmly. "Come and sit here. We've had a coup in Drumveyn land."

"Not Platt?" Joss asked with such fervent hope that there was a general laugh. "And I came rushing back because you were on your own," she told Madeleine in mock complaint.

"Oh, Joss, I'm so sorry if it spoiled your holiday. But I'm delighted that you came!"

"Come on, Joss, sit down. Sherry, gin, wine?"

"Tea," said Joss firmly. "I don't care what time it is."

Archie, though impressively filled out, looked much the same as when she had last seen him, laid-back, down-to-earth, his big grin as friendly as ever. But Lisa—what had been happening to her? The mutinous inarticulate teenager did not look as though she had found the happiness her mother had been so sure of last week.

And who was the kid? Gorgeous little thing she was.

Only Cecil was a little too polite. All the right things had by now been said about the baby, but too late. Her feeling of separateness had if anything increased. Archie couldn't leave tonight because this wretched new manager was coming up tomorrow, but could she slip away herself, perhaps persuade Archie to take her down to Edinburgh for the early morning flight?

There was almost a party mood among the rest, Archie euphoric about the deal with Tom, Lisa responding to being busy and needed, able to forget for the time being tomorrow and all the tomorrows after it, Madeleine pleased to have Joss back so soon—and to have put off for one more day dispatching Cristi to what would be at best a welcome on sufferance.

"Oh, good, are we eating in here?" Joss said, as space was cleared on the table and silver appeared. "That dining room gives me the willies."

Archie and Lisa winked at each other.

"Everyone seems to have felt like that," Madeleine remarked in wonder.

"Battleground," said Lisa briefly.

"Well, the kitchen may be warmer but it's terribly gloomy," Madeleine pointed out. And redolent of Platts.

"We could do away with all that rabbit warren of pantries and store rooms—they're stuffed with rubbish no one ever uses anyway. We could take the kitchen right through to the west side of the house, make one big cooking/eating area," Archie suggested.

"It sounds lovely, darling," Madeleine said politely.

He laughed at her. "Then do it. Cecil will make a plan."

"But I don't think—"

"It would be wonderful," Lisa leapt in enthusi-astically. "The old boot room has one of the best views in the house, clear across to Ben Breac."

"But what about the boiler? You can't move that."

"It's below ground level."

"Only semi—about eight steps down."

"Cecil? You're the professional."

Madeleine listened to them wrangling, enjoying the idea in theory.

Not until later, when they were settled in the drawing room and Cristi was in bed, could Joss catch up on all that had been happening since her last visit, or finally screw up her courage to tell her own news.

"By the way, I've chucked it," she announced abruptly, in a pause when Cecil had vanished, and Archie seemed deep in his own thoughts.

"Chucked what?"

"But Joss, why?" This really was startling. Even Lisa looked up from the *Scottish Field.*

"I know, charity workers don't run out of charity."

"I didn't mean that, of course—"

"Can't take it," said Joss, shoving a hand through her rough hair, her face grim. "I only seem to have had so much to give and the sup-ply's run out. Pretty contemptible, I admit, but there it is."

"Contemptible? You've given a hundred, a thousand, times more than most people give." Ar-chie abandoned his own preoccupations and broke in forcefully, to Madeleine's relief.

"I didn't imagine it could ever happen," Joss

turned to him, as though sure of his understanding. "Stopping caring."

"That must be hard to live with," he said quietly, and her face crumpled unexpectedly at his compassionate tone.

"What are you going to do?" Madeleine asked hastily. Joss, tough, unshakable Joss, could not be about to cry.

"Don't ask. Can't even begin to think," Joss replied, getting a grip with a visible effort.

"I don't suppose you'd consider staying here?" Madeleine asked longingly. "Would you? For as long as you liked, or till you decide what you want to do next. Lisa's living at home now," (Lisa warmed to that) "and it would be wonderful to have you too." Cajoling, tempting, but very serious.

"You'd never put up with me."

"You old curmudgeon, we could have a good try."

"Don't be daft, I can't accept that—"

"Why not? Perhaps it's time for you to accept things for a while," Archie suggested.

"Joss, do consider it. I think—I hope—things will be a little different here now." Madeleine could not yet put into words the vague images she had of warmth and laughter and voices.

Joss looked around at them, watching her, smiling; tried to speak, cleared her throat exasperatedly. "There's nothing I'd like better," she was finally able to say gruffly.

Chapter Sixteen

"We can't give Mr. Ferguson lunch in the kitchen."

"It's Tom," said Archie. "And he really wouldn't notice."

But the Maclaren image was too strong—and Charles's, since knowing that Mr. Ferguson's boys had been at school with her own son Madeleine saw him as Charles's age. It really wouldn't do.

Tom was driving up from Perth doing his best to temper an excitement he hadn't felt for years. He would inherit a can of worms from Maclaren, whose blinkered outlook he knew by reputation and from more than one professional skirmish. Archie didn't live at Drumveyn and would be out of reach for weeks at a time. There would be a horde of estate employees locked into their own way of doing things. And, more immediately to the point since he was shortly to meet her, the widowed mother was in situ and no doubt would be equally averse to change.

But to have the hands-on running of a place like Drumveyn, to leave the office and the problems of partnership behind as he had increasingly hankered to do, and break free of the strange isolation that comes after the ending of a marriage, that was the stuff of dreams and he could not suppress his exuberance.

Archie had raced up from Edinburgh not much ahead of him after putting Cecil on the London shuttle. If only she had agreed to stay one more day, to go around the estate with Tom, be in on the discussions and decisions from the beginning. When he had walked into their room last night and seen the packed bags he had felt as though he'd been kicked in the stomach. She had not pretended to be asleep but had slipped out of bed and come across to him, her face tight and unhappy, and had gone straight into his arms, pressing herself against him mutely.

"Oh, Cecil darling, what is it? Whatever is the matter?" he had asked, wrapping his arms around her, feeling her shiver and tremble. "Don't you feel well? Have you been sick again?"

She had shaken her head against him, not answering.

"Come back to bed. You'll freeze." He had lifted her, prepared for her to stiffen and free herself, with a token laugh to make rejection acceptable. But still she had clung, wordless.

"Do you hate it here so much?" he had asked, careful to keep the yearning need out of his voice, when he had put her back into bed and covered her up and was leaning over her with a hand propped on either side of her head.

"I just can't feel part of it." Or of anything, she could have added. "Give me time, Archie. But just now I must go back."

He knew her compulsion was more than the need to get on with pressing work. "Perhaps you'd feel more part of things if you knew more about them," he had suggested, careful to keep his voice easy. "Tomorrow, when Tom comes up to look around—" But he had known it was useless.

Cecil had reached up to link her hands behind his neck, feeling the warm skin, the solid strength. How can I explain to him this feeling of always watching a scene I have no way of entering, she had thought helplessly. The changed mood of the house, how much I want to share in it. But I can't take one step. To them I seem self-possessed, cool; how can they hear the pleading, "Let me in, make room for me."

Archie had waited for a moment, for the gesture had seemed like an opening, but Cecil had gazed at him with wretched eyes, and he had said softly, "Oh, my lovely Cecil," and slipping his hands under her shoulders had bent his head to kiss her.

"'Come to bed,'" she had whispered.

Their lovemaking had been silent and if its mood was more seeking than passionate neither would have acknowledged it.

Now Cecil sat rigid and oblivious in the crowded plane. Why had she run away again; why had Archie let her? Always this desperation to get clear of emotional situations, a desperation that over-rode even her own wishes. Then once she was alone this regret, the anger that no one had argued. Well, she would not be able to run away from the baby. She was committed this time. "For the full term," she thought ironically. At last she might find a crack through which to enter that world the rest of humanity seemed to take for granted—loving and belonging. And Archie would adore a child. She had watched him with Cristi. Her thoughts jarred. Cristi was a delight, outgoing, affectionate, astonishingly without hangups considering how she had been treated, and physically the sort of child Cecil could imagine herself having—but she hadn't succeeded in making any sort of contact with her. Joss, that unattractive creature with her yellowing tan and unplucked eyebrows and bitten cuticles, had hardly been in the house five minutes before Cristi was showing her a horribly realistic plastic tarantula the shepherd's son had given her.

I'm so prim, so orderly, Cecil thought with tired anger. If only I could be casual, disorganized, scruffy. I'll go back when the weather's better. I'll spend longer chunks of time there, unwind, plan for the baby. And I'll do the new kitchen. Thankfully, her brain snapped at the lure. She took from her bag the measurements and sketches she had slipped away to make last night. Absorbed at once, she set her imagination to its beloved work.

This couldn't be Lady Napier, Tom decided, this shapeless female in cords older than his own and dingy sweatshirt with some unreadable logo distorted by untrammeled breasts. The cleaning woman?

"Tom?"

Pretty much to the point. Perhaps after all—?

"Come in. Archie won't be a minute. Mads!"

Not what you would call a formal welcome, Tom thought with interest, but the house was much as expected. He'd seen fifty like it—"good" furniture and everything else the dead-grass color houses take on when carpets, curtains, wall-paper and paintwork fade unnoticed through the years.

Quick light steps. A smaller woman than the first was coming toward him. Tobacco-colored tweed skirt, cardigan exactly matching, all buttons done up; cream silk blouse with round neck pinned with pearl brooch; polished brown court shoes. His mother used to dress like that.

"Mr. Ferguson? How do you do? I'm Madeleine Napier. Archie will be here in a moment. This is Joss Barnes, a friend who is staying with us."

Her hand was small as a paw, chilly and shy. Her dark hair was very tidy. Her voice was soft and, charmed and intrigued, Tom realized that she was nervous. So this was the daunting dowager. In spite of the clothes she didn't look old enough to have a son of Archie's age. Archie had packed so much into his life that Tom, like most people, tended to forget that he was still in his twenties.

"I'm sure you'd like some coffee . . ."

Did they never use this room, Tom wondered, noting the best-parlor un-breathed-in air of the drawing room, though the morning sun was doing its best to find a way in past mature trees planted far too close to the house.

"Archie was telling me one of your sons had worked in Bahia with him . . ."

"Yes, that was Rob. He thoroughly enjoyed it . . ." Encourage your guest to talk about his own interests, Tom thought, amused. She was beautifully made, small and neatly rounded in a way he liked. She was clearly not intending to come around the estate with them, dressed like that. But why was she frightened, he wondered again, as they enlarged on the topic of Rob's time in Camargo. This was her home ground, she was a mature woman and he was the new factor, for God's sake, an employee to be.

"Tom, good, you're early." Archie came striding in, his chunky face beaming, Lisa at his heels with the coffee, followed by Joss and a small girl absorbed in trying to push a loop of wool back through a hole in her jersey.

I could just do with one like her, Tom thought longingly, as she abandoned her efforts to come and shake hands politely. But who is she? Not Archie's; too big to be the sister's; the friend's? Out of the question. Perhaps the child of that stunning wife of Archie's by an earlier marriage? Where is she today, come to think of it?

Hardly a second Mr. Maclaren, Madeleine was thinking with relief. Tom Ferguson didn't look like a man whose soul would be racked over the petrol book or a missing bread invoice. He looked at you with attention, as though he wanted to know who you really were, but with a kindness she already felt sure of. She suspected that he had known she was flustered, and hoped he had not guessed why. Not only that she felt lunch in the dining room without Platt in control would be a makeshift, and was annoyed with herself for worrying about it, but that she dreaded failing Archie. She must be ready to go forward, accept whatever changes were coming, but they loomed vague and daunting and she was unable to relax. Also she had the impression that Tom Ferguson observed a great deal and she had had a disconcerting glimpse of the house through his eyes—dull, correct, a house upon which she had been too meek and too unimaginative to stamp anything of herself.

Tom felt filled with elation and interest as he went out to the Land Rover with Archie, Lisa and the child. New job, new place, new people. He had not even had to launch into the chancy waters of freelancing, this had been handed to him on a plate. If he found he needed to supplement it he could surely find something else, but for the present he was grateful for a little slack. It had been more than time to put a bomb under his life. He would sell the Perth flat, that grim stopgap bought once Wilma was established in her bungalow in Scone, and the house with the big garden by the river at Meikleour had gone. The house where they had brought up the boys and struggled so long and so pointlessly to make their marriage work.

They came back late for lunch. Waiting for them in the kitchen with Joss, a game casserole in the bottom oven of the Aga and a mousse in the fridge, Madeleine relished the new simplicity of it not mattering.

"How did I ever endure those ghastly Platts?" she said luxuriously, spreading out on the table the *Times* Joss had just fetched from the village.

"Search me," Joss replied absently, absorbed in the property page of the local rag. "You always were a bit feeble."

Madeleine laughed. Maybe she was wrong, but she didn't feel she would ever be that feeble again.

Opening the fridge to press a finger on the mousse Lisa had made perhaps not quite early enough, she didn't notice Joss check, read an entry more intently, glance up to see if Madeleine had observed her, then hastily, furtively, turn the page.

Strange atmosphere, Tom thought, watching them all at lunch. Only Archie was his old uncomplicated self, full of new projects but for the time being sticking to those he thought would be of general interest. And Cristi was happy. She had been thrilled to speechlessness to see a pair of roe deer, hares still in their winter coats, and the wide views from the march five miles out which was the watershed between Glen Ellig where Drumveyn lay and Glen Maraich, the next glen to the west. Her excited recounting to Madeleine of all she had seen had broken the ice as they began lunch.

Lisa had said little during their circuit of the estate. What she had said had revealed the sort of knowledge and familiarity imbibed in childhood. It was obviously her scene, Tom thought. In those clothes, against that backdrop of mature plantations and farmland and moor, with the immense panorama of ridges and peaks beyond opening up as they gained height, she had looked strong, competent and at home. So why the bruised look about the eyes, the suggestion of holding herself carefully as if to fend off contact?

Joss too seemed to swing from dour preoccupation to hearty enthusiasm when her interest was kindled. Her heavy face could look stodgy, even grim, then Archie, with whom she seemed to be on excellent terms, would provoke a response from her and she would laugh or plunge into argument and her whole appearance would alter. Jolly had to be the word, Tom decided, watching her strong teeth flash in a big grin, listening to her powerful voice as they swapped stories about this butler who had just walked out and who seemed to have been as competent a racketeer as any quartermaster sergeant.

But Tom's attention was drawn over and over again to Lady Napier, so anxious and well-intentioned, so surprisingly unsure of herself. She was clearly uneasy about being made to sit still while Lisa and Archie transferred dirty plates to the sideboard and left them there, and Joss brought in cream in a pyrex measuring jug and a mug of tea for herself while the rest were doled out silly little demitasses of coffee. That unease could be explained by the absence of the butler, but her apprehension seemed to Tom to go deeper. She appeared to have no confidence in herself in relation to her children, he decided, watching her weigh everything she said and looking on the whole as though she had regretted saying it. She behaved, he decided, more intrigued than ever, like a guest who had arrived on what was obviously a bad day and felt very much in the way.

As a family they definitely lacked cohesion. And Archie's wife had cleared off back to London, it seemed. He couldn't pin down the keynote of their mood. They were not hostile, in fact they seemed anxious to defer to each other, but they were not at ease. Each seemed to be holding on to some private concern or apprehension. How easy would it be to fit into such a group, especially after this time on his own? And he too would bring his hangups, as he moved forward out of the isolation which had not suited his gregarious nature but which had been an essential interim between marriage and meeting the world again as a single individual.

Chapter Seventeen

Cristi, biddable Cristi, always so willing to please, startled them all by her reaction to Archie's careful approach to the subject of taking her home.

Distraught and sobbing, she clung to Madeleine with fierce little hands. "They said I was to stay with Lisa till they came for me—*minha mãe* said it was arranged—I am to live in England—*a casa está toda fechada*—" followed by a storm of Portuguese which Archie couldn't unravel.

"Who is Meenya My?" asked Madeleine helplessly, holding Cristi's burrowing head against her.

"Her mother. Cristi, listen—" Archie knelt beside her, drew her against him. "Come and talk to me. Come and sit on my knee, and we'll talk about it. It will be all right. Come on, we'll work something out."

"I won't go, I won't go—" The anguish in that wail brought tears to Madeleine's eyes as Archie lifted Cristi on to his lap.

"Oh, Cristi darling, don't upset yourself so. We'll see that everything is all right." But what promises could they make to her?

We've been so careful not to worry her about going back, Madeleine thought. But how blind of us that was. Cristi had naturally believed that her parents' plans would be carried out. She had settled in at Drumveyn with her whole heart, without a suspicion that this new life could be snatched away from her.

They calmed her and comforted her, and gradually persuaded her to talk. But to all Archie's gentle probing about her mother's family she would give only uneasy answers, frightened and uncooperative for the first time.

"Did you ever go to see your grandparents?" Archie asked. "Did you stay at the *fazenda*?"

"They hate me!" Cristi burst out, and the tears welled again.

"They surely can't hate you—" Madeleine began soothingly, but Cristi cut across her words violently.

"I am not *católica*," she cried out, looking up at Archie as though only he would understand this.

"Ah." That one phrase did indeed tell him a great deal. If Cristi were illegitimate that could explain rejection by the family. If she were also non-Catholic they were likely to disown her with a finality no ties of blood would affect.

"Archie?" Madeleine looked at him anxiously.

He shook his head at her briefly. "Cristi, don't worry. We shan't do a thing without telling you, I promise. We'll look after everything."

But she was not reassured, and with white frightened face refused to move from Madeleine's side. The courage and self-control which had been so striking when she first arrived had gone. She could not have put any of it into words, but here at Drumveyn she had found everything that had been missing in her enclosed and solitary life. Not only a new and challenging and beautiful world but a world of good sense and good humor. Instead of being petted, cosseted or ignored in turn, here she had found that things were expected of her, and in return she was given consistency, affection, mental stimulus and fun. Now the memories which had slipped from her mind—her mother's departure, the long journey with the stranger, the night in London and her arrival at the house where Lisa had not expected her, the car, coming to another strange house in the night—swarmed back terrifyingly. She felt all the agonizing helplessness of the child who can be dispatched like a parcel to unknown destinations by even the most trusted of adults.

She would speak to no one, pressing close to Madeleine or holding on to her clothes in a way that made Madeleine wince with guilt. To see happy positive Cristi transformed into this anxious wraith, beyond the reach of words or comfort, filled her with shame for them all.

Not surprisingly, bedtime brought problems. Cristi threw tantrums on a scale that reminded them forcibly of her Latin blood.

"What are we to do?" Madeleine asked, harrowed and exhausted, when Cristi had finally gone to sleep and Joss had offered to stay with her so that the others could discuss the problem.

"Not all the family may be so devoutly Catholic that they'd refuse to take her in, at least till her mother comes back," suggested Lisa, not looking at anyone. "I don't really see that it changes things that much."

"It's fundamental," Archie told her. "Her mother must have cut herself off from the family completely."

"We can't send her back without being sure someone will accept her," Madeleine pleaded.

"I agree. I wouldn't consider setting off with her unless something definite had been established. I'd hoped to get some names from her and make some contact before I left, but I think now the best plan would be to get everything organized for my trip, go out early and make contact with the family. If something can be arranged perhaps one of them could come over and fetch her. Or one of us might take her back. But would you be prepared to keep her here till then? It may take time. I shan't be able to set off at once."

"Of course, of course. You know that."

It crossed Archie's mind that he wouldn't have thought of suggesting such a thing a few days ago.

"Lisa?"

This was the crux. For Lisa there was still a painful duality in how she saw Cristi. The gay busy person, reveling in all Drumveyn had to offer, who was such fun to be with; and the child her husband had denied her, conceived in love with another woman, the child who had destroyed the hard-won self-esteem she had developed as Mrs. Armitage.

For one instant the rebuffs and loneliness, the awkwardness and longings of her early years rose up in Lisa in a surge of jealous spite. Why should she help this child; why should she have her in her sight one day, one moment, longer than she need? Cristi was someone else's problem. She should go back where she came from, and if possible cause grief and pain to everyone connected with her there.

Then a jumble of images of Cristi overtook the vengeful impulse—Cristi eagerly exploring this new environment that so thrilled her; shrieking ecstatically as Dougal swung her on a gate, then sliding down and racing off with the others in mad alarm at the approach of Donnie, though she hadn't the faintest idea what the panic was all about; squatting on the hearth of Steading Cottage bottle-feeding an early lamb, giggling as it dragged her off her perch with its violent sucking on the big black teat; doubtfully touching the dark cold fur of a mole impaled on the fence, allowing herself to be shown the long snout and powerful digging paws, but not very keen; Cristi this morning, held firmly by Archie as she balanced on the summit cairn on Ben Breac and gazed wide-eyed at the miles of hill and moor on every side.

So many times in recent days Lisa had recaptured through Cristi some flash of long-ago enchantment, had even recognized that in Cristi's delight she was being given the chance to come close once more to the essential core of Drumveyn life. Let the hatred be for Howard, for Justina, for her own inadequacy and blindness. Not for this child and her warm giving spirit.

"Of course she must stay," she said, finding her voice unexpectedly croaky. "Obviously something must be sorted out before she can go back." Only then did she realize how intently they had been watching her.

"And she must understand exactly what's happening," Madeleine said firmly, more to herself than to them.

Going wearily up to her room she found all quiet, Joss with her big backside wedged into one of the small buttoned velvet bedroom chairs, knees apart, elbows on knees, holding up her book to the light of a lamp. Joss was so used to discomfort that she often forgot to make the small adjustments, such as moving her chair or pulling the lamp closer, that made life easier.

She looked up over her reading glasses without moving as Madeleine came quietly in. "She's fine," she whispered, with a gesture of her hand toward the small bed at the other side of the room. "Though I have to say you don't look so hot yourself."

"Oh, Joss, thank heavens you're here. I don't mean here looking after Cristi. You couldn't have come back at a better time."

"Don't be soft," Joss said in genuine surprise. "You're surrounded by people, no longer at the mercy of Platt, or of Maclaren, come to that, and you've really never been—" She had been about to say better off, but she supposed you couldn't say that to a widow of four months.

Madeleine smiled faintly. No, that could not be said. "It's because of all the people that I need you," she said in a low wail. "I'm worried about Archie and Cecil—they're so nice to each other." Joss gave a little splutter of laughter. "Well, so careful with each other then. And Lisa seems to want to wipe out everything that's happened to her since she was somewhere in her teens, and that may do for the time being, but whatever will become of her?"

"But this business of Cristi hurts most?"

"You see, that's why I need you. You understand without being told. I feel so guilty. We should never have let her go on believing she was here for good. But I wanted her to feel secure after being pitched half way across the world—"

"—and rejected by Lisa, who was supposed to be expecting her—"

"Well, not absolutely rejected. Well, yes, that too. I didn't want her to worry. I should have seen that she was putting down roots, even in this short time. It was criminal of me not to protect her from this shock."

A movement from the bed arrested them, a murmur which sounded protesting.

"Dreaming."

"The dreams she had when she came perhaps." Cristi had not once mentioned Isaura today. It was as though she knew that she had moved on from the maid's possessive but stifling care for ever.

"Oh, Joss," Madeleine went on in a carefully lowered voice, "there's so much I want to get right. Archie's plans for the estate, for instance. I want to support him, but I've paid so little attention to all that side of things. I wonder sometimes what went on in my head. What did I do? I felt today as though Mr. Ferguson saw me as a complete cypher. Worse, an obstruction."

"Rubbish. But why do you call him Mr. Ferguson? He's about our age, a friend of Archie's, and an OK type even by your standards I should have thought. Are you trying to keep him in some sort of upper servant role?"

Madeleine felt herself blushing. In a way it was true, he was the factor. But also Tom Ferguson's eyes, though friendly, had been penetrating, and she had not liked to think how he might have assessed her.

"I suppose I will call him Tom. Well, of course I will. But it's going to be a bit of an upheaval, having him take over. I'm not sure I can cope. Having you here will be a help, because you're really the only person who knows me. I can talk

to you, be myself. You won't be rushing off anywhere, will you, Joss?"

Joss was still holding her book between her
knees—*Eight Feet in the Andes*. She flipped the
pages with a broad thumb, found a ragged fragment of newsprint, took it out and tossed the book
aside on Madeleine's bed. Pursing her lips in a
very unattractive manner, she seemed to reach
some decision, unfolded the bit of newspaper and
rammed her glasses up her nose with thumb
and forefinger.

"See what you think of this," she said.

Puzzled, Madeleine found herself looking at a
blurred photograph of a familiar cottage. "Ellig
Post Office?"

"Read it."

"For Sale . . . potential as shop . . . living room,
dimensions . . . view to the head of Glen Ellig
(well, yes, with one or two things in between I
should have thought) . . . two bedrooms, small
area of rough ground to rear of premises, garage/
shed in need of repair . . ." Madeleine looked up
bewildered to find Joss watching her, embarrassed, doubtful, but with an eagerness she
couldn't hide.

"Would you think it a cheek? I mean, on your
doorstep? I might not have a chance anyway, of
course. But it's the sort of thing I've been thinking
of. You must say if you think—"

"Joss! You? The Post Office?" In her excitement
Madeleine forgot the sleeping child but Cristi
didn't stir. "I can't imagine anything more perfect!
You'd be ideal. It's been for sale for ages, the living accommodation is tiny, I think, and there's no
proper bathroom. But would you, could you—I
mean—"

"I've got Mum's money," Joss replied tersely. "I need a roof of some sort. And I want to work, at something different. But the thing is, would you feel I was barging in if I got something near here?"

"Joss, don't be such an idiot. How can you think such a thing? You must know there's nothing I'd like better. But I don't think it will be much of a livelihood. I was wondering how I could persuade you to stay on here, but I didn't think you'd agree, you're so terribly independent. I'd half thought of asking you to be the new butler . . ."

They stifled their giggles as Cristi moved, calming down hastily.

"I saw the ad this morning but I wasn't sure whether to go for it or not."

"Well, it may be hopeless but at least let's go and have a look. Who do you have to contact?" Madeleine looked at the advertisement again. "Goodness, I feel so excited."

Joss felt warmth spreading through her. Since leaving One World she had felt not only adrift but somehow worthless, as though she no longer had anything to offer. She had told herself that her dread of seeming to latch on to Madeleine for support was unreasonable, but it had been real and since the moment when the words "Ellig Post Office" had jumped at her from the page this morning she had swung violently from negative to positive.

Nothing might come of it, but she had established one thing. She was wanted and for the time being needed here.

Chapter Eighteen

With a fearful rending that could be heard above the roar of the large new tractor, the last stump of the yew hedge which had first protected and now almost obliterated the west windows was dragged from its stony bed.

Jill, Dougal and Cristi, leaning from the window of what had been Charles's dressing room and was soon to be Cristi's room, cheered shrilly. Madeleine, looking out over their heads, resisted the impulse to hold on to Cristi. Dragging out that hedge was a bit like hauling Grannie's spirit, malevolent and spitting, from some lair where it had lain uneasily dormant. Looking down on the raw churned mess Madeleine saw for a moment a solitary pacing figure, wearing the inevitable dipping skirt of Napier tartan, purse-lipped and frowning. Gray wall, gray gravel, strip of mown grass, dark hedge. No curve, color or light. This, out of all Drumveyn, was where she had chosen to walk. The hedge had been allowed during her rule to rear and spread, shielding her not from the western winds but from intrusive eyes. The windows it had darkened were of her own sitting room.

"I hate views," she had said shortly, when Charles had suggested that the hedge was getting out of hand.

I hate views. How well that summed her up, Madeleine reflected.

Archie gave Craig MacNeil, the young tractor-man, a thumbs up of thanks as he ground down the bank and away to dump the last survivor of the hedge. Archie, Tom and Lisa surveyed with satisfaction the ravages he left behind. Cecil came out of the new door from the kitchen carrying a tray of glasses, and behind her Joss waved a couple of bottles for Madeleine to see.

"Champagne! This seems to be turning into a party, we'd better go down," Madeleine said, and the children pulled in their heads and stampeded past her.

"When was all this planned?" Glasses were going around. The children were supplied with coke. Everyone was gabbling happily. May sunshine struck for the first time in years the climbing stain of damp and lichen at the base of the house wall.

"Lots to celebrate," said Archie, tossing one bottle down and taking the other from Joss. "Tom's freedom—though it strikes me he's going to work a damn sight harder here than he ever did sitting on his backside in Perth—that pile of rubble indoors that Cecil promises will be a kitchen—" he grinned at the anxious look that crossed his mother's face "—but especially and particularly Cristi being part of the family."

His tone changed in spite of himself as he looked down at her bright face. He screwed the champagne bottle into a pile of earth and reached for her and swung her up above his head. She laughed down at him and he did his best to smile back in spite of the sudden lump in his throat. He tossed her up, caught her, set her down, and she beamed around the watching group as he steadied her.

The moment's emotion caught everyone; mouths made tight little smiles to hide it; people gulped, blinked. Cristi was theirs; the house would not lose the sound of her flying feet, her laughter, her eager voice.

They raised their glasses to her, calling out loving toasts. Jill and Dougal ducked their heads and gave each other sly grins, unable to cope with all this demonstrativeness.

Cristi had received without any apparent dismay the news that her parents would not be coming back. Delight that she was to stay at Drumveyn obliterated everything else, or perhaps that was the only way she could handle it. Later, when she was older, she would mind, but Madeleine hoped by then she would be so happy and secure that she would be able to deal with the pain of what they had done to her.

Cecil looked with professional pleasure at the chaos of yawning root craters, wheel tracks, mud and boulders. Space and light had been essential to her plan. Big curve of glass thrown out to catch the sun from south and west and give shelter from the north, glazed door to draw people out to a flagged terrace here of natural stone, those straggling rhododendrons around the lawn slashed back . . .

Tom thought in wondering relief, like releasing a long-held breath, "I'm here, I've done it, it's beginning." He had been coming up as often as he could at weekends, first staying in the house, then roughing it in the aired and scrubbed flat. Rob had come up for Easter and they had made a start on the painting.

Wilma had been furious. She still used the boys to maintain bitter and aggressive contact. Rob should have spent Easter with her, leading swiftly to outrage that their sons' whole future should be jeopardized by their father "waltzing off doing as he pleased and abandoning his responsibilities." Rob had competently and peacefully applied undercoat in silence for a couple of hours before he said, "We think it's great, Dad, all this . . ." Tom had said, "Good," and they had gone on painting.

Tom smiled now at the memory. Wilma had been too close in the Perth flat, the long dutiful endurance and the final ugly fight still fresh and raw in his mind, her petulant voice all too clear. Her power to anger him would surely not survive this sun and light and the sense of freedom which rose in him like the frail lines of bubbles in his glass.

The flat would be needed when Madeleine found a new couple to look after the house, and he and Archie had tossed around a few options—make a self-contained flat in the old nurseries perhaps, or there was a pair of empty cottages near the village which could be tidied up, or one of the unused outbuildings could be converted.

Tom was in no hurry. Slightly worried about his ability to fit into a family group again after being on his own for so long, he had found it surprisingly easy to adapt to the amorphous circle of Drumveyn. Although he had plenty of interests and resources and could be content alone he was not a natural solitary and he knew a lot of his new tentative happiness was based on the welcome he had received here.

*   *   *

Archie had come back from Brazil the moment he could, driven by urgency on several counts— primarily worry about Cecil, who was not coping with pregnancy as well as she had expected, but who resisted any discussion about her condition with a crisp insistence that she was fine. Then there was the problem of Cristi, plans to be made with Tom, and also, he discovered, a strong wish to be at Drumveyn. This last had taken him by surprise. He had intended to spend more time there and was bursting with ideas for its reorganization, but this actual longing to be there, this impatience with delays, even a certain rueful jealousy of Tom, those he hadn't anticipated.

He had been delighted to find Cecil not only ready to come with him this time but planning to stay, eager to begin work on the kitchen as a professional challenge and hoping, though she didn't put the thought into words even to herself, that this might prove a wedge she could drive in to make a place for herself in the family.

Also she was limp and dragged down by the persistent sickness she had to cope with not only every morning, but every time she saw or smelled or even thought of food. This had not been part of the plan. She had seen herself as one of those energetic lean types who carry their babies near-invisibly, sweep on with their normal lives, and are dined out on with comments like, "Cecil's incredible, drove out to Middle Wallop this morning to look at a house and had the baby in the afternoon, never turned a hair . . ." Reality was this lassitude, this struggle to bring her mind to bear, the greenish tinge of her skin, the ache in the small of her back and the distasteful and inconvenient business of dashing for the loo.

The only good thing was, Archie thought, shocked at her appearance and her tenseness, that she had voluntarily reduced her workload. Perhaps Drumveyn would be right for her this time, particularly as she would have a personal interest in it at last.

He had been troubled too about the news he had to bring concerning Cristi. Howard and Justina had slammed all doors behind them in Brazil as effectively as Howard had done in England.

Justina's father, receiving Archie in a dark over-furnished room in a pink and white house in Campo Novo, for like most of his class he did not live on his ranch, had been courteous and cold. He feigned surprise but no other feeling to hear that there had been a child. Archie, sipping the obligatory *cafézinho*, sugar half way up the tiny cup, coffee nauseatingly strong and black, was certain he knew all about her. Why else would he request, an edge of steel behind his suave tone, that Archie should not pursue his inquiries "outside the town." Or add, "The woman Isaura is the daughter of my head peon."

Walking down the steps, blinding white in the sun, and through the welcome shade of the orange trees lining the short path to the street, revolt had suddenly filled Archie. This was not the first of these encounters. He had run two of Justina's brothers to earth in Rio—the family was well known—and had been treated with the same thinly veiled disdain. Why was he doing his best to return Cristi to such people? Adoption by Lisa, which clearly she could not be expected to offer, was not the only possibility.

"Surely, among us all, some solution can be

found," he had challenged them, the afternoon he and Cecil had come back to Drumveyn.

Cristi was off around the lambing ewes with Donnie and was to meet the Galloway children from the school bus and go to Steading Cottage for tea. Tom was in Perth to finish the last of his packing and attend his send-off party which it seemed half the county was coming to. The rest were sitting on the south terrace having tea—unheard of in Charles's day. Like his mother, he had detested eating out of doors.

Joss had glanced with quick interest at Madeleine as Archie delivered his challenge. She knew how deeply Cristi had burrowed into the almost forgotten corners of her friend's heart. Would Mads go for it or not?

"Don't worry, Liz," Archie had continued swiftly. "I know you won't want to adopt her. No one expects it of you. It was a crazy idea of Howard's. But in the odd circumstances, with no one taking responsibility for her at the other end and all the paperwork in order, I can't believe it wouldn't be possible to adapt it somehow. Take her into the family by some other route. Make sure that she's safe for good and always. I don't know how you all feel, but I want to look after her, irrespective of her origins, because of the sort of child she is."

They had gazed at him in silence, sitting around the scarred old table Lisa had brought around from the gunroom till something better could be found. Each wanted Cristi at Drumveyn. Each hesitated to make a claim.

Madeleine had been shaken by daring, doubt and hope. She had done her best to face up to Cristi's departure, and this time had kept it clearly in front of Cristi herself, hating to see the quenching of her spirits whenever it was mentioned but determined to have no storms of shock and anguish when the moment came. But she knew now that the change that had come over this dour old house was only partly because Charles's grip was loosened, Platt gone and the rigid patterns broken. Cristi had brought the element that had been missing—happiness.

I mustn't pre-empt the baby, Archie reminded himself carefully, stifling not for the first time regret about the timing.

Archie would love to adopt her, Cecil thought. He does his best to say the right things about the baby but this is what he really wants. If only I could do this for him, plunge in now, say the right words, do the generous thing. But how could I manage, where would we live? Terror and inhibition clamped around her.

Joss had thought wistfully of her newly acquired cottage. That little bedroom up in the roof, someone to look after again. But what am I thinking of, grumpy old spinster who doesn't know how to deal with her own life let alone a kid's.

"Could I adopt her? Or am I too old? I suppose it wouldn't be allowed?" Madeleine had colored, looking around at the amazed faces. "Is that ridiculous? I just thought it might solve all the problems. Cristi could stay here—she really does seem so happy. Only would you find that bearable, darling?" she asked anxiously of Lisa. "And of course when Archie and Cecil come to live here permanently I'd be moving elsewhere, but I hope not far away . . ."

"Mum, do you mean it? You'd consider adopting Cristi yourself?" No doubt about Archie's reaction; his face had been a blaze of relief. "But I think this house will be big enough for everyone, don't worry about that." He longed to see it filled, humming with life. "But it's a tremendous commitment, to take on an eight-year-old child. Won't you need to think it out?"

"Legally, would I be considered too old?"

"We need Tom here."

Lisa had said nothing, in the grip of one last searing battle. Now she cut brusquely across the debate. "Look, this is silly. The legal side has been dealt with. At least, I suppose it's acceptable in English law, or Scottish law or whatever. Why don't I just sign what has to be signed? I'm not saying I could take on the responsibility, not yet anyway—I haven't even worked out what I'm going to do myself—but then at least it would be settled, wouldn't it? Cristi would be safe, in the family."

"Oh, Lisa!" Madeleine had got up impulsively from her cushion on the terrace wall and gone to hug her, too moved and excited to worry about how this would be received. And Lisa had accepted the hug, curling up her hands to press her mother's arm close, leaning her head for a brief moment against her.

I've never seen them do that before, Archie had thought.

Now he looked at his mother, raising her glass to Cristi, and saw the tears in her eyes. She looked so incongruous, soft silk bow fastening the neck of her coffee-colored blouse, gleaming shoes neatly together in the mud and stones. She had made no complaint about this destruction, was doing her best to be positive about the ripping out of the old kitchens. And what had she been feeling today, stripping his father's dressing room, touching objects which would inevitably bring back the physical presence known with the minute intimacy of marriage. How little he knew of her; and how she had surprised him recently. Joss had been good for her with her robust common sense and down-to-earth humor; it was excellent news that she would be living nearby. For Archie, one of his father's greatest crimes had been the severing of all social contacts for Madeleine as well as for himself. I wish I were here more, Archie found himself thinking restlessly again. I want to get to know this person better.

Chapter Nineteen

Joss's house-warming took place a couple of weeks after she moved in. As Ellig was a sub Post Office opening hours were limited and there had been plenty of time to do the minimal decorating she thought necessary. She had had plenty of help now that Tom's flat was finished. Cecil didn't welcome amateurs in the kitchen, except sometimes Tom, and though no one had expected Madeleine to wield a paint brush, Lisa, Tom and Archie had all put in a stint at the cottage.

Madeleine had been ready to furnish the entire place but had had to concede that few Drumveyn contributions would go through the door. Instead she widened her cultural horizons by racketing off in the van with Joss to rifle second-hand salerooms and eat pub lunches.

To avoid the boredom of choosing curtains Joss did accept Drumveyn cast-offs, happy with the first that came to hand, indifferent to surplus inches—or feet—buckling on the floor or cutting off the light at her small windows. It was Lisa who remade them.

Madeleine tried to offload some Drumveyn linen but Joss was firm. "Duvet and easy-care for me, and for you if you had any sense," and she bought the first covers of the right size she happened to pick up, patterned in brown, gray and black zigzags.

She did her best to stop them giving her housewarming presents. "I don't need anything else, and I'm not broke, you know. Well, for Pete's sake don't give me anything fancy then," she grumbled ungraciously when they told her she would be given presents and like it.

Lisa had run into an old friend, or schoolmate more accurately, one of the big Hay family from Sillerton near Muirend, and had heard about a pottery which had been started up in Glen Maraich. It wasn't open for the season yet but she and Madeleine had arranged to go over and had come back with a complete starter kit of blue and gray earthenware which they felt even Joss might enjoy using.

When Cecil announced that she was going to give her a painting Joss had become quite huffy. "It's no good giving me a picture, I'm bound to hate it. Why don't you give me a frying pan or something? Things on walls just collect dust."

"You'll never look at it," Cecil said, with her little cool smile, "so how can you mind?"

"Well, if I'm never going to look at it what's the point of having it?"

"It will change the room."

How right she was. The small McLeay oil, with its glowing color and Victorian exaggeration of Highland landscape wildness, enriched at a stroke the little sitting room, newly emulsioned by Tom three shades lighter than the color Joss thought she had chosen.

Tom gave her a wheelbarrow and Archie a load of logs. Cristi took time off from feeding lambs, heather burning and tree planting to make her a

peg-bag, copied from Jean's in the exquisite needlework taught her by the nuns.

Down they all came to lunch, bringing cream
from the farm, flowers and wine, and for one disgusted moment Joss thought she might shed a tear
as they trooped into her sunny low-ceilinged room
where lunch was already set out, the fire lit in
welcome and every chair in the house squeezed
in ready for them.

Her own house. Buying it had been more a
practical step than any wish-fulfillment. She had
the cash; she needed somewhere to live; she
needed work. She could still hardly believe that
she had acquired it so easily. Apparently there
had been a flurry of interest when it first came on
the market nearly a year ago but the minute income, limited accommodation, lack of a damp
course and an ominous dip in the roof had killed
most of it. Tom and Archie had made noises about
the value when she came to sell and protecting
her capital, but had agreed in the end that the
place was habitable. Since the retiring Miss Michie
had lived there for thirty-seven years and was in
excellent health Joss had remarked that it probably was.

She had done very little to it. Cecil had wanted
her to strip the woodwork, put in a wood-burning
stove, make one big room front to back with half
the attic turned into a sleeping gallery, the rest
removed "to give height." Great one for opening
things up, Cecil, professionally anyway, Joss had
thought, but the little house satisfied her as it was.
She couldn't be doing with anything posh. Just
the basics. Keep the hassle down. The garden
though, that might be a different matter. After the
years in the arid places, of never so much as both-

ering with a plant in a pot, suddenly she was burning to dig and clear and plant and sow and watch things flourish.

What she had not allowed for was the amazing sense of peace, of arriving. It was nothing to do with being near Drumveyn, or having Madeleine at hand. It was intensely personal, and very deep. For the first time in her life she had a place where she was dependent on no one, where her own needs and wishes prevailed. It wasn't the selfishness of this that she enjoyed but the straightforwardness.

Going to bed the first night in the little bedroom which looked out over rough grass to the river, listening to the village noises which would soon become familiar, a car pulling away from the pub, the brief barking of a dog, a snatch of voices, a door slamming, the sound of the river itself, she had felt herself relaxing voluptuously. And waking, there had been an instant awareness of being her own person, and feeling absurdly safe.

Madeleine, listening to the chatter and laughter in the crowded room, looking at Joss's careful preparations, felt as she often did these days that a strong tide of events was sweeping her along too fast to keep pace. Dear Joss, would she be happier now that she had this place of her own, a new job to tackle and the immediate future settled? Perhaps if she was busy, put down roots, the tormenting sense of failure would fade. It had been strange during these busy weeks to find that for the first time in their relationship Joss had needed support and understanding. She had spent a lot of time alone and had often been moody to the point of surliness, but to Madeleine's relief had finally managed to talk out some of the conflict tearing at her. She could not have gone on with her work with One World in the mental condition she had reached, had not wanted to go on, which was what had shaken and shamed her most, but she could not empty her mind of the immensity of the suffering and hopelessness.

Cristi, who had taken a fancy to a squashed leather pouffe Joss had acquired somewhere, had pulled it up to the fire and was cooking her face the same color as the scarlet Bermudas Cecil had bought her, and chattering animatedly to a relaxed-looking Tom. Cecil herself, in yellow canvas trousers and white and yellow striped shirt, was tucked away in a chair near the window, as far away from the food as she could get, contributing only her smile and her surface attention.

Observing them Madeleine thought again how strange it was that Cecil and Cristi should have not only the same physical stamp—line, conformation and coloring—but the same elegance. She did not see that she had it too.

Tom saw it, though. In fact, Tom, observing this splintered and uneasy family group with growing affection, had seen that Archie, unaware, had sought in Cecil the same female type as his mother, the fastidious, groomed, indoor type that cannot be untidy or ungraceful. Was this because his mother had eluded him, held him however unconsciously at a distance? From what Tom had gathered, Madeleine had been completely ruled by Archie's father. Certainly both her young had been driven from Drumveyn by strong feelings of resentment and alienation. Yet Madeleine was not a dominant or even a self-confident person. Indeed she seemed quite dazed at the changes sweeping through her world, eager for them but apprehensive. Would she miss Joss, the only person apart from Cristi with whom she seemed sure of herself?

Archie was pushing Joss into a chair. "Come on, Tom, we'll buttle. Shut up, Joss, don't move."

Tom got up willingly. The last thing he had expected when he had been offered the job as factor was to be drawn into the family, but that was how it felt. Those early weekends before the flat was ready had probably been the key. He had come as a guest to the house and had been made warmly welcome. Any reservations he had had about his own capacity to drop his carefully built defenses could be forgotten since he would soon be living in his own accommodation anyway, and a balance to suit everyone could easily be established. Meanwhile he found himself integrated into their group with astonishing ease and was more grateful than they would ever guess.

He set about carving a ham while Archie made great play of tossing the salad for Cristi's benefit.

Joss had briefly agonized over this lunch, then had laughed at herself. Guests could accept her on her own terms; another small moment of personal freedom. She had provided bread and cheese, salad, ham and fruit salad—only going as far as cutting up fruit perfectly edible in its original form because of the tempting Jersey cream. Accepting a plate from Archie she saw how beautiful the blue and gray pottery was and felt a quite unfamiliar satisfaction to possess it. She wasn't sure she approved of the reaction, but it was agreeable.

"Let's go and have a look at this garden of yours, Joss," Archie said, when Cecil was thinking the Benedicts mints she had brought were wasted on Nescafé and the mug of strong tea Joss was swigging down, and wondering how soon she could leave.

"Garden! Scrub and ashtips more like," Joss said derisively. But the room had grown uncomfortably warm with the fire and so many people and twice already she had had to go out to the kitchen and wait till the infuriating waves of heat subsided, leaving her crimson-faced and sweating. It would be a relief to be outside.

Tom had come down in one of the estate pickups. They took Joss to see what he had in the back—plants for indoors and out, tools, netting, bags of topsoil and dressing.

"This is now a working party," Tom told her, handing out picks and spades. "How would you like that front dyke tidied up and the gate rehung?"

"Perennials, flowering shrubs—say where you want them. Or we can heel them in somewhere for now and you can decide later where to put them," Archie suggested.

"Jean sent you some geraniums. She said you can put them out in the summer but it's a wee bit early yet," Cristi said seriously in Jean's exact intonation, unconscious of the smiles that went around.

Joss might protest about frilly pelmets and paint and pictures—and would have been appalled if she had known the value of the one Cecil had given her—but she made no objection to an afternoon's hard labor from everyone.

Except Cecil. "I really ought to get back. They're doing the arch and it's got to be exactly right." Why on earth didn't Archie send Malkie or someone down with a rotovator to do the garden? *I should have brought my gumboots, Madeleine* worried. I thought we were just bringing the plants. What shall I be able to do to help? Set to scooping up molehills and carrying the earth wherever she was bidden, she found the oddest thing not to be struggling with the unexpected difficulty of tough grass poked up in the middle of each heap, or teetering awkwardly about trying to hold a heavy bucket away from her skirt, but to be doing it under the gaze of the fascinated village. Cars and vans and tractors came and went. Pensioners creaked along to have a look at what was going on and settled on the wall to watch. Everyone who passed had a comment to make.

Joss will know every soul in the glen inside a month, Madeleine thought ruefully. I've never set eyes on half these people. She was annoyed to find she could not shake off her self-consciousness.

"How about tea?" Joss proposed at last.

"Down by the river?" suggested Lisa. "Though I suppose it'll be a bit plastic-baggy."

"But do you have enough for all of us?" Madeleine asked. "We were really only invited for lunch."

"Oh, Mads," and "Oh, Mum!" greeted this. Cristi was sent along the street to the shop with instructions from Archie, and came back with a box of four shiny tartlets the color of her shorts, which Archie identified as South American tree frogs and highly poisonous, three apple doughnuts, a Swiss roll with its ends showing signs of wear, and a packet of biscuits of her own choice.

"Jammy dodgers," she announced with satisfaction.

"She knows more of the language than I do," Madeleine said to Tom.

This is what living up here is all about, Lisa thought lazily, propped up against a cushiony tussock, watching the river slide past her feet disgusted only by a fertilizer bag caught on a low branch, a hoop of rusting car trim and a few lager cans. Being busy, being outside. We must put a boat on the loch again. And on Tuesday Tom's coming with me to look at that Highland pony. Wonder if we could find something for Cristi. It's getting too hot for these breeches and stockings. Wish I hadn't got such a big backside. Perhaps I could try jeans, Grannie would have gone mad . . .

"We could rotovate this whole patch for you if you like, Joss," Archie was saying. "How about vegetables? You're not too late. Or you could re-seed it . . ."

Two weeks ago I was in the office, Tom thought. That scene with Wilma—how can she think, even now, that she has any right to interfere in my life? But she was the sort of woman who never lets go of "her man." She would use the boys as a stick to beat him with for ever. Her airtight bungalow, her golf, her bridge, Slenderworld—none of it would really compensate her for being a woman alone. But twenty-three years. For God's sake, that had to be enough.

Chapter Twenty

The afternoon was warm, the bedroom windows open to drifting scented air. The house was empty, except for Cecil resting in her room. Archie had gone back to London, due to leave for India in a couple of weeks' time. Cristi was at school, Lisa off somewhere with Tom.

Slowly, deliberately, facing her long mirror, Madeleine took off her clothes.

Sometimes recently she had felt as though she was splitting into two people, one tumbling along eagerly in the spate of changes and the other, inner, person, struggling to adjust. Free of set-piece meals, stretches of time had become available in the day which she had barely known existed. That first morning when she had got up and gone out, as tentative and daring as Cristi herself, into the dew-drenched dawn where the pale heads of daffodils doubled down after rain and silver light strengthened through a soft blur of mist, she had stepped entranced through her own garden. Cold with a hollow shiveriness compounded of early rising, an empty stomach and the unearthly bleakness of dawn, still she had been swept by a sense of adventures ahead. Yet this beauty had been here all along while behind walls, windows, curtains, a different self had lain awake, waiting for morning tea.

This spring she had begun to look, with new care, at things it seemed she had never seen. The balsam poplars must every year have blazed with their shiny yellow-green which now constantly caught her eye. The pussy-willows must have glowed in mounds of gold among the dark bones of the later trees. She looked too this year with Cristi's eyes—at the tracing of green on a sticky cockroach-brown chestnut calyx about to burst, at larch needles opening into tiny green shaving brushes along the whippy branches, at the fragile cups of wood anemones not white but blushed and veined with pink.

Habit was strong. She kept to herself her tussles with it. How silly it would seem to anyone else that she felt quite reckless going out after dinner, wandering down to the barn or around the neglected paths below the lawn. And who would believe the sense of freedom it gave her to lean on a gate at seven in the evening and watch the lambs thundering from one favorite spot to another, the check, the pause, the bursting into mad bucks and another frenzied race.

Food had suddenly become very simple. Archie and Joss were uncomfortable with elaboration and extravagance. Lisa had no intention of putting on weight and Cecil seemed to live on fruit, muesli and Nutrilite vitamin products, and disappeared with faint apologies as soon as cooking started. Pasta when Archie was cooking, soups and casseroles as Lisa worked her way through the freezers, salads, fruit and yogurt. Platt had been too lazy to go to the cheese shop in Muirend but Lisa brought back perfectly kept Bries and Stiltons and local goat and herb cheeses to replace his supermarket horrors.

Madeleine had still not decided what to do about replacing him. She found it hard to see past the same arrangement but knew she dreaded it. Also the kitchen plan taking shape under Cecil's talented hand would hardly suit the old system. The space in the big curved window on the west terrace was intended to replace the dining room. This, Madeleine knew, was how things were done now, but where in such a plan was the inviolate territory of the staff?

In other matters too her mind stuck to set grooves. School for Cristi, for instance. Despite hating the prospect of losing her for months of every year Madeleine's only idea had been to send her if not to Lisa's prep school then to one just like it.

"Does Earnston House still exist?" she had asked, looking worried. "Or will it still be as good these days? How shall we find out? Tom, you're bound to know someone who has a daughter there."

"Yes, as far as I know it's still—" Tom began.

"*Earnston?*" All Lisa's misery in that place of exile rang in her appalled cry.

"Mum, what are you talking about?" Archie demanded more patiently.

"But surely—" Madeleine looked from one to the other in surprise, then in growing embarrassment. "I suppose I just thought school, you two, Lisa, Earnston. In fact, I didn't think."

"Do you want Cristi to go away?"

"I should hate it."

"Well, do you think it's the best thing for her?"

"I suppose after all the changes in her life it may not be. But then, what's the alternative?"

"There is a school in the village."

"The glen school!" she exclaimed, regretting it at once.

"We both started there, remember. So did Father, come to that."

"But Cristi's nearly nine. And how would she adapt to that sort of—?"

"You'd take her away from Jill and Dougal? From here?"

Tom had watched and listened. Had Madeleine never thought things out for herself? They were very patient with her, but now she was feeling inadequate and ashamed. Every day he saw her experimenting, testing her freedom. Sometimes it seemed that she and not Cristi had arrived at Drumveyn from a foreign land.

With the decision made to send Cristi to the Ellig school, which Cristi herself had been joyfully certain would happen the moment she learned that she was staying here for good, Madeleine found herself faced with making the necessary application. As Cristi's circumstances were unusual she had to go down to talk to the local education department. She had to drive. Flinching, she made up her mind to it, braced by the fact that Lisa had just taken the much more daunting step of going down to empty the house in Englefield Green.

At first she had said she wanted nothing from it; had asked Tom to arrange for the house to be cleared as well as sold. Since Tom was now acting as her solicitor he decided to go down himself to sort out papers and personal objects. At the last moment Lisa had seen what an imposition this was and how cowardly she was being and had said she would go with him. They had gone down two weeks ago and when they came back it was evident even to Madeleine that facing up to this had done Lisa good.

So now Madeleine in her turn, though cravenly longing to drag Joss away from the digging and clearing, hacking and burning which occupied every free moment, resisted the temptation. She had taken on the responsibility for Cristi; this was her job. And she would have to get used to the Volvo sooner or later.

She loathed getting into it. It enclosed her at once with hostile associations. In mirror image as she drove Charles was there beside her, stuffed tightly into his seat, never looking to right or left (had he been capable of looking to right or left?) bowling along at his arrogant unvarying speed. In profile he was a series of bulges, out-thrust disgruntled lip, chins, tweed waistcoat. His thick arms were straight out before him, hands so fat that the knuckles were invisible as he gripped the wheel. Being harried by the A9 traffic, driven to chicken-hearted detours in town, hot struggles parking, one or two scary misjudgments—it was not till she was halfway up the glen again that it occurred to Madeleine that she could sell the horrible thing. So obvious, and it had taken her six months to think of it. What was wrong with her? But was the car Archie's? And what would Tom say? Was it an asset?

Tom said, "Good idea."

"Is it mine?"

"It is."

"I wonder if I should—"

She looked at Tom doubtfully and saw that he was watching her with unconcealed amusement.

The image of Charles returned. I don't believe I actually liked him, she thought blankly. It had never really struck her before.

"I'll sell it," she said firmly. "At least, I'm not quite sure how to—"

"No problem," Tom assured her, and she sensed his satisfaction. "We'll have a look around and find you something you can really enjoy driving."

"Small,'" she said, recalling a bridge on the glen road where she should certainly not have swept on.

"Whatever you like." That was Tom; in his hands everything became simple. Lisa would never have faced the pain of going back to her house without him. Had she talked to Tom about Howard, or about the future, Madeleine wondered. Tom and Lisa. She put the idea aside, not wishing to trespass. But she thought she liked it. Tom had found a place in Drumveyn life so easily. She had worried at first about looking after him, finding things to talk about with him when Archie wasn't there, having a strange man suddenly part of the family circle. But she had soon forgotten even to think about it. Tom was independent and self-sufficient. He came and went, always busy and apparently content and already they turned to him when Archie was away with every question and problem.

Going to buy the car, which she had begun panicking about as soon as the decision was made, with him turned out to be fun. He put no pressure on her, she recognized gratefully. When she ducked the test drive he didn't attempt to persuade her, but took the Metro they'd been looking at around the block himself. Then with the deal more or less made she spotted a smart little Suzuki jeep across the saleroom and Tom saw a moment's longing cross her face. He checked the salesman's flow about warranty and took Madeleine by the arm and walked her over to the jeep.

"Fancy this?" he asked.

"No, no, of course not, it just caught my eye. Rather fun for Lisa perhaps, now that we're sending things to the laundry, and all the shopping, and running around the estate . . ."

"Rather fun for you too."

She looked at it with the momentary longing of someone tempted by an outrageous dress far too young for her.

"Buy it," Tom said. "For fun."

She blinked at him. His eyes were smiling, as though he knew exactly what was going on in her head.

So she owned a jeep, was sending Cristi to the glen school, was acquainted with dawn and dusk, had eaten pizzas in pubs and sent her husband's clothes to Oxfam, and now she asked her mirror who this person was? Had Tom's perceptive eyes made her want to know?

Kick off the brown shoes with the neat stacked heels—no, don't put them neatly side by side. Let the Munrospun skirt, lined, slither to the floor. Unclip, unclasp the daytime jewelry never looked at when it was put on. She unbuttoned the short silk blouse, creased at the waist as it hung over the full-length slip, tossed it aside. Did anyone wear slips like this nowadays? Discreetly colored tights. Lacy bra and pants. She felt her cheeks warm as she took them off. Her own body and she was embarrassed? Was she afraid of it or disgusted by it? She wasn't sure. Certainly she scarcely knew it. How did it look now? Forty-six. How should it look? And who would ever see it? Nurses perhaps when she was old.

As objectively as she could she studied what she saw; firmish round breasts, waist still there, hip-bones never to be visible again. She turned sideways to check the small bulge of her stomach, her neat bottom. Face, neck and forearms were lightly tanned. When had the rest of her body last felt sun and air? And her hair—naked as she was it looked ludicrous, unreal as a wig. She shook her head violently, combed it back with her fingers as Joss did.

This body of hers, what names did she have for it? "Breasts," she said aloud. Oh, very good, and what about boobs? "Belly." She never said that, she said tummy. Go on. "Bottom. Bum, ass, fanny," she added rapidly, getting into her stride. And? Well now, what did she call it? Honestly? She called it "there." That secret, unseen place, entered by Charles, exited by Archie and Lisa. It had produced two whole human beings. It must surely be important. And she had no better word for it than "there." "Vagina," she said aloud. Was that how you pronounced it? Surely no one said that, in everyday life. What had she read? She couldn't think. Had she glossed over in print as in life this unsayable reality?

My body. Will Charles's clumsy fingers, Charles's—she checked, failed there—be all it will ever know of intimate contact? No tenderness and no pleasure. Did they really exist? They must, they must, they have been sung and written about since words began. Or was I incapable of feeling them? How sad if that were so.

Well, she thought, I have looked at myself. I

have made some sort of acquaintance with the physical person I am. Now I must clothe this person to meet the things that are happening to her. She cannot be perpetually changing her shoes.

Chapter Twenty-one

Nobody took any notice of her. That included the sales assistants. It felt discourteous to start plucking clothes off the racks without speaking to anyone. But that, it seemed, was what one did.

What size? 32/32—what did that mean? Goodness, was this rack for men? She moved hastily away. A girl in a black leather jacket and nearly invisible skirt began to rattle the hangers around the rail, chewing. Madeleine crept back. Ah, HIS 32, HERS 14, that was better. Unisex. Had people's shapes changed too while she wasn't looking?

It appeared that one took things off the rail and dived behind those swinging flaps like saloon doors in a Western. They covered very little of the struggling customers behind them. And surely someone should invite one to do so? With two pairs of jeans in her hands she looked appealingly toward an assistant who, sighing, pushed her hip away from the till where she was leaning and came across.

"Stretch, 14, was it, narrow leg? That's a twelve inch, 98% cotton. And the indigo, that's what you want, is it?" And handing the jeans back she jerked her head towards the cubicles.

The shop seemed to close in on Madeleine, dark, hot, smelly, loud with pop music, crammed with strident colors. Behind those scanty flaps she would have to take off so many layers to drag on these unfamiliar garments. And twelve inch, 98%, what did it all mean?

Hot and flushed, she found herself on the pavement, hurrying away in panic. She should have brought Joss but had been too shy to tell her what she planned to do.

Am I frightened of everything, she thought in sudden fury, stopping short on the pavement. There must be better places than that stinking hole to find what I want. I'll go to the George for coffee, calm down and start again. In George Street she passed a dress shop of the kind that had called itself a boutique twenty years ago, perhaps still did. She must do something about her vocabulary. Her eye was caught by a pair of apricot-colored shorts with tailored jacket, the kind of thing Cecil would look marvelous in. Not exactly what she had in mind for her own new image but it was worth a look.

Soothing surroundings of pale blue carpet and white trellis-work, the smell of expensive objects, corseted gray-haired assistant coming forward. Easing the transition, Madeleine mocked herself, but it did help. The soft blue Chambray shirt and stone-washed jeans made her look astonishingly different—and she knew the moment she saw herself in them that she could do this. And there was better to come.

". . . of course the damson picks up the rhubarb so well . . . or madam would suit the aubergine . . ."

"Are all colors called after fruit and vegetables these days?" Madeleine asked with a little splutter of laughter, feeling suddenly much more light-hearted.

"It does seem so, doesn't it? Though this lighter one is hollyhock. You can hardly keep up with the names sometimes. With your coloring you could carry all these, perhaps you'd just like to slip this on . . ."

Familiar flattering background flow, half-heard, but there was nothing familiar about the figure that faced her. Mutton and lamb? But she knew, from what she had seen for herself now that she had begun to pay attention, that what the mirror showed her was perfectly acceptable. This new person looking back at her made her feel shy, but not ridiculous.

Dare I go home like this? But shoes? God, does it always come back to shoes? But how can I walk out of here in these clothes and my boring old high heels? Oh, shut up, who'll be looking? And there's a shoe shop not half a street away.

Tom never forgot seeing her walk across the courtyard toward him that afternoon, self-conscious and nervous, cheeks pink and eyes bright. She looked like a girl, that nice little body of hers free at last. Hair softer, earrings and brooch gone, comfortable-looking strollers on her feet. And that sweatshirt was a lovely color, just right for her.

"You look absolutely stunning," he exclaimed spontaneously, going forward to meet her with delight written all over his face. "Let's have a look at you." He took her hands and held them wide, studying her, beaming. "Yes, oh yes, I like it." He released one hand and spun her around with the other. "What a transformation. You look younger than Lisa."

"Well, don't let her hear you say so." But he knew from the shaky smile she flashed at him how keyed up she had been. She was thankful to her soul that it was Tom she had met first. No matter how tolerant one's young may be they are one's young, and to them one is old, fixed in a known image, and above all must never, never embarrass them.

"Come on, let's find someone and show you off. You were very brave to come home like that," Tom said, tucking her arm through his, and she knew that somehow he had guessed all the doubts, the temptation to stop somewhere and change, the defiant screwing up of resolution.

She was glad to have him with her as she went in. Cristi, spoon guiltily poised over a soup plate of ice-cream which an abstracted Cecil had let her take, looked thunderstruck, eyes wide. Then her face broke into a rapturous smile and she slid down and came eagerly to stroke and finger the new clothes, exclaiming in Portuguese, the admiring expressions of the Ellig school playground not adequate for this.

"Cristi, you're the one I should have taken to help me," Madeleine said, seeing it too late. "So do I look all right?"

"*Tão linda, tão bonita,*" Cristi crooned.

Madeleine glanced at Cecil, and Tom read the effort in her gay, "Well, what do you think?"

"You look so different," Cecil said helplessly, laughing but Tom was glad to see approving. "But so right. Lovely colors. You really do look like another person, and years younger." It was difficult to be tactful about such a change.

Cecil's approbation had mattered. Madeleine had been braced for damning polite murmurs. She

respected Cecil's standards and her sure sense of
color and fitness. Also she was very much aware
of the gulf that still lay between them. She had
hoped to establish some meeting ground over the
baby but it had, sadly, remained an almost taboo
subject and for this she blamed her first thought-
less reaction of distaste. She had over-compen-
sated with an enthusiasm she didn't quite feel
about the kitchen and Cecil had known. Now
there was a moment of sharing and warmth and
she was glad of it.

"What will Joss say, do you think, Cristi?" Madeleine asked. "Will she think I'm silly?"

Tom, who had gone to get tea going in the
screened-off section of the old kitchen where the
Aga was still functioning, smiled. The question
could be put in this form.

"But Joss wears jeans," he heard Cristi reply,
puzzled, and his smile widened. Trust her to keep
things practical.

"Shall we walk down to see her after tea?"
Madeleine suggested.

"Walk to the village?"

"Joss can bring us back." Madeleine felt that
her magically comfortable loafers would, like the
red shoes, take her on journeys of their own.

Lisa came along the corridor. "Oh, good, Tom,
you're making tea. Anybody about?" Should he
warn her? No, unfair. "Cecil next door?" Lisa
went on, without waiting for an answer. "Hey,
Cecil, tea's up."

She was getting the milk out of the fridge as
Madeleine lifted the dust sheet aside and came
through, still self-conscious but more amused than
anxious now. There might be outspoken com-

ments from Lisa but at least some members of the household approved.

"Mum!" Lisa gasped. "Where on earth did you get that lot? Are you helping Cecil paint or something?"

"I bought them," Madeleine replied composedly.

"Bought them?" Lisa made it sound quite scandalous. Then a grin began to spread across her face. "Well, who'd have thought it? By yourself? You actually went down and bought them all by yourself? Well, I must say you don't look half bad—" She broke off as Tom and Cecil laughed.

"Children," said Tom, "who needs 'em? Come on, grab the teapot, somebody. Where are we having tea? Is it warm enough outside?"

"No, really, Mum, I like it." Lisa was prowling around her mother in fascination. "It just takes a bit of getting used to. That's a gorgeous color. And you've got a decent shape for jeans, but blow me, really—"

Madeleine did literally feel a different person as she and Cristi followed the track down to the old bridge that had once carried the main drive from the village to Drumveyn. In her mind she leapt and ran, though translated into action this might have been deflating. But just to walk out of the house like that, not to worry about her hair, whether the track would be wet or muddy, whether she would be warm enough. It sounded so absurd; she was glad no one would ever know how deeply these inhibitions had been rooted.

Cristi chattered about school. Alison Mowat (younger daughter of the tenant farmer at the Lettoch, Madeleine worked out with a slight effort) had made up a story out of her own head about the flowers and trees asking people to take care of them. She had made it into a real book, with stables.

"Stables?"

"You know, with the stabler. And Dougal was best out of everyone at long jump, and tomorrow it's heats."

"What are heats?" By the way she had tossed off the word Madeleine knew she had no idea what it meant.

"I don't know, but we're having them, and we're to take a sack, and Dougal said he'd bring one for me as I'd surely not find one at the big hoose."

That was how Cristi dealt with everything. There were heats, and whatever they were she would be in them. You had to have a sack, don't ask why, and Dougal would bring one.

By the time it had been settled that she was to go to the glen school not much of the term had been left. Madeleine would have been happy for her to start in the autumn, thinking that she had more than enough to get used to already. Cristi had been devastated at the suggestion, which had been hastily withdrawn. Any worries about how her Brazilian convent education would equip her to fit into a Highland primary school could be forgotten. She floated over obstacles, deliriously happy to be part of it all at last. Accent, language, playground rites—she soaked them up like a bliss-ful sponge and her version of the day's events was a popular Drumveyn tea-time entertainment.

Joss, looking like a mobile compost-maker in borrowed waders, was fishing the wing of a car out of the river. "Damned thing kept catching my eye. It's hooked on to something, can you see what? Must have been here for donkey's years, just look at the rust."

Madeleine and Cristi looked at each other with conspirators' eyes and put their fingers to their lips. Not till the lump of metal was hoisted clear with their help (which Madeleine reflected she might not have offered in the ordinary way) did Joss notice what she was wearing.

"Good job you had on something sensible for a change," she remarked, trying to reach a fragment of blue plastic just out of reach, then added, "Blimey, what are you wearing, come to that?" and turning caught the suppressed laughter in their faces.

"Big improvement" was her verdict, as she laughed with them. "You're really getting quite sensible these days, Mads, did you know that?"

"Rather late in the day."

"Yes, well . . . Where's the jeep?"

"We walked."

"Did you indeed? And are you walking back?"

They looked at her.

"I see," said Joss, slinging the piece of car down by her dustbin with vengeful satisfaction.

"Come to dinner," Madeleine suggested.

"I might at that. Damn all here. Who's doing the cooking?"

"Tom. We're eating in the flat."

"He usually does something pretty substantial. You're on."

Squashing with the others around Tom's table an hour or so later, watching him dole out big helpings of a macaroni cheese with a good deal more bite to it than Mrs. Platt's pallid version, Madeleine said, "We're all a bit idiotic, aren't we?

The kitchen may be in pieces but the dining room isn't."

"But this room gets all the evening sun now the yew hedge has gone," Lisa pointed out quickly.

"The whole flat does," Tom said.

"Besides, we all hate the dining room," Joss put in.

"Bad vibes," Lisa agreed. Misery and mortification, she might have said.

I wonder, thought Madeleine. Maybe it's time I instigated some changes on my own account. I wonder.

Chapter Twenty-two

Tom could hardly keep his eyes off the new Madeleine. He had been attracted to her from the beginning, watching with sympathy her efforts to adjust to the changes that had followed her husband's death. He had seen a lot more than she realized of her secret struggles to adapt. He had recognized the resolve not to interfere, however lovingly, in Lisa's life, and the anxiety with which she watched this difficult daughter. He knew that Madeleine felt she should make the effort to get closer to Cecil but found her baffling and alarming. He had observed the strength of her friendship with the unlikely Joss, and knew she would be amazed to be told that Joss depended on it as much as she did.

But above all Tom enjoyed seeing her with Cristi, admiring the way she had stepped in to take the responsibility there. He guessed that with Cristi Madeleine was able to recapture happy times with her own children, free this time around of critical eyes. Yet she was so indoctrinated by Napier thinking that she had been resigned to sending Cristi away to school exactly as the small Archie and Lisa had been sent, regardless of their individual needs.

Archie was good for her, because he teased her

but showed his affection. Archie, however, was rarely there and when he was even his equable good nature showed signs of strain. Why had he chosen Cecil? Seeing them together Tom would be struck by their incongruity as a couple. He was sure there was love on both sides but Cecil obviously found it hard to show her feelings. She was hurting Archie, and knew it, Tom suspected, and the knowledge was driving her deeper inside herself. Tom was more than ever convinced that in choosing her Archie, unconsciously, had been pursuing an ideal, the mother inaccessible when he was young, and perhaps too the artistic creativity which he felt was lacking in himself.

In spite of her willingness to embrace new ways, while still wearing her middle-aged clothes, neat and correct, Madeleine had been distanced and separate. Tom recalled her at Joss's housewarming, determined to help but ineffectual and ill at ease, doing her best to pretend she didn't mind getting dirty or being watched by the slyly amused eyes of the village.

The change in her in the new style clothes was unbelievable. Amused that they could make such an impression on him, nevertheless his eyes kept going back to her. She had shed ten years, looked endearingly pleased with herself, even moved differently—and God, she was pretty.

Tom let one day go, knowing Lisa had a dentist's appointment the next morning. Also she had been muttering about sweltering in breeches and Tom suspected, seeing her eyeing her mother with increasing approval, that she would be doing some shopping of her own.

He caught Madeleine as she came back from seeing Cristi off with Jill and Dougal to catch the school bus. "I'm going out to the Lettoch beat today to have a look at those butts Archie wants rebuilding. How about coming with me?" he asked her.

Madeleine opened her mouth to say no, realized there was no reason on earth why she shouldn't go, and used the original breath she'd drawn to say, "I'd love to."

It had been so obvious that they both laughed.

"But what a shame that Lisa has to go to Perth," she added at once. "And Cristi would have loved it. But perhaps Cecil might like to come? Or could it be another day—we could arrange a picnic lunch."

Tom could see it all. "Today," he said. "Just you. And I've made a lunch."

"Well—" Why should she feel there had to be a problem? "Then I'll find something for me to bring—"

"There's enough for both of us."

It seemed the planning had been done. "Am I allowed to tell Cecil where I'm going?" she asked meekly.

"I think you might do that."

Madeleine came out carrying jacket and boots as Tom was reversing the pick-up to the gun room door. Heaven to go out, as she was, without fuss. And Tom thought, taking a quick look at her as he headed out on the Lettoch track, that it might have been Cristi beside him; the excitement bubbling up in Madeleine could be felt. Well, he was feeling pretty happy himself.

It was a day Madeleine never forgot. Her wings had spread, dried, and she felt herself lifting into flight. And like the dragon fly she didn't wonder how long or short her flight might be. She didn't notice how carefully Tom paced their climb to the butts, or how leisured his inspection was. It didn't occur to her as they propped their backs against the highest one and drank coffee from his flask that on his own he could have been up and down in an hour, the job finished. She was just glad she had managed all right so far. The sensation of flight had not extended to getting her up the hill.

It was a half-hearted sort of day, with a small wind chilly at this height and the sun coming and going but mostly going through light cloud. Even so, Madeleine gazed at the long ridges of Ben Breac, the peaks shouldering up at the head of the glen and the moors rolling away to the south with long fingers of vibrant early summer green reaching up between the dark patches of heather, and was ashamed.

"How can I not have come up here more often?" she exclaimed in disbelief. "It's so beautiful—and so near."

"But you must often have been out on the hill? Wasn't that all part of the scene?"

"Oh, yes, years ago. Shooting lunches, women and hampers brought up in the Land Rover and removed afterwards, unless one wanted to stand in a butt. I always dodged it. Just personal dislike of the whole idea—I didn't examine the morality of it. Then there were picnics with Nannie and the children, driven up to the traditional spots by the chauffeur. Never with Grannie or Charles, of course."

"How long is it since you were last up here?"

"It must be five or six years. Isn't that frightful, Tom? Though somehow you don't realize you've stopped doing it. It's all still there and theoretically, as you say, part of the scene." She was silent, thinking of those years, which now seemed one dark featureless stretch. "Now that I've got the jeep . . ." she said, out of her thoughts.

Tom laughed at her, very kindly. She was so transparent, so touching with her facing up to challenges which were ordinary life for everyone else. He was glad he was here to see it.

"If you hated shooting, how do you feel about Archie's plans to make it part of the economy of the estate again?"

"Well, I don't feel the wishy-washy way I did," she answered, surprising him. "I've thought about it a bit more this time. How else do you use this sort of ground? How do people in glens like this find a living? I still hate the idea of driving birds, but then I do have to remember that I'm prepared to eat them."

"Well put," he said, sounding teasing but impressed. He took in with pleasure her serious face under blown-back dark hair which today she had not bothered to cover with one of those damned head-scarves. Hopefully they'd gone for good with the cardigans.

"There's a lot for you to put right on the estate, isn't there?"

He could hardly say that between Maclaren and her inflexible husband a degree of decay and neglect prevailed which to correct would drain the resources of the place for a long time to come.

"Like the housekeeping books," she suggested with the glimmer of a smile, knowing exactly why he hadn't replied.

He liked the flash of humor. There was always the feeling with her that she would be great fun if . . . He hoped he was around for the "if."

She had been horrified when the iniquities of

Platt began to be revealed, and all the rest of the free-loading that had gone on over petrol, telephone, fuel and "borrowed" tools. The casual attitude of "it's a broad back" had been general and to Tom had fallen the job of changing it. He hoped for the support and maybe in time the loyalty of the estate people, but his first priority was to root out extravagance and inefficiency, and he had set about it with even-handed firmness. There would be a lot of moaning and bitching during the tightening up process, and Ross Miller, the grieve, had dourly set his face against every change, but Archie's plans, which Tom was already beginning to implement, for improvements to machinery and buildings and cottages should in the long run silence much of it. Men with families, settled for years in estate houses, wouldn't lightly throw up their jobs. They would grumble, threaten to go, but most of them, Tom knew, would make the best of it.

"Come around the estate with me and see what's going on," he suggested.

"I'd like that," Madeleine replied, envisaging with pleasure more days like this one.

"You could come and have a look at some of the cottages, see what you think should be done with them."

"But would people—?" She drew back, uncertain at once.

"You're Lady Napier. They'd be glad if you took an interest. Especially if they're going to get some benefit out of it."

She smiled but reminded him, "Cecil's Lady Napier."

"One of them. And I can't see her having much time to spare for the estate houses just yet." Tom found it hard to think of Cecil as connected with Drumveyn at all. When she appeared there it always felt as though she was making a professional visit.

They sat for a long time talking, Tom taking the chance, as well as expressing his relief to be out of the office and at Drumveyn, to put her in the picture about much that was planned.

"And what about a house for you, Tom?" Madeleine asked after a while. "The flat's very poky, especially with all the office stuff in it. You need room for Rob and Ian too, though of course you know they're always welcome to stay in the house. And I'm sure you must long for a place of your own when we use you as spare kitchen and dining room."

"I've enjoyed all that," Tom assured her. He had imagined he would live separately in the flat and if he had been asked at the beginning would have said that was what he wanted, not quite ready after solo living, however unsatisfactory, to be plunged into family life. But the Napier family itself was in a state of some flux at present and he had found himself drawn into it naturally and more and more agreeably. "But you'll need the flat for a cook or whatever soon," he added. He would be interested to see what she decided about that. "Archie and I discussed various ideas and I think, if it's feasible, I know which I'd prefer."

Madeleine had just discovered how much she had enjoyed having him on hand in the flat. That's you all over, she told herself crossly. You babble on making all the right noises about where he'll live, then get winded by the facts. "A house in the village?" she suggested, choosing the worst possibility.

"I want to live in the barn."

She didn't fail him. "The *barn*?"

"That large stone building below the steading," he began kindly.

"Yes, but, Tom!" Her imagination floundered.

"We'll stop on the way down and you can see what you think. I've a couple of plans for how it could be done."

"Cecil's?"

"No, not Cecil's," he said firmly and she laughed. She wasn't at all sure about the limed green oak and the Portuguese tiles that had been ordered for the kitchen.

"The barn is in a wonderful position," she offered, doing her best.

Tom laughed at her. "Let's go and look."

The tide was whirling faster, Madeleine felt, and she wasn't certain her head was always above water.

"One thing I've been meaning to ask you," Tom said, reaching a hand to pull her to her feet. "Do you dislike dogs?"

"Dogs? No, why?" Madeleine asked, taken by surprise. Then because Tom had a way of extracting accuracy, "Well, I've hardly known any to be honest." She had hated the way Charles treated his. "Grannie wouldn't allow them in the house, of course." And there came a quick memory of the glowing, polished Welshpool house, the refusal to let her keep a puppy she'd been offered and the sobbing hours of resentment and longing. (Had Lisa cried like that when she had been told she couldn't have a dog? Why didn't I wonder, why didn't I find out?)

"How would you feel about a dog in the flat? I could keep it out of the rest of the house."

"Oh, Tom, of course it would be all right. Anywhere." How awful that he had assumed it would be a problem.

"I must admit I've looked forward to having a dog again. Hopeless in the Perth flat of course." And living on his own.

"Cristi will be thrilled. Remember the dramas when the collie pups at the farm had to go? What will you get?"

"Black lab I suppose. We've always had them."

He rarely said we. It was hard to look at calm steady Tom and realize that his life too had been torn apart not so long ago. Would he ever talk about his wife?

"We'll have a little expedition to go and choose one," Tom proposed. A different "we," and one she found she liked.

She's fitter than I expected, Tom thought. That "Victorian ladies" walk of hers has kept her in reasonable shape. And air and exercise have given her a new sparkle; she's changing under my eyes. He savored with pleasure a sexual response far too long absent.

He's marvelous to be with, Madeleine thought as they dropped down a slope of miniature rock terraces, heather and grass. Easier than Archie even. He'd be awfully good for Lisa. Quite an age gap, of course, but she needs someone older than her, gentle and easy-going and tolerant.

It was an estimate of Tom she was forced before too long to revise. With his decision made to live in the barn, work had begun to make the roof sound, and a school-leaver from the village had been taken on to help Sandy Black with the initial stripping of slates.

Tom had walked up with Madeleine one after-

noon to see how they were getting on just as Ross
Miller, who had no reason to be there anyway,
had been sounding off about the number of broken slates. Although he was out of sight at the
back of the barn his voice could be heard from
the farm road. As Tom later discovered, the boy
had been unwise enough to reply that it wasn't his
fault as Sandy had reversed the van into one of the
stacks. Tom came around the corner of the building
in time to see Ross boot the lad clean off the roof
to land awkwardly on the stony slope with a yell
of pain.

Madeleine had never imagined Tom capable of
the rage he poured out on Ross Miller, the searing
but controlled anger of the humane man for the
bully and coward. Ross, an overweight bruiser of
a man, topped him by several inches but they
seemed negligible in the face of Tom's savage blis-
tering fury.

Madeleine was shaken by the scene but deeply
impressed, and a comment of Archie's came back
to her, "Oh, old Tom's a lot tougher than you
might think." But what impressed her even more
was his ruthless follow-up. Ross Miller he sacked,
never questioning Archie's agreement. But Sandy
Black was unwise enough to say sycophantically,
"Oh, aye, he could be rough on the youngsters,
could Ross," and Tom had been on to the comment like a flash. The classic excuses, "Well, but,
it wasna' my place to mention it," and, "I didna'
like to say anything at the time," protected no
one. Tom went in grim anger to every man, to
every house, on the estate, and left no one in any
doubt that if they ever witnessed brutality or bul-
lying on Drumveyn in any shape or form, and
were found to have said nothing, they would fol-

low Ross Miller down the glen with unhesitating dispatch. For a new factor, hoping for the loyalty of his work force, it was summary treatment indeed.

But Madeleine, talking it over with Joss, said tentatively, "Do you know, it seems strange, but no one really seems to have minded."

"Of course they won't," Joss said positively. "They hated Ross Miller and they're not fools. They can recognize decency and courage when they see it. Anyway, they value their jobs."

"It was quite daunting, you know," Madeleine said. "I would never have imagined Tom could be so—well, so hundred per cent. It was no holds barred. He'd seen something he couldn't accept and he just went for it."

She was glad, in some instinctive way she didn't examine, that she had witnessed it.

Chapter Twenty-three

I really can't put off advertising for a cook or a couple or whatever any longer, Madeleine thought, buzzing up the glen with the jeep crammed with shopping. The kitchen, which she could see was going to be more beautiful than she had dreamed possible, was almost finished. Lisa was more and more tied up, schooling the young horse she had bought with Tom's help, and now showing prospective buyers over the Achalder cottages.

Madeleine was still annoyed with herself over the "But your father would never—" that had slipped out when Archie had telephoned her about his decision, after lengthy discussions with Tom, to sell them.

He had been delayed in London, a survey he was due to make in Mysore put on hold as battle raged over the long-term effects of extensive eucalyptus planting on the traditional harvests.

"We need the cash," he had told her bluntly. "Something has to pay for all the new work we're doing."

"But selling?" The golden rule, hold on to capital, property and land.

"Those cottages have been empty for over three years," Archie had pointed out. "And we're never going to need them for the estate again. The number of employees will go down, not up. We could only rent them or use them for holiday lets, and frankly we don't have the money to spend on them at present. They're almost separate from the estate anyway on that bit of ground in the loop of the river."

So the pair of cottages, originally intended for superfluous members of the family and therefore well built and substantial, were put on the market and Tom had been glad of Lisa's help in taking around large numbers of the interested or merely curious. Archie, having kept the option for a private sale, had been firm that the keys should be held at Drumveyn so that possible buyers could be vetted.

Tom seemed to have gone up another gear without effort after Ross Miller's departure. It had taken all of two minutes for him and Archie to agree that for the time being anyway there was no point in replacing him. And the atmosphere on the estate had subtly changed with his going; the new order had been accepted and Madeleine had sensed in everyone a new respect for the strength Tom had so unhesitatingly displayed.

He and Lisa had established a good relationship, Madeleine's thoughts flowed on. She was more relaxed when he was around. He let her see that he valued her knowledge of the estate and they had many shared interests. She had started fishing again and often in these long evenings of midsummer they would be down together at the old favorite places. Did she remember being taught to fish there by her father, Madeleine wondered, and how upset she had been when he'd grown bored with her and refused to let her go with him any more? She pulled her mind hastily back to positive thoughts. The riding was good for Lisa too. Then there would be Tom's puppy for them to train when it was old enough.

Has Joss noticed what's happening, she wondered. Would it be disloyal to sound her out? Or am I hoping she'll say it's all rubbish, she asked herself, wryly honest. How good it was to have Joss in the village. Being able to walk over to see her, pop across in the jeep to take plants, borrow a book, drink coffee, gossip, laugh. There had never before been anyone nearby to whom she felt close, and it was a luxury she still relished. Joss seemed happier too, casual about the house but madly keen on her garden, out of doors for every available moment. Bluff and cheerful, she had been accepted with unusual readiness by the village and the glen, and as Madeleine had foreseen, already seemed to know every name and face.

But this cook advertisement—whatever was she going to put? The main problem was that as soon as she thought in terms of a couple she saw Platts and her stomach churned with repugnance. So if not a couple? And what help exactly was needed? Cooking. We can't live on salads for ever. And soon there'll be all the vegetables to freeze and the game to deal with. Archie would probably like to entertain the guns, though she dreaded the idea. Thank goodness that he would be too concerned over Cecil's condition to suggest that they actually stayed in the house. But the Cluny Arms in Kirkton would look after them adequately and it didn't take long to drive over from Glen Maraich. And Cecil really isn't well. She looks completely drained, far too thin, and so tense. It must be a nightmare for her, the sickness going on and on. She won't rest till this wretched job's finished either. Doing the tiling herself surely isn't necessary. And when the baby arrives there'll be so much extra work. Should I learn to cook—but no one has the time to teach me. Lisa always says anyone who can read can cook—well, she did agree there might be exceptions when that mousse I made bounced off the plate and across the table as though it had a life of its own . . .

Swinging around a bend, she slowed for an on-coming van pulling out around a walker who, encumbered by a large pack, was doing her best to flatten herself against the dyke. About to accelerate on her way, Madeleine caught not only the gesture of the girl's hopefully raised thumb, but her big smile.

Inconceivable not so long ago to pick up a hitch-hiker. Charles's views on the whole breed had been damning and trenchantly expressed. But Madeleine found herself drawing away from the corner and pulling in. It was the smile that made her do it.

The girl ran across behind the jeep, one hand behind her supporting the bouncing pack, and appeared at the nearside door. "Glad you spotted me," she said cheerfully as she opened it. "Can't walk on the left on roads like these. And I was getting really, really tired of this pack. Oh, but you'll have to shift all this stuff. What a pain for you. Don't worry, I can wait for something else. One good thing is, up here no one passes you. They just take a long time coming."

"This can all go in the back. I'm not in any hurry." Madeleine had forgotten the clutter on the passenger seat but hastily started to move it. Apart from the smile this girl had a lovely voice, warm and friendly—and educated and English, which was a surprise. She was wearing khaki shorts and what looked like a man's white vest with one shoulder fastened in a knot. She was clearly not wearing a bra, and Madeleine felt a sort of mental tightening of the lips before she caught herself up in annoyance. She looked again—those breasts were beautiful. The girl was no lightweight and her firm flesh was uniformly tanned to a shade not far off the color of her shorts. Her thick hair was a nicely blending milk-toffee color and looked as though it hadn't been brushed for a week. It would have been no surprise if the accent had been richly antipodean.

She helped Madeleine to transfer the shopping into the back of the jeep with great goodwill, pitching over anything that came to hand, chatting all the time. Madeleine made one or two ineffectual clutches as a new paperback sailed across to land among the cleaning stuff and a large piece of Brie smacked down on a net of oranges, but managed to say nothing.

"What a gorgeous glen. I was dropped off at Balna—Dalna—something a couple of miles back, by the shepherd. I had to go in the back of the van, very sheepy. Do I still smell of it? The dogs weren't too relaxed, thought they ought to pen me up in a corner. Walked from there. I like all the breathing and feeling but I could do without my entire wardrobe on my back. That'll do, won't it? I can put these bits around my feet. Oh God, I've forgotten the pack, nearly left it in the road. Idiot. I'll hold it on my knee. It was really good of you to stop."

"Where are you heading for?" Madeleine asked, starting off slowly. There wasn't much of Glen

Ellig left and she wanted to enjoy this girl as long as she could.

"Well, nowhere, I suppose. Just bumming about on spec. I generally try the hotel or the pub, just ask around for jobs. I like out of the way places but it does mean if you draw a blank you have to backtrack. Still, from here I can get over to Glen Maraich and the map shows a couple of hotels in a place called Kirkton."

"But where are you staying? Do you have a tent?"

"No, not that much of a masochist. There's always somewhere." She didn't think this nice upmarket female would approve of the lovely barman who'd let her share his caravan behind the pub in Dalcraig last night.

"And you're just taking the chance of finding work? How long have you been looking?" Madeleine hardly knew what questions to ask.

"Well, I set out—what day's this?—let's see, about four weeks ago. I've washed up here and there, did a weekend in a chip shop, saw a guy taking down a seven-wire fence and helped him for most of a day. His wife gave me a colossal supper—only thing was she made me do some death-dealing hip and thigh routine afterwards, she'd just got the tape."

Madeleine hoped this wasn't some mysterious sexual rite she ought to know about.

"Then I went up to Aviemore to see if there was anything doing in the hotels but it wasn't really my scene and it poured for two days anyway, so I made a loop around Spean Bridge and Fort William and came back here. These glens are fabulous," she ended yearningly.

"But what's your real job?" Madeleine asked, still searching for firm ground.

The girl turned and looked at her with a big grin. "You sound just like Mum," she said. She was so natural and friendly that it was impossible to be offended. "I suppose what I've mostly done is cooking. I'm really quite good at it. Messy, though," she added fairly.

"You've had some cooking training?" But it was the merest attempt to be sensible. Events once more had Madeleine in their grip.

"Oh, Cordon Bleu and all that. Though a fat lot of good that is in most jobs. How fast you can chuck the stuff into the fryer or the microwave is what usually counts. Who's interested in things like filo pastry and cheese sablés except watching other people slaving over them on telly."

"Would you like to come and cook for me?"

"Honestly? Do you need someone?" The girl glanced over her shoulder at the mountain of stuff behind them. "Well, I suppose someone will have to reduce this lot to bite-sized pieces."

Madeleine laughed. She had thought she was delivering a bombshell but the reaction had been totally matter-of-fact. This had happened before.

"My name is Madeleine Napier—"

"Hi, mine's Pauly."

"—and I have a large half-empty house, a more or less converted kitchen, a pregnant daughter-in-law tiling its walls, an uprooted Aga which was supposed to be reconnected yesterday only the men didn't come, an adopted child of eight, a son who comes and goes, a daughter living at home and a factor with a young puppy temporarily occupying the cook's quarters."

"Sounds great," said Pauly. She's more fun than I thought; shy though.

Madeleine opened her mouth, shut it again and smiled, at herself really. For her part, she couldn't imagine how anyone could contemplate working in such conditions.

"When's the baby due?" Pauly asked. "I love them when they're tiny."

A great simplicity flooded through Madeleine. It had become a phenomenon of recent times. It was something you almost had to learn.

"September," she said. "Could you stay that long?"

"Oh, sure. I'm not a rusher-offer," Pauly assured her, serious for the first time, as though feeling she should offer some credentials.

"Better come and see what you think then," Madeleine said, elation surging up in her.

Would the young horse Cuil face up to the bridge or not, Lisa wondered, taking him easily down the slope to the river. He'd come on very well. It had been a good idea to get a garron who could be used on the hill, as Tom had suggested. So many estates used only vehicles now, with raw new roads slashed hideously across grouse moor and deer forest. Tom seemed to know what he was doing around horses. Would he persuade Mum to ride again? He had certainly stirred her up to tackle a few things lately. She'd been so funny about the jeep, like a girl owning her first wheels, dashing about everywhere. And now there was Roxie the puppy, after all the fuss there'd always been about no dogs in the house. Mum spoiled her more than anyone.

The hay would need a couple more days like

this before cutting. Tom would get it right. Amazing how Ross Miller's swift exit hadn't left a ripple. You had to wonder how he'd actually spent his time. They could start clearing out the barn. Doing it up was going to be fun. Archie had been delighted at Tom's choice and the plans looked sensible, none of Cecil's fancy ideas. Shall I put down a marker for a cottage of my own on the estate? But it was the idlest of thoughts; Lisa knew she was a long way from knowing what she wanted to do with her life.

Glad to have something else to think about, she faced Cuil at the bridge, giving him a look, then taking him steadily on, letting him find out for himself that the hollow knock of his own hooves did him no harm. He snorted and tossed his head, but already he trusted her, and though he took the last few feet in an unsettling leap she praised and patted him.

A car was already parked outside the cottages. Now who were these people? There had been so many in the last few days. Oh yes, Quebell. Tom had been keen on them because they were interested in both houses.

As Cuil crossed the hummocky grass in the curve of the river, Lisa saw a man standing by the overgrown blackcurrant bushes at the end of the Archalder gardens. He was tall, pinfigure thin, faded gray shirt and jeans hanging off him, hair gray, knobbly face polished brown. As Cuil paced up to him, discovering he wasn't going to be allowed to make a fuss, the man looked up at Lisa with eyes as pale as his well-washed shirt and smiled. A smile of great sweetness. The phrase came into Lisa's head unexpectedly; she snorted at it as suspiciously as Cuil had done at the bridge. Then like Cuil she had another look and decided it was acceptable.

The man was relaxed and tranquil. He looked as though he was soaking in every detail of the scene, the air and feel of the place as well as the June richness of this sheltered part of the glen, the sprawling colors of garden survivors—lupins, climbing roses, Welsh poppies, the white froth of ground elder spreading everywhere. Suddenly Lisa realized what was odd about him. He didn't look like a stranger on new ground. She had the impression that he would look like this anywhere, unhurried, receptive, his own person.

"Best we've seen yet," called a firm female voice. "If only someone would turn up to show it to us."

With a crisp crunching of gravel a wiry woman with curly graying hair, wearing business-like dungarees and carrying a dog under her arm, came around the corner of the house, her energy raying up the sunny garden and bouncing off her husband's gentle calm. She was followed more slowly by an elderly woman with a stick in one hand and the leads of two small dogs in the other.

"Joyce Quebell," said the younger woman, nodding to Lisa and giving a quick raking look over Cuil. She might as well have slid her fingers under the chin-strap and checked the girth, Lisa thought, momentarily indignant, then amused. "We'd better tell you what we want the place for before we take up your time showing us around."

Chapter Twenty-four

Lisa came into the kitchen bursting to tell her news and found the Aga in its new place, Cecil already starting to tile around it helped by Tom, and the men who had installed it sitting at the kitchen table being given tea by an unknown female who looked like something out of a Castlemaine XXXX ad. She was presumably their assistant but seemed very much at home and had Roxie the puppy, prematurely aged with plaster dust, against her shoulder.

Madeleine had been staring around the torn cavern of the old kitchen, trying to see it as it had been, peopled by the figures of the past. How dark and huddled in on itself it had been compared to the sweep of space Cecil had created. She abandoned the grim phantoms as Lisa came in. "Darling, come and meet Pauly. Pauly, my daughter Lisa."

"New cook," said Pauly, raising the teapot in salute, while the Aga man whose mug she had been filling did his best to drag his eyes away from the lift of her breasts.

"What?" Lisa said, sinking down into a chair and beginning to laugh. "What's going on?"

Tom gave up tiling for the present. This should be rewarding. And getting another eyeful of Pauly was rewarding in itself. He thought he knew where Rob and Ian would spend the summer.

"Want some tea?" Pauly asked Lisa, leaning across the table to reach for a spare mug. The Aga man blushed.

"Well, yes, thanks, I'd love—"

Bang of the courtyard door, feet scudding along the corridor. "I was in the three legs with Jill and we beat Alison and Shelley and—"

Cristi checked at the sight of strangers, glancing at the men but her eyes going back at once to Pauly, recognizing with the unerring eye of childhood the not-a-real-grown-up. Pauly was nineteen, Lisa twenty-five. To Cristi they belonged to different generations.

Pauly gave her one of her slow warm smiles. "You must be Cristi. Going to take her?" She tipped the squirming excited puppy into Cristi's arms.

"Have you come to stay with us?" Cristi asked, through Roxie's ecstatic licks.

"To cook your grub."

"Is that food?"

"Sometimes," said Pauly, with a sidelong look at Madeleine. "When I'm concentrating."

Tom grinned and went back to work.

Cristi pulled up a stool close to Pauly.

How is it done, Cecil wondered helplessly. And will my back last out for this final job? Her mind skittered away from the question of what she would do when it was finished. On every visit to the doctor she was told to rest. Rest and let the fears flock in, the awful growing doubt. She needed Archie so much. Please, please, let me be able to talk to him when he comes, she begged some formless and unhelpful fate.

"We must think about a room for Pauly. The poor child hasn't been further than the kitchen yet," Madeleine was saying, as the door shut behind workmen not nearly so keen to head for home as the builders, joiners and plumbers of the past few weeks had been.

"I'm in the cook's flat, Pauly," Tom explained. "And you'd be very welcome to join me."

"That's OK," said Pauly. "Anywhere. I don't have much clobber," with a nod at the pack propped against a cupboard to whose subtle green Madeleine was totally reconciled.

"But you'd get the rest of your things sent up, wouldn't you, if you were going to stay for a few months?"

"There is no rest really. Well, books of course."

Doesn't she have a home? Madeleine felt she shouldn't ask.

"The nursery wing would give Pauly her own bathroom and little kitchen if she wanted it," she said worriedly, "only would it be too depressing, Lisa, do you think? Would the turret room be better?"

"Nothing grand," Pauly begged hurriedly. "Whatever the turret room is. I'm not very tidy."

"Let's go and have a look," said Lisa, and Cristi, who loved expeditions around the house, slid off her stool eagerly.

The nursery had no bad vibes for Pauly. Madeleine wondered if anywhere ever would.

"This'd be fantastic," Pauly declared, dropping her pack in the middle of the floor. "I can rough it up with coffee rings and fag burns in no time. And my own bathroom, great, I can be really squalid . . ."

Lisa laughed at her mother's face. "Mum, calm down, I bet she doesn't even smoke."

"Oh, wow, all of C. S. Lewis, *Bambi*, haven't read that for years, Ransome, *Heidi*, *Seven Little Australians*. Early bed for me tonight. Cristi, have you got into this lot yet—hey, don't let her chew that strap, the whole thing will fall apart—you're never going to see me in the kitchen."

Lisa saw her mother assure herself that this was another joke.

"So ask me about Achalder," Lisa prompted mock-aggrievedly as they fitted themselves around Tom's table for dinner.

"Oh, Lisa, sorry, I meant to ask," Tom apologized. "Events," one of which was very near his forearm as he helped himself to lasagna, "had rather put it out of my mind."

Pauly had plunged straight in to help with dinner, insisting to Madeleine, "You ought to eat something I've cooked before I empty my gear out all over the floor." This sauce was a glory of creamy richness but Tom wasn't sure his kitchen would ever look the same again.

"Are they nice people, darling?" asked Madeleine, and missed the face Lisa pulled.

"They want to run a kennels."

"A kennels! Oh, but of course they can't, that's really out of the question, isn't it? What—?" She managed to stop herself this time.

"Breeding? Boarding?" Tom's mind was already sizing up that piece of ground which he and Archie had thought they'd be lucky to get rid of, especially if the cottages went separately.

"Some boarding for friends, well, dogs of

friends of course I mean, mainly breeding—but just guess what they breed."

"What?"

"Dandie Dinmonts!"

"What are Dandie Dinmonts?" Cecil asked, taking some salad and feeling her stomach quiver.

"Oh, I know those," Pauly said. "Walter Scott's supposed to have invented them, though if he did I'm not sure how they exist. They're soft and plump, with huge eyes like baby seals, game as anything and gorgeously cuddly."

Not unlike you, lady, Tom thought in a pleasurable sexy haze.

"Can I see them?" Cristi demanded.

"They're not there yet, darling. The people just came to look at the house."

"But a kennels," Madeleine protested in spite of herself. "I mean, won't that be terribly noisy?"

"From here?" Lisa jeered almost as rudely as if she were fifteen again. "Don't be silly."

Tom looked quickly at Madeleine and knew the exasperation in her face was with herself and not Lisa.

"Kennels down there wouldn't interfere with anyone very much," he put in quietly. "What did you tell them, Lisa?"

"To go ahead and make an offer. They are nice, Mum." She had felt Tom's disapproval and he knew, if Madeleine did not, that this was intended to make amends. "Only it's rather funny—they do want both houses, but one for the husband and one for the wife. And Grannie, who is his mother, is going to live with her."

"What a weird arrangement," commented Cecil, trying to ignore the wafts of hot cheese from the lasagna.

Tom took a quick look at her pale face and got up to put the dish back in the oven.

"Isn't it? They said it so matter-of-factly it sounded quite normal for a moment. It wasn't till I was riding back that I thought, here, wait a minute . . ."

Now why do I instantly think this is immoral, undesirable, that we shouldn't sell the Achalder cottages to these people, Madeleine asked herself. Why do I think Lisa should have waited till Cristi was in bed before telling us? Am I just one mass of conditioned reflexes? It suddenly struck her how agreeable life might have been if she had lived in one cottage and Charles next door, though in their case Grannie would of course have lived with him.

"It sounds like an arrangement with certain advantages," she said thoughtfully, and laughed when Lisa gaped at her.

Good for Madeleine, Tom thought. For two pins I'd hug her. Pauly might be waking up a few sensations but this is the one I'd really like to get my arms around.

"He's an illustrator. Calls himself a hack artist. He's working on a series of environmental education books for children. Wife and Mum do the dogs. Wife's absolutely fizzing with energy, swarmed up into both lofts and looked at the water tanks, paced about counting, rootled in the sheds and all that, but she's good fun. Grannie's silent but capable-looking. He's very quiet, a bit dreamy, lets them get on with it." How could one convey his gentleness, the peace that seemed to flow from him? Even Cuil had felt it.

Archie turned west to head for Glen Ellig with weary thankfulness. The Mysore job was now definite and he would faithfully make his report but he wished more time had been allowed to see the effects of the original eucalyptus planting on the reduction of the water table. With a small movement of exasperation he made a conscious effort to drag his mind away from the whole thorny issue. The glen was looking wonderful. Still summer evenings like this were how he dreamed of it. Ribs of clear-cut shadow across gold-green grass, apple-green fields where hay had been cut, fat-plenty look of growing barley, trees still not darkened to the sameness of late summer, gardens bright. He wound down the window and the aniseed smell of Sweet Cicely cut down by the Council mowers along the verges floated into the car.

Good, Tom had got the new gates hung already. He'd never do a better day's work than that showdown with Ross. That fence would last another year but if they wanted to lamb in there next spring they'd have to do something about it. Thank God to be out of London, a London without Cecil. It had been odd being there with her here. Off guard, tired, he had been nagged of late by a feeling of impending disaster. Well, these few days snatched for the grand opening of the kitchen, another few weeks in London, then back up for a long spell, the grouse, the baby.

He was horrified at the sight of Cecil. Was no one taking care of her? She looked gaunt, the bulge of the baby stuck on in front of her like an actress's cushion, her eyes unhappy and vulnerable. He longed to go up with her at once to their room and caress and comfort that look away, make love very gently if love was what she wanted, hold her from anxiety and harm.

But they were all waiting for him, Cristi a warm eel in his arms, too eager to show him the puppy (in the drawing room?) to give him a proper hug; a young looking female in jeans and purple shirt coming to kiss him and turning out to be his mother; Joss nearly as brown as if she'd been back to the Sudan; the bruised shocked look gone from Lisa's face; Tom calm and at home; and a honey-skinned creature of mouth-watering contours, wearing a dress like a T-shirt that had stretched in the wash but not much, who was introduced as the cook.

As they were such a crowd and Archie was banned from the kitchen till the party, dinner to-night was in the dining room. The French windows were open as his father had never allowed them to be. The scent of the roses around them—they needed a bit of attention—filled the room, mingling with the smell of the trout Tom and Lisa had caught last night and Pauly had cooked with chives and cream.

"A farewell dinner," his startling new mother announced, "providing you agree." He felt almost shy of her. Apart from the clothes she had let her hair grow and it was softer and looser. She was browner than he had ever seen her. But more importantly and noticeably, she was braver and happier.

"Agree to what?"

"Well, Cecil and I thought we might switch the house around a little." Tom listened with interest. It had been Madeleine's idea. "How would you feel for instance about using Grannie's sitting room and this instead of the drawing room? We could open the arches—" on either side of the fireplace and closed off in Grannie's day—'then we could use the French windows more. And how would you like the drawing room as an estate office? All this stuff could go into the old morning room. Only you must say what you really think." She resisted saying that it was his house.

"It sounds ideal to me." Let the sun in to that frightening lair next door, wipe out for ever the conflicts that had boiled up in this room. He hoped for an input from Cecil but could tell from her polite expression that she had no view either way.

Everyone else had plenty to say.

"All I ask is that I never ever have to look at that épergne again . . ."

"We could sell the whole lot."

"The archways are rather elegant."

"But it might be cosier to use this as a small sitting room when you're on your own, Mum."

On my own. Madeleine was jolted by sudden fear. Tom will be living in the barn, Lisa will go off again when she's ready, Archie can't be here much and I'm certain Cecil will never make this home base even with the baby. But there's Cristi. I have Cristi. And Joss is close by. So will Tom be, come to that. And this engaging Pauly, dolloping out summer pudding with a generous hand onto plates carried chin-high by Cristi, may not vanish for a while. I never will be on my own again, in the same way as before.

Chapter Twenty-five

How can I tell him I feel perpetually alien in this place when he's rediscovering his love for it and more committed than he's ever been? How can I say I loathe and dread the prospect of having this baby, Cecil thought in despair, rigid beside Archie's sleeping body.

She knew what had happened. With his tolerance and readiness to enter into other people's feelings, Archie had come around not only to accepting the baby but to wanting it. She had read it in his eyes as he watched her, the reservations of her early pregnancy gone. Now that she was ill and wretched all his compassion and protectiveness were there for her. Tonight, holding her with a careful tenderness that had brought tears to her eyes (I can't expect him to want to make love to me when I look like this) he had said that nothing mattered in the world except her well being.

So how could she put into words the realization growing in her frightened brain? A mistake, a selfish idea she hadn't properly thought through and now wanted to jettison. No, more, it had been a determination to impose her will on events, possess something which had been denied to her. Greedy, arrogant. And stupid, believing that she could fit into Drumveyn life as and when she chose.

Drumveyn—the silence, the torpor of summer afternoons, the long dragging evenings, the semi-comprehensible conversations about Tom's problems with the farm workers, the weasel that had been after Malkie's mother's hens, that wretched horse of Lisa's changing legs. Changing legs? The peak of excitement pulling up a hedge or the roe deer getting into the garden or the puppy getting covered in paint. How I long for the wit, the jokes, the gossip, the sense of being at the center of things. We weren't particularly intellectual but our brains worked, there was always the drive of creativity. I hunger to be walking along Bond Street on a spring afternoon, wearing something new, slim, elegant . . .

Her mind drifted agreeably, filling in the details, came back with a jerk. What am I going to do now the kitchen's finished? I shall go mad. And this thing growing inside me, making me sick and ugly, I want to be rid of it, I want it never to have happened. There's only one way for it to get out now, and I am so afraid. But afterwards, if only we could . . . But how could I suggest that to Archie, with his broad humanity?

Leaving Cecil asleep (perhaps), coming down in search of breakfast, Archie found Pauly in the dining room, tidying up a dribble of marmalade from the pot with her finger.

"Oops," said Pauly, "the boss." She licked the marmalade off just the same.

"Keep me out of it," said Archie comfortably. "My mother's the boss. Madeleine." The new informality had been a pleasant surprise. "Proper porridge, I see, nice change. And crisp bacon. You're not a vegetarian?"

Pauly laughed. "Do I look as though I ought to be?" She sat down companionably as he brought his porridge to the table, leaning back in her chair and splaying out bare brown legs in what looked like Army olive greens sliced off through the map pocket. She was wearing thongs dark with dew; bits of grass clung to her wet feet which Archie noted were beautiful—broad, shapely and well covered, the same even fawn-gold as the rest of her.

"Tom said that to Madeleine," she told him, grinning. "Winding her up because she'd picked me up off the road and given me a job. 'Cooking?' he said. 'Nut roasts and pulse stews, I suppose. And what terms and conditions have you offered?' And your mother goes into one of her lovely little flaps. He's good for her," she added, jetting grape pips into her palm, "makes her laugh. God, I nearly forgot, do you want a kipper? I got some specially for you, beauties. You'll have to wait a couple of minutes, though, they have to be freshly done."

Archie waited with a sense of disorientation, this room already strange to him. The French window was open to a warm dull day. Morning scents were heavy, intoxicating after the polluted air of the city. He ought to take Cecil back with him, look after her. Or was that selfish, wanting her with him? It would be mad to take her away from here at this stage. The kitchen was finished, she'd be able to relax now. The bed was booked in Perth. Yet all the weeks here had brought her no closer to the family. For a moment he was angry with Lisa and his mother. Surely they could have done more. But Lisa had her own problems, and he knew his mother's shy efforts would make no headway with Cecil unless Cecil allowed it. And here was this girl, this cheerful casual Pauly, part of the place already, as he guessed she had been from the first moment she walked into it.

She sat and talked to him while he ate his kipper, indifferent to uncleared plates and waiting work. The dining room looked quite different under her hand, cereal packets on the sideboard, big slab of butter, crusts left on the toast, mugs for coffee.

"So these eucalyptus trees," she was saying, legs twined around the legs of her chair, battered flip-flops dropped toe to toe on the floor, and he had to suppress a release of laughter. She wanted to know. She had been thinking about what he had been telling them last night. The washing up could go hang.

"I'd better find Tom and get down to some work," he said at last, feeling better after a huge breakfast. "Via the gun room, I suppose, since the kitchen's still a secret."

"That's nice," said Pauly. "Lots of people wouldn't have bothered."

The kitchen party held one or two surprises. In the first place Ivy Black, Malkie and his mother were included, at Madeleine's instigation. Archie made no comment, but had never felt so close to her. Then Jean Galloway had agreed to come with Jill and Dougal who of course were head of the guest list. Madeleine had gone up to Steading Cottage herself to invite her.

"Oh, but I couldn't—the children are fair daft

with excitement though—but I'd best stay at home, I've Donnie's dinner to get—"

"Donnie is invited too."

"Oh, but he'd never—I mean, this is a busy time for him."

"Jean, I really wish you would come. It's just family. Or will that put you off more than ever?"

And since they could laugh over that Madeleine found the courage to hurry on. "I'm very grateful for the way Dougal and Jill have looked after Cristi. They spend so much time together I thought it would be nice if we could get to know one another better too. I've been so shut away in the big house all these years." She could not bring herself to be more explicit but perhaps Jean understood for she took the heroic step of accepting.

"Though what I've let myself in for I don't know. All very well for you, saying you're not able," she said crossly to Donnie, who hadn't said a word and wouldn't in the least have minded sitting in a quiet corner with a dram and an uninterrupted view of Pauly. "And the lord knows what I'll wear, and you're not going looking like that, either, so don't think it," she rushed on, swooping on a surprised Jill and plucking disgustedly at her favorite T-shirt.

Like an observatory the big window of the new kitchen curved high above the burn, looking across the folds of the moor to the imposing peak of Ben Breac against a purple sky. Madeleine need not have dreaded a stream-lined high-tech look. This was a sturdy, country, family kitchen, the blurred green of the limed wood repeated with yellow and white in curtains, cushions of window-seat and chairs, and again in the decorative tiles imported from Portugal by a friend of Cecil's.

Joss's present for the kitchen was a basket from some third world shop for Roxie when visiting. Pauly reached for one of the green and yellow cushions to throw into it and caught both Madeleine and Cecil.

Ivy Black, red-faced and giggly after two gulps of sherry, insisted on rushing about helping, and as she was patently happier being busy they gave up trying to stop her. Malkie's mother, in the black/green dress she wore for funerals, puttees of bandages under her gray lisle stockings, settled down to eat and drink and beam through crumby gums. Malkie watched Pauly.

"Could that be a problem?" Madeleine asked Tom.

He followed her glance. "I'm impressed it's occurred to you, but it sounds unlikely from what I've just overheard. Along the lines of, 'Just because I'm matey it doesn't mean I fancy you, you great berk, so don't get any ideas. Just look at my tits like everyone else and keep your hands to yourself, OK?' "

"Tom!"

"Just quoting."

Lisa caught Jean as she came in. "Come and have a look around. Isn't it a dream? Wouldn't have dared to show you though if Steading Cottage hadn't been first on the list for doing up. Not that we're promising quite Cecil's style . . ."

Madeleine joined them to say, "I'm so glad you came, Jean," with a shy smile.

"So am I then," Jean responded bravely. She had worried about the bairns coming so much to the big house. Were they in the way, did they behave themselves? Seeing them now so much at home, playing with the puppy, helping when called on,

she knew the barrier had been in her own mind.
And this kitchen was bonnie. No two ways about
it, young Lady Napier knew what she was doing.
Would there ever be room for a dishwasher in that
wee kitchen—and would the water pressure up
there be good enough if there was . . . ?

Pauly's food was voluptuous, mounded, piled
and overflowing. Fluffy little smoked fish creams
with fresh watercress, rough pâté (she fairly
socked the brandy into that, Archie thought ap-
preciatively) with crusty bread, avocado mousse
which she hadn't got around to turning out of its
ramekins so everyone had to do their own, with
varying success and a lot of laughter.

"There were meant to be prawns on top, but I
ate them. Oh, and don't go mad on the anchovies
if you want to taste anything else afterwards."

It's a pleasure to carve beef cooked like this,
Archie told himself, then stepped smartly aside as
a cascade of baked potatoes shot past his ankles.

"Oh, no, was it one of my two did that?" Jean
groaned, but unable to worry much after two
glasses of a fruit cup concocted by Tom and Pauly.

"Lucky I'd forgotten to slit them and put the
butter on," Pauly remarked. "They'll be fine.
Quick, grab Roxie, though, she'll burn her
mouth." Roxie, Pauly, Cristi, Dougal and Jill disappeared under the table.

And mother's not batting an eyelid, Archie noted.

"Can't wait for all those rasps and strawberries
and currants coming along in the garden," Pauly
said, cracking into the faintly golden-tinted towers
of an apricot hazelnut meringue with a careless
spoon.

"This doesn't look too bad to be going on with,"

Archie said moderately, receiving his stupendous portion.

"Afraid the blender's been sounding a bit odd since I did the nuts in it, though."

"What's different about this chocolate mousse, Pauly?"

"It's a soufflé."

Laughter. "But the flavor?"

"Orange Curaçao. I say, Malkie's going to hate all that fancy cheese, I should have put some Cheddar out, what a fool I am, I'll nip and get some . . ."

Only Cecil, whose party it should have been, walked among them still alone, flashing smiles at the congratulations, watching aloofly as they wrangled hotly about where the original passages and cubby-holes had been, taking steps from one spot to another, flailing their arms to sketch in walls. She tried to feel pleased with the job she'd done, but it was over, she had moved on. Yesterday, standing here alone, the cleaning waiting to be done by Ivy, it had seemed for a moment an achievement, a task completed against odds of weariness which only she knew about. Now it was just another job, another obligatory celebration.

Not quite. The original plan to eat out on the terrace had been abandoned as a fitful wind blew up towards noon. Engrossed and enjoying themselves, no one had been watching the sky or had heard the warning rumbles. The storm burst as Madeleine was pouring coffee, with a clap of thunder that sent Roxie first to the door and then in mad panic to the darkest corner she could find. Lightning lit the bow of the window with dazzling brightness, the rain hit it with a first smattering of huge drops, then with a solid sheet of water.

"Soon see if it leaks," Tom shouted cheerfully to Archie.

"Think we should have left the hedge up?" Archie yelled back, and they laughed uproariously at what seemed to Madeleine for a few moments not such a bad idea.

Once the children were persuaded that they liked storms, Malkie's mother had agreed that another dram would steady her, and Roxie was trembling in the warm darkness of Tom's sweater since in this appalling emergency only human contact would do, Lisa said she must go and check on Cuil.

"I'll come with you," offered Tom, drawing the puppy gently from her refuge and handing her to Pauly. No puppy could object to that.

"Right, come on then," said Lisa.

You mind, Madeleine accused herself blankly.

In the little flurry of advice and warnings, the grabbing up of coats and boots, the yelling dash across to the Subaru, she found herself startlingly, shakingly jealous. She wanted to share this moment of action and enterprise with Tom. She wanted to be the one that coped. She wanted him close to share the drama and beauty, the children cheering at the giants falling downstairs, the blinding rents of jagged light in the grape-dark canopy of sky, the fierce drumming of rain on the glass curve that framed the bright party scene like a stage set. She wanted him there to see Cristi's face vivid with excitement, her arms tight around Archie's neck; Cecil looking from the watertight roof to Archie's face watching hers, raising her eyebrows ironically; the puppy with her nose down Pauly's cleavage.

She wanted him. She just hadn't been admitting it.

Chapter Twenty-six

Was that a flash of light up at the barn? Could Tom be up there in spite of having been away so early this morning to go to the Field Sports Fair at Moy? He must be exhausted. He was probably just having a look at what progress has been made today and then he would come down and go straight to bed. But a day without seeing him had been too long and without really making any decision Madeleine drove on past the house and up the hill.

Tom heard the jeep and came down the stairs still open to the framed-up rooms of the lower floor, Roxie lolloping carefully at or on his heels. In the last light of a red sunset there was no doubting the pleasure in his face as he came out to meet Madeleine.

"What a nice surprise. I thought you were having dinner with Joss."

"I have been but she's thrown me out. She's been up since five, gardening, Post Office, a stint with her alcoholics in Muirend, then, as she pointed out, having a GUEST to cook for."

Does it show, this happiness at seeing him, this instant peace to be with him again? Time slowing; nothing looked for beyond the moment.

Tom grinned. "So what did she cook?" Joss's basic approach was well known.

"Steak pie from the butcher."

"And?"

"Salad."

It doesn't matter what we say, whether we speak or laugh. Just the sight of him, his well-muscled frame so different from Charles's flabby bulk, his healthy skin, his smile, the quiet dark eyes that see and do not criticize; just knowing that he knows me, everything about me, except the depth of these feelings that shake and amaze me. The little shock of pleasure when he comes into a room; the way when we're with other people my eye is caught by him again and again, the satisfaction of finding everything about him so right; this deep of-the-moment happiness in being with him.

The weeks since she had understood and acknowledged how she felt about him had been the happiest time Madeleine had ever known. There had been many days spent with him, like that first one on the hill. There had been calls made with him to neighboring landowners, not daunting social occasions, but business-like meetings in estate rooms or even standing in farmyards. The land that marched with Drumveyn to the north was owned by a reclusive old spinster and run, more or less, by her ex-shepherd, a big arrogant brute whom Tom wanted to keep an eye on, suspecting him not only of fleecing his boss but of having been a little too friendly with Ross Miller.

They had gone over to Alltmore for trout to stock the loch, and to Torglas to discuss peat-farming, both houses where Madeleine had dined in the early days of her marriage. More and more focused on her growing feelings for Tom, she had conveniently convinced herself that it was perfectly natural for her to make these as it were introductory calls with the new factor, since Archie was away and Cecil house-bound. She blithely ignored the fact that Tom had known Andrew Forsyth and Alec Blaikie for years.

The inevitable comments were friendly enough, however. "What a difference in Madeleine Napier since Charles died. She's really come out of her shell."

"Nice to see her out and about. They were lucky to get Tom Ferguson for Drumveyn, old Heriot down at Carrhill was after him."

"Did you have a good day up at Moy?" Madeleine asked. She had wondered if Tom would take Lisa but Lisa had been busy at Achalder helping Joyce Quebell. Had he asked her? Madeleine was still doing her best to think that would be a good thing.

"Long." She wouldn't know what he meant by that. He had so much wanted her with him but had thought she would be bored. "Met one or two people." In fact, of course, he had met dozens of friends and acquaintances and had been surprised by the warmth of their greetings, not realizing it had always been there but that of late they had recognized his need for solitude and respected it. Or that, in those who knew him less well, they had felt a reserve in him which had now gone. Today he had felt he was back in his own world again. "Come and have a look at what they've done here," he said.

The stone barn had been built on a slope so that carts could be driven into the upper story at one end. This arch was now framed and glazed, with French windows in the center. In the other gable the opening for pitching up hay from a load below was now a long window and a kitchen was taking shape around it.

Before Madeleine arrived Tom had been looking at the finished base for the wood burning stove and reflecting how this one job brought the whole thing so much nearer reality. Looking forward to having a place of his own, so suited to his taste and needs, he still knew how much he was going to mind leaving the flat.

He would miss being involved in family life, especially the gatherings around the big table in the new kitchen which had swiftly become the focal point of the house, eating Pauly's feast or famine meals depending on the state of her love-life or her hangover, for Pauly had dived into glen life with enthusiasm and a variety of raucous vehicles delivered her back to Drumveyn at hours Madeleine tried not to register. But he also knew he could cope with being alone now; the sour sense of failure the break-up of his marriage had left had faded.

But not to see Madeleine every day, not to listen for her step, her voice, her much more frequent laughter, and feel his body respond when he caught them. She was perfectly unaware of it. He was sure she thought sex had nothing to do with her any more. If she could know what the sound of that jeep coming up the hill just now had done to him.

He'll be so happy up here, Madeleine thought, getting his belongings properly unpacked at last, reading for hours, Roxie sprawled across his feet. Tying flies to pounding waves of Wagner. Fending for himself, fixing and improving. Rob and Ian coming and going—as long as Pauly is around anyway, she amended, trying to lighten the pang of loss.

"Pity about the stainless steel chimney," Tom was saying. "Not an object of beauty, though luckily it can hardly be seen from the farm road."

"You never notice things like that after a while," Madeleine said, making an effort. "It's going to be beautiful, Tom, this room. I'm so thankful you didn't put in modern patio doors."

"Cecil might have done things differently," he admitted, glancing around at the pointed stone walls, the floor and stair of Paraná pine he hadn't been sure Archie would allow, the simple kitchen. The whole room had a masculine look that satisfied him; space, clean lines, natural materials.

Madeleine gave an assenting laugh but he turned and caught the look of anxiety that crossed her face.

"Cecil not well today?"

"Oh, Tom, I'm so worried about her."

"Tell me." In the last light of the August evening they settled on the dusty floor before the great window, fending off Roxie's welcome, and watched the remnants of sunset fade and soft blue dusk fill the long reach of the glen.

"She's so withdrawn. It's as though she wants the baby to be something entirely private. And yet she's not happy about it. Archie begged me to look after her, but I dread intruding. And how haggard she looks, even though the awful sickness has stopped at last. I don't know how best to help her."

"The main thing is to let her see you care about her. Poor old Cecil, she hasn't had much affection in her life. But I know that's hard when she keeps you at a distance. And fundamentally you aren't drawn to her, she knows it, and she isn't a person who can be fooled."

"But I'm very fond of Cecil," Madeleine objected at once.

"Yes, fond. She's your son's wife. You want to accept her, more so now the baby's due. You can add up her qualities in your brain but you feel no warmth."

"That's awful," she said, not denying it.

"Yes, but it's not your fault. It goes way back to Cecil's childhood and it's the result of a flaw in her, not you."

"What do you mean?" He could surprise her but never for a moment did she doubt the accuracy of what he said.

"You knew Cecil's parents were divorced. But did you know how many removes she was from them by the time she met Archie?"

Madeleine turned to peer at him in the dim light, frowning, foreboding touching her with light cold fingers.

"When her parents separated she went to live with her father, who married again almost at once. He left his second wife after a couple of years and when he went he didn't take Cecil with him. She was adequately looked after by wife number two, but never felt she belonged. There were two younger children and whether they were treated differently or whether Cecil imagined they were doesn't matter. Rejection had set in. Stepmother married again, new husband agreeing to take Cecil on, though Cecil says he always hated her. Then stepmother died when Cecil was about thirteen. After that she was the ward of someone who had no connection of any kind with her, no interest and no affection. To give him his due he fulfilled his obligations—educated her, gave her a home, financed her training, but from the day she left school she was expected to live her own life."

"But Tom, I had no idea of all this. Archie has never said a word. Poor Cecil, what a ghastly time she must have had." Madeleine's mind went back to her own childhood; I should have been the one to draw this out, relate to it.

"Archie doesn't know. Not all of it. He thinks there was one step. She's never talked about it."

"But she talked to you."

"Oh, we used to talk when we were tiling. A very peaceful occupation, we blethered a lot."

We blethered. Everyone talked to Tom, reassured by his easy silences, his honesty, his readiness to listen. It had been Tom who had discovered that Pauly's parents, always referred to as, "dull old dears, can't help it, poor things," were a forensic scientist (mother) and a neurosurgeon called Alan Tobin, a name known even to Madeleine.

"What can we do?"

"Very little. I honestly think Cecil's capacity for love has been destroyed—"

"But she adores Archie—"

"Yes, she does, in her own blind, seeking way, but I think she knows she's incapable of giving him the warmth he needs and longs for him to break down the barriers for her. Of course the lifestyle they've established works against that—all this business of Cecil keeping her own name and having the studio as a bolt-hole to run to when she needs space and solitude. And my guess is that having the baby by implantation was entirely Cecil's idea but that Archie's come around to wanting it for her sake. He has a big heart, that son of yours."

"Does she want the baby?" It was a question Madeleine had been evading.

"I think she hoped it would provide an answer. No child should be brought into being for such a reason, and Cecil is intelligent enough to recognize that."

"And that yet again she finds herself outside the normal pattern," Madeleine said slowly. "She's worried that because she brought it about by her own will she won't love it. Oh, Tom, could anything be sadder?" Sad for Archie as well. Suddenly, passionately, she wanted happiness for him, wanted him to have his own child, born in the natural course of events, the waiting for it shared with warmth and happiness.

"Perhaps when the baby arrives she'll find that having some creature truly belonging to her, dependent on her, will give her what she needs. And that she and Archie will be closer with a child to look after together."

"I should have talked to her more. Made her feel she could talk to me. You're so kind and understanding, Tom. You help us all."

"You helped yourself." She could hear that he was smiling.

"Don't laugh at me," she protested. "I must have seemed a terrible old fuddy-duddy when you first came."

"I thought you were lovely." His voice had changed, was deeper, rougher. He leaned closer and the puppy rolled away from his thigh, flopped into a new position with a little mewing sound, slept again. Tom took Madeleine's shoulders, turned her towards him, bent his face to search hers in the near-dark, and she had barely time to think with astonishment, "He's going to kiss me—I want him to kiss me," when his lips were on hers, warm and gentle, and as though she had always known them.

She felt a response she had never imagined could exist, all the growing attraction of the last few weeks finding expression at last. Her lips, for one thing, woke to acute sensations, sending messages to those parts of her body recently acknowledged. Charles's kisses had been his pursed lips, ridged, hard and cold, pressed against hers, obediently pursed to meet them. After three or four of these brief uncomfortable pressures his right hand would move to her left breast and knead it through her nightdress. This had not been agreeable but had not lasted long. His hand had then moved down and there had been a pause while his fingers inched her nightdress up and she did her best to put a ditty about a spider out of her disengaged brain.

This memory flashed through her mind and spun away. Tom's lips were opening hers, or hers were opening of their own accord. Sweetness flooded through her, an instinct to flow and melt against him, but deeper than anything was a sense of complete trust in what he was feeling.

When he stopped kissing her she folded her face down into his neck, and for a moment they were very still, letting feeling recognized and shared sink slowly down.

"Surprising lady," Tom said after a moment, with an intimate tenderness she had never heard from anyone, quietest of voices against her cheek, but with a light teasing note he took some trouble over, terrified of frightening her away, all too conscious of the power of feelings long suppressed.

"Because I kissed you back? Believe me, it was a surprise to me too." Leaning against the circle of his arm, she drew back her head to look at the blur of his face, smiling. "I just learned it. Oh, Tom."

"And oh, Madeleine," he said, laughing. "Come here and practice."

Floating, given up to sensation, safe. When Tom's warm hand curved over her breast, just placed there, firm, it was comforting and wildly exciting at the same time, and she found herself saying inwardly, positively, "I want that on my skin." She had never felt anything like the golden fire that tongued through her body.

"I didn't know so many places were wired up together," she remarked, in this new freedom of voice breathed against voice, the world shut out.

"Oh, darling girl, what a lot of things we are going to discover together."

"But I thought it was Lisa that you liked. Fancied, as Pauly would say."

"Lisa? Oh, come on. I'm very fond of her, but—well, for one thing she's young enough to be my daughter—" One could hardly say to a mother, even in the circumstances, that a beefy wench with forty-inch hips and a tramping walk was no turn-on. He'd seen the hearty slaps dealt out to Cuil by way of approbation; alarming.

"I was jealous."

"You're joking?"

"I convinced myself you'd be good for her, and I did try not to moon about after you—"

"Moon about. What a nice phrase. And I've been doing my best to keep my hands off you."

"But why?"

Tom laughed delightedly. "When you ask me in that blank tone it's hard to tell. I suppose I thought I should give you time to find your feet, discover who you were, if that doesn't sound too pretentious. But you must have noticed I spent all the time I could with you. It was such a pleasure to see you take new steps, grow bold—mind you, I hadn't bargained for brazen . . ."

Chapter Twenty-seven

"Wow," said Pauly, coming in with an armful of washing she'd forgotten to bring in last night, which included every pair of shorts Cristi owned, and seeing the way they stopped looking at each other, "have you two got it together at last, then? That's great."

In one breath Madeleine rushed from instinctive reserve and the feeling that this was a bit much even for Pauly, to a joyful courage close to recklessness. Something wonderful had happened—why worry about the young finding it, or her, ridiculous?

"Yes," she said.

"No," said Tom.

Madeleine was utterly devastated. Had she got it wrong? Had the words and kisses of last night meant nothing? Was Tom embarrassed and ashamed this morning? All the doubts that had tormented her as a girl came rushing hideously back. After all, she had enlarged her experience very little since. The blood rose to her face but she caught at control. Don't show anything, behave naturally, think about it later . . .

Tom took one look at her betrayed astonished face and was out of his chair and around to her in a flash.

"Sweetheart, don't look like that. Pauly meant—"

Pauly, after one dumbfounded stare, dropped the washing on the floor and rushed to hug her as well. "God, my big mouth! Take no notice of me, it's none of my business. But you just looked so sort of lit up. But are you an item?" she added irrepressibly.

Madeleine took her face out of Tom's shirt and looked up at him uncertainly.

"We're an item," he said, giving up. "We just haven't leapt into bed yet—which is what Pauly originally meant," he added hastily to Madeleine.

That "yet" shot a response through Madeleine's veins that shook her. Still shaken, she began to laugh.

How Tom had wanted to leap into bed. He had wanted her for so long, it seemed to him, but he knew he must take it slowly. They had talked for hours up at the barn, indulging in the pleasure of piecing together the development of their feeling for each other, floating and drifting in the new delight of touch and caress. Roxie had given them up as a bad job and had gone to sleep properly and afterwards light puppy snores and dreaming yips would remind Madeleine nostalgically of those magical hours. Then they had stumbled down the open stairs, Tom with a sleep-doped puppy sagging under one arm, Madeleine with the torch because idiotically they still needed to hold on to each other, and Tom had driven the jeep down to the house and they had sat in it for a further unknown stretch of time, then had stirred themselves to go and make coffee in the flat and tell each other a few more things that couldn't wait till morning, now only three hours off.

But Tom had known lovemaking must wait. He

didn't want Madeleine bracing herself for it as part of the new order she shouldn't duck. He could gauge now her inexperience and knew he must tread carefully. He could wait—he thought. Wait until she wanted him, aware and certain.

"Pauly, did you find something for Cristi to wear? I've just stopped her coming down to breakfast in her pants. What on earth's going on? Mum, are you OK?" Lisa stopped short at finding Tom and Pauly still patting Madeleine.

"They're in lurve, as if we didn't know," announced Pauly. "Isn't it sweet? Only they haven't—"

"Pauly!" Tom's voice held a rare note of authority.

"—quite got used to the idea yet," Pauly swept on innocently. "And I don't know about anyone else but I could do with some coffee after all this emotion."

" 'Bout time you realized it," was Lisa's comment to her mother, softened by a grin. "Good, though."

And that was that, Madeleine realized in disbelief. Pauly and Lisa had seen this coming, accepted it all quite simply, if with a slight hint of "Let them dream on, poor old things." She must go and tell Joss at the first opportunity. Would she be as little surprised as the others?

"Mum's so funny," Lisa said, examining the ear of a small portly dog who was finding her natural protection of beseeching eyes and doleful face no help to her at all. "She has no idea we've all been watching her and Tom watching each other for weeks."

"Think they'll make a go of it?" asked Joyce Quebell, who liked things clear.

"Shouldn't think so. I don't think she had much

of a time with father, that might put her off. She'll be convinced she's too old, anyway."

"For sex? Well, it does become a bit of a bore— as far as I can remember," Joyce added with a rasp of laughter Lisa thought could only be called sardonic. Impossible to imagine Stephen and Joyce even holding hands. Poor Stephen, no wonder he'd decided his wife and his mother could get on with it.

"I don't think she's really interested—or does one always think that about one's mother? But Tom's definitely got an eye for the females. I thought he rather liked Pauly at one time."

"Pauly's younger than you."

"I know, but behind her scattiness she's quite mature. She has a knack of understanding people, and she's very responsible about things that matter. Cristi, for example. She looks after her marvelously. This ear's a lot better. Could we cut back the drops to once a day, do you think?"

"Let's have a look." The Dandie Dinmont's look of suffering deepened.

It was up on the kitchen table in West Achalder cottage, where cooking, veterinary care, meals, grooming, business correspondence, plans for the new kennels and no-nonsense drinking all took their turn or coincided. Both cottages had disappeared under a sea of clutter the moment the Quebells moved in. Unpacking was never finished, partly because they were all interested in other things but also because Stephen's mother had a small stroke a week after they arrived and was now in bed, her existence recalled at erratic intervals by her daughter-in-law and never, as far as Lisa could see, by her son. This offhand approach to patient care was accepted as normal and Mrs.

Q's main concern was to get back to the dogs. She seemed unperturbed at being shut away in a room furnished by cardboard boxes, with bare floor and uncurtained window.

Lisa, at home and school, had been trained to tidiness. In her own house—not that she had ever thought of it as that—she had devotedly maintained immaculate order. She saw this now as unnatural, neurotic, a propitiation not only to Howard but to undefined watching eyes.

Here other things were important. Stephen would stand for an hour at a time on the uncut lawn absorbing the scene around him, unselfconscious and relaxed, or would stretch out in his battered old armchair with his feet on the empty hearth for placid hours of inactivity. Sometimes he read all night. Sometimes he was up and out at dawn to fill his field notebook with drawings and observations. On the finest days of summer he could be found in his studio, windows closed, indifferent to everything outside.

Joyce thought, talked and worked dogs; would have dreamed dogs except that, as she said, "I've no patience with that sort of thing." She had partitioned the sheds and whistled up runs on the rough ground by the river, with the help of Ivy Black's husband Sandy, the Drumveyn handyman, at a speed that had much impressed Tom.

"You should hear Sandy," Ivy reported with relish. "He comes home just about on his knees. Swears something awful when it comes to morning again. There was one day he never even finished his piece, says the woman terrifies the life out of him and he's not surprised her husband lives next door."

It was a logical arrangement, arrived at years

ago. Stephen had made the fatal mistake of allowing a woman just like his mother to marry him—or perhaps it was the cleverest move he ever made. After a brief battle for supremacy, which he had erased from his memory as an agony too great to be borne, the two women had realized how much they liked each other and had formed a coalition which had left him in peace and gratitude on its outer fringe. They looked after him well, with fewer complaints for his handlessness than a wife with no other resources might have made. They gave him his freedom, said his drawings were very nice, and didn't expect him to provide for them. The Dandie Dinmonts were doing very well.

"God, when did I last feed Mrs. Q? I'll leave Flora's pad till later. You couldn't take Stephen something, could you?"

Lisa always wondered, as she went around the mossy path behind the cottages and stepped over the remnants of the fence between them, if the charm of peace would work again. It didn't fail. Just walking into the cool east-facing room, its chaos less earthy than the squalor next door, more liable to throw up glimpses of beauty to arrest the eye, satisfied and calmed her. Here was the room of someone safe in himself, focused by his creative talent, absorbed. It was extraordinarily restful, but it surprised her that she didn't feel in the way, or was never made to feel in the way. Stephen welcomed her with unvarying pleasure.

It's the sight of the food, she had told herself at first, with a gaucheness she still reverted to when unsure. But since Stephen often forgot to eat what she brought him, and even if he ate it was hardly aware of what he put in his mouth, she had to accept that he liked her being there. And he talked. She would not have thought that on the face of it they had a thing in common, but the gentle words would flow on, and she would feel ease wrapping her like a blanket around a disaster victim, and time slipping unregretted through her usually occupied fingers.

For she was busy these days. She was down at Achalder whenever possible to help Joyce, or look after Mrs. Q and see to the feeding and exercising when Joyce was away at shows or drumming up business. Then there was Cuil to have ready for the moor by the Twelfth. He was still too unused to the work to be handled by anyone but Tom or herself, so once shooting started a lot of her time would be taken up. And Pauly was always glad of help picking fruit and freezing the vegetables planted year after year by Malkie and allowed to rot by Mrs. Platt. Though Madeleine was getting into all that now, which helped a lot, and Joss often came up to give a hand.

Without noticing it was happening, Lisa was being drawn back into the world of Drumveyn, a hard-working world in which she was valued and needed. In it she could function competently, feel right, look right. She strode energetically through her days, trusting (wrongly) that exercise would work off the large meals Pauly's cooking and hours of fresh air tempted her to, her hair bouncing and glossy, her palms leathery, her nails ruined.

It was to Joss, for like Madeleine Lisa enjoyed the freedom of dropping in on her whenever she had the chance, that she said in naive surprise, "Do you know, I haven't thought about what I ought to do with my life for ages."

"Haven't had the time, I should think," Joss replied absently, sizing up stones for the facing she was constructing on the river bank. This was her favorite relaxation at present and no one came to call without gumboots and the prospect of leaving with aching shoulders and crushed fingers.

Lisa laughed. "That's just it. I seem to be living my life. I don't think I've ever done that before."

Joss paused long enough to give her a penetrating look from under her bushy brows. "That's right, you are. So why go anywhere?"

"Can it be that simple?"

"Don't see why not. What problems do you see? Mads, still? Surely not, she's too busy with her own affairs—or affair," with an uncouth cackle.

"Do you know, I find it hard to remember what the problem was with Mum. It seems to have faded away."

"Not before time. Here, hand me up that flattish one by your foot, would you. No, the next one, it's to go in here, you mutt. Yes, ye-e-es, that might just do . . ."

Lisa looked at the hunched shoulders, the wild gray hair, with affection. Joss was right; that was all that needed to be said.

Chapter Twenty-eight

Archie came up a couple of days earlier than first planned, bringing a weary and desperate Cecil with him. Unable to endure the boredom of Drumveyn once the kitchen was finished, and not interested in the humanizing of Grannie's sitting room, she had fled to London and had been dismayed to find herself neither comforted nor remotivated. Many friends were out of town; those left did not find her the stimulating company she used to be. The city was stifling under a pall of heat in enervating contrast to the squally weather flattening the barley in Glen Ellig. But worst of all her beloved studio seemed stripped of beauty just as she knew herself to be.

Contrived, precious, its colors lifeless, smelling of emptiness, it held aloof. Would she ever be able to regain the satisfaction of creative quiet hours there? Certainly at present she couldn't work. Nor could her mind reach forward to a time when she could see herself free to work again.

Back she came with Archie, trapped and frightened. She needed his presence, his nearness, but often too felt a burning anger that he had not moved forward with her in her feelings about the baby, feelings of anathema which now seemed more rational than her original blind need.

She knew she was being unfair. Over and over again she would beat down the resentful feeling that Archie had abandoned her. The opposite was true. He was more openly concerned, more tender and watchful than he had ever been, and he had kept this time till the baby was born free for her. Surely when it came she would love it. It had grown in her body, it was part of her; the natural maternal instinct would not fail, of course she would love it. She repeated it like a charm, feeling nothing but revulsion.

They had come back early because it was Cristi's ninth birthday and every adult in her circle except Cecil was determined that it should be a special day. Ellig School was coming to tea *en masse*— all eleven of them, from Dougal down.

Tom and Madeleine had gone to Muirend to buy a bicycle (Tom's present) and had talked so long in a pub garden after lunch that the shop was shut and they had to go back the next day. They had then set off to fetch a boat (Madeleine's present) from a friend of Tom's at Loch Insh and Lisa and Pauly had made pointed assurances about being there to look after Cristi that night.

How Tom was tempted. But essential as he and Madeleine found it to be together for every hour they could, sharing such romantic pursuits as mending cattle grids, sanding the bedroom walls in the barn, clearing ditches and hacking back the overgrown jungle around the lawn, he knew that she would find a planned overnight stay in a hotel totally inhibiting.

Pauly chucked everything in the delirium of party cooking, with Madeleine's willing but inexpert help. The kitchen looked like the retreat from somewhere.

Cecil had turned the headroom for access to the boiler room below into a tiled shelf with a window running around it, adding a couple of Chinese ginger jars and some pots of trailing geraniums. Made a nice feature, Joss had said. Cecil had winced. It was irresistible to the children, who lay on their stomachs on the warm tiles with their latest microchip toys and handouts from Pauly, and to Roxie, who found it a good observation post, particularly when the washing or ironing, not always distinguishable, were dumped there. It was a good height to park bottoms for passing chats, and was rarely free of the odd coffee mug or wine glass.

When Cecil walked in and saw this philistine mess her face looked so stormy that Archie thought an outburst inevitable. Then he realized he would welcome one. Cecil's introverted misery was wearing even his good temper down. He was worried about her physical condition, the stick-thin limbs and the dead texture of her skin, her makeup looking oddly extraneous in contrast to the professional blending of the past. But how much more disturbing was her air of in-held dread and her increasing separateness from everything around her. If the tension were once released perhaps he would be able to reach her with reassurance and love.

But Cecil tightened her lips, turned on her heel and went in silence up to their room, while Pauly, gloriously unaware, asked Archie cheerfully, "Want to see the cake? I've definitely excelled myself."

The cake was a whitewashed cottage with a slate roof. It had a garden with a dry stone dyke around it and a gravel path. It had a tree against the gable end and a vegetable patch behind it. Roxie and a collie and a cat were in the garden. The new bicycle leaned against the wall.

The children gazed and gazed at it.

"Is it all cake?"

"You can eat every bit?"

"There's wee cabbages here."

"Our cabbages aren't that far on yet."

"That cat wouldna' be there long with thae twa dogs."

The party had begun at the loch with a launching down the slipway constructed by Archie and Sandy Black that morning. A bottle of coke was successfully smashed and shrill cheers arose. As the maiden voyage was about to get under way the skies opened and there was a stampede for the house. Since good glen mothers had sent the guests well prepared they were in a mainly dry condition as they got their breath back in what had been Grannie's sitting room.

With the disintegrating silk wallpaper gone, the frowning furniture banished, the windows disencumbered of fusty velvet and the arches opened to the old dining room, it was unrecognizable. Madeleine had made a big effort to have it finished for today. The rigors of a children's party should scout Grannie for good and all.

Then came revolt. The knife hovered over the cake and the children's eyes flicked up at Pauly in horror.

"You're never going to cut it up?" Even manly Dougal was moved to protest.

The rest were transfixed, mouths open, waiting to see this dreadful deed.

Then Cristi startled them all by a long wail. "You're not to touch my little cottage, I won't let you, I won't—" Tears brimmed as she clutched Pauly's arm.

"Oh, Cristi!" Everyone in the room surged forward in consternation.

"Cristi darling, don't cry! It's all right, it's all right!" Pauly threw aside the knife, Tom and Archie closing their eyes as it missed all the children, and swept Cristi into her arms. "Don't cry, how awful of me! I shouldn't have teased you like that. I made another cake for eating. Come on, come with me, we'll go and fetch it. You can keep this one to look at."

Cristi leaned back in her arms, gave one huge sniff and broke into a sparkling smile, tears still on her lashes. The grown-ups, who had not been in the secret of the spare cake, muttered threats about what they'd do to Pauly if she pulled another stunt like that.

Shouts for help came from the kitchen and Tom went to see what was wrong. Pauly couldn't lift the second cake, welded by its icing to a massive breadboard. All the children gasped when it appeared, in the shape of a fluffy white rabbit.

"Oh, God, another candidate for the cake museum," Joss groaned.

"They'll never let her touch this one either."

"Just how many spares do you have, Pauly?"

"No more protests, you lot, this is it," Pauly told the children, lopping off an ear. Shrieks, mixed. "Only thing is," she added, licking icing off a sticky finger, "I wanted to get this furry effect so I used ordinary sugar. It might be a bit messy."

It was. Ivy Black rushed for damp cloths, she and Jean wiped every passing face and hand, and Malkie's mother, who had rather taken to parties at the big house and had in some mysterious way managed to include herself, soon had a white moustache added to her normal gray one which kept the children in muffled giggles.

"Whatever would Grannie—?" Madeleine said to Archie, in parody of herself.

"Isn't it marvelous?" How does Pauly do it, he wondered, the contrast with Cecil's cool remoteness dragging at him. She's so scatty, she does such idiotic things, but wherever she is there's laughter. No, that's wrong, she had Cristi in tears over the cake. But there's warmth, emotion, humanity. He watched the children flocking around her, watched her help Joss organize a couple of games, and minded having to say when she finally let them loose to play hide and seek through the house, "Don't let them disturb Cecil, will you?"

Driving the jeep up the steep twists of the track to the hallowed lunch place "back of the dyke," Pauly beside her nursing a game pie whose glazed crust she wasn't sure would hold together for the journey, Madeleine felt a buoyancy that was becoming familiar to her but which increasingly needed some outlet.

Enough to do for the moment, however, concentrating on the boulders and rock-ribs of the so-called road, and keeping up with Craig MacNeil in the pickup carrying the trestle tables, the alcohol and the children.

It was good to be part of the ritual and not a piece of baggage, to be out in the soft air, with warm heather scents billowing over them as they battled to fix the long tablecloths (Grannie's damask) in a wind much stronger than it had been below, and laid out the wonderful food. Jill and

Cristi with earnest faces arranged the silver in neat rows. Dougal helped Craig, who needed it with Pauly around.

"Archie won't see from the hill, will he?" Cristi asked anxiously, pulling Roxie's head out of a hamper.

All Archie was expecting was the sandwiches they had teased Pauly for making by the hundred and freezing a month ago, or perhaps ham and egg pie, certainly the traditional fruit cake which, black and moist, had been festering alcoholically in foil for weeks.

It had been Madeleine's decision to reinstate the formal lunch for the Twelfth, just as she had insisted, to Archie's great pleasure, that the guns should be invited to dine at Drumveyn. The day had a new importance this year; it had to pay. And satisfied clients meant returning clients. Archie had worked hard to promote the shooting and Tom to drag Jock Anderson the keeper out of his happy sloth to rebuild butts and deal with vermin.

Archie's face when he saw what they had done rewarded her. He hugged them all—Pauly felt as warm and succulent as one of her own puddings, and smelt of the chives she had just clipped into the salad.

Lisa, brown and windblown, came down leading Cuil with laden panniers, extolling his steadiness and sure-footedness to anyone who would listen. Rob thought he ought to give Pauly a hand, as literally as possible (also the food looked fantastic) but Joss, paid-up beater, insisted on retiring with the rest of the line to the lower side of the dyke. Jovial sounds soon wafted across to the champagne drinkers. Pauly had considered the beer allowance meager and had added a couple of crates.

Archie, watching the line of beaters wamble toward him later, doubted if many birds would think it worth their while to get up. Not that they'd be in much danger if they did. He hoped the guns would also miss the children, spaced along the line to do their share of beating. It wasn't quite what he'd planned but whatever the final bag the day was already a success.

Pauly revived another tradition she had heard them talk about, one which Archie certainly wouldn't have suggested in view of what he was charging.

"Don't we all have a dram and finish off the cake and pluck a bird?" she enquired innocently, when everyone began to turn to the waiting vehicles at the end of the last drive. "At least, I hope that's what happens because I don't think the cook's in a fit state to get enough done in time for dinner . . ." One bat of her lashes, one sad heave of her bosom, and every male present laid down his gun and set about the nearest grouse.

"Oh, just the young birds," Pauly murmured, making it sound delightfully sexy. "It is for your dinner, after all. Let me help you choose . . ."

Tom and Archie exchanged disgusted looks, delighted with her.

At dinner Archie watched his mother with love. He had been so surprised and grateful when she had pushed aside her reluctance and said that the guns should have dinner here as had always happened in the past. Then, of course, they had been family members or friends; this was a new scene and she had risen to it splendidly. He felt glad things had gone so well, relaxed after the hours in the sun and wind, delighted by that stupendous lunch which had so pleased the clients. Not that he and Tom had costed for it, but his mother and Pauly wouldn't have worried over such a trifle. Bloody good advertising, though. And Tom had organized the whole day superbly; he had certainly put a bomb under the estate staff in his short time here.

Madeleine was sitting in the center of the big curve of window, the fading lemon light of the western sky behind her. She must have taken a bit of the curtains with her when she went to buy that dress, Archie thought. She looked so pretty, alive and young, nervous about this dinner party, but glowing with the new happiness Tom had given her.

Pauly was wearing a white crepon sundress toward which hands strayed involuntarily as she brought to the table an ashet of young grouse on croûtons, crisp game chips tucked around them, and baby vegetables picked by Ivy that afternoon. She followed up with black current ice cream she prayed had set, and a pinnacled edifice of chestnut profiteroles drooling cream.

Rob scowled at the hands. Only Tom was immune, his eyes drawn to Madeleine with a look of love but not of possession. They haven't made love yet, Archie thought; he'll make it wonderful for her.

Lisa, with rather too much to say about Cuil's achievements, was keeping the stout owner of a Harrogate dip-and-strip business awake. He wasn't as fit as he had thought and was having trouble preventing his eyelids crashing down, Pauly or no Pauly.

*   *   *

Joss and Cristi were having a little party of their own, watching three soaps in succession, eating cheese on toast and two ice cream Mars Bars each, then having several roaring and slamming games of snap. Cristi was thrilled to be the first occupant of the attic bedroom and even more thrilled that Joss went to bed at the same time as she did. They had some companionable padding about in their nighties, or in Joss's case creased viyella pajamas with a faded flower pattern.

But once in bed Joss did not pass out with her usual readiness. She had no particular feelings about grouse. Creatures killed and ate each other. Man was carnivorous. And she did not imagine it mattered much to the birds that they'd been killed for sport. Shooting was a source of income and jobs in otherwise unusable terrain. But the whole rigmarole, the money lavished, the expensive kit, men, dogs, pony, vehicles, ammunition all committed for a day to the securing of what, seventy, eighty meals? The elaborate food, the champagne. So why should it be less acceptable for champagne to be drunk in connection with blasting a few grouse out of the sky than in other circumstances?

But she knew, really, where her unease was founded. The wealth of the few, the vast incurable wretchedness of the many. She could acknowledge that, but not her restlessness. That she pushed away; she'd eaten too much toasted cheese, drunk too much beer at lunch. She banged her head into the pillow, setting her face in a sleeping scowl.

Chapter Twenty-nine

When Madeleine had run into Penny Forsyth in Muirend and been invited, plus entire household, to the famous Alltmore lunch on the Sunday after the Twelfth she had almost refused automatically, before she remembered there was no Charles to object. And it would be quite different going with Tom.

Archie was delighted that she'd accepted. He was pleased she had begun to re-establish contact with the glen friends he had always remained in touch with and also, at her own pace, to meet the hosts of Tom's friends who were so glad to see him emerge not only from his temporary isolation but from his highly depressing marriage.

Archie wanted to go to Alltmore himself; it was always an excellent party. But Cecil, he knew, wouldn't consider it and he couldn't leave her.

Lisa had one moment of panicky reluctance as instinctive as her mother's, then her mind went back to childhood friendships before the onset of her surly teens. It might be fun to see what had become of everyone. "Penny said nothing smart," Madeleine had said. That clinched it for Lisa. She'd be able to do some of the morning chores at Archalder on the way.

At Alltmore the sons of the house were on park-

ing duty and they to Madeleine's surprise directed
them down the lawn stretching between mounded
rhododendrons backed by weeping birches to the
loch. Madeleine paused for a moment, fascinated.
Not a scrap of floral print or well-cut tweed to be
seen. There was old Lady Hay of Sillerton, formidable sparring partner of Grannie's, in dungarees
Malkie might have refused to wear. And fussy old
Peter Semple who had that nice house overlooking
Muirend was turning sausages on a barbecue as
big as a bed, wearing a faded sailing smock and
a Para Handy cap.

No one could exactly say, "Thank God frightful
old Charles has dropped off his perch," but they
could and did welcome Madeleine warmly, and
Tom, whom most of them knew already, as their
new neighbor. Any comment about their appearing together moved swiftly from surprise to
amused approval. Cristi was an intriguing addi-
tion, and Pauly, splendidly filling a washed-out
pink and chocolate rugby shirt, was cut out from
the Napier party in seconds.

Madeleine found catching up on gossip like trying to remember a book read long ago, except that
all the characters had jumped a generation.

"... come and say hello to Robin Thorne,
though I think he was rather hoping to see
Archie . . ." Robin Thorne, the small boy who
always produced some living creature from his
pocket at children's parties, now a wildlife pho-
tographer. And hadn't his mother left his father—
there had been some girl, very LSE and un-
shaven legs . . .

And what had happened to Philippa Galbraith
after her father drank himself to death, and Affran, lovely Affran, had been shut up? "Philippa?

Joined the Air Force of all things. Oh and by the
way, Janey Buchanan's looking for you. Says if
you're shooting again on Drumveyn she wouldn't
mind doing a deal about game, she's always keen
to get hold of it for Grianan guests . . ."

How they talked. Madeleine had forgotten that
unstoppable chatter, and the laughter. She was relieved to see Lisa absorbed into it, then laughed
at herself. Had she expected to find her scowling
and kicking holes in the lawn?

Tom was clearly enjoying himself but Madeleine felt a constraint in him. The glow of arriving
with him instead of a boot-faced Charles faded.
He was there, with her or near her most of the
time, easy, friendly, but the magic link between
them was not there today. She guessed his mind
was on last night's events, and under all the greetings and chatter her own mind kept returning to
them.

Rob and Ian had been with their mother in
Scone for Ian's birthday. Wilma had done her best
to make Tom go, for the sake of the boys, etc.
Every instinct in him rebelling at the thought he
had sounded out Rob, not sure what the boys
would want. Rob had said cheerfully that it would
be a disaster if he went as his mother was spoiling
for a scrap. She had managed to have one anyway.

Rob had done a long day's ghillie-ing, foregone
the drams in the game larder and left half an hour
late in the jeans he'd worn all week and a T-shirt
crumpled into a pattern of small pinkish triangles
by Pauly putting it through the hot wash with her
red scarf.

An hour later there had been a telephone call
for Tom. He had taken it in the kitchen, listened
for five seconds, then put the call on hold and

said grimly, "I'll take this in the flat." Two minutes later he had come back, in the state of controlled anger that had shaken Madeleine on the day he had sacked Ross Miller. His face was pale except for high color along his cheekbones and there was a line of white around his lips.

"I shan't be here for dinner," he told her brusquely. "There's something I have to sort out."

She had nodded, saying nothing, awed by this anger which so transformed him, and he had turned on his heel and gone.

In the narrow hall of the Scone bungalow Wilma with mottled neck and unsteady hands tried to replace the receiver. In the sitting room the boys sat without looking at each other on the new Parker-Knoll recliner chairs.

"Think it would help if I changed?" Rob asked eventually, when their mother didn't appear.

"Too late now. Anyway, this isn't about us, it's about Dad. Candles on the table. And you should see the stuff she's cooked."

"He'll never come."

"She's going upstairs." They listened, then Ian picked up the remote control, clicked on some mindless game show and turned up the sound. Would Dad get it together with Madeleine, Rob wondered. But he and Ian weren't ready to talk about that yet.

Their mother was down and clattering in the kitchen when the Subaru pulled up outside. They came to their feet as they heard her hurry to the door.

"I knew you'd come," they caught her triumphant cry, then their father's furious, "Don't be a bloody fool!"

They had seen in their boyhood, very rarely,

glimpses of his temper, the blazing rage of the normally easy-going man goaded beyond endurance. They utterly respected it.

"I'm sorry, boys," Tom said, coming in. "This is something that has to be sorted out once and for all. Here," his wallet was out, 'take yourselves off to the pub. Sorry about your birthday, Ian."

"It's OK, Dad." Get out, leave them to it; this looked nasty. It was Rob who had the courage to turn and say clumsily, "Good—I mean—coming down, you know—" before he hastily followed Ian out of the house.

Tom took Wilma by the arm and marched her into the sitting room and shut the door.

It had needed to be done. He could not have allowed her to maintain her stranglehold on his life, or to go on using the boys in such a way. But it had left a bad taste and today he needed a little space and found himself not quite ready to appear as half of another couple.

Madeleine was aware of it and minded. Don't be ridiculous, she told herself, trying to remember the name of an elderly admiral stumping determinedly toward her, it's only two weeks since he first kissed you. But she realized with a small stir of excitement (the admiral dealt with very simply as it never occurred to him she wouldn't know who he was) that the knowledge of another side to steady, obliging, reliable Tom made him more attractive to her than ever. There was a strength in him which he didn't often reveal and she admired it.

At first she hadn't even known her recent restlessness was sexual. I have never felt desire, she had decided, then had giggled at the way these phrases caught one out. I have never wanted anyone, she had amended, but I want Tom. My body needs him. He makes it feel alive and desirable. What Charles did to me cannot be all there is. Then the check. The body drawing in on itself, a shudder at the memories . . .

These thoughts revolved in her brain as she waved Cristi off in the Alltmore dinghy, gaily hiding alarm, located Pauly by a roar of male laughter, and watched Tom steady as a rock putting up an impressive score at the clays. He looked so good in that check shirt with one of Pauly's scorch marks on the shoulder, muscular legs in well-worn jeans. Last night when he returned, looking in briefly to say he was back, he had looked a different person, dark-faced and formidable.

Suddenly, jealously, she wanted the right to stand beside him, close, touching (when he'd finished shooting of course). She wanted to take his hand, feel his skin, wanted to hear his voice, deep, quiet, for her alone. So swept by sexual possessiveness that she could hardly remember who she was talking to, she stood clawing back concentration with an effort she was sure must be visible.

Voices around her rattled on cheerfully. "Devolution? I should simply up sticks and go and live in England—" "—if you squeeze it into a ball and freeze it you can just grate what you want—" "—her list's at Jenners, horrific prices. By the time I phoned everything had gone except two champagne flutes. I ask you, imagine giving someone two glasses—"

To live forty-six years and never have known these feelings. Anyway, Madeline thought fiercely, I know this much now, this wanting, whatever happens.

Then unexpectedly they were alone.

First Pauly. "Do you mind if I go to—oh, God, what's the place called? Anyway, there's a party but they'll bring me home. Oh, and Penny's trying to get rid of leftovers, says everyone brought more contributions than she'd put out in the first place, so do you think you could grab some of those for dinner . . . ?"

Then Lisa. "I promised Joyce I'd do the feeding as she'll be late. And Cristi wants to see the puppies, so I'll take her with me . . ."

Beside Tom in the Subaru, rejoicing to have this unlooked-for privacy, Madeleine was pitched back into despair when he looked at his watch as they drove through Kirkton and said, "Mind if we look in at the Cluny Arms and say hello to this week's party? They should have arrived by now."

"That's a good idea." I do not want to sit on a bar stool and talk to unknown people. He's gone, he's lost. I've got it all wrong. He's affectionate and likes to spend time with me but that's all. I want to burrow into his arms. I want to talk to him. I want these waves of feelings to reach some shore, to break and die. Sex made one very fanciful, she decided. But mocking herself didn't help.

Lisa pulled up on the now weeded gravel of Joyce's half of Achalder cottages with relief. The day had been all right, better than she had expected, but goodness, how they all did yap and gabble. It had been quite good fun to meet people again but this was better, the evening sun on the curve of the river, work to be done, Mrs. Q appearing in a pink lacy jumper and brown nylon stirrup pants, carrying a bucket, one eye screwed up against the smoke from her cigarette. And Stephen next door, busy in the quiet room.

"Put that bucket down, Mrs. Q. Go and give her a hand, Cristi."

Cristi was out like a flash. "Can I see the puppies?"

"Want to see them first?"

It was always like that here, Lisa thought. Uncomplicated. The puppies were very up-market cuddly toys with suede paws and limpid eyes and the softest coats in the world. Cristi was ravished by them, and Lisa and Mrs. Q left her on the kitchen floor with Meg the mother's chin on her thigh and puppies everywhere.

Joyce arrived as they finished feeding, with a Best of Breed and a huge amount of shopping only approximating to the lists she'd lost. "I just made up Stephen's. Could you take it around for him, Lisa, and tell him to come and eat with us if he hasn't got anything for supper. And you and Cristi will stay of course."

This is the best part of all, Lisa acknowledged at last, heaving the bulging carrier bag over the fence. This is what I have been waiting for all through this day of voices and faces. She had been conscious of her own wariness, wondering if people knew about Howard, giving non-answers to the friendly question, "Lisa! Hi! What are you doing these days?" Here there were no demands or judgments.

"Want to see?" Stephen stood up, stretching, his eyes smiling at her.

She looked silently at the detailed precise work, the delicacy of color. "You could pick them."

He laughed. "No better praise."

"Oh, Joyce said if she'd brought all the wrong shopping you were to go around for dinner."

"I'll find something. Was the party hard going?"

"No, good really. Just that I don't feel part of that scene any more."

"Come and walk by the river. I've been in here all day."

Lisa hesitated. "I'd love a walk, but perhaps I ought to help Joyce, she's asked us to dinner too."

"Ah. Then I'll come after all." But he left the decision about helping to her. He allowed other lives to take their course. Nor did it occur to him to offer any help himself.

Lisa put her head in at the kitchen door of West Achalder. "Stephen would like to eat. Can I give you a hand?"

"Shan't be thinking about food for ages. Just hotting up a quiche anyway and chucking a salad together. Cristi's going to help me groom the Briard, he goes home tomorrow."

Peace. Like being alone without feeling lonely. Seeing through Stephen's eyes, learning the minutiae of a landscape she had thought she knew. Talking when she was ready about the feelings the day's encounters had woken. Talking finally about Howard. "I don't suppose I was ever married, isn't it weird?"

"That matters? How? Does it hurt you, make you angry? Or does it worry you with regard to other people and their perception of you?"

Questions put so simply she found she could deal with them as if she were asking them of herself.

"The confusion between sacrament and civil contract seems to me an extraordinary thing for society to cling to," observed Stephen. "Couples should be able to enter into whatever commitment they choose. I let Joyce organize me into marriage," with a smile that acknowledged responsibility, "and I was wrong. But we have arrived at a simple arrangement. Just be yourself, Lisa, if you can, putting the questions behind you."

"Be myself," she repeated slowly, her eyes on the swirl of dark water beneath an overhung bank where alder roots were already laid bare. "Who am I?"

"An honest, hard-working, able person, with a capacity for happiness and for giving which you hardly realize."

And vulnerable, he thought, unformed, and that moves me. After the positive women I have known!

I ought to get Cristi home but I love all this, Lisa thought later, in a haze of malt whiskey and overfed contentment. Good job school hasn't started yet. The kitchen was warm, crammed, stacked, poorly lit, richly smelling. A raft of letters and leads, bills and pills, dead biros, cigarettes, books, spectacles and dog whistles was swept to one end of the table. Dirty plates with knives and forks between them were piled lopsidedly in the middle beside a wedge of Edam, a packet of cream crackers and a dented enamel coffee pot.

I like this mixture of zeal and indifference, this disregard for appearances, this cozy squalid comfort. I like watching Mrs. Q's brown hands fondling that fat silky puppy, the way they treat Cristi as an equal. And I like the way these three people co-exist, the quietness Stephen carries with him, and the way time flows by.

Chapter Thirty

Madeleine, startled into awareness by the first ground frosts, the rowan berries turning, the end of the holidays for Cristi which at the glen school came so early, realized that she didn't want this summer to be over. Archie and Cecil would go back to London after the baby was born, Tom's cheerful helpful boys would vanish, and lovely Pauly, how long would she stay? They had been so lucky to have her this long but she was bound to get restless soon and how would they ever replace her? Thank goodness Joss was there—for of her own moments of restless doubt Joss had never spoken.

And the barn would be finished. Madeleine dreaded Tom moving out of the flat. Even now she hardly ever saw him alone. The shooting took up most of his time, though the other demands of the estate didn't conveniently stop for it—machinery breaking down as harvest began, calves to sell, tanks to check and water to pump after the dry summer, Sandy and Ivy vanishing to Wick where Sandy's father was ill just as work was starting on Steading Cottage and Ivy was needed for extra hours in the house. Everyone was busy at this time of year so only Malkie's mother was available to help out, but she did her rough and ready best.

Madeleine was busy herself. Cristi had shot up several inches and needed new things for school, and now had her own views on what she wanted. Visits to the dentist had to be hastily fitted in, there was Roxie to look after while Tom was on the hill, a large household to shop for and so much fruit after all the sun that she and Pauly could hardly keep up with the freezing and jam making.

Through all this activity Cecil went her solitary way, taut and uncommunicative, as comfortable to have around as an explosive device with an unknown length of fuse. They did their best, consciences bothered by the still figure lying for hours on a long chair on the terrace.

"I know it can be very alarming, the last part of the waiting," Madeleine said bravely, shivering to remember her own ignorance and loneliness and desperate wish to match up to everything expected of her in the weeks before Archie was born. "Do talk to me if you're worried, Cecil, won't you?"

Cecil turned expressionless eyes on her, as blank and black as a pool in the heart of a wood, and said politely, "That's kind, Madeleine. Thank you."

Of course I can't help her, Madeleine thought, ruffled by the coolness of that stare. She's perfectly right to find me absurd.

How could I begin to tell her the horrors that beset me about this baby, Cecil thought helplessly. It was so different for her. She was in her own home, about to produce the heir, her husband's son. I belong nowhere; this baby is no one's.

The only person she could have talked to was Tom, who had been able to break down the barriers of reserve in those uninterrupted hours when they had worked on the kitchen together, but Tom was busy. Also his attention was centered elsewhere at present and they both knew it.

"She should do more," said Pauly flatly, bashing on through her day—making packed lunches with her eyes half open, cooking breakfast, helping Cristi staple together a favorite belt Roxie had chewed through, skimming cream she'd set last night, making butter, loading the washing machine, putting bread to prove, getting the pudding into the fridge, nipping to the village, unloading the washing machine, re-loading it, hanging out the first lot, knocking back the bread, fly-mowing the bank below the lawn, having a quick lunch with Madeleine and a languid Cecil, washing the kitchen floor, emptying the washing machine, taking Roxie down to meet Cristi and Jill off the school bus (Dougal was now at Muirend High School to Cristi's great grief), remembering the bread and finding Madeleine had put it in, giving the children tea, all going down to pick the last of the raspberries, then diving off for a quick bath while Madeleine gave the guns tea. She had just started to wash her hair when she remembered with a yelp of horror that she hadn't taken the ragù for the lasagne out of the freezer.

Three large beef-fed Americans, looking forward to dinner in a stately home, were lost the moment a damp-haired Pauly rushed on to the scene with wails of despair and contrition. Going down to pick spinach as an alternative to the ragù, then sitting on the terrace with huge drinks stripping out the mid-ribs with the baronet, his mother, his cook and his estate manager became a much-told story back home. The one who found himself in the garden with Pauly putting down slug pellets by torchlight enjoyed it even more but had less to say about it.

Archie was torn between wanting to get on with pressing work and feeling he should be with Cecil. She made no demands on him—if only she had. Nor did she give him any support. She was ill, he would remind himself angrily, God knows what she was going through. But she could have talked to their guests, given Madeleine some back-up, not cut herself off so completely from all that was going on. Or not despised it, for there was a contempt in her aloofness that hurt.

Archie saw to it, aware that it was as much to satisfy his own conscience as to look after Cecil, that when he could he drove her down to the doctor for her routine checks. She accepted this without comment, but left him feeling his concern was derisory.

He had hoped these brief intervals alone together would give them a chance to talk but she blocked every attempt. He even tried to whip up a row to break the stalemate, pointing out that he had a stake in this child too. Cecil merely turned to look at him with a small ironic lift of her brows. Anger did not come naturally to Archie and he had not persisted. Cecil, desperate to be forced into a confrontation so that she could admit at last that she had been mad to embark on this pregnancy and pour out her secret terrors, had turned away shrugging, but clenching her jaw against rising sobs.

Questions dragged at Archie as he slogged across the moor, socialized with clients, found time to look at work in hand, or sat up late in the new estate room planning the months ahead with Tom.

Cecil hated Drumveyn. Well, Tom was here now and had shown a resolution and drive in his handling of things that had exceeded even Archie's expectations. He and Cecil had never intended to live here full-time and he was almost certain that a major job offer would be coming up soon which he would have to consider very carefully.

But deeper and more instinctive than all the practical considerations he was aware that his feelings about Drumveyn had changed, or rather had emerged from the welter of resentment and frustration his father had created.

Seen from here, what he and Cecil had regarded as personal freedom seemed mere flirting with the demands and sacrifices that weld a marriage. He had been as selfish as she. And even in their lovemaking, which had been so important to them both, Cecil had always eluded him to some degree. Would they ever recapture that precarious delight? And without it what did they have in common? A need for someone in the background of lives otherwise full? That would never be enough for him again, and it was not enough to offer a child.

Even Joss had made some effort over Cecil. "Look, if you ever want to chat to someone who's not family, just pop over. You know where to find me. Drumveyn can be a bit overpowering . . ."

Cecil, who found Joss unappealing to the point of repulsiveness, had flashed one of her brilliant smiles and murmured, "So kind . . ." in a social way that made Joss grind her teeth and go off muttering.

Lisa felt much as Pauly did, that Cecil would feel a lot better if she did something useful. Also, even in her slowly emerging self-assurance, she was wary of Cecil's mockery. That was what she read in Cecil's eyes, never guessing Cecil's envy for the simple answers Lisa was finding.

No shooting was arranged for the day of the Kirkton Games and they went over in a big crowd, taking Jill and Jean Galloway, and Malkie and his mother. Dougal and his elder brother Donald, who never missed this annual event, had gone early with Donnie for the morning stock judging. Archie too had put in an appearance to support Donnie, but had come back to be with Cecil as the others left.

Joss joined them with the Quebells. She didn't have a lot of time for Stephen's serene brand of selfishness, but Joyce and Mrs. Q were women after her own heart. Lisa had hoped Stephen would be with them, but of course this sort of crowd was exactly what he'd loathe. For a moment she thought wistfully of being with him in the cool east room at Achalder, or in the shaggy scented garden, then the jumping started and she became absorbed. They must get Cristi up on something soon.

"I'm not going to do a thing today," Joss announced, collapsing with a thud on to one of the Drumveyn rugs at the ringside, heaving one ankle across the other and batting her skirt belatedly down between her thighs. "I'm not even going near the WRI tent, they're bound to haul me in for something or other." She had been ear-marked as secretary for the next session, and had recently been co-opted on to the Ellig Hall committee. "I shall just let people flow around me." Madeleine was amused to note how many flowed toward her during the course of the afternoon.

The aggression that had so beset Joss had died away, worked off in gardening she said herself. But talking more seriously one day to Madeleine as they picked their way down a long row of Drumveyn red currant bushes, she admitted it was because she had begun to put down roots.

"I was never much into visits home, as you know, but when Mum died there was an awful feeling of belonging nowhere. And batting around the world I'd met hundreds of folk but none of them were really friends, and that made me think a bit. The old menopause didn't help—not so much the effects, though they can be a real pain in a hot climate, but, you know, realizing all that part of me, that function, was over and I'd never had a child. Come to that, I'd never had a bloke," with a sudden uncouth guffaw. "Being here, even if I were to buzz off again one day, I've realized there'd always be somewhere to come back to and that makes all the difference." Then she had become embarrassed and dived down to strip the lower branches and Madeleine had left her alone.

"Archie should be here," Madeleine protested inwardly, as the Range Rovers gathered, the backs opened, the gin came out and more and more familiar faces from the past appeared. But to be fair, Cecil did only have about five weeks to go, this wouldn't be much fun for her. Yet there was Lady Hay's granddaughter, who had been at school with Lisa, round and brown and happy in a smock intended for a much earlier stage of pregnancy and looking as though she might give birth at any second, laughing helplessly as her husband and brother tried to haul her out of a folding chair clamped around her hips.

Though it didn't occur to Madeleine, the eyes were on her too. "Whatever's happened to Madeleine Napier?" startled voices inquired. "She's a different person."

"Isn't it great?" Penny Frosyth said. "She came to our barbecue looking about the same age as Lisa. I'd always thought of her as my mother's age!"

"Looks happy. Charles was such a cold-blooded so-and-so. And where does Tom Ferguson fit in?"

"New factor."

"That's not what I meant, you idiot."

"Not sure yet. Be a nice idea, though."

"Wouldn't she be a bit dull for him, too meek and mild? He's just got rid of one dim wife."

"She's not as meek as you think. My guess is she could be quite fun, given the chance . . ."

Cristi was second in the Girls under Ten, watched with passionate envy the serious-faced little girls in kilts dancing undeterred through everything going on around them, then took part with Roxie in the chaos of the Most Obedient Puppy class, which drew a huge hysterical audience. Joyce had been asked to judge and had trouble in finding a winner.

Pauly, powerful, scarlet-faced and determined, battered all comers on the greasy pole and won after bursting her pillow over Dougal's head and covering the spectators in feathers. Ian Ferguson took her off to partner him in the bucket and pole and made sure they lost. Pauly, soaked from head to foot, wearing only brief shorts and a skimpy pale blue singlet, was a sight long and enjoyably remembered in Kirkton and the neighboring glens.

On the way home Cristi was full of Roxie's cleverness and Donnie's (not Drumveyn's) success, throwing away such lines as, "he reckoned he'd do well with those Leicester crosses from a Blackface dam." Jill was more interested in her mother's success in the ambiguous "Three Sultana Scones." Pauly let Rob gloat over their victory snatched from Penny Forsyth and her son Patrick in the musical cars, while dreamily playing back the sight of a sunburnt Craig MacNeil leaping down the final section of the hill race looking as fit as when he'd started. If only Archie had been there. Things weren't complete without him. He was so much the boss of the household, the linchpin that held everything together. Donald Galloway might be worth checking out, though.

Madeleine was nagged by growing uncertainty about Tom. As at the Alltmore barbecue, he had been with her for most of the time this afternoon, but always carefully part of the group, never letting them be seen as a couple. Was this discretion on her behalf or how he preferred it to be? And in their precious moments alone, though he was clearly as eager to get her into his arms as she was to be there, though her body responded instantly and his kisses reduced her to dizzy delight, he always called a halt, letting feelings calm down, delivering her back to normality with a little quizzical smile she couldn't interpret.

Was she doing something wrong, not giving him the signals he was looking for? Or had she misunderstood—was this all he wanted? It wasn't all she wanted, but even as she thought of making love, she shrank. Always the two levels—imagined longed-for pleasure with Tom, remembered reality with Charles. How could she want that? Yet her body insisted that she wanted something.

Chapter Thirty-one

"This pie will still be warm—I hope they think it's meant to be."

"Like quiche. It'll be fine. We'd better take Roxie's lead. Those downtrodden dogs of Martin Arbuthnott's might take out their misery on her. Where is Roxie's lead?"

"She bit the end off it," said Cristi.

"Well, run and find another in the gun room."

"Have you two got your boots and jackets?" Pauly demanded as the children came racing back with a lead that ought to slow Roxie down considerably. "Right, chuck them in the jeep and then help with this lot. You'll have to put your foot down, Maddy, I'm afraid I just don't know where the time has gone today . . ."

It was the last drive of the season and though not as grand as the lunch for the Twelfth, Madeleine had decided to make it special, particularly as Andrew Forsyth and Martin Arbuthnott were among the guns. Andrew she wanted to enjoy himself, but Martin belonged to the old style Drumveyn school and she had suffered a few pompous dinner parties at Dalquhat over the years and wanted to show him what Drumveyn could do these days.

Pauly and Rob had been over at the Cluny

Arms in Kirkton last night where a piper had been in the bar and an impromptu ceilidh had developed. The Belgians shooting on Drumveyn had wanted to learn 'Ighland dancing; the Americans had wanted to take photographs; the locals had nudged forward their empty glasses. On the way home Rob had moved in ardently and when Pauly had beaten him off for the umpteenth time things had suddenly become heavy and they sat for hours up on the hill road while Pauly tried to make him understand that she liked him a lot but didn't fancy him, without saying why.

This morning she had never caught up. Apart from her hangover and only having had a couple of hours' sleep, the summer had been hectic and even her splendid resilience was wearing thin. She had been so busy ironing a shirt at the last minute for Archie, going over the collar again and again in the hope that he wouldn't notice it was still damp, that she had let the bacon burn and there wasn't any more in the house. There wasn't time to make the syllabub for dinner; it would have to wait till she came back from the hill. She'd helped Tom pack the glasses and plates into the pickup, quivering at every rattle, then had come into the kitchen to find Cecil swaying greenly by the Aga and asking faintly if it would be too much trouble to squeeze her some orange juice.

About to say, "Squeeze it yourself," and whirl on, Pauly suddenly noticed the dark circles under Cecil's eyes, the veins standing out from the thin hands clutching the Aga rail. Too thin now to wear her rings, Pauly thought with a pang of compassion and of something else, even sharper, which she didn't want to think about.

Malkie's mother, set to cleaning the new potatoes Malkie had just dug, had asked, "Scraped or scrubbed?" which had suggested she knew what she was doing. But on being told scrubbed she had been found ten minutes later with three potatoes done, abraded to perfect whiteness and egglike smoothness.

"That's the toffs for you with their daft ways," giggled Madeleine, after halting this barbarity, listening for a moment in case zeal took over again the moment her back was turned. She'd never have made a joke like that when I first came, Pauly reflected, then wished she hadn't laughed.

"Oh, God, I should have done this yesterday, oh God, I should have got up earlier," and, "Oh God, I should never have got up at all," she moaned as they rushed around. Cecil, very pinched about the face and remote about the eyes, sat hunched at the table till it occurred even to her that she might be in the way, when she laboriously hauled herself to her feet and took herself off.

"You'd think she could shred a cabbage or something," Pauly muttered crossly, dragging her head out of a low cupboard and taking a couple of deep breaths before diving in again, wishing she could remember where she'd put the tupperware box for the coleslaw.

"She doesn't look well," said Madeleine with concern. "I wonder if I should stay with her."

"Oh, Madeleine, no, I'd never manage to get everything done without you. Ouch, where is the bloody thing?"

"Is this what you're looking for?"

"What's it got in it? Oh, Winalot—I remember now, I grabbed it when the bag split. Here, let's have it." Before Madeleine could stop her she was chucking apples out of the Worcester bowl on the table and emptying in Roxie's biscuits, then sweeping salad into the dusty container. "Be fine, don't worry about a—"

She broke off. A vehicle had come screeching into the courtyard at speed. Running feet came along the corridor.

Rob burst into the kitchen. In spite of the drama of the moment a part of his brain thought how gorgeous Pauly looked with her eyes wide and startled, her lips parted, the salad container clutched to her breast like a threatened child.

"There's been an accident on the hill—no, really, it's OK—" A masculine way of imparting news.

Archie! Tom! thought Madeleine, with an awful feeling of going pale inside. Lisa was safe at Achalder. And, *Archie*, thought Pauly, with an agonizing jab of fear Rob would certainly be happier not knowing about.

"One of the Americans got peppered, manic Belgian swinging around the horizon. He's insisting on going down to the doc and his chum's coming down with him, says he feels arbligated to accompany his friend. Archie's going mad at having two butts empty. He's put Dad in one. I've got to belt back as Dougal's looking after Cuil till I get there. Pity Ian pushed off this week."

"Dougal's good with Cuil," Jill put in defensively.

"I know he is." Even in his haste Rob paused to answer her courteously and give her a smile. How like Tom he is, Madeleine thought with pride and the little tug of need that never seemed far away, no matter what else was going on.

It was evident that Rob's dramatic arrival and

haste were all to do with the success of the drive
and nothing to do with the wounded American.

"But where are they?" Madeleine asked.

"Going down slowly to wait at the lunch place.
I ran down the Lettoch burn to the pickup."

Bet you moved, Pauly thought, wishing she'd
seen him.

"But how is he injured, this American?" Madeleine asked worriedly.

"Just a couple of pellets in his hand. Nothing
really. Hey, this lot looks good," Rob added ap-
preciatively, reaching for a sausage roll. "I'd better
get back. Do you want me to take any stuff with
me? The kids?"

Indignation from the little girls.

"No, I'd better have them with me to hold
things down."

They all looked at Madeleine.

"Dad said to take the Subaru," Rob said. "The
keys are on the hook in the flat."

Madeleine felt one wave of panic, then steadied.
She had done plenty of driving this summer. The
injured American had his friend to look after him.
"But Cecil," she remembered.

"She'll be OK," said Pauly. "We were going to
leave her anyway while we did the lunch. I'll
come down off the hill as soon as I can, but you'll
probably be back before me anyway."

"I'd better tell her what's happening. You two
take Roxie and go and get into the jeep. Take those
things with you—and help Pauly all you can."

"We will," Cristi and Jill shouted, racing off
with the first things they snatched up, eager to be
off so that they could see a shot man.

Madeleine soon discovered that a rallying approach to the accident would not do. Being shot

was a serious business. The sufferer was solici-
tously helped into the back of the Subaru by his
comrade, who then got in beside him to be sup-
portive. Madeleine, feeling like a taxi driver,
stopped making encouraging noises and concentrated on driving the big car, and found she was
enjoying it. It was nice to have some power in
hand to get past the meandering tourists. And the
car was redolent of Tom.

The Americans thought they were an emergency. The elderly housekeeper at the Muirend
surgery did not. "The doctor's at his lunch. Surgery starts at one forty-five," she said firmly, ush-
ering them into a horribly modernized waiting
room with lighting so concealed they might have
been in a wartime train, and a tank of fish which
looked as though they too were waiting for medical attention.

The Americans were all for rushing off to the
hospital instead but Madeleine assured them they
would have to wait a lot longer there. As the doctor light-heartedly extracted the pellets, knowing
as soon as he heard his patient speak that he
would have had every known jab, he further incensed him by saying, "You were lucky to be
shooting at all. I was invited to Sillerton today
and had to be on duty."

Madeleine had assumed that as soon as the pellets were out she would be rushing at least the
supporter back to take his place for the last drive,
and was working out how soon Pauly would be
down with the jeep, which might be able to get
him nearer to the butts than the car. Her passen-
gers, however, thought they should have lunch,
and were not impressed when they found that

most places in Muirend stopped serving at two in the good old-fashioned way.

They found a dismal café and embarked on a lot of cultural confusion about cow's milk and ground beef while Madeleine surreptitiously looked at her watch, worrying about Cecil and whether she had found anything for lunch, and about Pauly hurling herself down the steep track in the jeep.

Madeleine was halfway up Glen Ellig before it emerged that the Americans thought they were being taken back to the Cluny Arms. It hadn't occurred to them that Madeleine would take them anywhere else. Would it be quicker to go back to Muirend and up Glen Maraich or over the hill? Nothing in it now, Madeleine decided, pushing on. Pauly would probably be back by now, Cecil resting. There was no urgency if the Americans didn't intend to go back to shoot, she told herself as she started up the narrow hill road thick with cars, caravanettes and even idiots towing caravans, crawling around the switchback bends. The smell of deodorant and aftershave and unworn-in tweed overtook the friendly Tom smell of the car.

I want all this tedious business to be over, and the dinner-party tonight. I want to be alone with Tom, up at the great window of the barn. I want his hands, I want him to want me so much that he doesn't stop—

An approaching car, coming level with a passing-place on Madeleine's side just before she did, swerved unexpectedly into it, doubtless meaning well.

"Different," said Madeleine breathlessly, managing to pull over in time.

"Don't worry, Duane, we'll soon have you sedated," she heard from the back, reassurance and reproof nicely blended, and she crushed down giggles as she drove on.

"And I wish you joy of them," she said wearily, as she drove off from the Cluny Arms leaving Ian Murray sinking under a deluge of demands for iced water, the use of the office phone, a stimulant-free meal for the patient and new reservations for the flight home. The wretches had had no intention of coming to Drumveyn for dinner and hadn't even mentioned it, let alone apologized—though she supposed she shouldn't complain about two less to feed.

Pauly came running out with a white terrified face as she pulled up in the courtyard. Madeleine felt her insides liquesce in new fear—Cristi beating, Tom, Archie—

"It's Cecil, she's started, waters have broken—the pains are awful—I found her collapsed at the bottom of the stairs and got her up to bed—"

They raced upstairs. Cecil was lying on her side, hunched around the bulge of the baby as though denying its right to fight free of her body with this unendurable pain. Tears were trickling from her eyes.

"Oh, Cecil, poor darling, is it agony?" Madeleine soothed her, tears pricking her own eyes as she put her arms around that resisting body.

"So horrible, such a mess, sorry," Cecil gasped out.

Madeleine looked up at Pauly in frowning query.

"She was upset. It was such floods, she hated it happening, I think." Pauly looked baffled and uncomfortable. She would tell no one of that hysterical scene, Cecil striking out at her helping hands, the things she had screamed, shuddering at her soaking clothes and shoes, her own helplessness. Pauly knew she could not even imagine the agonies Cecil was facing, but stubborn common sense insisted that it need not be like this, not at this stage anyway.

Then a pain hit Cecil, and her screams lifted the hair on Pauly's neck.

"Have you managed to time them?" Madeleine asked as Cecil relaxed again, freeing her crushed hands and rubbing them.

"God, of course I should have. But there have only been a couple as bad as that. I couldn't even guess how far apart."

"We'll have to get her straight down to Perth. Thank heavens we've got Tom's car. But Archie will have to be told."

"I'll do that. I know where they are." The afternoon drive was the Lettoch Beat, and Pauly's heart sank at the prospect of the stiff pull up to the butts.

"Are Cristi and Jill beating?"

"Yes, we needn't worry about them. Plenty of people to look after them."

"Where's Cecil's bag? I know Archie made her get it ready." When he had finally grown angry with her for not preparing for the baby she had phoned Harrods and told them to send everything necessary. She hadn't even unpacked the boxes; Archie had done that.

Her own bag for the hospital was sketchily put together; another refusal to face up to reality, in telling contrast to the organized Cecil of former days.

"Give Lisa a ring at Achalder. Let her know what's going on, but say there's no reason to come back. And Pauly, don't worry about dinner, anything will do, everyone will understand. At least we've two less to worry about."

Thank goodness she's here to take over, Pauly thought with relief. "It's OK. Tom and Rob will turn to. We'll be fine. And I'll send Archie down as soon as I can."

They had difficulty in persuading Cecil to move and when she finally gave in she swayed down to the car like a zombie, indifferent to what she took with her and who was looking after her.

Apprehensive but resolutely calm, Madeleine set off down the glen once more, driving as fast as she dared.

Chapter Thirty-two

Pauly paused to catch her breath in painful gulps, bending nearly double and putting a hand on a lichened outcrop of rock to steady herself. Bilberries were growing in a narrow cleft and a few dark berries still clung to the tiny bushes. Gratefully she crammed them into her mouth. It was maddening to have to lose height in this corrie and then have to claw it back to reach the long spur of the Lettoch ridge. A stir of wind chilled the damp hair on her neck and she scratched impatiently at the rash of prickly heat rising on her burning arms in the cool air.

The flank of the hill hid her from guns and beaters alike. As she reached the crest she would be between them and very near the butts. Presumably if she yelled and shouted no one would shoot her—unless for ruining the drive. Grinning, steadying her breathing, she clung for a couple of seconds more to the friendly anchor of the rock.

Then the memory of Cecil's agonized face came back and she pushed herself upright and tackled the slope again, hauling herself up the smaller ledges, by-passing rock faces, following peat-black sheep tracks through patches of heather wherever they led her upwards.

Poor Archie, he would be frantic when he

heard. He adored Cecil, and who could blame him? Cecil's beauty, even haggard and ravaged as it had become, her wonderful sense of color, her glorious clothes and stylishness all seemed hopelessly enviable to Pauly. Another ball-game; not for her. Cecil was definitely a grown-up and even Pauly's unquenchable friendliness had not been enough to bridge the gap between them. If only she'd be nicer to Archie. Not that they quarreled, but if Cecil could just lighten up sometimes, give a bit. It must be wonderful to be looked after as she was, but she hardly seemed to notice.

Was she going to be all right, having this baby? Cold fear drove Pauly on, the sound of Cecil's screams coming back all too vividly. Would Madeleine be all right, driving her to Perth alone? Perhaps they should have phoned for an ambulance after all. But Madeleine had changed this summer. Even Pauly, from the unobservant standpoint of the next generation, had noticed how much more positive she had become, yet how much more relaxed and fun to be with.

Hurry, hurry, Archie must get to Cecil as soon as possible. The pain shooting down the front of her shins was agony, her hair was flopping dankly around her scarlet face, her fingers were sore where she had pulled herself up the rocks, an unbearable stitch was starting in her side. She didn't know what she shouted as with gasping relief she came at last onto the shoulder of the hill and picked out through sweat-stung eyes the dark shapes of the butts. She didn't know who spotted her, only thankfully heard answering shouts, the shots die out, saw figures coming toward her, Archie running and leaping past them all.

Then Tom was there, his arm around her, Archie, his face oddly gray under his tan, gripping her shoulders, staring into her eyes with desperate fear as she hurriedly assembled the essential facts for him. Then he was gone, hurtling down to the jeep, and she was sinking down with hands patting her, Tom uncapping his flask, Rob kneeling beside her so that she could lean against him.

The evening was in tatters. Andrew Forsyth and Martin Arbuthnott had made themselves scarce, Andrew phoning Penny and taking the two Belgians, who scarcely deserved it, to have dinner at Alltmore. The other Americans, polysyllabically concerned and all too ready with gruesome medical stories, revealed that they had already decided to go back to the Cluny Arms.

"What? What about my dinner?" Pauly was sufficiently revived to protest, but it was the merest token.

That left the anxious remnants of the family. Lisa, having made sure there was nothing she could do to help, was still at Achalder. Joyce and Mrs. Q had taken Joss off to a show, and Lisa was looking after Stephen and the dogs. Questions had been gently asked as to why Stephen couldn't look after the dogs and himself too, but no one had seriously expected an answer.

Dougal was bringing down Cuil, but when a wide-eyed excited Jill was delivered home and told her mother what was happening Jean came down at once to offer to have Cristi.

"I'd best have her for the night maybe," she suggested to Madeleine. Their eyes met. Nothing was said, but in both their minds was a premonition that all might not be well. Odd that, thought Jean, as she walked home with Cristi, I never used to feel I knew her at all, she always seemed so snooty, but she's not a bit really, once you get to know her.

Pauly was the most overtly upset, sniffing her way through the tedious job of unpacking lunch baskets and unraveling half-made preparations for a big dinner-party. After her exertions it wasn't surprising that she needed a little comfort which Rob, genuinely concerned but seeing a chance to regain lost ground, was happy to offer. None of them could know that the fear in Archie's face was still vivid before her eyes, or that she was desperately willing everything to be all right, not only with the baby, but between him and Cecil.

"He deserves to be happy," she told herself savagely, slapping unwanted food into containers, pushing back her straggling hair with a hot wrist, rubbing her foot against a shin stinging with heather scratches.

Madeleine was silent, pale, helping mechanically, in her mind the vision of Cecil's thin racked body and memories she herself had long ago shut out. She had offered to stay with Archie but he hadn't wanted her to. Indeed, seeing his tortured face as he hung over Cecil, folding her thin hand in both of his, Madeleine had been frighteningly conscious of areas of dark and private pain into which she must not intrude.

Tom, seeing off clients, paying beaters, locking the gun cupboard, having a word with Jock Anderson, checking the bag, could hardly wait to get back to her. He knew exactly how she would be feeling and going at last into the kitchen and seeing her white face and look of hard-held calm he went straight to her, indifferent to the presence of Pauly and Rob, and took her in his arms.

"You've had a hell of a day, haven't you?"

Thankfully she laid her head against his shoulder. "She was in such awful pain," she said, and the tears at last welled up.

Over her shoulder Tom saw Pauly's face, as appalled as a child's when its mother, incredibly, cries; saw Rob turn his head to register her shock and move toward her protectively. She would be all right. His arm firm around Madeleine he turned her and walked her out of the room and along the corridor to his flat.

". . . she should probably have been lying down—we should have made them send an ambulance—but it would have taken so long—I tried to go fast but the corners are so dreadful and she kept crying out. Then when we got there everyone was so busy—they were very good really, but of course we had to wait—then it seemed ages till Archie came. I would have stayed with him but he told me to come home. They said nothing would happen for hours, but I don't see how they could be sure, the pains seemed to come so close together . . ."

Out it all poured, the nightmare drive, the doubts, the helplessness, and the deeper inner fears.

"She seemed so—angry. I can't describe it. Fighting it, furious. As though she'd forgotten that the pain meant the arrival of the baby she'd wanted so much. I tried to remind her but she—well, she almost seemed to spit at me not to be a fool. I don't think she wants it, Tom. At least, that can't be true, it must just be the agony she's going through. But it really did seem like that for a moment."

Sobbing unrestrainedly, releasing all the strain,

she leaned in Tom's arms and he held her close, his face set. He could only too well believe that Cecil did not want this child; he had suspected it. What kind of performance was she going to throw now, he wondered grimly.

He kissed the top of Madeleine's head, drew her hair back from her wet cheeks, kissed them till she lifted her face to him, kissed her tear-clogged lashes, then reached across her and ripped off a couple of sheets of kitchen roll.

"Here, blow your nose."

She obeyed, grateful and ashamed. "Sorry, Tom, I don't know what I'm crying about. Nothing awful's happened. It's a baby being born, it should be lovely and exciting."

"It will be." He drew her comfortably against him.

"We should do something about dinner. You must be starving."

"I've probably done better than you today. Did you get any lunch?"

"Oh, yes, my shot Americans insisted." She began to giggle weakly. It had not been for her benefit. "But poor Rob and Pauly—"

"They're fine." Tom didn't think Rob would welcome company any more than he would at the moment, and grinned briefly. He bent his head and gently kissed Madeleine's still trembly mouth.

"Oh, Tom, you're so good to me. Hold me, love me," she said with sudden fierceness.

His body responded with a swiftness that startled him. Careful, he warned himself, go steady here, she's had a lot to contend with today. But as he kissed her he could feel her need, her abandonment of restraint. He had waited a long time for an unequivocal signal from her and he was getting it at last.

With a muffled exclamation he swept her up and carried her through to the bare little bedroom. Her eyes were closed, worries and inhibitions forgotten, conscious only of the immediate sensations of his lips, his arms, the strong barrel of his body against her own, warm, solid, astonishingly right to every sense.

When he began to undress her she stilled, kept her eyes closed for a moment, then slowly opened them to stare into his, intent, questioning not him but herself. Tom felt his throat tighten at the vulnerability he saw there.

Gently he unbuttoned her shirt, peeling it back from her shoulders, dropping it to the floor. He bent his head to kiss the swell of her breasts above her bra. His hands smoothed down her back, came around to unfasten her jeans—and with a sharp movement that shocked him out of his sensuous mood of desire and expectation her small hands seized his, checking them—worse, sharply pushing them away. He froze, head still bent, not looking at her, allowing the first hurt jar of surprise to subside.

Madeleine felt an aching tension clamp her body, hating herself for that involuntary movement but quite unable to prevent it. Conflicting emotions buffeted her—Tom was strength and comfort, and her need for him on this day of drama and exhaustion and the looming threat of unknown troubles was immense. But devastatingly she had glimpsed herself, standing naked as she had stood in front of her long mirror, naked in the full light of evening, exposing her middle-aged body to Tom's eyes. All the inhibitions of the past rushed back. They should be in bed, decently covered. There should be some intermediary stage between the surging up of desire and the appalling step of nakedness. And, fatally, she remembered where she was. This had been the inmost burrow of Platt, of Mrs. Platt; here in this room, stale-smelling, littered, their bodies had lain, perhaps conjoined (oh, surely not) in the bed which had stood where Tom's bed now did.

"It's all right," he was saying, his hands quiet, still gripped by hers. "It's all right. We'll go at your pace. We've all the time in the world."

"Tom, I'm sorry." She could barely speak. She had wanted this, longed for it, but she saw now that the longing had been childish, imprecise—worse, she saw as Tom pressed his head against hers and she knew it was to hide his eyes from her, selfish. She had dreamed that one day, leaping all the prosaic details of undressing—and goose-pimples, she thought, feeling incipient hysteria curl up in her—there would be some magical rapturous resolution of all the doubts and self-conscious fears. And memories. For as the reality of what Tom had been about to do hit her what surged up in her brain was not the delight of touch and caress she had discovered with him, but a vision of Charles's summary grasp, the invasive greedy exploration of her body, brief, insensitive, and then—

With an exclamation of despair and disgust she jerked back, freeing herself from Tom's arms which opened to release her instantly. I wanted him to resist, to hold on to me, she thought fiercely. I have everything to learn. For looking at his shut eyes and tight face, she witnessed for the first time the intense primitive male pain at rejection. Also, alarmingly, she felt his anger. She had seen it unleashed before and each time had been glad it had not been directed at her. Now she saw that his whole self was concentrated on getting it in hand; he had no spare capacity to offer her comfort. She had dealt him a terrible blow; she was on her own.

She knew that she must somehow try to assuage the pain for him, if she dared. "Tom." Her voice was tiny, useless. "Tom, I'm sorry. I do want this, truly. Dear Tom, you know I love you. I just— Tom?"

For his head was still down, his body rigid, his mouth a tight line.

Mustering her courage, she put out a hand to touch his cheek and saw her hand was trembling. If he blazed out at her, if he jerked away his head, if in fact he did to her what she had just done to him . . . But he held still, and after one fractional moment of allowing her hand to touch him in the most hesitant of loving, contrite caresses, his own hand came up over hers and held it against his cheek.

In thankful relief, she whispered, "Tom, I truly couldn't help myself. I wanted it as much as you did."

Not quite, thought Tom, getting the anger at his own stupidity in hand, managing with a heroic effort to dredge up a wisp of dry humor. He dragged in a huge breath, released it slowly, consciously relaxing the tension that had gripped him in that moment of disbelieving shock when Madeleine had pushed him away. "It's all right, I should have waited."

"No, no, Tom, it's not your fault. It was right, it wasn't too soon, it wasn't that. It was just . . ."

But what could she tell him of those hateful buried memories, Charles's blundering and indifferent haste, her own ignorance and passive endurance and deep distaste? She had no words for any of this, and to her in any case these were things of which one never spoke.

"I suppose emotions are all a bit wrought up today," Tom said, sounding unintentionally brisk as he gathered up his control, his good sense, his care for her again.

"Come on, put this on." He stooped to pick up her shirt. "We'll find some food, make coffee, and we'll talk about this. It was just the timing, sweet, just the wrong moment. I should have had more sense."

She let him believe it. She saw with a chill emptiness that if she were to insist that he had not misjudged things, that she too had believed the time right, then they would be left with a much more frightening question—would the real problem ever be resolved? Would all the terrors and self-doubt and shame she had hardly realized Charles had created in her always rise up like this and push back the warm tide of need and passion and joy? Putting on her shirt again, Madeleine felt very self-conscious, anxious and alone.

They were sensible, of course. They occupied themselves with putting together a supper neither of them wanted. They ate some of it. They talked about the day. They did not talk about Rob and Pauly, to whose possible whereabouts both their minds turned with a desolate simple envy. They even talked about what had just happened, minimizing it, establishing it in an acceptable context of wrong time, wrong place. They even laughed about Madeleine's sudden realization of being in

Platt's bedroom. Platt had indeed rarely been so welcome a topic. For there was a long evening to get through and their bodies were separate and drawn into themselves, as though actually fearful of contact. And when Madeleine at last decided thankfully that it would be reasonable to plead tiredness and go to bed, all they could achieve was the bumping unpracticed embrace of strangers.

How can that be, Madeleine thought in wild exhausted sorrow, as she went through the silent house and up to her room. We made the identical movements, placed our arms in the identical positions. But an inner resistance, inner questions, made the gesture mechanical and meaningless. What have I done? What have I done?

Chapter Thirty-three

Rob and Pauly, with a kindly instinct to give Tom and Madeleine a clear field, drifted through to the sitting room, oppressed by a sense of large events they weren't part of, edgy because of their own unresolved feelings. Rob turned on the television; a white corridor, a green-gowned figure.

"Oh, Rob, not hospitals! I couldn't bear it," Pauly cried.

He went to her quickly. "Come on, you've had a lousy time. Cuddle up." He put his arms around her and found her shivering, so unlike warm imperturbable Pauly. "Hey, she'll be all right. Archie'll phone any minute with the news."

"I don't want you to get the wrong idea," she muttered miserably, succumbing to the lovely comfort of his arms.

"It's OK, I know." But holding her glorious body he could barely cope with the ache of longing. After a while he said, his voice so husky he had to start again, "Listen, you've told me I don't turn you on and all that, but I'm not sure why. I mean, we get on pretty well, I fancy you like mad, you seem to like having me around, so what's the problem?"

She struggled up to look at him—not quite what

he'd intended. The unhappiness in her face startled him, but he also saw there a pity which he knew was the end of any hope he had had.

"You really are a lamb, Rob," she said earnestly (just what a virile twenty-year-old wants to hear), "and I'm really, really fond of you, but I just—"

How tempting it was to pour out her heart, put into words feelings she had only truly recognized today. But sense prevailed. To Archie she was just a kid, a scatty and scruffy kid at that, amusing, nice to have around maybe as Cristi was nice to have around, but that was all. She thought of sophisticated, intellectual, cool Cecil and blushed in shame.

"I'm sorry, Rob. It's just no use . . ."

He drew her down into his arms again, unable for the moment to find words for her. The first big thing for him. She needn't know that, it would only upset her more. Soft-hearted lump that she was, he thought, his throat aching. He'd be off to college in a few days; she wouldn't be here at Christmas. But at once he knew how desperately he wanted her to be.

"She's fighting the pain," the sister said, doing her best to sound explanatory and not exasperated. "She's refusing to push. There's absolutely nothing wrong."

"I'd like to be with her."

"She won't have you there, she's quite positive."

"Christ, I need to be with her," Archie exploded.

"Did you go to classes?" Sister began brightly, then seeing the fury in his face rushed on hastily, "I'm sorry, but she really does insist that you don't come in. She doesn't want you to see her like this."

"Is that what she said?" It sounded like Cecil, he thought with rueful amusement in spite of his baffled anger.

"We'll keep you in the picture," Sister promised, and made her escape.

Archie phoned when they were at breakfast, or lingering at the table in various stages of sexual deprivation, remorse and self-recrimination. Lisa, even she dimly aware that no one was very forthcoming but putting it down to worry over Cecil, had given up bracing remarks like, "I suppose she's bound to have a bad time, those tiny hips . . ."

The baby had been born just after midnight, Archie said. It had been a forceps delivery in the end. A boy, who had weighed in at just over seven pounds and though bruised about the head was otherwise fine. Cecil was fine.

They had barely had time for the first wave of joyful relieved exclamations when Cristi came scorching down from the farm on Jill's bike to say that Donald Galloway had left a jacket behind when he was over for the Games, "he had such a head on him," which she thought meant he was forgetful, and Jean was going over to Killin to return it to him.

"I'm to ask if I can go, and we're to have a picnic, and Donnie says not to forget my wellies because this sun won't last the forenoon, and if I want to take Roxie Jean doesn't mind. Darling, darling Roxie, did you miss me?"

She was ecstatic about the baby, even hesitating

for a moment about the picnic. "Can I go and see him, what's he called, how big is he?"

Only when she had been assured that she couldn't see him today and had been packed off with a contribution hastily grabbed up by a tired-looking Pauly, and had raced off again yelling at Roxie who was jumping around her wheels, did the rest begin to voice more sober questions.

"Why didn't Archie phone at once?" Lisa demanded. "He must have known we were dying to hear."

Why indeed, Madeleine thought fearfully, trying to persuade herself her feeling that all was out of kilter in her world was only the result of her long night of appalled regret and yearning need for Tom. A Tom whose too-evident determination to reassure her by behaving as though nothing had happened made him seem this morning utterly beyond her reach.

And Archie didn't come home.

"I should ring. Something must be wrong."

"Leave him. He'll phone when he wants to."

"But he must need clothes. He didn't take anything with him."

"Leave him." Tom had never before used that tone of terse authority to her.

"I know you're right," she admitted, "but I just feel so afraid."

"He'd tell us if anything had happened."

Madeleine wasn't so sure.

Pauly crept about looking pale and somehow diminished, her ebullience crushed. In a sort of numb desire to do everything right for once she decided to empty the dog biscuits out of the fruit bowl and dropped it on the floor. Seeing its two-hundred-year-old beauty in fragments among the

Winalot she knelt beside it and sobbed her heart out. Strange things were in the air, and Pauly couldn't cope with intangibles.

On Monday Archie came home, cloaked in a terrible reserve, looking ten years older. He brought the baby with him.

"But where is Cecil?" Madeleine asked helplessly, taking the light warm bundle from him as he thrust it toward her. "Oh, Archie—"

He gave her one look and she stopped. Whatever he needed now she would give him, silence included.

"Cecil's still in the hospital. She's going home tomorrow. Home, that is, to Chandlers Yard."

Madeleine gazed at him, feeling her face sag in shock as her reeling brain tried to take in the implications.

"I should think we'd be able to look after the baby between us, don't you?" Archie said, making a huge effort to speak more lightly. "He's called Nicholas. Come and look, Cristi."

Over her head he looked at Pauly, and smiled bitterly as he saw her drawn as by a magnet to the sleeping baby.

"Oh, his poor head, the little love. Can I hold him, I adore them when they're new . . ."

"I've got all kinds of kit for him," Archie began. No one was listening. He felt weights and chains lifted from him and drew a long tired breath.

The problem everyone had foreseen, that Cecil would have a long and difficult, perhaps dangerous, labor, had not been the ordeal he had had in the end to face. True, she had battled against the whole process, had prolonged it by her dread of pain and her resistance to what was happening to her, but even so the baby had been born in a few hours. Not that he would ever minimize what any woman went through to give birth; he shuddered again to think what had happened to that slender elegant body. The real problem had begun when Cecil closed her eyes, turned her face away and utterly rejected the child. She would not look at it or touch it and drew back in revulsion when they tried to lay it against her breast.

"This often happens," the nurse lied glibly. "She'll be better when she's had a good sleep. They all want to hold the baby first thing when they wake up, you'll see. Come along then, my wee man . . ."

Cecil had not wanted to hold the baby when she woke; had given way to a storm of violent weeping protest when they tried to insist.

Archie, harrowed and exhausted after a sleepless night, found this unnatural and incomprehensible. Worse, he found it contemptible. He had made himself come to terms with the idea of this baby for Cecil's sake, doing his best to understand her need, and in time he had come around to wanting it. Now from the first moment of feeling its helpless fragility, looking at the battered head, the delicate skin, the tiny puckered mouth and screwed-up eyes, he had been flooded with protective love. Everything was simple now for him, everything forgotten in the one fact, this was his child to be looked after always.

Now Cecil talked, reserve torn away by what she had suffered, and he discovered the depth of her rejection of the baby and her loathing of what she had done. She talked to him as he had begged her to talk in these last fraught weeks, and he could scarcely endure it. She wanted to have the child adopted. She wanted to wipe out the whole expe-

rience. But in all she said, hurried, panicky, deaf
to reason, she never told him how she felt about
him. It was as though love was the least important
factor; there was only order to be reestablished,
work to start again, a disastrous mistake to be
glossed over.

Yet under all the selfish desperation a voice inside her cried, "Love me, love me." Perhaps Tom
could have heard it, for in his quiet way Tom had
come closer to Cecil than any of them. But Archie,
shocked by an egotism he couldn't forgive, found
he couldn't bear to touch her, let alone find words
to help her.

Back at Drumveyn, with Cecil safely in London,
he said nothing, and Madeleine asked no questions. She knew he phoned Cecil, but the calls
were always brief.

"Can we cope with this baby?" she asked
Tom doubtfully.

"Oh, there has to be a bit of know-how amongst
the lot of us," he said comfortably.

"Not from me," she confessed with shame. "I
handed them over to Nanny."

"And not from Pauly, I suppose, except that
she's a natural. We could always call on Jean Galloway in a crisis, and there'll be the usual district
nurse visits, or whatever they call themselves
these days. Archie read the instructions on the
packet before he left hospital, evidently. He seems
to know what he's doing."

So Nicholas, without a drop of Napier blood in
his veins, with his down of blond hair and his
light skin and dark blue eyes as unlikely a child
as Cecil could have produced, took his place at
Drumveyn, sleeping for astonishingly long peri-
ods, yelling for food the moment he woke and

putting on weight in no uncertain fashion. To Madeleine, taking her turn at feeding, changing and bathing him, things she had never done for her own children, he was simply Archie's son. Just as Archie had felt, in that first moment of holding him, uncomplicated protective love, so for her Nicholas had become not some other man's alien child, but himself, known, loved, her grandson. It seemed odd that she had had to make an effort to accept that one day he might inherit Drumveyn; now that seemed irrelevant, something that would take its natural course.

Chapter Thirty-four

On a Monday in October Madeleine went into the estate room, one-time drawing room, to put the day's pile of business letters on Tom's desk. He'd hardly been in here all weekend with the excitement of the pony arriving for Cristi. He and Lisa must have trotted miles leading the two little girls up and down. Clearly for Jill, slipping about in the saddle, clutching Iona's mane, giggling and shrieking, it would be a short-lived craze. But for Cristi, her face ablaze with joy and determination, it was equally clearly going to be the great new love of her life. Lisa, co-opted to give a grooming lesson this morning, had been wondering aloud whether it had been a good idea to acquire Iona during half-term week.

Idly Madeleine flipped over Tom's desk calendar, having to think about the date. The large black 7 stared at her. Guiltily she stared back. The day Charles had died. But at once she queried that guilt—at forgetting, or because the anniversary should mean something to her? It didn't. Truthfully, she thought, I am glad, not literally that he died, but for all that this year has taught and given me. Had Archie and Lisa remembered? Lisa had said nothing.

She went to the window. No shrouding trees

now, but light, the crisp light of autumn reaching into the busy room with its two desks, its filing cabinets and computer and maps and reference books. Where the big trees had crowded there was an unsightly mess, but new growth would cover it in the spring. Archie had not consulted her. He had said only, "It won't look too good for a while, I'm afraid," and attacked the job as soon as he returned from seeing Cecil in London, a meeting about which he had volunteered no information. It was as though he needed to do something physical and positive, with visible results. Making a statement about Drumveyn and himself.

It appeared that Nicholas would be staying here. Madeleine didn't ask about that either. He was a joy to all of them, and for her he had provided a much-needed focus for attention and time and loving care.

She stood for a moment, testing memories of this room, finding they had lost their teeth. It was hard to recall its chill oppressiveness or the futility of the hours she had spent here.

Tom's desk. Drawn to it again, she ran her hand caressingly along the curved back of his swivel chair, the dark hide smooth and shining with years of use. He would be in at lunch-time. Only two hours to wait. It was absurd to think in such terms but that was how the hunger for him gnawed her, a hunger only briefly satisfied by being with him again.

They had never talked again about the fiasco when he had begun to make love to her the day Nicholas was born. Not really talked, in a way which cut through the tangle of hurt pride, remorse and the sense of inadequacy which lacerated Madeleine every time she remembered the scene.

Tom seemed on the surface no different in his behavior toward her. Steady, kind, affectionate— no, openly loving. But Madeleine often wished that he had not controlled his anger that day, wished he had simply battered down the barriers, damned her for her coldness, carried them both to some glorious conclusion.

There had been an intensity of emotion about these last weeks that she had never experienced in her life before: her own feelings for Tom which seemed to have nowhere to go, her pain for Archie's pain, and the loving pleasure they all took in Nicholas. She closed her eyes, her finger-tips alive to the texture of the leather, her body restless, her whole being waiting till the moment when she would hear Tom's voice, Tom's tread.

She was roused by the sound of Pauly talking to Nicholas as she brought him downstairs. "Now listen, buster, you'd better learn to count. You've had two breakfasts already, three if you include that little snack at five-thirty—five-thirty, for God's sake, what are you doing to me?"

Madeleine smiled, then laughed as a memory came back of the day she had asked Pauly if she would stay. She had begun so ineptly. "Pauly, darling, you know how much we've loved having you here, but I do understand that you'll probably want to move on before long."

Pauly, making a cake and about to crack an egg against the mixing bowl, startled her by pitching it back into the basket to splatter messily among its mates, and turning to her with a face of despair.

"Oh, Maddy, I know I've been a disaster and

smashed and burned everything. I know that shell and seaweed Worcester bowl was worth a fortune, and I did chip the big teapot, but it was only the spout" (did I know about that, Madeleine wondered), "and I'm always forgetting the ironing and meals get a bit late and my room's a tip, but I really try. I'll write everything down and keep Roxie off the beds and I honestly don't want to go out and get smashed when I have to get up for Nicholas . . ." Her voice wavered and her mouth began to pucker ominously.

"Pauly, whatever are you saying? I was going to ask if you'd stay. I'd hate to lose you, we all would. Darling girl, don't cry, whatever you do, don't cry, I really cannot bear it—"

"You'd let me stay? Honestly? But I thought you'd want to get a proper cook, and a proper nanny. Could you put up with me?"

"There has never been a cook like you," said Madeleine, folding her in her arms. (How I do understand all these men lustfully pursuing.)

"You can say that again," sniffed Pauly, giggling and hugging her back. "I've been terrified you'd want me to go. I was only supposed to be filling in for the summer, till you got someone real. But if I had to leave Cristi and Nicholas I'd die."

"The only thing is, you've worked so hard this summer, perhaps we ought to have more help for you."

"No way. Ivy's back now, and old Ailsa's good fun to have around and she can do with the cash. We can cope," Pauly promised, swinging as easily as Cristi from despair to eagerness. "A baby's nothing."

For her that was how it seemed. She howked

Nicholas around in his rocker like a bag of shopping, handled him with a loving firmness he clearly enjoyed, and wasted no time worrying about problems that hadn't arisen yet. Madeleine didn't think there would be any unfriendly nursery spirits to trouble this child.

Archie had gone to see Cecil because in spite of all she had revealed to him while she was still in hospital he didn't feel he could abandon their marriage as summarily as she seemed ready to do.

Very thin, hair cut short, elaborately made-up, looking as though she'd just spent a fortune at Max Mara, she had confronted him, unnaturally glossy, wretchedly uptight. They couldn't agree about Nicholas.

"We can find somewhere to live that would suit us both and get a nanny for him," Archie urged.

"I won't have anything to do with him. Ever. He must be adopted, he's nothing to do with either of us."

"He's my son."

"How can you say that?" An almost vicious note in her voice made Archie wince.

"You are my wife. You bore him. I have accepted him as my son. You can't play with a life like this, Cecil. He exists, he's a human being. We brought him into the world, I as much as you, since I agreed to the plan."

"That's utterly false. It doesn't make him your son. There are thousands of people out there longing for a baby, waiting lists years long. We can't give him a proper loving home." Still that deep-seated need for her.

"Why not?" Archie's voice was deadly quiet.

"Because we—" She broke off and stared at

him. I need him, she thought. I need his strength and his calm and his tolerance. But do I love him? Do I only want to take from him? But no, there is love. There is that heavenly desire and fulfilment—and there is the slipping away, a small cold voice reminded her, the final refusal of yourself. But I can't do without him; his love will be enough for us both.

She made one tiny movement toward him, so tiny that it was more an instinct than a visible gesture, and in that instant looked into his eyes and saw that she had lost the only thing she wanted in the world. His eyes were kind, concerned, but they no longer found an irresistible beauty in her. She had done that, with her denial of the child. Worse even than destroying his love, she had destroyed his respect.

She didn't lack courage. There were no scenes, no pleading, no hostility. Only the efficient plucking apart, thread by thread, of a marriage which had once held a flawed but marvelous happiness.

The barn was finished, its long upper room satisfying to the eye with its solid proportions and natural materials, but Tom hadn't moved in. Partly he wanted to stay under the same roof as Madeleine, partly he knew she was upset about Archie and Cecil and felt everyone was slipping away from her. Except Pauly, who had largely given up her wild ways and was leading an admirable life of baby care and domesticity. True the pack of admirers was still at her heels, augmented by a Hay grandson, Robin Thorne from Baldarroch and Donald Galloway who had suddenly found Killin much nearer home than he had previously thought. But on the whole Pauly seemed unmoved, and Tom wasn't entirely satisfied that it was only absorption in the children which had brought about the change. Perhaps, even, she was missing Rob. But attractive as the idea was he couldn't convince himself it was the explanation for her subdued mood.

The news which made Madeleine feel more bereft than anything was that Joss was off again. She had seemed so happy, to Madeleine anyway, with the Post Office, her garden, her friendship with the Quebells, the jobs she'd taken on in the glen and her alcoholics support group in Muirend. At this turning point in her own life too, Madeleine realized just how much she relied on Joss's familiar rock-like presence.

"I thought you were so busy and contented," she protested, not attempting to hide her dismay.

"This? This is just playing," Joss said, then made an effort not to be too dismissive when she saw how shattered Madeleine was. "Retirement stuff. I've a few more years left in me yet."

"But you work all the time here. And you were so frustrated about how everything was done in OW. And the political corruption and the waste. Joss, you hated it, you know you did."

"No reason not to go back," Joss said shortly.

"But you love your cottage and having your own place."

"Mads, listen, stop whingeing and I'll try and tell you how I feel. I'd hit a low last year, worn out probably, and I was fighting with everyone and everything. Rolling up here and finding that nattering to you and being with you was just as good as it had always been, in spite of the years, meant a lot to me. Then getting this place, finding I could fit in here, it kind of steadied me and gradually put everything into perspective again. As I said to you that day we were picking currants, knowing that when I've done another stint and am really on my knees I've got somewhere to come back to makes such a difference. Not the old Post Office, of course. I'd have to sell that. But this place, and all of you."

"Oh, Joss, you do have somewhere. This is your home, it truly is. I shall talk to Archie and make sure that there will be somewhere for you, always. He'll be delighted. I only wish you'd settle for it now You've done more than your share, as he once said."

Joss reached out and gave her arm a squeeze which would certainly leave its mark. "No, I haven't," she said. "Try and see that, Mads. For me, I mean, it hasn't been enough. My conscience would never let me give it up so soon. You've no idea what it's like out there, the helplessness and the need . . . And by out there I mean all of it, vast areas, whole countries. I can't walk away from it. I tried, but somewhere deep down it's nagged at me all along. But to go back—wherever they send me—knowing there's a place I can come home to, where there's—well, it's been more than friendship, it's been love—"

She ended on a treacherous gulp, and for the first time in their long relationship they embraced, closely and warmly.

"We'll miss you so much," said Madeleine, openly in tears.

"Yes, and in the first five minutes I'm going to ask myself what the hell I've done, chucking all this away . . ."

Chapter Thirty-five

More startling and just as drastic in its way was Lisa's departure. She came in one evening when Pauly was upstairs bathing Nicholas, helped by Cristi who adored him. Tom was putting in a couple of hours at the accounts before dinner. The kitchen reeked of reduced vinegar and Madeleine was busy labeling an army of jars of the plum chutney she and Pauly had been making.

"Mum, could I talk to you for a minute?"

"Of course, darling." But Madeleine looked up in surprise. As a rule Lisa's life went on its way without much reference to her.

"Would you mind very much if I went to live with Stephen?"

Winded, Madeleine stared at her, a sticky label poised on the tip of her finger. She opened her mouth, realized her first word was going to be "but" and shut it again.

"Only, well, I don't want any fuss—if you don't mind," Lisa added, with a vague idea that mothers were entitled to fuss about this sort of thing.

"To live with Stephen?" Was she really questioning the "live with" rather than the "Stephen"? How could she, when if only she hadn't wrecked everything with Tom she would have longed to do this very thing herself. Then she started up impulsively. "I'm sorry, darling, that was only being taken by surprise. I want you to do whatever makes you happy."

"Honestly?"

"Honestly." And so it was, she found. If only Lisa should not be hurt again. Certainly from what she had seen and heard of Stephen he could not be more different from Howard.

"Well, Stephen doesn't particularly chat me up or anything," Lisa said, doing her best. "But I know he wants me and it feels right, as though I've found the place I'm meant to be. I can't describe it. I know he's selfish—well, he's used to having everything done for him—but I want to look after him, and in other ways he's the least selfish person I've ever met. He understands about people. He makes me feel needed, he likes me the way I am. And then the way they live, it's all so down to earth and it suits me. Growing up here— the way it was, I mean—" seeing her mother's face, "and afterwards, with Howard, a cash value put on everything, the endless striving. With Stephen I'm just myself."

She was looking at her mother appealingly, her strong-jawed face tentative and vulnerable, wanting her not only to understand but to share her happiness. Her mother was mad about Tom; would that help her to understand this?

"Oh, Lisa, I'm so glad. I've seen how relaxed and settled you've grown—and how much time you've been spending at Achalder cottages," Madeleine added with mock severity, reaching up to kiss her large, embarrassed but relieved daughter.

"You can't imagine the mess they live in," Lisa said fondly. "Not the dogs of course. I love it."

"Can I ask though, please don't mind, are you and Stephen—would you like to be married?" On the assumption that Lisa's marriage to Howard had been legal a divorce was going through on the grounds of desertion.

"Neither of us think that's important. He's married to Joyce at present, of course, which we all tend to forget, but they'll sort that out."

"Ah—well, that's good." Really, what else was there to say?

"The only thing is, though—" Lisa looked worried now, not meeting her mother's eyes, and Madeleine wondered what was coming. "Well, about Cristi. I mean, I did sign all the papers and everything, for her adoption, so now that I'll be having a home of my own again would you feel— I mean, am I dumping a responsibility rather? I wasn't sure what you'd think . . ."

"Oh darling, you mustn't worry about that for one moment," Madeleine exclaimed, with a surprisingly sharp pang of possessiveness almost overtaking her wish to reassure Lisa. "All that was decided long ago, and this doesn't change anything. Of course Cristi stays with me, Drumveyn is her home."

"It isn't that I'm not fond of her and all that," Lisa mumbled in embarrassment and relief. "But I'm not sure that Stephen . . ."

"Don't think about it ever again. Anyway, you'll be nearby, you'll still see Cristi all the time. In fact, nothing much will change, you'll just be sleeping in a different place."

Oh dear, could I have put that better?

"Well, if you're sure that's all right?" It was clearly a token question. Madeleine could tell from Lisa's grateful face that she would do just as her mother had told her and never give the matter another thought.

"Of course it is. So, when do you think you might move down to East Achalder?"

After Stephen's divorce? Will Joyce leave? Will they do any work on the cottage or need things from here? Will there be some kind of party to arrange? Madeleine suppressed all these questions.

"Well, now, this evening," Lisa said. "That's what I wanted to say, really."

"Lisa!" But Madeleine was laughing, shock overtaken by the beautiful simplicity of it. Why not? Why not just walk down the hill and across the river, past the barking wagging ever-hopeful dogs, and take up life with Stephen? "It sounds wonderful."

Laughing, tears close, they clung to each other.

"I never thought you'd take it so well," Lisa admitted. "You'd have hit the roof a year ago."

"I certainly would," Madeleine agreed equably. "Perhaps I should now. Oh, but I'm going to miss you."

"No, you're not. You'll see me every day. You know I'll always be in and out, and in any case I'd really like you to come down and get to know Joyce and Mrs. Q properly."

"Not Stephen?" Madeleine inquired smiling.

"Oh, he's hopeless," said Lisa lovingly. "But Mrs. Q isn't all that well again, she'd love more company. Joyce and I are always busy outside."

It struck her mother that Joyce was almost as important in all this as Stephen and wondered if it wasn't the whole ménage which drew Lisa. She couldn't wait to talk it all over with Tom, a pleasure still thankfully unspoiled.

"So, will you be having dinner here or there?"

she asked, playing up the practical briskness, and was rewarded with a great happy laugh.

So the household dwindled again as November closed in with a sky like steel wool and a slow plopping from neglected eaves that drove Tom mad. Last year Platt and Mrs. Platt and I, thought Madeleine, this year Pauly and the children and I, and Tom till he goes to the barn, which he surely must do soon.

Yet how different it was. The dismal weather didn't matter in the beautiful chaotic kitchen, or in the sitting room with its scatter of children's things, Roxie sprawled in front of the fire, often opera pouring out, a taste Pauly unexpectedly shared with Tom, and Nicholas asleep in spite of it in the former dining room next door.

Archie too, tired after a tightly-scheduled trip to India, trying to put Cecil out of his mind but shocked to find how antagonistic he felt toward her, had braced himself for the depressing atmosphere of winter all too well remembered from other years. Coming into the bright sitting room after a slush-pelted drive up, with Cristi and Roxie jostling to welcome him, with Pauly smiling up at him from the floor where was she cutting up— *what*, the Melton cloth for recovering the billiard table?—to make a stuffed frog, Nicholas burbling in his rocker on one of Grannie's inlaid tables, he felt with a sharp rise of spirits that gloom would never get a toehold here again.

It was a brief visit and for the few days he was at Drumveyn he was mostly out and about the estate with Tom. Every building on the place seemed to need attention one way or another, and every piece of work undertaken led to at least two more. One job in progress was putting in a damp course at Malkie's cottage. Archie had been ashamed at the state it was found to be in when work began.

"Aye well, it is ca'ed the Birnie," Ailsa had pointed out with a sly cackle. "That's the oozy place, is it no'?" She was so used to the damp she was indifferent to it but some new wallpaper that would stay on the wall would be fine.

Craig MacNeil, who had wasted no time in repining when he had finally given up his hopeless quest for Pauly, was now engaged to Ivy and Sandy's daughter Trish, and they would be needing a house.

Archie finally brought himself to talk about Cecil, on a bitter afternoon spent with Tom looking at sites for next spring's tree planting. For the first time he put into words his guilt at failing her, and admitted that his love had not survived her rejection of Nicholas.

"I shouldn't have agreed to the pregnancy in the first place. I should have seen neither of us was sufficiently committed to our own relationship, never mind starting a family. A whole life, brought into being for a whim. And how could she refuse even to hold him, a beautiful child like that, totally dependent, our responsibility? Then I find myself wondering if it was just post-natal depression. Perhaps she's longing for him now and can't bring herself to say so."

"Would you like me to go down and talk to her?"

"You're the only one she might talk to. Would you mind doing that, Tom? I'd be so grateful. I need to be sure she's all right."

Tom found Cecil sad beyond words, brittle and

dismissive. "I'm just not capable of loving, Tom—Archie or the baby. Water under the bridge."

"Weren't you and Archie happy together before your pregnancy?"

"Happy?" She remembered the reserves never broken down, the frustration of never being able to give herself completely. Could she tell Tom, lose for one moment the sense of being forever outside emotions which other people took for granted? Impossible. "It suited us at the time, I suppose, but it was all rather a travesty, wasn't it?"

Tom knew she had come as close as she ever could to reaching out, and had drawn back. Nothing he could say would help. "What will you do?" he asked quietly, much moved.

"Does it matter?" she asked with a shrug of her thin shoulders, turning away from his compassionate eyes. "It's always been like this. To touch is to destroy," she added with a laugh. Not a pleasant laugh. "I'm going to work in Paris for a while. I've had a rather flattering offer. Then I'll decide where I want to be."

"You'll keep the studio?"

"This?" She glanced round disparagingly. "Oh, I'm tired of this. So pretentious, don't you think?"

She was right, Tom thought driving home, full of pity for her yet glad to be out of her rarified aura. There was a deadly chill of destruction in all she touched.

He took the journey slowly, a little startled to find how much he wanted time alone. The feeling he had of his relationship with Madeleine, indeed his whole life, being on the back burner was beginning to weigh on him. He blamed himself entirely for misjudging Madeleine's readiness to go to bed with him, and found it hard to forgive his naivety and blindness in acting as he had. Fatal anyway to choose a moment of harried feelings and heightened drama, after being so determined that when they made love it would be because Madeleine wanted it enough for every other consideration to vanish.

He had not imagined so many weeks would pass without their sorting it all out. Where had the time gone? With Archie away, he, Tom, had certainly had to spend a lot more time on the hill than he had anticipated, right through stag stalking and well into the hinds. Archie had wanted a thorough cull this year, and certainly old lax habits had led to a damaging increase in the deer population, both red and roe. And though he had never for a moment regretted the departure of Ross Miller it had meant a lot of extra involvement in the direct running of the farm for himself.

On Madeleine's side, though Pauly was always on hand, it seemed possible to waste an awful lot of hours on Nicholas, enjoying him in a way Tom knew had never been possible for her with Archie and Lisa. She also spent lots of time with Cristi, feeling that after a day at the glen school she needed more than the exclusive company of Jill and Dougal. A good many books and games had found their way down from the nursery to Grannie's ex-sitting room and Madeleine found it a nostalgic pleasure to share them with this different child in an atmosphere free of critical observation and comment.

But it's not just time, Tom told himself impatiently, shifting in his seat in frustration at the whole situation. It hadn't just been his crassness of choosing that damned flat for the big moment, or of starting to strip off poor Madeleine's clothes like some over-eager schoolboy—Madeleine had obviously had a bad time with Charles and all that should have been brought out into the open, cleared out of the way, before he waded in himself.

Well, there was something else to be brought into the open too, he reminded himself. What if he'd simply turned her off? What if he was a lousy lover? No one could have described sex with Wilma as glorious and though he'd been unfaithful to her twice during their marriage, neither affair had had much substance, being principally escape, and both were a while ago. He'd never worried about the idea before, but after all, how did one ever know? And Wilma had turned sour on him quite soon after they were married; it had never occurred to him that it might have been because he didn't satisfy her.

The decision to move to the barn nagged at the back of his mind all the time. With Lisa at Achalder and Archie away no one had thought twice about his remaining at the big house. Or had they? Might Madeleine herself have wondered why he stayed? Another thing they hadn't discussed. But he felt that if he moved out it would be a decisive, perhaps distancing move. A year ago it would have been all he could have dreamed of. A new and absorbing job, this perfect dwelling created to his own specification, a place where the boys were happy to come (or had Rob too received a wound that would keep him away for a while?) and the new affections and friendships so generously offered. There was no excuse for staying any longer in the flat, but day after day he had put off making the move. After Christmas he must go. Till then they all had more than enough to do.

It was as well that the two children held this little group together in a workable surface cheerfulness, for all the adults during that foggy, mild and damp December had withdrawn into their own doubts and preoccupations. Pauly in particular was forcing herself to have a good look at her circumstances and she was not satisfied with what she saw. Honest and direct to a fault, she knew that she had begun to slide into the sort of fantasies about Archie that could only lead to grief.

She could only imagine what he must be going through to have lost Cecil, and when she thought of Cecil's talent and looks she was furiously ashamed of her childish dreams. So what are you going to do about it, she would ask herself angrily, pummeling bread dough or making ferocious and frequently destructive attacks on linen room or cluttered cupboards. You can't just sit here year after year mooing and bawling like a cow whose calf's gone to market.

And she thought of the children, of the casual way Cristi had been tossed into a new world, and needed more than anything stability and security. For her, as far as possible, the years of childhood should be settled and unchanging. Commitment. Pauly thought of Nicholas, inevitably bonding with the person who handled and fed him most, the person who was there at waking, who appeared in the night when he cried. He was too young to know now if this figure disappeared or changed, but soon he wouldn't be.

Do I want to spend the next ten years in this house, with Archie coming and going and all that brings of anticipation and wrenching loss, pushing down feelings, perhaps having after a while to see him with someone else, letting these children, who are not mine, burrow deeper and deeper into my heart, and know it's all hopeless?

And dishonest. This was where she really jibbed. It would be a pretense and one that she wasn't sure she could handle. But she had promised Madeleine she would stay. Anyway, unthinkable to let her down now, just before Christmas. But afterwards she must be responsible and face up to it all properly.

Her parents were to be part of the Christmas party. Madeleine had been trying for some time to persuade Pauly to invite them up and she had finally agreed, with a big show of kicking and protesting.

"I suppose they are getting a bit desperate to see me, poor things. Aren't parents odd? What a drag. I'll tell them there's no room here though, they can stay in the village, or better still at the Cluny Arms, that's further away."

"You'll do no such thing. I shall write myself."

"Oh God, no sex, no dope, no alcohol, some festive season . . ."

Not even in childhood had there been a Christmas like this at Drumveyn, Archie thought, loading the twelfth plate with turkey. Tom had just gone around again with the wine and sitting down again by Madeleine had given her a little smile that sent a stab of loneliness through Archie. They were taking things at their own pace, these two, which presumably suited them, but the strong base of their affection for each other, perhaps not acknowledged yet as love, was plain to see.

Tom would have liked the boys to have been here but that would have meant Wilma being on her own and he had not made a fight of it. So Rob and Ian were sitting primly at the small table in the dining area, making one pheasant go around and staying sober on Hungarian Riesling.

Joyce and Cristi were less interested in what was on their plates than in what was going on in a box near the Aga, where one of Flora's offspring was celebrating Christmas by being wrested from kith and kin. Mrs. Q's face was the exact color of the wine-red velvet jacket with puffed sleeves she had dug out of some forgotten box. Archie was glad they had a doctor on hand—if a neuro-surgeon would know how to deal with a merry old dear subject to coronaries. But Alan Tobin looked as though he would be able to deal with most things.

Amanda Tobin, a riper and even more voluptuous Pauly in a suede shirt that matched her caramel hair ("not my idea of a forensic scientist," Tom had been startled into muttering) was looking after Stephen, who seemed amused and more than content. Lisa had been positive he wouldn't come, but he wouldn't let her miss this. He understood what she had suffered in this house and he most lovingly wanted to be sure that she was part of its changing mood. He still couldn't believe his luck in winning the trust of this gauche affectionate girl. To him she was a magical combination of the competence he would always admire in a woman, a yearning to be needed which made her endearingly dependent, and a firm young body which generously welcomed him. He'd almost forgotten how wonderful that was. Nor would she ever want to change him or try to program his life. As for the party, he thought he could stand

it on the whole as the sort of food he never saw
at Achalder kept arriving, the lively noise swelled,
and Amanda Tobin, leaning closer to be heard,
also swelled enchantingly.

Archie had been impressed by the change in
Lisa, her cheerful confidence bringing back vividly
the plump, tough, boisterous sister of early years.
Stephen was a lot older than she was, of course,
but seeing them together Archie had to concede
that, like Tom and Madeleine, they had found
some secret which had eluded him.

He also watched Pauly, hair wild and cheeks
flushed to a lovely peachy glow, rushing about
keeping the perfect food coming, picking up Nicholas for a quick cuddle, giving Cristi a hug of
thanks for helping, beaming to see the parents she
clearly adored so readily at home here. She was
looking dramatically different today, in a blouse
of emerald and silver stripes with huge sleeves
and high collar which belonged to her mother.
The vivid color was spectacular on her, Archie
thought—and what those stripes did to her shape
as she thrust out her bosom, demanding, "Well,
which do I look more like, Christmas wrapping
paper or Madame Cyn?"

They drank a toast to wish Joss well wherever
her new assignment would take her, and blushing
and gruff she made a few ungracious remarks in
reply, to the effect that she supposed now she was
letting down everyone in the village, and trust her
to have just got the garden straight.

This effort was wildly applauded and Archie
had trouble making himself heard. "I think the
WRI will scrape along till you come back, Joss,
but remember that there's a house here for you
when you do." His eyes met his mother's, who

managed a wobbly smile of thanks. "Until then your home is Drumveyn, and we want to see you here as often as you can manage."

Joss banged at her eyes and couldn't find her napkin and everyone tried to hug her and Cristi flew for the kitchen roll. Madeleine was choked with tears. It had meant so much having Joss turn up on that awful day last winter and to have her nearby all this year. And somehow, with things still unresolved with Tom—or perhaps not unresolved, but over, she felt she couldn't tell any more—the thought of not having Joss on hand was truly dismaying.

Pauly, trying to subdue the ache in her heart to see Nicholas grinning gummily in the crook of Archie's arm, knew she couldn't bear this torture much longer. She must go back—to what? What had she done before? What in all that careless, transient, irresponsible life had meant anything at all compared to this?

She did not meet her father's eyes and would have been amazed at what he was thinking. Nothing would save her from grief and hurt.

Chapter Thirty-six

The landscape was clamped, iron-hard, in a spell of bitter weather which seemed to go on and on. Still, leached of color, the days succeeded each other with hoar-frosts at morning and freezing fog holding the rime on ground and trees well into the day, sometimes all day. Everything seemed to be waiting—for the soft touch of snow, for the blast of a gale, or, utterly remote as it might seem, for some sign that spring would eventually come.

And clamped in icy suspension Madeleine felt her own life to be. Often and often during those days she would feel her throat ache with threatening tears that all the promise of last year seemed after all to have returned her to frozen waiting and loneliness. There are the children now, she would remind herself. But they were part of the problem. Much as she loved and enjoyed them they tied her utterly. Tom at the barn seemed as unreachable as Pauly, now at home in Buckinghamshire with her parents.

Oh, Pauly. How much they had all depended on her and how devastating it had been when she had suddenly changed her mind and said she wanted to go. "Not much good at settling down," she had said with a surprising off-handedness. "I suppose it always was a bit temporary, wasn't it?"

"Of course it was," Madeleine had rushed to agree, anxious to exonerate her of all blame. "It's been wonderful having you here so long. Of course I understand you'll want to be off on your travels again."

What had gone wrong? What had upset her? Had one among her pursuers hurt her in some way? All Madeleine could do, hating to intrude, was offer to help if she could. She could not miss the distress beneath the uncharacteristic abruptness, but Pauly was keeping it stringently under control. Even when she said goodbye to the children, her face tight and pale with stress, she hadn't shed a tear. Perhaps she knew if she did there would be tears in torrents and waterfalls, Madeleine divined correctly, for that moment of all others nearly broke Pauly's hard-held control.

To Madeleine at parting on Perth station she had said only, "I'm sorry, Maddy. Thank you for everything you've given me. It's just that—oh, restless, you know, hopeless case . . ."

But it seemed that she hadn't taken off anywhere yet, according to Amanda Tobin, with whom almost unnoticed Madeleine had begun a correspondence, growing from her reply to Amanda's Christmas thank-you letter.

Besides the huge gap left by Pauly there had come Tom's long-deferred departure. He seemed quite contented in his solitude, settled in at the barn exactly as she had first envisaged him, with Roxie, his music, his books—his impossible books that were all called things like *Cradock on Shotguns* and *Robson's Guide to Still Water Trout Flies: an Alphabetical Survey in Color. Rites of Autumn* had sounded more promising, but had turned out to be *A Falconer's Journey across the American West*. Thinking of them evoked loving amusement, then a pang of vivid envy. He was so peaceful, so self-contained.

Tom wondered if he would ever be free of the nag of self-reproach and doubt. Had he missed his chance for good? Madeleine was always so busy with the children, with the house, with Mac-Ivor the Dinmont puppy who had been Joyce's Christmas present to Cristi. She was always welcoming, always of course courteous and charming, but the early days when they had first admitted their feelings for each other now seemed far away. Kisses and embraces had begun to seem self-conscious, for him anyway, and he was no longer sure she wanted them. How in hell had they got themselves to this point? But deciding to go down and confront her, sort it out one way or the other, he would be racked by uncertainty about whether he still attracted her. Perhaps the whole thing was dying a natural death? As in the beginning, he felt he needed an unmistakable sign from her; the prospect of it seemed increasingly remote.

Archie tossed the letter aside and dropped his head into his hands with a groan. Here was the offer he had thought might come, an excellent offer; a one year lectureship at the university of Pôto Alegre in Rio Grande do Sul.

And he knew he didn't want to do it. He didn't want to accept anything that took him halfway across the world or even kept him here in London. He wanted to be at Drumveyn. With the sharp frustrated anger of one who has reached this stage in his thoughts many times before, he got up brusquely and went to pour himself a dram. Swilling the large tot he'd given himself around the glass he suddenly checked. Was that really the only recourse he had? It was a habit he had never had to worry about before but making a rapid check he realized how much he'd been drinking over the last few weeks. He put the glass down and turned back to his desk.

He felt actually incapable of making a decision about the Brazilian job. He would go up to Drumveyn to be there for the meeting with the Forestry Commission. Tom, as he had amply demonstrated, was more than capable of handling it on his own, Archie reminded himself. Well, he would see how his mother was getting on with this girl she had taken on to replace Pauly. Replace Pauly! He let out a harsh bark of laughter. The very words were ridiculous. But of course there had to be someone to look after the children. At least his mother hadn't insisted on a butler.

He knew the excuse was thinner than the forestry planning one, but he had a powerful compulsion to go north and examining it found it was based on a fear that without Pauly the mainspring of the big house's daily life would have failed. Had they all been blind to what she had given them? It seemed so now.

A memory returned of the night when all the Christmas and Hogmanay festivity had died down, when Tom had been flitted into the barn, though refusing a house-warming party, and Pauly's parents had left for home. The remnants of the family, worn out by celebrations, had gone early to bed. Only Archie had not felt like sleep. He had sat over a last drink in the quiet kitchen, looking around the big room still full of the good food smells of the day, and had observed Pauly's unmistakable stamp super-imposed on Cecil's elegant design. The tiled shelf was submerged under a miscellany of objects. Two messy saucers were on the floor beside MacIvor's bowl. A draught reached him from an open window and a little dirty track across the green and yellow cushions showed where the cats came in and the central heating went out. Pauly would be bottle-feeding lambs in here come April, he remembered thinking—and the next day she had delivered her bombshell. Why? He still didn't understand it.

He remembered another occasion when he had found, scrawled in one of Cristi's felt pens on an opened-up sugar bag which was obviously all Pauly had had to hand, a roughly hatched diagram covered with notes in her huge writing, "Lovage, fennel—v. tall. Rosemary—hedge? Tarragon—spreads like mad, MOVE." Warmth had spread through him as he had recognized plans for reclaiming the herb garden. A promise for the future.

His mind ranged nostalgically over other pictures—the day Cristi had finally wheedled Pauly into riding. Pauly had pretended she was frightened, had begged Tom to tell her what to do, finally hauling herself with a struggle on to a circling Cuil to the hysterical delight of the children. Then she had jumped the pony neatly out of the field and back again, surprising him as much as anyone.

There had been the day when he had arrived up for Christmas to find the house empty, a couple of hundred mince pies cooling on racks on the kitchen table, the cats asleep in the puppy's basket, the ironing board out and the iron on. I suppose I should be grateful she left it on its heel, he had thought, without being able to raise much indignation. He had gone out to look for signs of life, heading up the road to the farm, and had met a little group coming toward him. Even before he picked out its component parts the words "my family" had leapt into his mind. Pauly had been pushing the pram, Cristi was on Iona, Jill on her bike with Roxie prancing around her, and who was that on Cuil? His mother, with the easy seat of someone taught to ride as a child, looking very young under her hard hat, cheeks bright in the brisk wind. The sight had taken him back twenty years. She looked marvelous.

They had surrounded him with shrieks of welcome and surprise, since he'd managed to come a day earlier than expected. MacIvor had put his head questioningly over the side of the pram, where Nicholas was profoundly asleep. This is where I want to be, Archie had realized, with an odd weakening lurch of his stomach. Everything I want is here. And the core of it all had been Pauly and Pauly had gone.

Madeleine sat alone in the sitting room. Even through the closed door she could hear the ceaseless blare of Radio One. Perhaps after all she would have to go back to using the drawing room, since at least it was out of earshot of the kitchen. But surely Carol had said she was going to bed early after last night's disco in Kirkton? Madeleine walked into the brilliantly lit kitchen to find the radio yelling away to itself. At the closed window the faces of the cats pressed wistfully. Carol hated them. Madeleine let them in and as she turned from the window took in the state of the room.

It had taken on a different look, a sort of barren cleanliness. Carol got very aggressive about hygiene, went through miles of clingfilm, always had the place smelling of some horribly scented cleaning product, had done away with the plants and kept the laundry in the utility room, where Mac-Ivor's basket had also been banished in spite of Cristi's tearful protests. Yet Carol personally was not tidy, and now on the table lay a turned-back paperback, a much thumbed *TV Times* (for the kitchen now had its own television, the dread phrase "live as family" not having survived twenty-four hours for Carol and Madeleine), a dirty mug and plate, and a white sliced loaf, its wrapper torn and open, its crust tossed down beside it.

Madeleine stood there, riveted, and the months reeled back like film. Platt and Mrs. Platt and their long uncouth dominion. That single object, the white sliced loaf, suddenly crystallized everything for her. She had come full circle. She had been subservient to others all her life, had freed herself, had truly believed she was free, and now was sliding straight back into the trap.

Had her freedom depended so entirely on other people? Now that they were gone was she going feebly to succumb to the first challenge she met? What had happened to her new image of herself, her confidence? Ten minutes ago she had actually thought of retreating to the drawing room again. This girl, this undeniably hard-working girl, competent with Nicholas, accepted by Cristi, with her adequate food and rigorous time-keeping, wielding her squeegee mop and spraying the loos with hideous air fresheners, would take over just as Platt had done. If I let her.

I must control what happens. I must take the initiative. Surely, surely in this last year I have learned something. I will not let my life be channeled and restricted again. *I* must make the moves. And suddenly she knew what she must do. Give this drab child notice, certainly, find some arrangement that would really work but also she knew what she must do, now, without delay, about Tom. That was what mattered.

Checking only that Carol was in her room and the children both asleep she pulled on coat and boots and let herself out into the freezing night. Her torch shone on the glitter of freshly rimed tarmac and lit a bowl of silver fog in which she hurried forward, her breath trailing white, her fingertips icy in the gloved hand that held the torch, the other holding her collar close at her throat.

If there was any light at the curtained window of the barn it wasn't strong enough to penetrate the fog. She let herself in, and thankfully saw the warm flood of light coming down the open stairs, heard Verdi, reasonably muted, rolling splendidly above, felt warmth enfold her. But she would have come in, she knew, even if Tom had gone to bed.

Roxie heard Madeleine when she was halfway up the stairs and gave one soft whuff of welcome. She expected only friends to arrive. Reaching the top of the stairs Madeleine paused. The room looked wonderful, its wood and stone and the tawny velvet curtains which covered the great window softly lit by two big low lamps. Tom was sitting by one of them, the light gleaming on his brown bald pate, looking up at her in surprise over his reading glasses. Then putting down his book he came quickly to his feet.

"Madeleine, what's wrong? Is it one of the children?"

"Nothing's wrong with anyone."

"Thank God for that." He was looking into her face, puzzled but trying not to show it. She saw him not look at his watch; dear Tom. "Well, it's lovely to see you. Would you like a drink—or I can make coffee—"

As he turned to gesture her to a chair, begin the hospitable stir of making her welcome, she clutched at his arm to stop him, releasing it at once as though that was assuming too much. He looked at her in query.

"Tom, would you mind—could we talk?"

But before he could answer she saw that here too she was ready if not to off-load the initiative, then at least to share it. "No, I mean, I'd like to talk. I'd like to say to you things I should have said long ago." Infuriatingly her voice had begun to shake.

"Maddy, of course we can talk." At a loss, anxious because she was clearly wound up, but with a great joyful hope beginning to coil inside him, Tom tried to draw her forward gently to the circle of light and the chairs.

"I never get a grip on things." She seemed rooted where she stood. He could feel the cold air off her coat; there was foggy dew on her dark hair. "Joss would say that," she added with a little strangled laugh which he was only half relieved to hear.

"Sweetheart, it's all right—"

"I've let all this time go by," she went on as though he hadn't spoken. "I'm just as useless as I've always been. I saw it all tonight. Carol's just going to turn into another Platt."

Tom wasn't sure the ex-butler had a relevant role here but wasn't going to hurry her.

"And I was so awful to you, so cruel. And afterwards I did nothing about it. I just waited for you to decide. I've always done that, waited for other people to make decisions for me. But now I want to tell you this. I love you very dearly, I've missed you desperately since you came to live up here, I hurt and ache when we are so polite to each other. I wanted you to make love to me, I needed it. No, no," she cried as, voice hard to summon, he tried to offer reassurance, "I must say all this. Maybe you don't feel the same way any more." He made a sharp movement of protest to which she shut her eyes. "I don't know if it would be good for you, I don't know what will happen, I may have hang-ups I'll never be free of, I just don't know. But I want you. I want that loving. I've wanted it for months."

"God, Madeleine." Shaken, intensely moved by her honesty and courage, his body making its own uncomplicated response even while his brain was warning, "Go gently now," he seized her by the arms and stared into her face.

She nodded, answering the question in his eyes. "I've been such a coward. Perhaps I've left it too late. Perhaps you don't want me after all." Always that sort of ingrained politeness, ending on a little sob of half-laughter.

"Want you." His eyes wet, the muscles of his mouth oddly out of control, Tom wrapped his arms around her in a consuming crushing grip.

"Tom." Wordless moments had passed, their bodies molded close, peace returning. Roxie had given them up as a bad job and padded back to her beanbag.

"Yes."

"I want to stay now. Would that be all right?" Still the good-little-girl deference she had never lost. It sounded absurdly, deliciously funny now.

"I think that would be in order," Tom said gravely, but his voice sounded queer and he didn't seem to be breathing very evenly.

In the warm, secluded room, where the bed was a few steps away, it seemed suddenly so simple to take off her heavy coat and go on taking things off, Tom's hands coming to help her with the high-necked sweater, their eyes on each other, smiling, sure. In this light I might not look too bad, she thought, but it was cheerful, unimportant, a worry belonging to the past.

Tom thought, there ought to be a lead-up to this, this is where I blew it before. But he too went on taking off his clothes, and the thought had no impact. He was a second and a half ahead of her and she stood for a moment looking at the chunky well-muscled body on the bed, the duvet thrown back, the curve of his arm waiting for her. That was where she wanted to be.

Roxie lifted her head to give them a long considering stare. Because she was three-quarters asleep it made her look owlishly disapproving and they laughed at her.

"Mind your own business, dog," Tom ordered as he drew Madeleine comfortably down beside him.

"I might be hopeless," she warned him again, with a sharper edge of anxiety this time.

Tom suddenly remembered that he had feared he might be "hopeless" too. How absurd it seemed; now he was filled with the vigorous confidence of the male who knows beyond all doubt that he's

welcome and wanted. "I never heard anything so
silly," he said, beginning to kiss her. "And remember, this is us. Just us."

Madeleine had never, never imagined anything
like this. The warm sensuous tide, the encapsu-
lated intimacy, the feeling that whatever she was
or did was right for Tom. And she had had no
idea of the startling things her body seemed to
know, released and satisfied at last.

She slept beside him, drifting out of sleep into
moments of intense happy awareness to find herself there, sleeping again with an incomparable
feeling of arrival, of safety. Once Tom asked her,
"Do you think you should go back?" and she
mumbled, "Carol's there. I pay her, don't I?" and
he pulled her closer, grinning. What had he done
to this woman?

Chapter Thirty-seven

Archie walked down from the barn burdened by the feeling of intense loneliness that had become all too familiar in the last few weeks. It was accentuated, he knew, by the unashamed glowing happiness of Tom and his mother. She was so funny. He found he was smiling broadly as he came past the first of the buildings that straggled out behind the courtyard.

She had said so openly, "As you're home, darling, I'll stay up here tonight. I don't altogether trust Carol, particularly now I've given her a month's notice. But of course if you're there it's perfectly all right." Just practical concern about the children; a blithe unconcern about what he might think of her staying with Tom.

But certainly, there had to be some better solution to finding help for her with the house and the children. His thoughts swung at once and inevitably to Pauly. He had barely realized, till this first visit since her departure, how all his reviving pleasure in Drumveyn had been tied up with her. Had depended entirely on her, he was beginning to think, remembering how he would walk in on some family group, busy, contented, instantly welcoming, and it was the sight of Pauly that made his heart lift—Pauly pink-cheeked and spice-smelling, flour and egg-shells everywhere, in full flow of creating some exotic pudding—Pauly harassed and wild-haired beside Cristi at the kitchen table, homework spread out before them, exclaiming in relief, "Thank God you've come, you can do these horrible sums for us." That had to be worth driving five hundred miles for.

Why had she gone? And how could he hope that she would ever come back? She was nineteen years old, for God's sake, a natural wanderer. She needed new scenes, new people, people her own age. Someone her own age, you mean, he amended doggedly, someone who could be a focus for all her warmth and capacity for love, who would love her in return; someone who could give her children.

Yes, that was the crux. He checked, faced at last all that final thought revealed. He, Archie, could give her all the love in the world, and longed to do so, but he couldn't give her children, and for a girl like Pauly not to have children was unthinkable. He had failed Cecil there; he would not inflict such a wound on Pauly. But he could give her Cristi and Nicholas, an inner voice persisted. She adored them both. Yes, and like a complacent fool he had thought she would never be able to tear herself away from them, would somehow, without any decision or action on his part, be always at Drumveyn. And now she had gone, quite rightly, to get on with her own life . . .

His attention was caught by a high crying sound, thin on the cold air. A buzzard? Not at this time of night. A rabbit in the grip of a weasel? It came again, a doleful whimpering. A puppy? MacIvor? Surely he hadn't been left out by mistake? The sound led Archie to the old game larder, now used as a store. The slatted door was shut; he heard the wheeking of the puppy change to an excited note as it realized someone was near. But as Archie opened the door MacIvor didn't hurtle out to meet him. Puzzled, he found the puppy in his torch's beam, and a sadder spectacle he'd seldom seen. Muddy, draggled and shivering Mac-Ivor shrank back uncertainly, one paw raised, huge eyes pathetic and pleading.

"Poor old boy, what's happened to you?"

Longing for comfort, MacIvor crept forward on his belly, but as Archie reached out to pick him up he shrank back instantly.

He's been hit, Archie thought in disbelief. He's been shut out here cold and wet for God knows how long, and someone's given him a fright as well. Carol. It could be no one else. The cold-hearted little bitch, she was always complaining about the animals being allowed in the kitchen. Talking gently to the puppy Archie soon persuaded him to let himself be picked up. In his four months of life MacIvor had on the whole encountered only lavish love from human beings and today's traumas were soon forgotten.

Archie took him in and rubbed him dry, warmed some milk for him, fetched his basket and pulled it close to the Aga. Standing watching him plummet into sleep, belly round and full, he felt as his mother had felt seeing Carol's harmless loaf of bread, that this was a moment of catalyst. They had somehow let this mean-minded alien girl into their home, into their lives, when they had had Pauly—darling, slapdash, clumsy, beautiful Pauly, pouring out on them her generosity and energy and time and care, stinting nothing.

Just as his mother had done in that moment of

sharp awareness which had given her the courage
to go to Tom and tell him how she felt about him,
so Archie saw with salutary clearness how ready he
had been to let others make decisions for him. He
had seen himself as independent, shaking free of
his father's repressive hold, but in fact he had
been far too ready to let life slide easily along.
The firm grip Tom had taken of estate problems
had freed him of worries there. He had lived with
Cecil according to her laws. He had let Pauly slip
through his fingers because he had assumed she
would always be there, without any effort on his
part. He hadn't even tried to find out why she
had gone. Now he wanted to know that much at
least, to contest her reasons if he thought fit. And
he wanted her to know his feelings for her, so that
she could take those into the equation.

He looked around the bare kitchen, no longer
the hub of warmth and company and laughter
that Pauly had made it, and he saw that his own
life was equally drab without her. His house in
Richmond, where the clutter of a past he didn't
want to hold on to gathered dust, his lack of moti-
vation about the work which had once been of
such burning interest to him, the loneliness of
even this beloved place without her.

The contentment of Tom and his mother seemed
in this bleak moment impossible of achievement
for him. He thought of Lisa up to her ears in All-
in-One and worm pills at Achalder, of Joss with
her conscience once more at rest doing the job she
saw as hers. They all had their place. He thought
of the children asleep upstairs. We promised to
look after them but we're still handing them
around like parcels. They, and Drumveyn, are my

job, and I shall do it. But not alone, please not alone.

The lane ran along the ridge, large houses in big gardens succeeding each other on his left. He drove slowly, near her now, not quite ready for the problems of whether she would be there or not, busy or free, with people or alone. And he discovered too, with a wry amusement, that he was greedy for every detail of her environment, the home where she had grown up.

Amanda Tobin herself opened the door, a hall wide as a room behind her, the glow of her toffee-colored hair under the porch light bringing instant stabbing physical longing for Pauly.

"Archie, what a lovely surprise! Come in." Welcoming, warm, but Archie didn't miss the fact that her brain was swiftly assessing this unannounced arrival. Nor did she immediately offer to call Pauly. Did that mean Pauly wasn't there?

Alan Tobin, hearing Archie's voice, came out from a room on the left, his face lighting up in pleasure, and Tom was drawn into a big and beautiful room. Nothing younger here than the eighteenth century, he noted, soothed in spite of himself by its well-used, well-cared-for air.

"I'm sorry to arrive like this without warning." At least they weren't entertaining and didn't look as though they were about to. He knew he couldn't deal with any social preamble either. "I'd like to talk to Pauly if I may. Is she here?" Three small crucial words. His voice failed to ask them naturally.

"She's here."

But in spite of the surge of pure relief Archie

knew at once that it wasn't going to be quite that simple.

"Have a drink, Archie," Alan Tobin was saying, going across to a well-stocked walnut table which bore the signs of long service. Well, a drink would certainly help. Had he come from Scotland today? The journey, the roads, the snow further north . . .

The whiskey hit the spot and steadied him.

"This isn't a casual visit, I take it?" Alan asked.

Amanda's grave awaiting expression told Archie it was the question she too would have put.

He placed his glass carefully on a porcelain coaster with a fishing fly painted on it—old-fashioned double-hooked Blue Charm, he registered with the astonishing irrelevancy of the brain in moments of tension—while his stomach started slowly to churn. "I want to ask Pauly to come back to Drumveyn."

They nodded, neither making any objection, yet in some way Archie sensed they were not quite satisfied. A small silence stretched.

"She's very unhappy," Amanda said at last, not making an accusation of it, rather sharing her deep anxiety with Archie.

Pauly, unhappy. Suddenly he could bear it no longer "If I could . . ."

"Of course."

Blessed people, they let him go to find her alone. She was in a small room at the back of the house, half sitting room, half conservatory, prone in a shabby old armchair, staring at a screen where Michael Fish mouthed and gestured at black raindrops over England and blue patches over Scotland. She had the remote control in her hand and Archie had the impression that she had been slumped here clicking through the channels for a long time.

"Pauly." His voice had no texture, no depth.

She turned her head and came to her feet in one violent movement of shock, her face registering disbelief and then a sort of helpless utter thankfulness he knew she couldn't master and would barely be aware of.

"Pauly." No better, husky, effortful.

She was coming toward him in a huge bound and his heart leapt as he braced himself for the impact of that hefty body. But she caught herself back. The Pauly of this lonely winter was not the spontaneous girl of last summer. She had taught herself some hard lessons.

"Archie, how lovely!" she said as her mother had done. "How's everyone at Drumveyn? Why didn't you let us know you were coming? I didn't hear you arrive. Have you seen—yes, of course you have, or you couldn't have got in, how silly of me . . ."

Flood of words to help her through the moment, while she warned herself, "Don't hope, don't go mad, just keep it cool, it doesn't mean anything . . ." But to see him there, so completely unlooked-for, solid and strong, his eyes smiling at her, made it hard to summon calm.

The children, Tom and Madeleine, Lisa—and the dogs, cats and ponies, naturally, Archie thought with resigned love. It was easy to talk, to fall at once into rapid chat, leaving sentences half-finished, releasing emotion in gabble and laughter.

"And how is my replacement getting along?" Pauly asked gaily, biting the bullet.

"Pauly, she's a disaster." He would take this chance. He told her about MacIvor, and the ready tears sprang to her eyes. "But worse, she keeps the kitchen tidy, hasn't scorched the ironing since she arrived, and hasn't smashed a single heirloom."

With the tears still on her lashes he watched her mobile face break into her big happy smile. "So you see, darling Pauly, you'll have to come back." Her eyes fixed on him, delight dawning. "You can see that we really need you, can't do without you in fact—"

Somehow the radiance was fading. She looked down, her eyes hidden from him, and he saw her visibly take control of her reactions.

"Pauly? Will you come? Or perhaps you've got something else set up by now. I should have asked you what your plans were, of course." His mother speaking. He didn't want to know her plans; if they existed he wanted to sweep them into oblivion.

"No, no plans." A different Pauly now. Quiet, very much in control. "But I won't come back, Archie. Thank you very much for asking, and I'm sorry if you came all this way specially for that. But no, I think that bit of my life is over. Must move on. Much as I loved it, of course . . ." Not quite so much in control there.

"But Pauly, won't you even think about it?" He had never imagined there would exist this icy sense of finality, as though a steel band were tightening around his heart. "We do need you. We could get some help for you, Trish might come in—"

"No!" For once in her life Pauly sounded really sharp. "No, Archie, it's nothing to do with that. Honestly, it wouldn't work, and that's all there is to it. Now let's go and have a drink with the parents, they're bound to want to talk to you . . ."

He drove a hundred yards along the lane and pulled up, blind and shaking. Was that it? Was he going to accept dismissal without, as he felt, even being given the chance to talk. Being given the chance. Was this the fatal Napier flaw—or the flaw inherited from Madeleine—this courteous acquiescence, this readiness to see another person's point of view? Was he going to give up this matchless person without even making her understand how he felt about her? Without ever having time alone with her, getting to know her properly, for herself? He had thought she would respond to the children's need; he hadn't talked about his own.

He left the car where it was and went back. Alan opened the door this time, took one look at Archie's face and nodded, a hand indicating the sitting room door. Pauly was where she had been before, the television off now, her supple body curled up in the big chair, shaking with muffled sobs.

"Pauly, no, I'm not going to let this happen. Here, come here." He knelt in front of her, pulled her against him. "I'm not going to let you go. If you won't go back to Drumveyn I'll take you somewhere else. My life has been completely meaningless since you went away. You are the only woman I want and I'm not going to let you leave me again—"

"I thought you just wanted a cook," she sobbed, searching vainly for something to mop up her streaming tears.

"A cook?" Even in that moment, laughter rose

from somewhere. "You complete idiot, do you think I'd drive all the way down from Scotland to ask you to come and cook for us again?"

"But you know what I mean," she said, struggling up and cleaning her face with a wild swipe of her arm. "You said you all missed me and needed me. I know and I hate the thought of it, but I can't come back because of that. I couldn't be there and spend all my time longing for you to turn up and then breaking my heart every time you went away again. It was *awful*, I couldn't face it again."

"Pauly." His anguished concern at this revelation was stark in his voice. "Oh, come here. What a fool I've been."

"I assume we can take it that matters have moved forward somewhat?" Alan Tobin queried dryly as they came plastered together into the drawing room. Amanda took one look at them and came to kiss her daughter's drenched and beaming face and to hug her delightedly.

"I'm going to take her back with me," Archie said, when the excitement had died down a little.

"You amaze me," commented Alan.

"I meant now."

"We do have beds," protested Amanda. "Or bed, if you must."

"Mum!" Pauly exclaimed, her nineteen years betrayed in that shocked reaction.

"I think if you don't mind we'd rather start for home tonight," Archie said, feeling rather like nineteen himself.

"A bit dramatic, but perhaps drama has its place," Alan remarked, surveying Pauly, her expression quite fatuous with happiness, her nose and eyes red, her hair looking as though she and Archie had already spent the night together.

"Not to be too boring, but were you thinking of taking anything with you?" Amanda enquired mildly, as Pauly seemed besottedly ready to head off into the night with her hand in Archie's.

"Taking what?" she asked, surprised.

"Are you sure you can cope with this?" Amanda asked Archie.

With some hasty packing by her mother, some food produced by Alan in spite of Pauly's assistance, with loving embraces and more tears, they went along the lane to the car.

"Frankly, I think you're doing us a favor, Archie," Alan commented, as he tucked his daughter in. "She's been nothing but a pain in the neck for weeks."

Pauly bounced out of the car again to give him another hug, effectively cutting off further insults.

Laughter again, Archie thought in surging euphoria, laughter and understanding and affection. Laughter, and this heavenly girl to look after, the family made whole once more. He started the car and headed north.

Drumveyn lay sleeping, big gray house quiet in the gray frosty dawn.

"Shouldn't we wait?"

"They won't mind." The bell pealed far away in the kitchen.

"They'll never hear."

"The dogs will."

"Dogs?"

"What do you bet Roxie's visiting?"

Down they came, alarmed, thrilled, amazed, excited, shivering in the icy air, laughing, hugging, kissing, drawing them in, Cristi snatched up by Archie because she hadn't bothered to put her slippers on, MacIvor torn between yipping hysterically and rolling over on his back in pleasure.

"Morning, Tom," Archie said.

"And good morning to you. Come to your senses at last, have you?"

"Can I be the one to get Nicholas? Please?" Pauly was away, bounding up the stairs, Roxie at her heels.

"Where's Carol?" Archie asked.

"Done a runner," said Tom.

"Well, she did tell us she was going," Madeleine put in fairly.

"Said she felt she wasn't valued here," Tom added seriously, and Archie laughed.

Down came Pauly with a beaming Nicholas, so good-natured that he didn't care whether he was summarily snatched out of sleep or not, just so long as he didn't miss the party. And a party breakfast it turned into in the warm kitchen, while the early sun laid an apricot gleam on Ben Breac's white crown and warmth crept into the day.

"And are you going to stay here for ever and ever?" Cristi asked, having pulled her chair as close to Pauly's as she could get it.

"For ever and ever and ever, amen," said Pauly, leaning to hug her, giving a gay child's answer to a child's question, not looking at Madeleine.

Archie smiled to himself, seeing his mother telling herself to accept the answer in just this way. But when they finally made a move and began to clear the table he exchanged a quick look with Pauly and reached for Madeleine's hand and drew her gently away. "Come and talk to me." She de-

served to know first, herself, and what he planned
and hoped.

They went into the sitting room and by a mu-
tual instinct through the arch and to the French
window. Standing there looking out onto the still
garden, the lawn white under the trees, spongy
wintry yellow-green where the sun had thawed
the frost, Archie asked, smiling, "Are you pleased?"

"I cannot tell you how pleased," Madeleine said
softly, smiling back at him.

"I nearly lost her."

And I nearly lost Tom. She put both her hands
around Archie's arm and gave it a little loving
shake.

"I've been offered a lectureship in southern Brazil. For a year." He looked away from her, down
the lawn to where the loch lay frilled with white
cat ice. "I've decided not to take it. I want to be
here." He turned to her now, looking into her face.
"It won't affect Tom's position, of course, God
knows there's more than enough for us both to do.
And there are one or two jobs I'm still involved in
which I shall have to finish off. But I want this to
be home base from now on—and I want to marry
Pauly of course. But how do you feel about it all?
And particularly about Cristi? You were the one
who took on the responsibility for her when no
one else was ready or able to do it."

"How do I feel about it? I feel happier than I
have ever felt in my life."

"You're laughing at me."

"Of course I'm laughing at you. You know perfectly well the children will stay together in this
house, with you and Pauly. And now I can move
to the barn, where Tom and I intend to lead an
utterly simple and peaceful life together. You can-

not imagine how I long to have *one room* to worry about!"

"Oh, Mum." He so much wanted her to be happy. "You're such a different person . . ." But it was not something a son could adequately put into words. He pulled her close for a big hug and as Madeleine felt the steady beat of his heart she found herself thinking with thankfulness and confidence, it's like the new heart of the house beating.

SIGNET ONYX

WOMEN OF PASSION AND AMBITION

☐ **HOMECOMING by Susan Bowden.** Tessa Hargrave is going home to a town she fled in anger and in shame many years ago, to the family she has never been able to call her own, and to confront the man who broke her heart by marrying another. Tessa will learn that it is not too late to make a wrong choice right—if she dares to risk all for love again. "Moving, insightful."—*Romantic Times* (185870—$4.99)

☐ **MEMORY AND DESIRE by Lisa Appignanesi.** Driven by inner demons and rare passion, Sylvie Jardine, brilliant psychoanalyst leaves the Continent for New York, pursued by the choices she has made, by the deceptions and illicit obsessions—until there is nowhere left for her to run. Now her estranged daughter must solve the tantalizing mystery of her mother's past—or be destroyed by it. (175530—$5.99)

☐ **WORLD TO WIN, HEART TO LOSE by Netta Martin.** Alexandra Meldrum stormed the male bastions of oil and property, using anything—and anyone—to win back her family's honor. Now she has it all. There's only one thing more she desires. Revenge on the one man who is her match in business and master in bed. (176863—$4.99)

☐ **BLOOD SISTERS by Judith Henry Wall.** The best of friends—one had brains, one had beauty, one had talent, one had a deadly secret. From the day they pricked their fingers they swore they would always be friends through thick and thin. And they were. All except one who made them question their friendship—and their husbands. The one who disappeared with a deadly secret ... (404149—$4.99)

☐ **THE RESTLESS YEARS by Lucy Taylor.** In an era of social upheaval and sexual liberation, when women suddenly had so many choices and so few guideposts, the Marcassa sisters were swept up in the turbulence of the times and their own surging desires. An emotion-packed saga of sisters divided by ambition and desire, conflict, and change. (173333—$5.50)

*Prices slightly higher in Canada